Praise for *The Revenge List*

"*The Revenge List* checks all the boxes of what a thriller should be. Brilliant premise? Check. Mounting tension? Check. Jaw-dropping twist? Double-check. I couldn't put it down!"
—Riley Sager, *New York Times* bestselling author of *The House Across the Lake*

"I flew through this twisty, original thriller through the dark side of self-help. *The Revenge List* is a breath of fresh air that ends with a jaw-dropping gasp."
—Heather Gudenkauf, *New York Times* bestselling author of *The Overnight Guest*

"It's always a delight to see a justifiably angry woman in fiction, and McKinnon handles Frankie's story with ease in this twisty thriller."
—Kelley Armstrong, #1 *New York Times* bestselling author

"A propulsive page-turner of a thriller, and a gripping and important deep dive into the power of grief and the dangers of revenge. *The Revenge List* is an absolute triumph!"
—Hank Phillippi Ryan, *USA TODAY* bestselling author of *The House Guest*

"*The Revenge List* is both twisty and twisted, and that's a good thing. Compulsively readable from start to finish."
—Samantha Downing, internationally bestselling author of *For Your Own Good*

"A thrilling page-turner with a protagonist you can't help but root for—even when she makes you mad."
—Cate Holahan, *USA TODAY* bestselling author of *The Darkness of Others*

"Taut, furiously paced, and immensely entertaining."
—Jennifer Hillier, internationally bestselling author of *Things We Do in the Dark*

"McKinnon is a clever master of surprise, dropping subtle clues and changing course often enough to keep you glued to the pages. A read-in-one-sitting thriller with a stinger in the tail."
—Kimberly Belle, internationally bestselling author of *The Personal Assistant*

THE REVENGE LIST

HANNAH MARY McKINNON

mira

ISBN-13: 978-0-7783-3346-3

The Revenge List

Mira
22 Adelaide St. West, 41st Floor
Toronto, Ontario M5H 4E3, Canada
BookClubbish.com

Printed in U.S.A.

To Jenny & Sonica
More than Book Friends Forever

Also by Hannah Mary McKinnon

Never Coming Home
You Will Remember Me
Sister Dear
Her Secret Son
The Neighbors

THE
REVENGE
LIST

If I die, I forgive you; if I recover, we shall see.
—Spanish proverb

FRANKIE'S FORGIVENESS LIST

WHO	WHY	FORGIVENESS SCALE
The bastard who killed my mother	Needs no explanation!	~~X~~ 2
Finn Morgan	Dad, there are so many reasons...	4
Edith Bryant	Ugh! Worst neighbor ever!	
Chelsea Fischer	Made school hell for years	3
Adrian Costas	Ruined my life	3
Tyler Vance	Thanks for nothing, college m-fer	3
Trina Smith	With colleagues like her...	
Patrick Davies	Misogynistic dick of a client	3
Shay Callan		
Geraldina Hoyos	Ha! Ha! Ha!	10
FRANKIE MORGAN	The worst ☹	①

CHAPTER ONE

The sharp sound of a high-pitched scream filled the air. A noise so unrecognizable, at first I didn't register it had come from deep within me, traveling up my throat in stealth mode before bursting from my mouth.

The remnants of the yell reverberated around the car, forcing their way into my ears and penetrating my skull, urging me to *do* something. Survival instincts kicked in, and I fumbled with the seatbelt, my other hand grasping for the door handle. The need for the relative safety that solid, stationary ground would bring was so intense it made my stomach heave. A loud click of the central locking system meant my captor had outsmarted me again, obliterating my immediate plan to throw myself from the moving vehicle.

When I looked out the windshield, I knew there was no time to find an alternate escape. The end of the road— the edge of the cliff—announced by signs and broken red-and-white-striped wooden barricades, had been far enough away seconds ago but now gleamed in the car's headlights, a looming warning yards ahead. I couldn't comprehend what was about to happen, couldn't do anything as the vehicle kept going, splintering planks and racing out the other side with nothing but air below. I let out another scream, far louder than my first, the absolute terror exploding from my lungs.

For the briefest of moments, we were suspended, as if this was a magic trick or an elaborate roller coaster. Perhaps, if I was really lucky, this was all a dream. Except I already knew there were no smoke and mirrors, no swirling track leading us through loop-the-loops and to safety. It wasn't a nightmare I'd wake from with bedsheets wrapped around my sweaty body. This was happening. It was all terrifyingly real.

As the car continued its trajectory, it tipped forward. The only thing to stop our momentum was whatever we were rushing toward, obscured by the cloudy night skies. Pushing my heels into the floor, I tried to flatten my shoulders against the seat. My hands scrambled for the ceiling to brace myself, but I flopped like a rag doll, my loosened seatbelt tearing into my shoulder.

They say your life flashes before you when you're close to death. That didn't happen to me. Instead, it was all my regrets. Choices I'd made. Not made. Things I'd said and done. Not said. Not done. It was far too late to make amends. There would be no opportunity to beg anyone for forgiveness. No possibility of offering some.

As the finality of the situation hit me full on, I turned my head. The features of the driver next to me were illuminated in a bluish glint from the dashboard lights. His face had set in a stony grimace; his jaw clenched so tight he had to have shattered teeth. But what frightened me the most were his eyes, filled with what could only be described as maniacal delight.

He'd said we were both going to die. As the car hurtled to the bottom of the cliff, I closed my eyes and accepted he was right.

CHAPTER TWO

Ten days earlier

Seven minutes. Four hundred and twenty seconds was all it took before I gave shoving a fistful of coffee stirrers deep into my eyeballs some serious thought. *Seven*. As I'd begrudgingly trudged into the church hall on Chestnut Street in Portland, Maine, at exactly 6:59 p.m.—no sense being early for a torture session—I had promised myself I'd make it to thirty.

Lack of motivation wasn't the only problem. Before I'd arrived, I'd hoped the seating arrangements would allow me to duck and hide at the back of the room, but the counselor clearly had other ideas. She'd arranged the chairs in a circle with two dozen spots in all, so I'd chosen an empty one with a space on either side, plonked my bag at my feet, folded my arms across my chest, and abandoned any good intentions of trying to look like I wanted to be here.

My initial and arguably naive understanding of these anger management sessions, to which I'd agreed under duress and against my better judgment, had been that they would make me calmer. Slightly less irritated, at the very least, but so far, it wasn't working.

"Come on, Frankie, pull yourself together," I whispered, garnering a glare from another woman on the opposite side of the circle, a petite redhead wearing ladybug-patterned pants and dangly silver grasshopper earrings. I gave bug lady a smile, hoping it translated into something close to *girls gotta stick together*, and uncrossed my arms. Maybe the gesture would make me appear more receptive and approachable to the counselor, who sat a few chairs to the left. If there were extra marks to be had for a friendly attitude, I was in desperate need.

It was a crisp evening in mid-October, a little cooler than usual on the Northeast coast, the sidewalks slippery with leaves, the trees already partially bare thanks to Old Bastard Winter making an impromptu appearance over the past few days. On any other Monday, I'd have either been at work catching up on my construction project management duties, or at home, eating dinner while reading from my out-of-control stack of crime novels. Maybe binge-watching Netflix until I woke up dribbling into a cushion and shuffled my sorry ass off to bed. I swallowed a sigh. Some people were terrified of dining alone, but with the last few weeks I'd had where I'd been inundated with work, it sounded like absolute heaven.

My visiting a church on any day was an unusual occurrence. I only frequented them for the occasional wedding, christening or, thankfully rarest of all, funeral. While I'd never been to this particular place of worship, if memory served, it smelled the same as the others. Musty books and burnt coffee mixed with faint body odor, Grandma's perfume, and pine wood polish. A smell not even the electric air freshener behind me, which sprayed out the occasional *pffft* of lavender-scented grossness destined to give me a thumping headache, could adequately hide. I wondered for how long I could hold my breath without passing out. Then again, maybe fainting was my escape plan. Definitely a lot less painful than those coffee stirrers.

As the counselor said something about the various benefits of group therapy and what fabulous exercise we'd try tonight, I switched my brain to selective hearing. I looked around the circle, glancing at the other adults who'd joined. We were a mixture of gender, age, and ethnicity. A few actually appeared enthusiastic, making eye contact with the counselor, nodding like a gigantic set of bobbleheads. Some looked openly bored, checking their watches and sliding their phones from their pockets as often as I did. Most, as one might expect from this group, appeared *angry*, with scrunched-up faces and narrowed eyes, expressions filled with disdain.

I let my gaze fall on a tall, lanky person—from my vantage point I couldn't tell if it was a man or a woman—who'd pulled an eggplant-colored hoodie halfway over their face and sat hugging their knees. Kind of comforting, knowing I wasn't the only one wishing I could manipulate time or had a DeLorean parked outside.

I forced myself to concentrate on the counselor for more than two seconds, dug around my memory to recall she'd introduced herself as Geraldina Hoyos. I shouldn't have forgotten the name, considering she was a friend of my boss—who also happened to be my father—and he'd mentioned her five times at work in the past week alone. She was perched on the edge of her chair, which sat atop a stained frayed blue rug bunched beneath her black leather boots. Her smile was not only unwavering but genuine, and her gray hair cascaded past the bright orange scarf wrapped around her neck, over her narrow rust-colored jacket, and halfway to her ankle-length tangerine skirt. If I squinted a little, she resembled a giant happy pumpkin who might roam the place until Halloween.

For the millionth time in what was now eight minutes,

I wondered if corralling a bunch of individuals with temper issues in the same room was a good idea. The smallest of sparks could ignite one of us, unleashing a chain reaction that would explode like fireworks across the room. Except they wouldn't be colorful and pretty, but an ugly, dangerous pyrotechnic display with the potential to blow off the roof. As I bowed my head, I allowed myself the smallest of grins and half crossed my fingers, because if it happened, we'd get to skip the rest of the hour, collateral damage be damned.

"Again, let me take this opportunity to thank you for joining the group this evening," Geraldina said in her so-cheery-it-was-annoying tone. "Please remember everybody is welcome here. This is a safe space filled with mutual respect."

I tried hard not to roll my eyes at her language du jour. Bug lady pursed her lips, and eggplant hoodie didn't say anything, either, but folded into themselves like an accordion, now appearing half their original size. As I sank lower in the old wooden chair, which had already made my butt numb, I hoped Geraldina wouldn't ask me to *share*. I'd seen similar groups on TV, where people bared their souls before bursting into tears and piling in for a group hug, the idea of which made me shudder. I tucked in my chin, wishing to be invisible, and thought how counselors like Geraldina got any satisfaction from this job was a complete mystery. We were more akin to a bunch of sullen teens than adults, so moody I half expected to end up grounded if I didn't change my attitude. Maybe I'd be sent to bed before the session was over.

I glanced around the room again, counted nineteen other individuals who'd either been forced or, like me, had kind of, sort of, *maybe*, agreed to these sessions of their own accord. At thirty-three, I wasn't the youngest or the oldest. As I pretended to listen to what Geraldina was saying, I continued observing one participant after the other, trying to guess what had brought them here. Anger issues, obviously, but what kind?

One guy sitting a few chairs to the right might've been at home in a UFC cage and capable of tossing my weathered Ford F-150 truck with one of his sleeve-tattooed arms. He had his elbows on his knees, fingers steepled beneath his chin, seemingly hanging on to Geraldina's every word. Why was he here? It was easy to make stereotypical assumptions. Road rage? A bust-up at a bar when someone side-eyed his partner once too often? Or had his partner done the side-eyeing?

The older woman next to sleeve-tattoo sat straight-backed, fingers spinning her gold wedding band on her left hand. She wore a tailored black suit and killer red-soled heels probably worth twice my monthly rent. When I arrived, she'd made eye contact, seeming open and friendly, not the type to lose her shit. Most people would think she belonged at a business networking luncheon or a parent-teacher meeting rather than a session like this. After all, women, in particular, weren't supposed to burst into fits of rage, we were taught to swallow it down, keep ourselves in check.

"You're an angry woman, Frankie." How often had I heard that? As if it were an emotion exclusively tolerated and understood in men, something they felt was completely justified, and yet we felt the constant need to apologize for it. I barely scraped five feet three inches on a good day, yet my temper had been compared to an offensive lineman, a Tasmanian devil, or a sun bear, depending on who was asked. Until I looked it up, I'd assumed the latter might've been a compliment. Turned out sun bears aren't cute and cuddly as the name would imply, but vicious marsupials who'd rip your face off if given a fraction of a chance. I mean, come on, I wasn't *that* bad.

Truth is, we all carry some degree of anger inside, every

single one of us, and anyone who insists on the contrary is a goddamn liar. Some ignore it; many stuff the sentiments into a little box and keep it closed, maybe ridding themselves of tension through breathing exercises, meditation, or a deep tissue massage. Others, like me—and probably many of the people in this old church hall—didn't fare as well. We could explode in a nanosecond if the wrong button got pushed. Become red-faced and feral, noticing the verbal or physical damage we'd caused only in the aftermath of the carnage, when it was too late. My temper could turn into fire, wild and impetuous, unpredictable. Able to get by on a tiny ember until it was fed. It wasn't a part of me I liked but it was difficult to ignore, one of the reasons I often preferred my own company so I didn't piss anyone off but myself.

"Okey-dokey." Geraldina clapped her hands, startling me into sitting straight as if school were in session. "Time for our first reflection exercise and an opportunity to get in touch with our feelings."

A soft groan escaped my mouth. Not quiet enough because Geraldina glanced at me, put her head to one side, and gave me one of her dazzling, cherubic smiles. Despite her cheery facade, I couldn't help but wonder if she was thinking *your dad said you were a shit-stirrer.*

"It'll be beneficial, I promise." Her gaze flicked around to the others in the circle. "It can help you let it go."

I bit the inside of my cheek, promised myself if she broke into the Disney song, I'd shove those coffee stirrers into my ears as well. Willing my legs to resist making a mad dash for the beverage supply table, I sat on my hands and waited for further instructions. Ones I'd already decided to ignore.

"Forgiveness is a process," Geraldina said, and bug lady let out a snort. Tough crowd. Apparently, I wasn't the only cynic. Like a trouper, our counselor pressed on, undeterred.

"It takes time and commitment. It's hard and can be painful. At times it may seem impossible. However, if you're willing to put in the work, it might be the best decision you make." She put a hand to her chest, tapped lightly a few times. "You might lose some emotional baggage for good."

"Lost baggage has a tendency of showing up," the woman in killer heels said, garnering a few snickers from the rest of us. "I should know. I travel almost every week."

"Let's see if we can help you get rid of it forever," Geraldina said.

"How?" sleeve-tattoo guy asked. "The way I see it, sitting in a circle won't cut it."

"One of the things we'll do is work on a forgiveness list," Geraldina said.

"Forgiveness?" Bug lady practically spat the word.

"Not all in one go. It's a document we'll come back to over the next six weeks." Geraldina paused, smiled at us. "For today, take some time to think about anyone you feel has wronged you, and whom you have anger toward. Make a note of the people you haven't been able or may not yet want to forgive, and write down why."

A ripple of indecipherable murmurs spread across the room, and Geraldina smiled again as she held up her hands. "Again, it's not something you'll finish tonight. The aim is to be as close as possible to letting the anger you currently feel go by the end of the sessions."

"What if we can't?" a woman of about sixty with corkscrew curls said. "Or if we don't want to? What then?"

Geraldina nodded. "We'll work on that, too. For now, think about the concept. About the possibility of forgiving. If it feels too much, take a break, walk around, get a drink, and—"

The double doors to the room swung open. We all looked

over as a guy dressed in ripped jeans, a fitted white shirt, an anthracite hooded parka, and a slouchy beanie strolled in. He carried a black Nike backpack over one shoulder and ran a hand through his hair as his face beamed, eyes crinkling at the corners. If killer heels lady belonged at a business event, this man wouldn't have looked out of place on an Instagram influencer shoot. His scruffy but I'll-be-damned-if-it-wasn't-cute stubble made him ridiculously trendy, as did his brown hair flopping over his eyes *just so*. Midtwenties or so. And hot. *Way* too hot. If my brother, Rico, were here—a nonsensical notion because he was more placid than a puddle—he'd have leaned over and whispered to look away, stat, because slouchy beanie guy was too young for me. He'd have been correct. Probably. *Definitely.*

"Apologies for being late," hot guy said, pulling a face, his voice a deep and rumbling sound coming from somewhere in the broad expanse of his chest. "I'm Evan. I was at the wrong address, waiting outside and wondering if I'd got the time wrong."

"Idiot," bug lady whispered under her breath, but if he heard her, he didn't react.

Geraldina let out a little laugh, her face slightly flushed as she waved a hand and repeated her spiel about everyone being welcome. "Grab a seat. I was explaining our exercise for today."

Hot slouchy beanie guy aka Evan moved to an empty chair three away from mine, a waft of soap and citrus hitting my nostrils as he strolled by. I watched him set his things down and shrug off his parka. When he turned and caught me staring, he frowned. I dropped my gaze, opened my bag, pushed aside the latest thriller I'd been devouring, and pulled out my trusty ring-bound notebook, the one Rico had given me for Christmas. As I opened the sunflower cover, I half listened to Geraldina recapping our forgiveness list assignment, thinking these sessions really were going to be a total waste of time. By the sound of it, I wasn't the only skeptic because a baby-faced bald guy wearing a SpongeBob SquarePants T-shirt grunted and said, "I'll be here all week if I write down the names of everyone I'm angry with. I'm fifty-two. It's a helluva list."

Considering his tone, I didn't think SquarePants T-shirt was joking, but Evan laughed anyway. It was a warm sound, instantly making my stomach perform involuntary flips that I could've done without. This wasn't a place to meet someone. Not for a hookup or anything remotely more consequential. We were in anger management sessions, for God's sake. I needed to get a grip, not get laid.

I imagined the conversation with my father.

Him: How was your first anger management session, Frankie?
Me: Terrific, Dad, I screwed a hot guy's brains out. Can't wait for next week. Yay!

Erm, *no*, particularly since my father was the one who'd convinced me to attend these sessions in the first place. Actually, *convinced* wasn't strong enough. First, he'd verbally twisted my arm hard enough to annihilate all of my objections, said he knew Geraldina from a Mediterranean cooking class and pulled a few strings to get me into her group before I could protest again. The fact he knew my counselor socially gave me more than a sneaking suspicion he'd be quizzing her about my progress or lack thereof. But I'd made a promise to come tonight, and if nothing else, I was a woman of my word.

I'd agreed to six sessions, vowing to myself I'd be on my best behavior, so neither Dad nor Geraldina had a reason to suggest I attend more. I had to stop looking at Evan and not gawp as he extended his arms in a languid stretch. Except the *Breathe* tattoo on his left forearm and the acute definition of his biceps rippling beneath his shirt wouldn't let my gaze break away quite so easily.

Telling myself to knock it off, I grabbed a pen, deciding Geraldina's exercise might be a welcome distraction after all. Thinking about people who'd pissed me off in the past was easy. Listing the names of everyone I was angry with? Same as the other guy, I'd need more paper. As for the concept of forgiveness, that was another matter entirely. Some actions, some *people*, would never deserve it.

I turned to a blank page in my notebook and penned *FRANKIE'S FORGIVENESS LIST* at the top. Translation: *BIGGEST ASSHOLE LIST.* Slowly and methodically, I drew two columns, writing *WHO* and *WHY* as the headers. Trying to control the tremble in my fingers caused by bubbling fury, I added *The bastard who killed my mother* on the first line.

Pardon them? Never.

CHAPTER THREE

Not that I enjoyed keeping score all the time, but so far it was Frankie 1—Forgiveness 0. After some slight hesitation I wrote *Finn Morgan* on the second line. This was a private exercise, not something I'd share with anyone, so I decided I might as well be truthful. Listing Dad was a given for multiple reasons. Our relationship had always been complicated. Direct, for the most part, at times painfully so. He said maybe the mix of his Irish heritage and my mother's Italian genes had made me an impulsive bigmouth. Considering I was sitting in an anger management session, I couldn't much argue.

Edith Bryant. The words flew from my pen now, as if it had a brain of its own, and no wonder. My septuagenarian neighbor had detested me from the instant I'd moved into the apartment next to hers three years ago. Her vitriol wasn't necessarily personal. As far as I could tell, the miserable old bag hated everyone.

We'd been in the hallway the first time we'd met a few hours after I'd moved in, and Edith gave me the distinct impression she'd been hanging around, waiting to ensure I wasn't some kind of criminal. I'd introduced myself hoping to make a reasonable impression, trying not to wince when she'd crushed my fingers between her bony, beringed digits. The old woman might have been shorter than me, but she had the grip strength of an American Ninja Warrior.

"What on earth kind of name is *Frankie*?" she tut-tutted in a raspy voice, her face looking like she'd chewed an entire bulb of garlic. "You're not a *boy*."

"It's short for Francesca."

A click of the tongue. "So be it. None of this *Frankie* nonsense."

Things had plummeted downhill from there at alarming speed. She'd bang on my door when I dared listen to music at low volume, yet practiced her ancient and out-of-tune violin whenever she pleased. She gave me a verbal lashing when I called her fluffy feline, a nasty creature constantly baring its teeth or doing an astoundingly accurate impression of Grumpy Cat, *Penny* instead of Penelope. My fault. I should've remembered she was a stickler for full names.

The next day Rico and his husband, Noa, had come to my apartment to drop off some books and had found Edith snooping through another stack I'd ordered from my local indie, and which had been left on my doorstep. When I'd confronted her about it, she insisted she'd simply been making sure the courier hadn't mixed up our deliveries, never mind she'd once told me online shopping was for *lazy losers*. Yes, Edith was the pain in the ass neighbor who, despite being rude to me, regularly banged on my door to ask for money for obscure charities and proceeded to tell everyone in the building if I didn't comply. The woman really was an asshole.

I tapped my pen on my notepad. Who else deserved a spot? *Chelsea Fischer*, school bully extraordinaire. Writing her name sent a jolt of anger through my body, making me question if Geraldina's assignment was a good idea. The counselor had called this a *safe space*, but what happened when we walked outside, all riled up after thinking about our enemies, both past and present?

For the second time, I told myself to get a grip. Most of us had dealt with a school nemesis at some point, someone who'd made our life a misery. At my age, we were supposed to be over that crap, yet I found it impossible.

I urged myself to add a few more names and reasons, ignoring the desire to include another, someone I barely allowed myself to think about. I glanced left and right, reminded myself this was a private exercise. I'd been advised to get in touch with my feelings. Mission accomplished because they hurt like hell, so I gave in and wrote *Shay Callan*, each letter a piercing stab of guilt to the heart. There was no time for me to elaborate on the reason for including Shay, because Geraldina was walking over. I hoped she'd keep going, but when she knelt beside me, I put my hand over my scribbles so she couldn't see them.

"I'm pleased you're here, Frankie. Your father spoke highly of you during our pasta making class the other day."

"Erm, thank you," I said, unintentionally making the last word go up so it came out as if I'd asked a question. I looked around, caught Evan staring at me again. What was his problem? I turned back to Geraldina. "How, uh, kind of him."

"He's a sweetheart," she said, and it took me a second to register she meant my dad, not Evan, as another of her smiles danced on her lips. "How's your list coming along?"

"It's…okay, I guess."

"There's no need to rush. You know, much like making ravioli from scratch, which, by the way, I failed at five times until Finn helped me, you'll likely find the work we do in this group is a process."

"Uh-huh." I tried not to squirm in my seat. I didn't want

a process. I didn't want to *feel* anymore. What I wanted was an exit.

"What I'm saying is you should expect progress, not perfection. Something to remember as we move through the sessions, okay?" She stood and took a step before stopping, her face glowing. "Please tell your father I said hello."

A blush appeared to be creeping across her face, but she turned too quickly for me to be certain, and I frowned as she walked away. Why was she… Oh, *God*, were Dad and Geraldina more than cooking together? I groaned on the inside. While I'd been on his case to find a partner for years, and he'd had a few relationships since my mother died almost two decades ago, I rather wished it was someone other than my saccharine pumpkin counselor.

I grimaced as I imagined future holiday celebrations peppered by her sweet smiles and probing questions. *How did your father's gift make you* feel, *Frankie? What was the significance of the ugly Christmas sweater you gave Rico?* Ugh, I'd have to roast my own head and serve it to them for dinner, stuffing and all. I grinned. Mom would've laughed at that. She and I had often shared the same sense of humor.

"Great job, everyone." Geraldina clapped her hands again, and as a joke to myself, I added her name to the list for being so irritatingly sprightly. "As we go further into this exercise, you'll rate the names on a forgiveness difficulty scale from one to ten, with one corresponding to the hardest, and ten being the easiest to forgive. During the sessions, we'll get you to focus on the easiest first and work our way up. Think about what it might take to…"

My thoughts drifted as she babbled on. I scribbled a couple of ratings, gave a few of them the same one as their level of assholery was about equal. Pretending to be deep in thought, I tapped my pen and hoped Geraldina might mention to my father I seemed an engaged student and didn't need to return. Providing she didn't see my list, of course. In any case, I put her down as easiest to forgive, figuring once I got out of these pointless sessions in a few weeks, my minor annoyance toward her would disappear. Well, maybe it would linger if she became a permanent fixture in Dad's life, but I'd handle it somehow. Despite everything that had happened between him and me, I wasn't the kind of daughter who'd begrudge him happiness.

I glanced over the ten names, wondered if it was a lot, and tried to see what my neighbors had come up with, but couldn't get a proper look. I closed my eyes for a few beats, decided there was one more person who deserved a place on my list, and I wrote this one in capital letters.

FRANKIE MORGAN

I underlined my own name twice, added and circled the number one next to it. Not a doubt in my mind, my past self was who I detested the most. I'd never forgive myself for the things I'd done, no matter how many times I attended these anger management sessions.

A short while later, Geraldina suggested we take a break. Before she finished her sentence I'd jumped up and beat the line to the drink supplies table at the back. Slouchy beanie guy—aka Evan—was three steps behind. He wrinkled his nose when I filled a paper cup with brown liquid from a stained, white plastic thermos, which had to be older than me.

"You might regret it," he said with a chuckle.

"What?"

"The coffee." He smiled again as he cocked his head to one side.

Hold on. Was he…flirting with me? Nah, surely not, so I shrugged and poured in some cream, not wanting to admit he might be right because the coffee smelled charred, and tiny white pieces now floated on the surface. I took a sip, doing my utmost to not grimace. I wouldn't give him the satisfaction.

"Figures," I said.

"That it's bad?"

"That a guy like you won't drink this stuff."

He raised an eyebrow, his lips forming into a wider smile. "A guy like...*me*?"

"Uh-huh. One who's been fed barista nightmare concoctions since birth."

Evan burst out laughing and put a hand to his neck. "Oof. Straight for the jugular."

In order to disguise a smirk, I took another sip, trying to make a point of demonstrating how delightful and delicious it tasted. It didn't. In fact, the second mouthful was far worse. My cup now smelled of locker room socks and if Evan wasn't observing me with his deep brown eyes, I'd have long spat it in the trash.

"Gross, huh?" he said. "I warned you."

I managed a strangled sound as I swallowed the coffee, along with my pride and any hopes of cracking a wiseass comeback. "You win."

"There's a coffee shop not far from here," he said, leaning in. "If you want to go—"

"Three more minutes," Geraldina said with another clap of her hands. I swear she must've taught grade school at some point. "Let's get ready to connect, explore, and share how the forgiveness list made us *feel* today."

I watched as she headed for the small hallway leading to the bathrooms, then glanced at Evan, who, up close, looked so delectable my stomach did some more of those involuntary flips. This wasn't a fair fight, and I bet he knew it.

"About that coffee," he said. "If we leave now, Nanny McPhee won't spot us."

I wanted to grab his hand and run away faster than an Olympic sprinter but instead I feigned nonchalance. "Sure, whatever."

We fetched our things and darted out of the room, laughter catching in our throats as we burst through the church's main doors and stumbled outside like a pair of adolescent truants. It was gone seven thirty, the skies dark, the air heavy with the smell of a storm, making me cinch my coat tighter around my waist.

"I'm Evan," he said as we speed walked from the building, and I glanced over my shoulder, half expecting Geraldina to rush out, demanding our return.

"Frankie Morgan."

He seemed to stumble on the uneven road, said, "Nice to meet you…*Frankie*."

I smiled at the soft, almost tentative way he said my name until I reminded myself I'd agreed to have coffee with someone I'd met less than half an hour ago in anger management sessions. This probably wouldn't go down as one of my better life choices, but to hell with it. Coffee didn't mean I was asking for his hand in marriage. Besides, we were in downtown Portland. Plenty of people around on a Monday evening, despite the cold. Providing Evan didn't try anything obnoxious, I wouldn't graduate from voluntary to court-mandated therapy. Or a jail cell.

"There's a place on the corner of Temple and Congress, about a five-minute walk away," Evan said. "Jake's Cakes. Do you know it?"

"No. What about the bar on—"

"Not really my scene. I don't drink."

"Ever?"

"Nu-uh."

"Is that why you were at the session?"

He shrugged. "Might have something to do with it. Got some long-standing issues I'm trying to work through. Thought a group might help."

At least he hadn't been forced to go, and I decided not to pry in case he turned the question my way. "Coffee's perfect, especially after gross sock juice."

He let out a snort. "Jake's Cakes is really cool. I stop by every morning on my way to work. Did you drive here?"

"No. I live within walking distance."

"Same. This your first time with Geraldina?"

"Yeah. You?"

"Yup. Want to discuss how bailing early made us *feel*?"

"Not if you want to live." I grinned and as we carried on in silence, I stole another glance. The glow of the streetlamps made Evan's skin appear smoother, flawless almost. I forced myself not to ogle, but he was one of those people who looked effortlessly good. Ridiculously good. *And he's too young for you, big sis*, I heard Rico say in my head. *Waaaaay too young.*

As I pushed my brother's sound judgment from my mind, a glowing sensation a fair way south of my bellybutton bloomed. I gave my head a shake, told myself sex wasn't on the agenda. Evan inviting me to a coffee shop was completely innocent and any other ideas presumptuous on my part. I hoped I was wrong, because while Geraldina might've thought making a forgiveness list was a great way to exorcise some demons, I could think of a far better alternative to get rid of my frustrations.

CHAPTER FOUR

We got to Jake's Cakes, one of those cozy but trendy places filled with handwritten chalkboards and a clientele closer to the age I presumed Evan was than mine. Huge red letters hanging on the wall behind the counter announced the coffee shop's name. Open shelving displayed an eclectic mix of cups in all shapes and sizes, which complemented the assortment of dented and old wooden tables and chairs. I imagined the owner had spent hours curating the perfect homely environment to make it seem it had been thrown together in a laissez-faire way, and one you'd be happy to spend hours and dollars in.

My eyes darted to the fridge next to the counter, filled with delicious treats already making my teeth ache. The scent of specialty coffees invaded my nostrils and I gulped it in greedily, detecting a hint of vanilla, caramel, and a waft of cinnamon. Combined with the warm air and smell of freshly baked pastries, it almost made me weak at the knees.

I nodded to the barista behind the counter who was busy making an elaborate coffee order with dark syrup, whipped cream, and sprinkles. More of a meal than a drink. "Jake, I presume?" I said.

Evan shook his head. "Nope. Nobody knows who Jake is. He's a total enigma." He took off his parka as we approached one of the only empty tables close to the back and away from the windows, a little nook decorated with glowing fairy lights.

"What can I get you?" he said.

"I can get my own."

"I know, I know. Tell you what, how about you get round two?"

I raised an eyebrow. It seemed I wasn't the only presumptuous one, and why was this guy even in anger management? He seemed so...*nice*, then again, I did too, most of the time. "You're assuming there'll be a second round..."

He flashed another dazzling smile and I told myself this time my stomach would hold still. It didn't. "I drink fast, you'll see. And we have to, they close in about twenty."

"Fine, fine. Regular coffee, one cream, one sugar. Nothing fancy."

"Hold on, lady. You mean we've come all this way and you *don't* want a soy milk caramel booster crunch Frappuccino with extra hazelnut drizzle?"

"God, is that a thing?"

"I hope not, it sounds hideous." Evan pulled a face and walked to the counter while I didn't even bother trying to not look at his ass as I dumped my bag on the chair and covered it with my coat before heading to the bathroom.

As I washed my hands, I looked at myself in the mirror, thinking I could've made more of an effort. The humidity had made my curls tighter, but they looked fun and playful. Rico said they took five years off me compared to when my hair was straight, although he generally followed up his pseudo-compliments by teasing me about my being two years older. I tilted my head to one side, wondered if

Rico was right about my looking younger and Evan somehow thought we were the same age. If all he wanted was a night of fooling around, chances were he didn't give a crap. Truth be told, neither did I.

"You sure this is a good idea?" I asked my reflection, wishing I'd brought my bag so I could apply a fresh layer of mascara and some lip balm. I'd never used a lot of makeup. Didn't have the skills or the patience and wearing too much at work wasn't a good idea. In my role as project manager, being too dressy on a building site attracted all kinds of negative attention I refused to think about because it would stir up all kinds of negative emotions I wouldn't want Evan to see. Better put my best foot forward, if only for one night. I gave myself another once-over. "You're really thinking about bedding hot young dude from anger management?"

A sly smirk spread over my face because I already knew the answer. It had been a while since my last brief encounter, a man I'd hit on at a bar and gone home with. I preferred meeting people in real life and had never taken to online dating apps. Too many lies, too many weirdos. At least if you spotted someone in the flesh at a bar or a club you could observe them for a while before deciding if you wanted to strike up a conversation, let alone anything else.

"Have a coffee, go home, *alone*, and leave the kid be," I whispered, imagining it was what Rico would say if he'd stood next to me. My brother had been lucky, though. Met his soul mate—a concept I refused to believe in—a few years ago and they'd recently adopted a baby girl. Although Rico and Noa didn't shove their blissful happiness down my neck, I couldn't ignore it every time we met. I was happy for them. I *was*. Truly. Maybe if I said it often enough and with a little more conviction, the envious streak in me would fade away to nothing. Not that easy, even if I'd concluded years ago that

I was crap at relationships ever since my first one fell apart with disastrous consequences at the tender age of fourteen.

I pulled the bathroom door open, looked over at our table, expecting Evan to be sitting there with our drinks or at the counter chatting with the barista. Neither was accurate. Instead, he stood next to my seat, with my open wallet in his hands. When he glanced up and spotted me, his eyes went wide, and he shoved my things away, the gesture not making the slightest bit of difference to the immediate anger shooting from my stomach to my throat.

"What the hell do you think you're doing?" I yelled as I stormed over, the level and intensity of my voice enough to make other patrons stare. I whipped my head around, glaring at them, too, almost daring—hoping—they'd shush me or tell me to calm down.

"I wasn't—"

"Going through my stuff? I saw you. What were you doing? Stealing?"

Evan's cool exterior disintegrated. "N-no, I—"

I held up a hand, tried to regain control by vowing I wouldn't allow my temper to go ballistic all over Jake's fine establishment, not when it might prove to my father I needed those sessions with Geraldina after all. "Save it. I don't care."

Without letting Evan get out another word of protest or attempt to make a pointless apology, I grabbed my bag and coat, knocking over both cups of coffee in my haste, sending scalding brown liquid spilling across the floor as I stomped to the exit, ignoring Evan's pleas.

In the short time we'd been inside, the clouds had burst, and a deluge of icy drizzle fell from the skies, sending people scurrying down the street and darting into alcoves for temporary shelter. The perfect, ominous storm. It was about a twenty-minute walk to my little apartment on Grant Street, and there was no way I'd attempt it in this weather or mood.

"Fuck it!" I let out a stream of multicolored expletives, not caring who heard as I pulled my phone from my pocket. A few taps and swipes, and I'd summoned an Uber, which was a few blocks away.

Glancing over my shoulder, I saw Evan mopping his shoes and the floor of Jake's Cakes with handfuls of paper napkins. When he stood and looked through the window, I wasn't sure if he could see me or his reflection, and I urged the driver to hurry. Must've worked, because not sixty seconds later a car pulled up. I grabbed the handle and yanked open the door.

"Frankie?" the driver said as he looked in the rearview mirror, from which a Barney the Dinosaur figurine swung side to side.

I was about to reply when I slipped and lost my footing on the wet curb. As my butt landed on the sidewalk with a thud, my open bag flew into the air, and turned upside down, the contents spilling not only across the ground, but bouncing underneath and inside the car, too.

I swore again, more loudly this time, scrambling to retrieve tissues, tampons, and a pair of sunglasses from the ground, as well as my wallet and lip balm, which had landed on the back seat. The driver hadn't moved. Jerk.

"Are you all right?" he said, his voice so quiet I barely made out the words.

"I will be once I get home," I muttered, ignoring him, as I busied myself with repacking my bag, thrusting the items inside, and pushing them down, much the same as I tried to do with the anger I had for Evan for being such a dick.

When we pulled up in front of my apartment building, I thanked the driver, who'd mercifully remained silent the entire way, got drenched during the six-yard sprint to the building's broken main door, and headed upstairs. I tiptoed past Edith's, hoping I wouldn't wake my beast of a neighbor—her or Penelope—but I didn't do a good enough job because two steps later, her door flew open.

She scanned me from head to toe, her usual brand of disapproval forming on her face, her eyes narrowing. "Do you have to be *quite* so loud when you come and go, Francesca?"

"Do you have to be *quite* so infuriating, Edith?" I said, stomping past her, digging my teeth hard enough into my cheek to draw blood.

We'd had another argument in the hallway a few weeks ago after she'd accused me of being noisy the evening prior despite the fact I hadn't been home. When the building's superintendent, Mrs. Clayton, had rushed up the stairs to find out what the fuss was about, Edith expertly wound her around her little finger by bursting into tears and accusing me of trying to make her believe there was something wrong with her memory. The look of triumph on Edith's face when Mrs. Clayton gave me a stern warning about tenants being kind to their neighbors, an expectation she wasn't prepared to compromise on, made my insides boil.

I'm still not sure how I managed to keep my mouth shut other than not wanting to be kicked out of the building. I adored my little apartment with its old parquet floors, working fireplace, and the reading nook I'd built by the living room window. And I wouldn't let an old battle-ax like Edith make me leave.

Once I unlocked my door, I turned and looked at her, my chin raised. With a cold smile I gave the door a good shove, figuring I might as well hand her a real reason to be pissed. I took off my sopping coat and dumped it on the hook, kicking off my shoes and refusing to let out the scream building inside me because Edith would've heard it and known I'd let her get to me. Still, I shouldn't have gone to the anger management session tonight, all it had done was make me feel more riled. Instead, I should've stayed home, binge-watched TV, and read my latest Lisa Unger book before crashing out.

Maybe I'd give Rico a call, which would definitely cheer me up. We hadn't spoken in a few days. That would've been so unusual a year ago I'd have sent out a search party, but since he and Noa adopted Azumi, their schedules were all over the place as their priorities had shifted. Regardless, Evan would soon be a distant memory, at least I thought he would be until I remembered he'd probably show up at the next session with Geraldina.

"*Asshole,*" I grumbled as I emptied my bag on the kitchen table, ready to sift through the contents and determine if anything was too wet to salvage. Inspiration struck as I dug through the items, searching for my sunflower notebook so I could add Evan's name to my forgiveness list considering he deserved a prominent spot. Ironic to include someone I'd met at an anger management session, and I doubted Geraldina would see the funny side.

I looked at the things strewn across the table, some of them leaving water streaks and grit behind as they rolled across the wood. I frowned as I plunged my hand back into the depths of my bag, and searched through each pocket, a surge of anxiety traveling throughout my body when my fingers came up empty.

My notebook was gone.

CHAPTER FIVE

Without bothering to put shoes on, I headed out my front door and retraced my steps down the hallway, ignoring Edith's shouts to keep it down. I scoured the floor and the stairs, hoping my notebook had fallen out of my bag on the way up, but when I reached the main exit, I still hadn't found it.

I raced back to my apartment, where I grabbed my phone, pulled on a jacket and a pair of sneakers, and dashed to the lobby again. Once I'd flipped the hood over the back of my head, I pushed the door open and went outside. The onslaught of freezing air immediately found its way into my bones as the rain fell in steady streams and bounced off the sidewalk, splattering my jeans. Undeterred, I used the flashlight on my phone to search the ground, walking thirty yards each way from the entrance in case it had got blown down the street.

When I looked up, I saw Jeff, another neighbor who lived on the first floor, standing by the building's entrance.

"Everything all right, Frankie?" he said.

"No," I snapped, unable to help myself.

"Can I help?" he said gently.

I was about to bite his head off again but thought better

of it. Jeff was a charming elderly man with bad hips and a perpetual smile, who was the perfect antidote to Edith and her perma-scowl. He always had a kind word for everyone, and his tiny terrier was friendly, too, although by the looks of things, Terry wasn't impressed with Jeff's idea of going for a stroll in the rain. Anyway, I couldn't afford to antagonize more of my neighbors, and definitely not the kind ones.

"I dropped something," I said. "But why are you out with Terry? Didn't you find someone to help until your hip replacement?"

Jeff grimaced. "Things didn't work out with the new dog walker."

"Oh?"

"Uh-huh. From what I gather, there was a good reason Terry didn't take to him. Did you ever see the two of them out?"

"Only a glimpse, a few weeks ago. The guy seemed in a hurry."

"Yeah, Mrs. Clayton said she heard Terry yelp a couple times in the stairwell."

"Wait a sec…are you saying the dog walker might've hurt him?"

"Not sure, but that was it for me. I told him not to come back." He clicked his tongue in disapproval. "Anyway, what did you lose? Maybe I can help find it."

"Why don't you let me help you instead? I'll take Terry for a quick stroll now, and you can ask me anytime until you find someone regular. You know how much I love this fluffball."

"Bless you." Jeff handed me the leash. "You're the best."

"Can you please let Edith know?"

"I could," he said with a smirk. "I'm not sure she'd listen and would probably beat me to death with her violin because she knows I don't care for cats."

Jeff hobbled into the building, and as I walked down the street with Terry trotting by my side, my mood soured again when I searched for Jake's Cakes' phone number and dialed, only to find nobody would pick up. When voice mail kicked in, I left a message, asking them to contact me urgently. I vaguely recalled Evan saying something about them closing soon and, after consulting their website again, saw they already had. Not only that, but they wouldn't reopen until Wednesday.

Thinking of Evan made me a) fume some more, and b) wonder if he'd taken my notebook, but it didn't make much sense. When I'd walked out of the bathroom he'd had my wallet in his hands, nothing else. There had to be a simpler explanation.

I imagined the paper sunflowers lying on the ground in front of the coffee shop, drenched with rain. Crap. Last Friday I'd made notes of a conversation with a prospective client as we'd discussed their plans for a major main bedroom and bathroom reno, as well as their ideas for a total basement revamp. Both during and after our chat I'd sketched a few ideas and worked out a rough estimate of the costs. If I lost those details, I'd have to contact the client—providing I could somehow remember their name and find their number—and go over what we'd discussed for a second time. I'd seem a total amateur.

There was only one thing for it. After I'd handed Terry back to a grateful Jeff, I was in my truck and on the way to Jake's Cakes. Turned out to be a pointless exercise because my notebook wasn't outside the coffee shop either. Perhaps a customer had found it and handed it to the barista. Maybe it was sitting on the counter, only a few dozen feet away. Frustration built as I tried the handle and the door wouldn't budge. I banged on the glass, cupped my hands against it and peered inside, hoping someone was still there. Nothing. *Shit.* Where else could my notebook be? Maybe I'd dropped it in the rideshare. I opened the Uber app, tried to register a lost item, but the trip hadn't yet shown up in my history.

Defeated but still furious, I drove home, where I didn't bother lounging in front of the TV but showered and headed straight to bed with my book. Bad move. I couldn't concentrate on the pages, and sleep ignored me as I flip-flopped on my mattress, getting increasingly riled by Evan's snooping stunt and my missing notebook, making it impossible to rest for more than half an hour at a time. When morning came, it was as if I'd stuffed my head with cotton balls or partied all night with a dozen tequila shots. I wish. At least I'd have had some fun.

With a grunt and a groan, I rolled out of bed before my alarm clock went off at six. I dragged myself to the bathroom, hoping a splash of cold water would wake me. When that didn't happen, I decided I'd either need to set myself up with an intravenous drip of coffee or attach jump cables to my heart, neither of which seemed particularly appealing. At least the rain had stopped, and I crossed my fingers hoping work would be calm and uneventful. Still, if history told me anything, I'd be butting heads with Dad well before the day was over.

I'd joined my father's company, Morgan Construction, over thirteen years ago, after I'd been unceremoniously ousted from my psychology degree during the first semester of college. I'd limped home, mentally battered and bruised, my dreams of becoming a criminal psychologist gone, and I was thoroughly pissed off. Dad had offered me work, but I couldn't stand the near constant disappointment in his eyes, and I'd refused, bummed around a few crappy jobs on a road to nowhere for over a year until he convinced me to change my mind.

Sometimes I regretted being a project manager for him,

often contemplated the paths not taken, but I'd been shit out of options, and I'd caved. The pay was decent, and as I'd grown up around building sites, I'd had a good idea of how things worked well before my first official day. My current role may not have been giving me the warm and fuzzies, but I was damn good at it, and my stubborn streak wouldn't let me quit over a few arguments with my father.

When Mom was alive, she'd shake her head, and say our disagreements were because he and I had such similar personalities, which I'd refused to take as a compliment. Rico had agreed with Mom's assessment, but only once because the bruise from where I poked him in the ribs with my fork had lasted a week.

Now in his early sixties, Dad was still obsessed with getting to wherever he needed to be early, regardless of traffic. I'd never known him not to be a hard worker. He was the kind of man who kept his promises, a trait he'd instilled in Rico and me since birth—for better or worse—and always looked out for his crew, whom he considered family. A bit of a fitness nut, and while he may have been close to the age of retirement, Dad had the muscles I remembered from when I was a kid. He had no intention of slowing down.

"Things will fall apart if I'm not around," he'd said on more than one occasion. The fact he was conversing with his lead project manager—me—didn't seem to factor into the equation. Speaking my mind without the ability to always filter or sugarcoat was a less desirable characteristic he'd bestowed on me. Hence the regular butting of our equally tough-nut skulls.

I forced myself to get moving, dressed, and had a breakfast of coffee and toast before heading to the truck Dad had given me when he'd bought a new one. It had the blue-and-white company logo and phone number on every side of the cap on the back. Morgan Construction was located in Riverton, the Portland neighborhood where Dad had lived since he'd arrived from Ireland when he was five, and the place he'd chosen to raise his family. Quiet and respectable, exactly like my father. No wonder I didn't quite fit in.

The drive took a little over a quarter hour. The company was in a small commercial facility where we had decent and secure storage space plus a functional but lackluster office. The latter had mostly open-plan seating filled with gray and beige cubicles, and a conference room with a reclaimed timber table and six chairs. There was a single office with a door that shut properly, which my father had insisted our finance person take as she needed the peace and quiet more than we did. Dad wasn't a big believer in spending money on our *mothership*, as he called it. He preferred clients to see what his ten-person crew was capable of by showing them the portfolio of new builds ranging from simple bungalows to luxurious dwellings, quick kitchen remodels to high-end, top-to-bottom renos, and all the commercial buildings he'd built in between. I had to admit, it was an impressive collection.

It was barely after 7:00 a.m. and Dad was the only person here so far—no surprise, he'd been known to sleep at the office on occasion—and as soon as I walked in he waved me to the kitchenette in the far-left corner, where he proceeded to press the button on the chrome dual-cup coffee machine, the only thing he'd splurged on because after he'd met my mother and she'd introduced him to Italian-style espresso, he couldn't bring himself to drink anything else.

"How was anger management?" he said, as the noise and aroma of freshly ground beans filled the air. "Make any progress?"

"Good morning, Dad. Lovely to see you. How was your evening? Do anything fun?"

He crossed his arms, blue eyes piercing mine. Clearly, he wasn't in much of a mood to make or take a joke, and I wondered if Geraldina had already ratted me out for disappearing early on her last night. Not that it would've been ethical, of course.

"You went to the session, didn't you?" he said.

I rolled my eyes. Ever since I was a kid, Dad had major trust issues, thinking everyone was out to screw him, which was ridiculous, considering he honored every agreement he made and never overcharged his clients. A little voice in my head told me I had the same trust issues, and I shoved it away, covering its mouth with a few layers of duct tape, trying hard not to revert to sulky teenager mode. I'd never understood how parents did that—it was almost as if they had an invisible switch they could flick at a moment's notice, sending their offspring tumbling through a wormhole and into acne-filled, brace-faced pasts.

"I told you I'd go, didn't I?"

"Doesn't mean it's true. If I call Geraldina—"

"Seriously, Dad. I'm not a kid."

He took a sip of coffee, standing with his feet hip width apart. I hadn't inherited anything close to his height, which had all gone to Rico, but my father's size and dominant body language had long lost its effect on me, and I stared him down.

"This is important, Frankie. You know darn well we almost lost the Davies contract."

"I know, I know. And I still can't believe I ended up in these sessions because of him."

"No, your temper landed you there."

"Because he touched my ass."

"You said you weren't sure, and he denied—"

"He's hardly going to admit it, is he?"

"No, you're right." Dad waited a few beats. "But you still embarrassed him."

I sure had. Humiliating Davies had been my full intention seeing it was one of the only ways creeps like him learned. The *misunderstanding*—the word made me grit my teeth— had happened here at the office, exactly one week ago when the three of us were going over the plans for Patrick Davies's Super McMansion (not kidding, that's what the pompous ass had called it), a house my father had spent hours working on, getting the plans and details as close as possible to our incredibly fickle potential client's near impossible vision. Open floor plan with hidden beams that were structurally mind-boggling, a kitchen I could've fit my entire apartment into twice, and a garage big enough to make Lewis Hamilton weep.

Davies, who was about the same age as my father but had disregarded every single memo about feminism and equality, informed us in no uncertain terms he'd done the rounds of multiple construction companies to weed out *the boys from the men*. "No offense, missy," he'd added. "Anyway, you get an honorary guy badge, seeing as you own a pair of work boots."

As he'd chortled too loud, long, and hard, I'd squeezed my tongue between my teeth to stop myself from telling him he was a total prick. He was a wealthy prospective client, after all, and I tried my best not to tune out completely as he droned on about expecting the *best of the best* because he *worked hard and played harder*. The guy was a walking cliché if I'd ever seen one, with a fancy shiny suit and open shirt, a gold Rolex, and buffed shoes. He must've taken his fashion inspiration from the *Miami Vice* dudes. The eighties version, not the newer one. Everything about Patrick Davies screamed slimeball, and I'd considered him harmless enough until we walked out of the conference room. As Davies ushered me ahead of him, something I'd mistaken as a surprising yet gentlemanly gesture, his hand brushed over my backside.

It wasn't the first time something like this had happened. It had been years, but the #MeToo movement still hadn't reached the macho depths of the construction world. I'd been called *sugar tits* so many times I'd lost count. Same with the number of instances I'd been asked how well I handled wood. Same crass jokes that never got funny.

At first, I'd gone on the counterattack (*I can handle wood harder than you'll ever get*) or challenged all of them on their bullshit (*do you call all your colleagues that or just me?*). Sometimes I repeated their statements verbatim and watched them squirm. On other occasions I pretended I didn't understand what they meant and requested a more detailed explanation (*can you please spell that for me?*).

Unsurprisingly, my behavior led me to being seen as someone who took herself too seriously and had the inability to see the funny side of anything. *Combative* was the word Dad had once used, until I'd sat him down and explained how being one of the only people with a pair of boobs on a jobsite could feel. He'd grimaced and promised he'd be more supportive, had confronted a few subcontractors when they'd made lewd comments about women in construction.

I hired female staff as often as I could and became friends with some of them while we worked together, leading to whispers about my sexuality, which I ignored. In time, people understood not to mess with me. I knew a large part of it was because I was the boss's daughter and therefore in a position of power. That bothered me, too, as it meant they'd still direct their bullshit at someone who wasn't.

After over a decade in the industry, there was no question my fighting spirit had been eroded. Dealing with every battle was impossible, so I picked them carefully. Part of me knew I should've done whatever I could every time to defend the sisterhood, past, present, and future, except when I was the only or one of the only females on site the vast majority of the time, and male allies were sparse and largely silent, I'd decided the better strategy was to ignore them.

But touching me like Patrick Davies had? Hell, no.

I spun around, grabbed his wrist, and thrust his arm high into the air, waving it around. "Anyone lost a hand?" I yelled. "Because I found this slimy one on my ass."

Davies yanked himself away and stumbled as my words bounced around the office. Aside from him, Dad, and me, there were only two other people there. Sal, our contracts guru, who let out a snort and ducked behind the partition of his desk. The FedEx delivery agent standing next to Sal grinned so hard I thought she might give me a standing ovation. My father, however, was not amused. For a few seconds I worried if he opened his eyes much farther, they'd pop out of his skull and bounce across the floor like Ping-Pong balls.

"Thank you for coming, Mr. Davies," he said, grabbing our visitor's right hand as I let go of the left. "I'll get the final quote to you by tomorrow evening, and we can discuss once you've reviewed it. Thanks again. Thank you."

Davies, who for once didn't appear to find an appropriate cliché for the situation, stormed off, his face a deep shade of scarlet. It took no time for him to find his voice, because Dad and I weren't more than a few sentences into our argument when my father's cell phone rang.

An incensed Patrick Davies spoke so loudly, he may as well have still been in the room. He told Dad I was imagining things, he had children, *for fuck's sake*, and his briefcase must have grazed me by accident. Dad spent ages calming Davies down. Even longer to convince him there was still room for collaboration and I shouldn't be fired, and he ended the call by making yet another profuse apology for the way I'd acted.

"You still want to work with him?" I shouted when he rang off, the FedEx delivery courier slinking by us and out the door, while Sal ducked behind his screen. "Are you kidding me?"

"Calm down, Frankie, hold on. He swore he didn't touch you, and—"

"Are you accusing me of lying, Dad? What the *hell*?"

"Wait, listen to me, please. He insists it was his briefcase."

"Of course he does."

"Are you sure it was his hand? Because if you're absolutely certain, I'll call him right now and tell him to forget the contract." He shook his head, looked at me and frowned. "This counts as sexual assault these days, right?"

"*These days*, Dad, really?"

"I know you're upset. Look, we can tell the cops, but you have to be sure, and I'm sorry, but if they ask me what I saw, I'll have to tell them I was in front of you. I didn't see anything."

I stared at him, breathing hard, trying to figure out if I'd been mistaken, overreacted because I'd jumped to conclusions. Jesus, wasn't this self-doubt typical female behavior? I'd been so certain it was Davies's hand, and now I was attempting to talk myself into believing I'd got it wrong, been my usual impulsive self. No. I knew what I'd felt, didn't I? And it hadn't been a briefcase. Or had it? Had I assumed it was his hand because he'd been such a misogynistic ass during the meeting? Expecting the worst because it was the type of guy I'd decided he was after sixty seconds of being in the same room with him?

Dad was right, this did count as sexual assault, but what would going to the cops do? It would swiftly be brushed away as another *he said, she said* situation. There was no proof, I *may* have been mistaken, in which case I'd ruin a very lucrative contract for the company, not to mention the damage Davies could inflict on our reputation after what he would insist was a false accusation.

"Fuck!" I yelled, the word booming around the room, making Sal flinch. "This is such bullshit!" My anger had nowhere to go. I didn't know what to do with it, how to rein it in—or if I wanted to. As we were still standing by the door, I slammed it as hard as I could before giving the wall a good kick, gasping as my boot went straight through the plasterboard.

"Stop it, Frankie," Dad said, catching me as I was about to topple over. "You need to seriously calm down."

"Don't tell me to calm down," I shouted. This wasn't the first time I'd lost my temper because of a male-related issue, and I knew it looked bad, but I couldn't help it. If word got out, I could already hear what would be said about me: I was emotional. Having a bad day. On my *period*. I had to get out of there before I did or said something I truly regretted, and so I'd followed Davies's example and stormed out of the office, clamping my lips together so I didn't utter another word.

The situation made me so furious I wrote *I QUIT!!!!!!* a dozen times that evening, ready to send the message to Dad, but I knew in doing so I'd put him in a financially difficult position. Earlier in the afternoon, as we'd prepared for the meeting with Davies, Dad had asked me to step into the conference room and closed the door; something he never did.

"We need this deal," he'd said quietly, his face grim. "Prices have increased dramatically. I've overcommitted on two projects and lost out on the last three bids. If Davies walks, we'll hit a wall with cash flow, and I might not be able to pay the guys."

"It'll be fine, Dad," I'd said with one hand on his shoulder. "I've got your back."

In the end, I hadn't sent the text to my father and when he'd called and informed me Davies had agreed to the project because it was the best design, but he didn't want me working on it, I complied.

"Frankie," Dad said, his voice stern. "We need to do something about your *issues*."

"My issues?"

"Your anger. You can't fly off the handle like that and you know it. If you weren't my daughter…"

"You'd fire me? Then why don't you?"

"Because I want to help."

We'd had another loud argument before I'd agreed to attend a few anger management sessions with a woman called Geraldina. "It's only six weeks," Dad said quickly. "And she's a lovely lady. I'm hoping it'll help with some of your moods." There was that classic Morgan directness again, and I'd hung up before it made me change my mind about everything.

Standing in the office now, the day after my first session with Geraldina, I looked at Dad. The concern on his face, not only for me, but for his suppliers, his employees, people who depended on him, was unmistakable. "Yes, I went to the session," I said, omitting the part about leaving early with the hot young guy who'd turned into a weirdo before I'd managed to have a sip of decent coffee.

"Thanks, Frankie," Dad said, his shoulders dropping. "Call me if you need me."

I spent the rest of the day at the building sites I was responsible for where I had a long and arduous debate with the plumber about moving the bathtub six inches, thanked the new tiler for an outstanding job with a complicated kitchen backsplash pattern, and sorted out a logistical lumber head-scratcher. By the time I sank into the seat of my truck to scarf down a capicola and pickle sandwich I'd picked up from my local deli for lunch, it was shortly after four.

Between bites of food, I called Jake's Cakes again and left another message, hoping someone would hear it and phone me. Next, I opened the Uber app so I could retry registering a lost item, but my frown deepened as an uncomfortable sensation snaked its way into my stomach. Because almost twenty-four hours later, yesterday's ride still hadn't appeared in my history.

What the hell was going on?

CHAPTER SIX

Trying to brush the growing discomfort away, I told myself there had to be a simple reason for the blip in the history. Maybe the driver was new and hadn't processed the ride yet or there were other tech issues—Uber updating their system or something. Apps always had glitches and bugs, so I decided I'd wait another few hours before trying again. As I sat in my truck, my brain working through other scenarios about where my notebook might be, a flash of inspiration hit.

"Hey," I said to Dad as soon as he answered. "Can I have Geraldina's number?"

"You're not thinking of bailing on the sessions, are you?"

"No." I drew the word out to three syllables as I closed my eyes to keep my temper in check long enough to get what I wanted. "I may have forgotten something at the church hall, is all. I want to know if she found it."

"Maybe I should call her."

"Why?"

"She might not be up to taking any calls, and—"

"Dad," I snapped. "Give me her details. Please."

After I pressed him again, he caved, but when we hung up and I tried her number, my call went straight to voice mail. Kind of a relief, really, because although I wanted to retrieve my notebook, I hoped she hadn't found it. If she flicked through the pages, she'd see I'd added her to the bottom of my forgiveness list. No sense denying the notebook was mine considering my name and address were on the inside flap, and while Geraldina was all sweetness and pumpkin spice, something told me she wouldn't appreciate my sense of humor. Neither would Dad if she told him.

With another sigh I dropped the rest of my sandwich in its wrapper, took a swig of water from my bottle, ran through my task list in my head, and decided to call it a day. Shifting my truck into gear, I headed to the grocery store to pick up some food for my sad and lonely fridge.

My culinary skills weren't remotely close to gourmet chef level no matter how far I stretched my imagination, but I wasn't hopeless in the kitchen either. Somewhere between my twenty-fifth and twenty-eighth birthdays I'd decided I needed to master more than a badly boiled egg, especially as having my favorite take-out places on speed dial was getting old and expensive.

And so, on a whim I'd taken classes at a place on Congress. I'd managed to convince Rico and Dad to join me for the *Happy Cooking for One* lesson as we were all single at the time, and we'd lovingly renamed the class SBC, short for *Sad Bastard Cooking*. After almost setting his eyebrows on fire, Rico had thrown in the kitchen towel after the first night, but my father declared he'd found a new hobby. Nowadays, not a week went by without him discovering a new use for leftover egg yolk or lemon juice, and he recently revamped his signature dessert, a chocolate Charlotte Russe, complete with homemade lady fingers.

Dad said we could only get out of our monthly Sunday dinners if *all* our limbs fell off simultaneously, and Rico swore they were why he'd put on five pounds in the last three months. "Or it might be my not-so-secret stash of M&M's," my brother had said. "And the fact I sit on my butt all day drawing comics and writing music."

As I walked around the grocery store, grabbing fruit and veggies, thinking of Rico reminded me I still hadn't heard from him or Noa. I made a mental note to call them later, and once I'd added cereal, yogurt, orange juice, and milk to my purchases, I headed to my apartment.

Thankfully, Edith didn't yank her front door open as I snuck past, and I hoped she'd fallen asleep with Penelope on her lap. Or she'd moved out. As I fumbled for my keys, my toes hit something resting on the floor against my door. I looked down, saw a bunch of flowers. Strange. My birthday wasn't for almost another three months, and I wasn't celebrating anything before then.

Stepping over the flowers, I let myself into my place first where I set the bags of food on the kitchen table before going back for the bouquet. It was beautiful—vibrant yellow sunflowers, pink roses, white lilies, and lavender-colored Limonium, all elaborately wrapped in white tissue paper and ribbon and set in a rectangular slate gray opaque glass vase. As I inhaled the delicate perfumes I examined the arrangement more closely, searched for a card or a store label, an indication of who had sent it, or where it had come from, but found none.

Had Rico bought them for me? Unlikely. He was more of a living plant kind of guy with a particular penchant for succulents, and he'd given me cut flowers exactly twice. The first was when he was seven and had stripped the chocolate ganache from the top of my ninth birthday cake a few hours before the party. Mom had marched him down to the local bakery for a new cake, and then the florist, where he'd spent all his pocket money on a bunch of sunflowers. He'd stuck googly eyes on them in an attempt to cheer me up, and they'd been my favorite since—precisely why he'd given me the sunflower notebook I'd lost.

The second was a few years ago. Before he and Noa had a whirlwind romance that swiftly became the stuff of legends among our friends and family, my brother and I had been at a local bar, people watching. I'd pointed out a guy I liked, and with whom I'd flirted for the last half hour.

"No chance," Rico announced, waggling his finger.

"Says who?"

"Me."

"Oh, really?"

"Tell you what. Whoever gets his phone number first, wins."

"Wins...what? You won't have a one-night stand with him, Mr. Hopelessly Romantic."

"No, you cover that department for the both of us."

"Shut up."

"You know it's true."

I grinned but didn't deny it—there was no point. "Whatever. Okay, so bragging rights, but I'm telling you, if I get his number, I'm going to—"

Rico stuck his fingers in his ears. "La, la, la, la. Things not to say to your brother."

I lost in ten minutes flat. Rico's, uhm, *apology* had consisted of a half-eaten box of Oreos and a bunch of wilted chrysanthemums, both of which he'd picked up at a gas station on his way over to my place when he came to gloat some more. No, these sunflowers that had mysteriously arrived at my apartment weren't from Rico, and there was no way they were from an ex. My last attempt at a relationship with a guy named Valin had ended over six months ago, and no words had been exchanged between parties since. Not surprising considering I'd threatened to cut off his dick when I discovered he'd slept with someone else.

"You're a nutjob, Frankie," he'd shouted as he'd leaped from the sofa. His reaction wasn't overly harsh considering I'd been in the middle of wrapping a gift for Rico at the time, and had pointed the scissors at Valin's pants, insisting I didn't need him to take them off for me to carry out my threat. The scary thing? I'd meant it. I hadn't seen him since and there was no way he'd left this gift for me in an attempt to reconcile.

This bouquet wasn't from my more recent hookups, either, and I knew that for a fact because I'd gone to their places for the night and snuck out before dawn. They didn't have my number, had no clue where I lived, and to be honest, it wouldn't have surprised me if neither of them remembered my name. It had been sex, the great, no-strings-attached variety that always worked best for me. Didn't need therapy to figure out that catastrophic relationship in my teenage years had left a massive—and negative—dent in my heart and on my psyche, but at least this way my behavior prevented me from getting hurt again the way I had all those years ago.

Another thought clambered into my brain, and although I wanted to push it away, it got stuck and wouldn't let go. Evan. Had he sent the flowers to apologize? It was possible. He'd held my wallet in his hands when I'd come out of the bathroom. It would've given him ample opportunity to look at my driver's license, which meant he had my address. The more I thought about it, the more convinced I became he was the mystery florist, especially when I realized the only way he'd have known I liked sunflowers was if he'd got his hands on my notebook after all.

Forget about cooking dinner, I wasn't hungry anymore,

and I couldn't work out with whom I was angrier. Evan for stealing my notebook, or me for not believing it until now. As I yanked on my jacket and shut the front door, I first snuck past Edith's before doubling back and knocking gently, for once hoping she was home.

"Yes, Francesca? What is it?" she snapped when she saw me. "I'm busy counting charity donations. You know, the one you didn't contribute to."

I smiled, overly sweet and calm, including when Penelope stuck her head through the crack of the door and hissed at me. "Don't mean to disturb. I was hoping you might've seen who delivered flowers to me earlier."

Edith let out a grunt. "First of all, if you didn't mean to disturb, then why did you? And second, I've got better things to do than watch your place all day."

I clenched my teeth. "Did you see anything or not?"

"Not, and I'm busy. With *charity* work."

She picked up Penelope and shut the door in my face. I had no idea what had caused Edith's perpetual contempt, or why she insisted on directing it at me so often, but it was clear she'd be of no help. I bounded down the stairs as loud as I could, ignoring her muffled yells to stop making her walls shake, and headed for my truck. On my way, I gave Geraldina another call, ecstatic when she answered after the second ring.

"Oh, hi, Geraldina, it's Frankie."

"This isn't Geraldina. I'm Oksana, her sister. Who did you say this is?"

"Frankie." I hesitated, not wanting to announce I was in anger management sessions to a stranger. It was bad enough knowing it myself. "I know Geraldina in a professional capacity. Can I speak to her?"

Oksana let out a deep sigh. "I'm afraid not."

"It's urgent," I insisted.

"Maybe so, but my sister had an accident."

"Oh, no, what happened? Is she all right?"

"We think so." Oksana's voice sounded more than a little strangled. "She took a tumble down the front steps this morning when the handrail came off."

"Oh, wow. How awful."

"It was scary. She broke her nose and passed out. She's never been good with blood, you see. Good thing I was staying over."

"Please give her my regards." I paused, trying to phrase my next question so I didn't sound like the uncaring ass I knew I was being, particularly when I recalled Dad saying something about Geraldina maybe not being up to taking calls and me not asking why. "Maybe you can help. I called because—"

"Oh, Geraldina's asking for me. I'll let her know you rang. Franny, was it?"

"Frankie."

The phone went dead, so I fired off a text, stating how important and urgent it was before asking if Geraldina had found a notebook with a sunflower cover at the church hall last night. Three bouncing dots appeared, followed by the message She says she didn't find anything.

Could you ask if she'll give me Evan's number? I almost hit Send, added Please.

The swift, to the point, and utterly unsurprising response arrived almost instantly.

She said definitely not!!!

Damn. No clue how to locate Evan. I tried calling Jake's Cakes again, but still didn't get a reply, so I drove to the church hall. When I couldn't find an office, I went back to the anger management session room, interrupting a youth group midexercise. They were dotted around the space in groups of four, silently building what appeared to be newspaper towers.

I waved to the only adult around, a man I presumed was their leader. As he walked over, trough-like dimples grew in his cheeks. "Keep going, teams," he said over his shoulder. "And remember, no talking. This is all about finding other ways to communicate and work together."

"I'm looking for the pastor," I said as he grabbed my hand.

"Seek and ye shall find." Tapping a finger on his chest, he added, "I'm Father Joe."

I couldn't help my gaze from dropping to his bright blue T-shirt featuring a cartoon Jesus hovering on a cloud, the letters *BRB* underneath.

When Father Joe caught my eye, his grin widened. "You wouldn't believe how many cool-kid points I scored when they saw this. They think I'm majorly lit or rad or whatever it's called these days. Anyway, how can I help?"

He listened intently as I told him I'd been at the church hall last night and had mislaid my notebook, but before I had a chance to ask if he'd located it, he was already shaking his head.

"There was nothing in the lost and found. Nothing in this room either. I checked first thing. Maybe Geraldina found it?"

"Apparently not."

He grimaced. "I wish I could help. Perhaps one of the other group attendees has it?"

"Yeah, maybe," I said, my stomach contracting, red rage bubbling around in there as I pictured Evan going through my bag, taking my notebook, looking at my plans, reading the names on the list I'd written. My jaw clenched. It was my personal stuff, none of Evan's nosy—but tasty-looking—ass business. I told myself to stay calm, to not let my frustrations show, and after I'd thanked Father Joe and apologized for the interruption, I walked back to the truck. I was about to curl my fingers around the door handle when my phone rang.

"Hey, are you Frankie?" a woman said.

"Yeah, who's this?"

"It's Cleo from Jake's Cakes. You called a few times. Something about a book?"

Another round of explaining what I was looking for ensued. I crossed my fingers, hoping Cleo would immediately tell me she'd found my notebook and had set it aside, ready for pickup whenever I wanted. Wrong again.

"I'm afraid I didn't see anything," Cleo said. "But I left early because of the rain. My basement flooded during the last storm, so—"

"I was there around seven forty-five."

"Ah, I'd gone by then. I'll check in the morning."

"Could we go now?"

"Afraid not. I'm out of town."

My fingers had tightened around my phone, squishing it hard, and I forced myself to loosen my grip, counted to three, said, "Maybe it fell under the table or something? I was in the left corner with, uh, with my friend Evan."

"Evan Randell?"

My back straightened. He hadn't mentioned his last name, but if I could get Cleo to confirm it, I'd have something to go on. I forced my voice to turn smoother than the whipped cream Dad had mastered in dessert class. "Yeah. He's *really* good-looking. Has a *Breathe* tattoo on his arm. He's a regular at the coffee shop. Comes in every morning."

"That's him," Cleo said, her voice bubbly. "Even after he

moved to his new place on…Forest Street, I think he said, right? Anyway, he still stops by without fail."

"Uh-huh," I said, silently thanking her for the fantastic little nugget of information her loose tongue had provided.

"Oh, we *love* Evan," she continued. "He's practically family. Did he tell you he made the big Jake's Cakes letters for us? The ones hanging on the wall behind the counter."

"Sure," I fibbed. "Is Randell *dell* at the end, like the computers?"

"Yeah…wait, hold on. You *do* know him? Only, I'm not in the habit of handing out client information to random strangers."

"No worries, he and I are practically family, too. Thanks so much for your help. Bye."

I dropped my phone in my lap. Family, my ass. In my experience, where there was family there was conflict, and while Evan and I weren't remotely related, a definitive storm between us had brewed, ready to wreak havoc.

CHAPTER SEVEN

Trying to locate Evan's phone number while I sat in my truck proved pointless. Not everybody had a landline these days, and if they did, they often weren't registered online thanks to the incessant spam calls. I didn't find an Evan Randell on Forest Street when I looked on whitepages.com, and with over two dozen Randells in this area alone, calling each one to see if they knew him would take ages.

I abandoned Google and turned to social media for clues. There was no Facebook profile, which didn't come as a surprise. Evan probably considered himself way too cool and more than a decade too young for what the more recent generations regarded as a geriatric app, hobbling toward it's inevitable decline in popularity one scandal at a time. Couldn't say I disagreed much. I may have been a few years older than Evan, but my account had been gathering cyber dust for years.

Moving on, it took a single search to locate his Instagram account. Evan was immediately recognizable from his profile picture, a black-and-white moody affair in which he looked directly into the camera, a sexy smile playing on his lips. I shoved the *ooh, he's so hot* thoughts aside, chastising myself, insisting the photo confirmed he was pretentious. Evan was also a snoop, and if it turned out he'd stolen my notebook and sent an anonymous bunch of flowers by way of apology, I'd add thief and creep to his résumé. No denying Evan was good-looking, I wasn't immune, but it didn't excuse him for being a weirdo.

I drummed my fingers on my steering wheel, calculating my next move. No clue what other platforms he used. Dating sites and hookup apps? Possibly, although Evan oozed charm that meant gaggles of women had to be fawning all over him as soon as he walked into a place. Hell, I'd almost been one of them, never mind my usual fail-safe intuition. In any case, I didn't have the time, energy, or patience to search for him everywhere. I needed a different, more immediate play that wouldn't mean sending a direct message via Instagram, which Evan could ignore or delete. I wanted a good old-fashioned face-to-face meeting, meaning I'd have, and keep, the element of surprise.

The sun had already set, and as I sat in the church hall parking lot, the dark skies had filled with clouds again, making my surroundings oppressive and ominous. I thought back to what Cleo had said about Evan living on Forest Street, debated walking but decided against it as I lived in the same general direction, although I could've used the time to clear my head. Maybe work on a better approach than *where the fuck is my notebook* if I found him. Sure, the tactic was direct and to the point, but unless my sole intention was to piss him off, it likely wouldn't yield the desired results. No, to get what I wanted I'd have to play a role, be the good girl, otherwise he'd immediately label me irrational.

I switched on the engine and turned onto Cumberland, crawling as slowly as I could, running imaginary scenarios through my head of what I'd say. When I arrived at Forest

Street, I parked in a Pay & Display and pulled my coat tighter as I headed north, walking building to building, door to door, stepping inside wherever possible, scanning the names on buzzers and mailboxes.

Ten minutes of sleuthing, and I'd found nothing. I crossed the street, did the same thing while moving south. Another bucketful of choice cuss words later, and I'd reached the last apartment building left to investigate. The place was far bigger not to mention fancier than the one I lived in. Red brick facade, a tightly locked, see-through glass and wrought iron door that appeared to lead to a sparkling marble foyer with two elevators. For sure this was a hell of a lot more expensive than what my budget stretched to.

I hung around outside, hoping someone would either go in or come out of the front door. By the time a man dressed in a plaid suit and peacock blue fedora walked out, my toes had gone numb from the cold, and I thanked him when he held the door for me as I slipped inside. Once I'd made sure I was alone, I searched the mailboxes, made progress at last when I spotted E. Randell marked on apartment 2D.

The elevator was full of mirrors, and I couldn't stop myself from straightening my shirt and buffing the toes of my boots on the back of my jeans. It was the kind of place that forced me to do stuff like that, all the while making me think I was a street urchin. No clue what job Evan had—our conversation hadn't lasted long enough to find out—and I didn't care. I'd come for one thing only. My notebook.

The hallway smelled of lemon and cookies, the ambient lighting illuminating abstract artwork hanging in gold frames, giving them an opulent glow. I walked past the doors, half expecting an Edith-type neighbor to yank one open and demand to know what I was doing here. If my sense of orientation was correct, apartment 2D faced the street, and

I hit the buzzer with my thumb, anticipating Evan's foot-steps, but heard none. I rang again, and a third time, longer and more persistent, before pressing my ear to the door. Still nothing. *Balls.*

It was Tuesday night. The guy was probably out some-where on the prowl for other women's bags he could rifle through, or at the gym working on those *ridiculous* mus-cles. No. I would *not* think about his body. No good would come of it, and I couldn't wait here much longer because my bladder was already shouting *empty me* in protest. Defeated, I went downstairs and out the main door, stood looking at the building as I tried to decide what to do next. Locate a café or something nearby where I could pee and find a good enough vantage point to watch the place for a while and see if Evan came home. The alternative was to come back early tomorrow or wait at Jake's Cakes, hiding behind a newspaper in case the barista recognized me from yesterday's outburst, but I didn't want to wait another night to reclaim what was mine. As I dithered, shifting my weight from one foot to the other, I heard a voice.

"Frankie?"

I spun around. Evan's hands were thrust deep into his pockets, a slouchy beanie perched on his head. He'd slung his Nike backpack over his shoulder and with the zipper open I saw paintbrushes and a blank canvas sticking out the top. How unexpected. I hadn't painted him as a...painter.

"What are you doing here?" His expression was that of someone with something to hide, including an *oh-balls-I-wasn't-expecting-you-and-now-I-don't-know-what-to-do* widen-ing of eyes, and despite the dim light I could tell he'd had the decency to blush. Him looking like he might drop his bag and run confirmed the belief he'd done more than search through my stuff. I waited until he came a little closer before throwing away all my good intentions and deciding a verbal attack would be my most effective weapon of choice.

"What did you do with it?"

He frowned, gave his head a slight shake. "What?"

"My notebook? I want it back. *Now.*"

"I've no clue what you're talking about." His frown eased, face filling with something like relief, and damn it, if I hadn't caught him rummaging through my bag, I'd have said it looked genuine. "What notebook? You mean a laptop?"

"Stop pretending. You know I'm talking about the one I used at the group session last night. The one in my bag. The bag *you* searched through, remember? I know you took it. Give it back."

He grimaced. "About the searching thing. I'm sorry."

"Don't give a shit. I want my notebook."

"I really don't know—"

"It has sunflowers on the cover. Same as the ones you sent."

"Huh?"

"Stop messing about, Evan." I lowered my tone to a whisper as I leaned in, punctuating every word. "Give. Me. My. Notebook. It's got important work stuff."

"I swear I didn't take anything. Maybe Geraldina—"

"She doesn't have it."

"Have you checked the church hall?"

"Stop deflecting. You took it when you were going through my things, didn't you? Did you think it was my journal or something? Grabbed my wallet knowing I'd leave as soon as I caught you so I wouldn't notice you'd taken something else? Smooth move."

"I—"

"What the hell is wrong with you? Do you get off on snooping through women's things?"

"*No!* I, uh…" He swallowed, looked away, and because he

now had his back against the front door of his building, the light behind him obscured his face, making his expression almost impossible to read. "This is going to sound ridiculous."

"*You're* ridiculous. You stole from me."

"I didn't steal *anything*," Evan boomed, his voice loud enough to make me take a step back. I reminded myself I'd met the guy at an anger management session. I had no clue why he'd been there, or how bad his temper could get, and I needed to be ready for anything. Except Evan's shoulders fell as he withered like a deflated balloon, blowing out a long puff of breath.

"Listen, Frankie, I, uh, I can explain. I...I thought we hit it off."

I opened my mouth to argue he was wrong, which he wasn't, not really, so I closed it again. "Go on."

"And, well, I didn't know whether you'd call if I gave you my number—"

"Except we go to the same anger management sessions."

"Yeah, well, I had no idea if you'd show up again. Especially considering you'd ditched the first one so easily."

"I still don't get it. Educate me in your creepy snooping ways."

"Uhm, I wanted to check your driver's license to have a peek at your address."

"The *hell*?"

"To see you again," he said quickly. "Accidentally on purpose or something, you know? That's it. I didn't take anything, I swear. I don't have your notebook. I promise. I don't."

My face contorted itself into a bizarre grimace, settling somewhere between confusion and disgust. Was he under the illusion I should be flattered by his blatant invasion of privacy? I should be wooed or charmed or some ridiculous insipid romantic comedy bullshit? He probably assumed that because he was so damn hot, he could get away with stuff like this. Evan must've noticed my expression, because he raised his hands, his palms facing me, and waved them around.

"I didn't mean—"

"To be a thief and a stalker?"

"I'm *neither*," he said, his face clouding over again as his tone grew a little louder, more adamant. "And by the way, your statement's pretty bold considering you're the one standing in front of my building. Want to elaborate on how *you* found *me*?"

"Never mind."

Evan crossed his arms. "I do mind. And I know. Cleo called. Told me she may have inadvertently given a woman named Frankie my address."

Discomfort squirmed in my stomach, but not nearly enough to make me apologize. "Stop turning things around. The work stuff in my notebook is important."

"For the last and final time, I didn't take anything from you. I saw you trip outside Jake's Cakes. Maybe it fell on the ground or—"

"If you didn't take it, how the hell do you know I like sunflowers?"

"Huh? What? Can we please focus on one issue at a time because you're confusing the shit out of me."

"It doesn't take much, does it? The flowers you sent."

"I don't—"

"You saw the sunflowers on the cover of my notebook. It's why you chose them. What were you doing? Taunting me? Making fun?"

He shook his head as if to rearrange my words in his thick skull. Hands on hips he said, "Wow, okay, do me a favor and listen to what I'm about to tell you. You ready? Pay attention—"

"Don't patronize me."

"I. Did. Not. Take. Your. Notebook. And I certainly didn't send you flowers. Are you kidding me? What for? You don't strike me as a flower-loving girl."

"What's that supposed to mean?"

"With your temper, I'd expect you to rip off their heads, cackling."

"How dare you—"

"No, enough. I've no idea what you're talking about but more importantly, Frankie, I don't care. Take your bullshit to someone who *gives* a shit. Because I don't." He dug a key from his pocket and unlocked the front door before turning around again. "Do me another favor, yeah? If you come back to group sessions, don't talk to me."

"I wouldn't talk to you again if you were the last man on earth."

"Sweetheart," he said with a wry smirk. "If I were the last man on earth you'd be trampled to death in the rush."

The door slammed behind him, leaving me with my jaw hanging, any kind of retort dying in my mouth as I watched him disappear up the stairs. I tried to reconcile his words and reactions with what I'd seen last night. His responses to my accusations about the notebook and the flowers had been rude, sure, but they'd seemed sincere. Except I'd met the guy yesterday. Had been in his direct vicinity for less than an hour. For all I knew he was an aspiring actor, or a seasoned one considering he had the Hollywood looks for it, and he was making me doubt myself on purpose.

"Evan Randell, you're an asshole," I shouted. I searched for the corresponding buzzer on the ones outside, pressed my finger to it and held it down, my pulse tap-tapping in my neck as I refused to let go. Nothing happened for almost a full minute, not until I heard a window above me opening.

"What the hell are you doing?" he yelled. "Give it up and go home!"

"Not without my notebook," I shouted, finger still firmly in place.

I kept ringing his buzzer and hoped he'd come downstairs with an apologetic look on his face and my stuff in his hands. Wishful thinking. Nothing happened so I kept pressing—on, off, on, on, off, on, on, on, off—a rhythmic pattern I knew would bug the crap out of him. It must've, because without warning, what had to be two gallons of ice-cold water splattered on the ground, soaking the backs of my legs to my knees. I screamed and jumped to the side before looking up. Evan stood at a window with a huge smirk on his face and a large orange plastic bucket in his hands.

"Ready for round two?" he said. "Because we can play this game all night."

"You're an *asshole*," I screamed.

"You said that already." Evan shrugged coolly before closing the window and lowering the blinds, leaving me not only fuming, but drenched.

I made that Frankie 0—Evan 1.

CHAPTER EIGHT

"Asshole," I shouted again because I couldn't come up with anything more intelligent before stomping to my truck. I only made it five steps when the heavens burst open, sending another downpour of water my way. In the minutes it took to reach my Ford, freezing rivulets snaked their way down my neck, and the bottoms of my jeans felt like a pair of squidgy squid clinging to my calves.

No way could the evening get any worse. If Evan had taken my notebook—and despite his Oscar-worthy performance I was still convinced there was more than a distinct possibility he'd done so—there was no way he'd return it tonight. And if he *had* sent those flowers, he wouldn't be admitting it anytime soon either.

The guy was a Grade A douchebag. He'd invited me to Jake's Cakes, only to go through my stuff, and for what? Because he was so insecure and desperate to see me again and positively *had* to have a way to find me? I wasn't buying it, which meant he was a liar. And a creep. As for the anger management sessions, I knew Dad wouldn't let me bail after only going once. I decided I *would* attend the next meeting, if only to confront Evan again. Maybe I could do something to irk him enough to leave (coffee stirrers, anyone?) or I'd ask Geraldina to move me to a different group.

Thinking of her made me wonder how she was doing. I debated calling Dad for info, but I didn't want him to go on the defensive seeing as I suspected I wasn't supposed to know they were potentially more than cooking buddies. I definitely didn't want to get sucked into a discussion about Patrick Davies, and why I'd ended up in the anger management sessions in the first place.

I yanked the truck door open and flung myself inside, shivering as the relative warmth enveloped me like a tepid blanket. It was time to take control wherever I could, prove to myself Evan had stolen from me by shutting down all other avenues. I retrieved my phone and opened the Uber app. The ride still wasn't showing in my history.

A sudden brain wave hit. About a year ago Rico had been an Uber driver for a few months to make some extra cash. He hadn't enjoyed it much, especially when one of his clients vomited over the back seat and left him a negative review, complaining he'd made her throw up with his *aggressive driving*, which I knew firsthand was ridiculous. The fact she'd been off-her-face drunk didn't seem to matter, and after he'd paid for the car's cleaning bill, he'd stopped chauffeuring people.

I sent him a text, asking if there was a help number for Uber drivers.

Problem? he answered.

No. Got a number?

Five seconds later he sent me a screenshot with the details. After thanking him and agreeing he'd call me in the morning, I dialed the number he'd given me, reprimanding myself for not thinking of this before, and wishing the next available agent would hurry the hell up so I could get home and change out of my soggy clothes.

Finally, a woman named Amélie came on the line, her voice so friendly, it had the opposite effect and managed to turn my mood as bleak as the skies. As swiftly as possible, I explained how I might've forgotten an item in the car I'd got a ride home in twenty-four hours earlier.

"This help line is for Uber *drivers*," she said, cutting in, her scary vocal fry unnecessarily emphasizing the last word. "You need to open the Uber app. Select the ride from your history, and—"

"Yes, I was getting there," I said, not doing a very good job of hiding my irritation, and thinking that if she'd let me finish, I'd have had time to explain. "The ride isn't showing yet. I think there's a technical issue."

"How odd, from what I can see, the system's working perfectly. Hold on. I'm not supposed to do this but… I'll hop over to your passenger account." She asked me a few security questions to confirm my identity, finished with, "When did you say you took the ride?"

"Yesterday. Around seven forty-five p.m."

A long pause. "You didn't take an Uber yesterday."

"Yes, I did."

"Not that I can see."

"Exactly my point!"

"Did you use a different service?"

"Uh, *no*."

"You're sure? Wait, let me check something… Oh, yes, here we are."

Progress, finally. "Great. I need to register the lost—"

"That's impossible. It says here you didn't take the ride. There's a no-show fee."

"Huh?"

"And, uh-oh. The driver didn't exactly leave you a favorable rating."

"I don't care about the rating, and you don't understand, I got *in* the car."

Amélie waited a few beats. When she spoke, her voice was lower and deeper, as if she were recording a corporate educational video or a hemorrhoid cream commercial. "For passenger safety, we recommend riders always verify the make and model of the vehicle, and match the license plate with the one in the app before—"

Heart thumping, head spinning, I hung up. She'd made a mistake, logged into someone else's account with a similar name, maybe. It didn't ring true seeing as I'd verified my identity with her, so I flipped to the Uber app, scanned through the recent charges. And there it was. Damn it, Amélie was right, I'd been billed a no-show fee. Desperate for a different result, I logged in to my banking app, where I checked my credit card statement. Same charge. What was going on?

I replayed what had happened yesterday evening after I'd found Evan snooping through my bag. I'd marched out of Jake's Cakes, called an Uber, *definitely*—it was the only rideshare I used—and the car had arrived almost instantly. Faster than anticipated but surely that wasn't unusual. I was no tech guru but as far as I knew, GPS locations indicated on an app were an approximation, especially in an urban setting, not an exact science a hundred percent of the time. It'd been dark, too, the rain pouring harder than it was now. I'd been way too pissed off at Evan's stunt to follow Amélie's recommended safety protocols, regardless how sound and wise they were.

I hadn't paid attention to the car's make and model, hadn't as much as glanced at the license plate.

I forced my brain some more, tried to recall what the driver had said when I'd got into the car. Had he known my name, or had I announced who I was? I couldn't remember. If Mom had been alive, she'd have given me hell for getting into a stranger's car, especially after drilling it into Rico and me when we were kids that it was something we should never, ever do. "Once you're in the vehicle, you're in big, big trouble," she'd told us. It had given me nightmares, made me dream of faceless kidnappers trying to grab me.

Except it was the norm now. Summoning a ride via an app was much like everything else we did these days. Convenience was key. Trips. Books. Clothes. Food. Furniture. Appliances. We were so used to handing out our address to anyone who could make our lives easier, get us something more quickly, we often did so with little to no question.

As all these thoughts swirled around, another realization smacked me around the face. While I couldn't recall if I'd given the driver my name, I knew for certain I hadn't told him my destination. There was no need as he would've had the details in his app. But if I'd got in the wrong car…how had he known where to take me?

I drove home, struggling to stick to the speed limit as my heart raced, pushing me to go faster while my pulse throbbed in my temples. My thoughts kept scuttling around as I attempted to understand what and how this had happened. I'd got into a man's car, and…wait. It *had* been a man, hadn't it? The brief exchange we'd had was too short to be classified as a conversation, it had been a couple sentences at most because for the rest of the trip I'd sat in the back, repacking my bag, and thinking about Evan holding my wallet. The encounter with my Uber driver had fuzzed at the edges as I'd instantly deemed it neither relevant nor consequential.

I had no proper idea of what he looked like either. Couldn't offer any real description of skin or hair color, let alone distinguishing features such as an earring, scar, or tattoo. Even his clothes were a distant memory. Had he worn a jacket? If so, what color? Red? Blue? The only thing I remembered was the Barney the Dinosaur figurine hanging from the rearview mirror. That was it. Other than that trivial detail, there was nothing.

Shaking my head, I forced myself to refocus, clenching the steering wheel harder. The whole situation made zero sense. Amélie the Uber lady had to be mistaken. Tech glitched all the time, it wasn't infallible, and neither were humans. Maybe the driver had tapped the wrong button when he'd picked me up and claimed I was a no-show by mistake. It had to be a regular occurrence, surely. Maybe he didn't know what he was doing, particularly if this was one of his first days on the job.

Whether I'd given him my name or he'd said it was up for debate, but he'd known my address, had dropped me off at my front door without my guidance. He couldn't have done so without being an Uber driver. I decided that detail settled it, and my heart rate slowed. App or human glitch, which meant I got a ride for a cheap no-show fee.

Somewhat relieved to get back to my place, I parked the truck, trying to rid myself of the remaining anxiety. I still glanced over my shoulder a few times when I got out of my vehicle, though, wishing the front door to my building was always locked like Evan's. My fellow tenants and I had requested the security improvement multiple times, but our landlady had yet to order the repair, and we didn't have any cameras in the building either. Perhaps it was time to pressure her again into taking these matters seriously.

When I reached the entrance, I stopped and turned, looked both ways, the hair on the back of my neck standing sentry as I squinted into the dark. A cyclist biked down the road, after which a squirrel darted across the street and made its way to safety up a nearby tree. Berating myself for being paranoid, I headed upstairs, sighing with relief when Edith didn't accuse me of being loud, and again when there were no new flowers at my door. Neither my nerves nor my temper could've withstood either.

As soon as I got rid of my wet clothes and changed into a soft blue hoodie and a pair of aging sweatpants with holes in the pockets, I sank onto the couch with a bowl of cereal. It quickly became apparent I was far too jumpy to watch TV, and when I'd finished eating, I grabbed my laptop, making the humongous mistake of typing *fake Uber driver stories* in the search bar of the browser, which sent me tumbling down a terrifying network of cyber rabbit holes.

There were horrifying stories of theft, assault, rape, and murder, enough to turn my stomach and make me never want to leave the house again...except, I reminded myself, it was a hiccup in the app or the driver's fingers, that was all, especially considering I'd been dropped off here without issues. Save for my notebook, nothing was missing, and odds were still high Evan had stolen it. If a fake driver was going to take something from me, it would be my money, not an old notebook with irrelevant information. If I had dropped it in his car, he'd probably thrown it out by now, which was total crap because I had to restart the sketches and estimates for our potential new client. The quote wasn't due until the end of the week, meaning it was a less pressing issue for now.

I grabbed my phone and checked the Uber app again, hoping Amélie had discovered a bug somehow and I'd see my ride history had been updated so I could register my missing item, but nothing had changed. I flung my phone on the coffee table, shoved my laptop to one side, and flicked on the TV. I stayed there until I woke hours later, only to find the remote control had left indentations in my forehead, and sleep had provided me with exactly zero answers about what had happened last night.

CHAPTER NINE

"Are you going to tell me what's up with you?" Dad said.

It was Wednesday afternoon and he'd called while I was checking progress on one of our construction sites, a mini mall where an independent grocery store called Monastery had taken over another of the vacant units, the fourth in as many years, and had tasked Morgan Construction with the renovation and expansion.

Up to this point Dad and I had enjoyed a perfectly reasonable conversation, spending the first ten minutes going over the project and costing details and what was left to do by month end. As I'd been on the verge of hanging up, he sprang the *what's up* question on me. Frankly, I thought I'd done a decent job of injecting a good amount of sprightliness into my voice, but apparently Finn Morgan, human lie detector, was onto me.

"I'm fine," I said, flicking a stray piece of chipboard off my jacket. "Everything's great."

"Hmm." A single, short noise was all it took to know he didn't believe me. "If that's true, then how come you bit Sandy's head off this morning?"

My annoyance shot up like a high striker fairground game,

dinging the virtual bell loud and clear. "Come on, Dad, *really*? He cut the drywall in the wrong place, so I made him do it again. I can't believe he came crying to you."

"Actually, he mentioned you seemed a little off, asked if you were okay."

"Ergo he came crying to you."

Dad snorted. "Don't be ridiculous. I called him for his birthday."

"Oh…crap."

"Thought you'd forgotten. Honestly, Frankie, I keep telling you it's the little things that make the biggest difference. Put a reminder on your phone or in Outlook. It's not tricky these days with all the tech we have."

It wasn't worth an argument. "I'll take care of it."

"Before you go," he said, and I pressed my teeth down on my tongue, waiting for him to continue, which he did after he'd let out a big sigh, full of displeasure. "Sandy said you were so angry, he thought you were going to rip off his head, scoop out the contents, and use his skull as a fruit bowl."

"Pfft, I wasn't that bad. And he was late this morning. I believe it's a cardinal sin in the Morgan rule book."

"According to him it was all of sixty seconds."

"Which in your world is longer than an eternity."

"His wife's pregnant. She was sick. He needed to do the daycare run for the twins."

I let out a spiteful laugh. "Sure, whatever, expect me to be all motherly while you take the guy's side. Big surprise."

Dad exhaled slowly. I pictured him with his cell phone clenched in his hand, his eyes closed as he counted to *Zen*. Ever since I was a kid, it made me want to push his buttons faster and harder. See what it would take to make him explode. It hardly ever happened, which infuriated me more. I was jealous of Dad's calmness, envious of Rico inheriting it, too.

"Should I assume your comment is actually about the Davies situation?" he said.

"You know what they say when you assume? It makes an ass out of you and—"

"I'll take that as a yes. Listen, Frankie, we've been over this multiple times. What happened with Davies has nothing to do with Sandy. You can take your frustrations out on me, but I draw the line when you make it everyone else's problem, especially my crew. They deserve your respect."

I was about to launch into a retort about how respect was a two-way street, but Sandy had always shown it to me. He was a good man, decent and kind, a hardworking employee who never made any kind of sexist remarks or microaggressions. He didn't care who his boss was if they were good at their job. I closed my mouth while I searched for an appropriate response. Thankfully, I didn't need one because my phone buzzed. My brother, *finally*, saving me by the literal bell.

"Rico's on the other line. I've got to go."

"Fine," Dad said. "Tell Rico I expect them all for Sunday lunch. I'm making a trifle."

"*Trifle?* You know it's not the eighties?"

"It's a Gordon Ramsay recipe, so pipe down, cheeky, or you won't get any."

"Oh, *no*, for whatever will I do?"

"Yeah, yeah. Bye."

"Bye, Dad."

I disconnected our call and tapped on the incoming one from Rico, way too eager about giving him hell for not being in touch for the best part of a week. "Hey, stranger," I said. "And I mean that quite sincerely because where the hell have you been?"

"Frankie—"

"I swear when you didn't call this morning I considered

sending out a search party to see if a stack of comic books had toppled over and you couldn't dig yourself out."

"Listen—"

"What's going on with you? How's Noa? And my gorgeous little Azumi? Does she want to come live with her favorite aunt yet?" As the seconds passed, doubt wriggled its way in, devouring my cheeriness. It was taking Rico far too long to answer, which was unusual. So was him not yet making a quip about my verbal diarrhea. Maybe it was a bad line, or we'd got cut off, because my brother was always ready for some verbal sparring. Shit, most times he started it.

"Hey, fleabag?" I said. "You there? Cat got your tongue?"

"I heard you."

The way he said the words sent a shiver rushing down my spine. "What's wrong?"

"It's…it's Azumi."

"What's happened?" A few seconds passed. "Rico? Talk to me."

"They're not sure," he whispered, a sob escaping his lips. "They're running tests. The doctor's supposed to be here soon."

"Where are you?"

"Maine Medical. We were in the ER, but they moved us to a room."

"I'm on my way. Text me the details. Is Noa with you?"

A stifled sob. "Yes."

"Have you called Dad?"

"I will after I speak to you."

"Let me call him. I'm coming to you now. It'll be okay, Rico. Whatever's going on, I'm here for you. I won't be long."

After he whispered a thank-you and we ended the call, I phoned Dad, gave him the sparse details Rico had shared as well as the room number my brother had already texted me. I grabbed my things from the worksite, yelled a quick goodbye to Sandy and the rest of the crew, and sprinted to my truck, cursing myself when I noticed the tank was running on empty. As usual, I'd left it way too late to fill up.

I gunned it to the nearest gas station, forcing myself to reduce my speed so a cop didn't pull me over, and swore again, more loudly this time, when I saw each of the four pumps was taken. I hedged my bets and got in line, and within moments a car pulled up behind me, boxing me in. I swore the woman in front had to be a not-so-distant relative of a sloth. A triple coat of paint in the rain would've dried faster than it was taking her to start filling her snazzy Range Rover.

Instead of paying at the pump, especially given the line continuing to form behind me, she headed into the store. Five minutes later, I could still see her inside, taking her sweet, sweet time as she perused the snack shelves, picking up a bag of pretzels and putting it back, selecting some popcorn before changing her mind.

"Enough," I said, jumping out of the truck and running inside. As soon as I got within a few feet of her, I told myself to keep my voice as light and friendly as possible. "Excuse me, ma'am. I'm stuck behind you and I was hoping we could speed things up a little."

She turned around, *slowly*. Early forties. Designer jeans. Long, ruby red fingernails. Expensive-looking cream-colored coat, the kind I wouldn't dare touch in case I left dirty fingerprints all over it. Her gaze drifted at an equally leisurely pace, sweeping all the way from the top of my now fluffy, hard hat–shaped curls to the tippy toes of my dusty scuffed work boots. Then it traveled back up again, her smile as fake as the friendliness of my initial request.

"I'll move once I'm done," she said, taking a few steps to the left so she was now directly in front of the freezers.

"Please, it's an emergency."

Before I finished my sentence, she actually, for real, gave me a dismissive wave. My mouth dropped open as I watched her take a tub of double fudge ice cream and peruse the label, put it back and select another. I couldn't stop my anger from surging. It raced from the pit of my stomach and sped throughout my entire body at warp speed, setting every part of me on fire. For a tiny fraction of a second, I imagined grabbing her hair and shoving her face-first into the frozen treats. I closed my eyes, balled my fists.

"Oh, I'm so terribly dense," I said, my tone sharp enough to cut glass. "I didn't realize the entire world revolved around your incredibly selfish ass."

The woman whipped around, eyes wide, her expression telling me she usually got her way and it had been a long time since anyone had put her in her place. "*What* did you say?"

My turn to look her up and down, just as slowly, a wide grin on my face. "Are you always such a stuck-up bitch or are you making a special effort for me today?" Without another word I turned and stomped to the door, holding both hands, middle fingers raised, over my shoulders. "Have a shit day."

I regretted my actions before I got in my truck. Mom had always said it was easier to catch flies with honey than vinegar, and goodness knows as a music teacher she'd dealt with her fair share of difficult students and parents alike. If I'd kept my calm, gently explained my niece was sick and I was trying to get to the hospital, I may well have been on my way. My family needed me. My behavior was ludicrous. Then again, so was the woman in the store.

My short moment of introspection didn't last. When the woman finally emerged, her heels clack-clacking on the pavement, her strides were smaller and slower than before, sending me over the edge I precariously dangled from. I laid on the horn, making her jump and almost drop her grocery bag. She ignored me, and instead of putting her purchases on the front or back passenger seat of her overlord SUV, she walked to the trunk.

I put down my window, leaned out, and yelled, "Hurry up!"

Without turning around, she held her two slender middle fingers over her shoulders. Yeah, I deserved it, but it still pissed me off. Finally, she was in her vehicle, and I started my engine, expecting her to pull ahead but as my truck lurched forward, it tapped the back of the Rover.

"Shit," I muttered, cutting the engine, smacking my steering wheel with both palms. "Shit, shit, *shit.*" I backed up as she got out of her vehicle, her face more thunderous than a summer storm, and took in the little dent the impact had made. Seconds later the cashier strode out of the store, rushing over and asking the woman if she was all right.

"She did that on purpose," she shouted, pointing at me. "Look at my car. *Look* at it!"

"I didn't mean to hit you," I said as I jumped from my truck.

"Sure, you didn't." She yanked her phone from her pocket and held it to my face. "You were harassing me in the store. You insulted me. Said if I didn't hurry up you'd follow me."

"What the hell are you talking about?" I said.

"What's wrong with you?" the cashier said, voice raised. "You can't threaten my customers."

"I didn't threaten anyone," I yelled back. "She's lying."

Before either of them could answer, two older men who had exited the rusty pickup truck behind me made their way over, scowls on their bearded faces as they rearranged their baseball caps in some kind of wacky hat duet. Taking another step, the bigger one looked at the cashier. "Need some help here?"

"Back off, Deliverance," I snarled. "Mind your own god-damn business."

"Wow, that's not very ladylike," the store clerk said with a click of his tongue.

"Jesus, what next?" I scoffed. "You going to tell me to fucking smile more?"

"Holy gee willikers," the other ball-capped man said, letting out a long, high-pitched whistle. "You're quite the charmer, aren't you? You kiss your mother with that mouth?"

The mention of Mom, the rising anxiety because of Azumi's as yet unknown condition, the woman being so deliberately obtuse in the store, the hat men practically thumping their chests, plus the fact I knew this could have been avoided if I'd shut the hell up and played nice—everything mixed to-gether and boiled over at the same time. I couldn't bring my-self to apologize or back down. I felt cornered, threatened, and my fight instincts went into overdrive. Judgment had written itself all over their faces, and I took a step toward the baseball-capped men, getting in their faces.

"I said, mind your own business. Get back in your shitty truck and fuck the fuck off."

"You're unhinged," the woman said, still aiming her phone at me, but when I turned around, she scuttled back to her car, and I heard the click of the central lock. That was when I noticed the store clerk had pulled out his own phone and had it pressed against his ear.

Too late to protest—he was already speaking with the emergency dispatcher, giving the address, and saying some-one was threatening his customers. I wanted to jump into my truck and get out of there, but hat dudes and Rover lady had me boxed in and abandoning the gas station on foot wasn't an option.

Five minutes later—must've been a slow crime day in

Portland—a cruiser arrived. It took a half hour for everything to be sorted out, during which I took responsibility and apologized profusely for the sole purpose of speeding the process up.

Notes were taken, insurance information exchanged, and tempers went from boiling over to a gentle simmer. I learned the woman was named Nicole Nelson, and although the damage to her Range Rover wasn't extensive, I'd still be out of pocket. When she finally drove away, the cop looked at me.

"Not going to cause any more trouble are you, Ms. Morgan?" she said, one eyebrow arched.

I gave her a salute. "Scout's honor."

After she'd left, I went to grab the pump to fill my truck at last, but the store clerk rushed out. "No," he shouted, waving his hands. "Leave my premises before I get the cops back."

By the time I'd filled up at the next gas station and made it to the hospital room, more than an hour had passed since I'd spoken to Rico. Dad was the only person there when I walked in, and he jumped from his seat, laying into me within seconds.

"Where were you? You were supposed to be here ages ago."

"I stopped for gas."

"In Canada?"

"There was an argument."

"With whom?"

I waved a hand, looked away. "Some woman. Doesn't matter."

"Jeez, Frankie, what is it with you?"

"It wasn't my fault."

My lie immediately backfired. "It never is, is it?" he said, staring at me for a long moment before shaking his head, his expression full of the special brand of Dad Disappointment he reserved for whenever he decided I'd let him down. I'd seen it so many times and yet it still cut deep, opening old, festering wounds. "You're here now," he said, forcing a smile. "That's what's important, and—"

Dad's sentence got cut off by my brother walking in with Noa two steps behind, followed by a man in scrubs who pushed Azumi's hospital bed into the room and excused himself once he'd put it in place. I looked down at my two-year-old niece. She appeared tiny, her face a peculiar shade of green, her gorgeous brown eyes sunk into the back of her skull. Exhausted, terrified, as she clutched Spotty, the Dalmatian stuffy I'd given her last Christmas, and which she'd never slept without since. Her thumb was firmly planted in her mouth, something she hadn't done in at least six months because Noa had weaned her off it by bribing her with Wonder Woman stickers.

I gave her a soft kiss on the forehead, grabbed Rico and Noa, pulling them in for a hug before peppering them with questions about Azumi as fast as my mouth would allow. What was going on? Why was she here? What happened? What was wrong with her? How serious? What treatment? The words all tumbled out in a rush, and I could barely keep up with them myself.

"Frankie, stop," Rico said, closing his eyes. "Slow down."

Dad put a hand on my shoulder, making me jump as I'd almost forgotten he was there. "Give them a chance," he said before turning to Rico and Noa, waiting for details.

"She was complaining about a sore stomach a few days ago," Noa said.

"A few *days*?" My voice rose. "Why didn't you say?"

"Frankie," Dad warned. "Let them speak."

Noa grabbed Rico's hand and gave it a squeeze, his eyes

welling up. "We went to the family doctor and he said she was fine. It was probably just an upset stomach."

"This afternoon she kept saying it hurt really bad," Noa said. "Then she threw up."

"We gave her some medicine, but it didn't help," Rico added, his words so strangled, I wasn't sure he'd continue. "She kept crying but this time it sounded different, you know? We took her back to the pediatrician, and they sent us here immediately."

"What do they think it is?" I said. "Bad food poisoning or something?"

"Worse," Rico said. "Appendicitis."

I let out the breath I'd been holding, was about to say that wasn't too bad when my brother spoke again.

"They think it burst," he said. "She needs emergency surgery now."

It was as if I'd taken a hundred kicks to the stomach and my guts had spilled all over the scuffed floors. My sweet baby niece had a ruptured appendix? While I didn't know the details, I understood this was bad news because it could lead to serious infection if anything got into her bloodstream. What antibiotics had they given her? How fast could they operate? Before the questions made it to my mouth, the door opened.

My stomach dropped again when I recognized the person dressed in blue scrubs. Someone from my distant past I'd hoped to never see again. A man who held a prominent place on the forgiveness list I'd written in my still missing notebook.

Tyler Vance.

CHAPTER TEN

A decade and a half had passed, but I recognized him instantly. The years had been more than a little kind to Tyler. Not that I'd have admitted it, but he looked better than when we knew each other in high school.

When his eyes met mine and he gave me a courteous nod, my back stiffened. Writing his name on the list in my notebook had been justified. Even with what he'd done, he had zero recollection of who I was. Why would he? Individuals like Tyler Vance used people, discarded them, and never changed. They took whatever they needed, consequences for, and harm to others be damned. No doubt Tyler had sailed through life as entitled and self-assured as he'd been when I'd first set eyes on him.

It had been four days into our senior year, and I'd already known Tyler by reputation. Everyone did. He'd caused quite the stir across the school when he'd arrived, and no wonder. Tall, tan, with long blond hair, and a muscular body from years of competitive swimming, I'd heard whispers about him resembling Brad Pitt in *Thelma and Louise*. Rico and I had watched it at least twenty times. My favorite part was when Geena Davis and Susan Sarandon blew up the gasoline truck, which always made me cheer and whoop, but Rico regularly paused the scene where a half-naked Brad acted out a robbery with a hairdryer, both of us sighing at his impeccable physique.

I didn't sigh when Tyler Vance walked up the front steps of the school, the light shining behind him, but the rumors were true—he could've been Brad Pitt, or perhaps some Nordic god gracing us mortal peasants with his presence. Trouble was, he knew he looked good, meaning his ego had grown ten times the size of his massive deltoids, and his attitude rendered me almost immune to his charisma. Not that he ever showed any interest in me. I was the short, skinny girl with a mop of curly brown hair who'd acquired a sordid history, bringing with it an unflattering reputation I couldn't hide or get away from until I left school. Unsurprisingly, Tyler, along with everybody else, mostly avoided me.

I learned he'd recently moved to Portland from Texas with his parents and younger sister, who'd been equally blessed in the looks department. Unlike her brother, she had the soul of a saint, volunteering for as many clubs and extracurricular activities as her schedule would allow. Apparently, their father was a hotshot real estate broker who'd teamed up with a well-known and wildly successful developer in the area, and consequently the Vance family oozed money.

Tyler drove a shiny black Corvette, and instant legend had it he'd got into a spat with a teacher on his first day when she'd complained about him parking across two spaces. He'd given her a nonchalant bow and informed her in his charming Texan twang that he was doing it to protect the school. After all, if his car got damaged, his father would sue. The teacher didn't care for his attitude, but when she'd taken the matter to the principal, he'd shut her down. Everyone stopped wondering why when brand-new equipment showed up in the science lab the next week, courtesy of a generous donation from the Vance family.

Throughout the year I spotted Tyler at a few parties my ever-popular brother dragged me to, but I'd barely exchanged more than a few words with the unchallenged King of School by the time we graduated.

Until the first week of the fall semester when he plonked his butt two rows in front of me for our biology class, I'd had no clue we were both headed to Northwestern for a psychology undergrad. When he saw me afterward, we had a minuscule *what a coincidence* exchange, and I thought that would be it until he approached me five weeks later and invited me for a drink.

I didn't accept at first, but he asked again the next day and my roommate told me if I didn't go, I was being absurd, and she'd have to slice my skull open to see if it contained anything. Considering she never went anywhere without her ankle-length black overcoat no matter the weather, framed her eyes with thick black kohl, thereby unintentionally turning herself into an evil-looking raccoon, worshiped The Cure and Sisters of Mercy, and had watched every episode of *Dexter* at least eight times, I relented. The next day I told Tyler we could go for a coffee after class, my plan being a swift escape if necessary, and under pretext of having homework to finish.

"I always admired you in high school," Tyler said after he insisted on paying for my Starbucks and we sat outside the library. Good job I didn't have coffee in my mouth because I'd have choked from shock.

"Me? Why?"

"Come on, Frankie. Really? You got a full ride here, didn't you?"

"How did you know?"

"I guessed, but it's hardly surprising. I mean, you were always top of the class, and you made it seem so goddamn easy. Me? I needed three tutors to keep my As. Good job I know my way around a swimming pool, or my father would've drowned me."

I shrugged. "I didn't mind the schoolwork. Not great at sports, though. English was my thing."

"Not surprised. Your essays were amazing. Most of us were scared to read our work out loud in class after you because we sounded like a bunch of first graders."

He brushed his golden hair from his face, and I imagined how it might be to run my hands through it, particularly if he were on top of me. I looked away, the heat of a blush darting from my neck to my cheeks, burning me from the inside out. Where the hell had that thought come from? He *was* attractive, obviously, but after what had happened to me in the past there was no way I'd act on it. Besides, I'd never been remotely interested in Tyler. It had to be the change of state, the Illinois winds, or he'd slipped something in my cup.

I glanced over, watched as he took a sip of coffee and set the drink on his knee. "How are things going?" he said. "Classes okay?"

I relaxed a little. This was a friendly conversation. Nothing to it. We hailed from the same place—sort of—that's all this was. "Yeah, they're great. I worried my grades would drop but so far they've been consistent." I shifted my butt, for whatever reason gave in to the need to brag despite an awkward discomfort ensuing whenever I did. "I'm ranking pretty high in most of the classes."

"That's what I heard." He gave me a wink, leaned over. "It's why I asked you here."

"Oh?"

He sighed, big, long, and overly dramatic. "Yeah. I'm struggling like hell with the Darwin paper for bio."

"But it's due Monday."

"Let me guess…you handed yours in already?"

"Yesterday."

He smiled, shaking his head. "Wild. I have swim practice most nights. I'm not going to make the deadline for the paper."

"You want my advice on what to write?" I said, imagining us spending time together at the library or in my room, heads bent over books, leaning against one another. Tyler drained the contents of his cup and when his Adam's apple bobbed up and down as he drank, my thoughts went from saintly to dirty. I cleared my throat and hoped it would do the same for my mind. Didn't work, but Tyler broke the spell when he spoke.

"Not exactly," he said. "I think we can come to a much better arrangement."

The hairs on the back of my neck rose, a sudden and intense premonition inside my head screaming this wasn't a *let's study together* proposition, and I should leave. I didn't move but instead sat there like a mouse trapped in a tank with a snake, waiting for it to strike. When he didn't say anything, I let out a strange noise, too shrill, too loud.

"Tyler, what do you want from me, exactly?"

"Isn't it obvious? For you to write the paper for me."

"Har, har," I scoffed, my face dropping when I looked at him. "Wait, you're serious?"

"I'll pay you. A lot."

"No, you won't. Because I'm not doing it. What if we get caught?"

"We won't."

"It's unethical. Not to mention illegal, probably. I won't do it." I stood, and as I reached for my bag, Tyler gently put his hand over mine. He left it there without exerting any physical pressure, but the gesture came over loud and clear: he expected me to follow his instructions because Tyler Vance always got what he wanted.

"Get off me," I said, my voice low, and he dropped his hand.

Before I took two steps he spoke again, his tone amicable, friendly, as if his question were the most natural thing in the world. "How's Rico?"

I turned around, more than a little bewildered. I'd had no idea they really knew each other. "He's fine. Why? What's it to you?"

Tyler stared at me. "Planning on coming out of the closet anytime soon?"

My heart thumped, and I forced myself to plant my heels firmly in the ground so Tyler didn't see the tremble in my legs. Nobody knew Rico was gay. His sexual orientation had been our secret for years, after I'd found a few bottles of pills stuffed in the side pocket of his bag and had refused to leave his room until he told me what he'd planned on doing with them and why. Ever since, he and I made sure it stayed secret until he was ready to tell the world.

No question, it infuriated us that people believed his sexuality was anybody's business but his own, but we didn't yet live in the tolerant and accepting society we wished for.

None of Rico's friends knew the truth, and definitely not our father, whom my brother feared telling the most. He didn't think Dad would understand or accept, worse, Rico worried he'd order him to pack his bags and leave. If that happened, he'd have nowhere to go, especially with me so far away.

"I don't know what you're talking about," I said, staring Tyler down, thinking Rico's private life wasn't my story to tell and this jerk could bite me. Except Tyler wasn't done.

"Come on, Frankie, drop the act. I learned a lot of useful things about people during my year in Portland." He grinned his slow, sly smirk, making me want to whack him. "I might've needed tutors for class, but my observation skills are killer."

"Again, I've no clue what you're going on about."

"Really? My source—"

"What *source*?"

He tapped the side of his nose and shrugged. "They tell me Rico's still pretending. Doing a pretty good job, but you know how quickly rumors spread, and once they do..." He shrugged again. "You wouldn't want his last two years of high school to be hell, would you? Of all people, with what I hear you went through—"

"Which is none of your business."

"You're right, you're right. I'm just saying, you know how damn cruel kids can be."

I took a step forward. "If you say anything about my brother, I'll kill you."

"Relax, don't worry," Tyler said. "Nobody will utter a word as long as you help me."

"You can't extort me, you asshole."

"Who said anything about extortion? You obviously misunderstood. Frankie, I'm willing to pay you a lot of money. I'm purchasing your services."

I was about to shout at him—rant, rave, scream—before heading to the dean's office and telling her what Tyler had said. For once, my brain shut down my mouth as I realized Tyler would deny it, of course, and I had no evidence. My legs gave way and I sat back down. Tyler might as well have put me in a headlock because Rico was adamant he'd finish school—the place he referred to as a *gigantic man-eating lion's den*—before he ever went public, and he wanted to move out before he told Dad. I'd have done anything to protect my brother. *Anything*. But I wouldn't be the victim. Not this time. And I could save most of the money for Rico's education, and pretend it was from a local job or something.

"I'll help you," I said, deciding to turn things to my advantage. "But whatever you were thinking of paying me, you'd better double it. And if I hear you've breathed a word to anyone about my brother, I'll make the paper so bad, you'll fail instantly. Then I'll come for you in your sleep."

I'd thought it would be one and done, but Tyler needed more. He paid me, very well, in fact, so ultimately when we got busted by an overzealous teaching assistant with a photographic memory, even I no longer believed I'd been forced.

The one transgression they'd found cost me dearly. It went on my transcript, I lost my scholarship, and couldn't afford to continue my course. I withdrew before the end of the first semester.

Tyler on the other hand, well, as one might expect, the family fortune spoke volumes. He got a slap on the wrist, as did I, but his education hadn't depended on handouts. Last I'd heard he'd left psychology and gone to a different college where a brand-new full-ride Vance scholarship had been created. Equal opportunities my ass.

As Tyler now stood in the hospital room, I still detested him as much as I had back in college. He'd never apologized or offered a smidge of comfort. I'd been collateral damage he wouldn't have lost a moment's sleep over. My name had more than likely never crossed his mind since I'd left, and if it had, it was only because he was pissed we'd got nailed for cheating before I'd completed one of his papers and he'd either had to write it himself or find someone else. However, my education boarded the express train to Crapville, taking my intended future along for the ride.

I never told Rico or Dad why I'd written someone else's work, or for whom I'd done so, had let them both assume it was to make a fast buck. Unsurprisingly, Dad and I had the second-biggest argument of our lives and didn't speak for nearly three months despite my having moved back in with him and Rico.

After bumming around for a year, beating myself up daily about my life choices, being resentful toward everyone and everything, taking odd jobs including working at a grocery store and a hole-in-the-wall pizza joint, making me permanently smell of week-old oil, Dad convinced me to join his company. God, could the Tyler debacle really have happened so long ago?

He looked up from his tablet now, and introduced himself, his voice low, the hint of his Texan accent still present. "I'm Doctor Vance, pediatric surgeon."

I waited until his eyes met mine again, expected them to widen or narrow when he finally made the connection. Nothing. He didn't react at all. Clearly the prick had no idea who I was. I'd spent years berating myself about what I did—what *we* did—and detesting the man who'd been at the root of my decision. Meanwhile, he couldn't recall we'd met. I worked very, *very* hard to shove my feelings aside, including how conflicted I felt about the fact we needed his expertise. I didn't want any of us being at his mercy. I wanted nothing to do with him.

"Let's get straight into what's going on with Azumi," he said. "The ultrasound confirmed she has acute appendicitis, and I'm afraid there are definitive signs it has—"

"Burst?" Noa whispered. "Oh my God. How could the other doctor have missed it?"

"It can be very hard to diagnose in young children," Tyler said, and I grabbed Rico's hand and held it tight as we listened to him. Azumi needed immediate surgery, the OR was being prepped, and she'd go in as soon as it was ready. He talked about the risks of surgery, and the danger of infection—peritonitis that could lead to septicemia, something I knew could be fatal—the paperwork and consent forms, which would be handled swiftly. I looked at Noa, his skin so pale, I thought he might pass out and collapse on top of his daughter.

"Will she be okay?" he whispered.

"We're doing everything we can," Tyler said, making me want to scream at him for giving such a noncommittal answer.

Rico looked at Noa, then dropped his gaze to his feet. "I…uh, I don't know if we can afford all this," he mumbled, his cheeks alight.

"Don't worry about that now," Tyler said. "The finance department can help you with the logistics."

Despite the softening of his face, it made me want to yell only a wealthy person would say that. I knew where Rico was going. He worked freelance, made designs for comic books and graphic novels, wrote music. His work was sometimes more in demand than others. Noa had a good job in IT as a software developer, but it was a start-up he was involved in, so the insurance coverage was minimal.

"It's important we don't delay the operation," Tyler said. "We need to get in there now."

After another fire round of questions, Tyler excused himself to get ready for surgery. As the emotions of what was happening to Azumi threatened to wrap their thick fingers around my neck, I excused myself and slipped away to the bathroom in the hallway so I could regroup and try to process what was going on.

I pressed my head against the cool white tiles, took in a few gulps of air to calm down. How was this fair, a two-year-old getting violently sick like this? An innocent kid who'd never hurt anyone, loved Dalmatians, shortbread, and dancing in the living room with her orange rubber boots on her feet. She didn't deserve this. Not any of it. It made me want to punch the wall until my knuckles bled.

Thankfully, a woman walked into the bathroom before I did something I might or might not regret. I flicked on the tap, cupped my hands underneath, and splashed water on my face. Once calm enough to be of any use to Rico and Noa, I opened the door and headed into the hallway. Two steps later, Tyler called my name, stopping me dead.

"Frankie," he said again, waiting for me to turn before he continued. "It's been a long time. I'm so sorry about your niece."

"How nice of you to pretend you care."

He looked at me, his eyes downcast, and he gave me a smile I didn't know what to do with. "You have my sympathies, and—"

"I don't want your sympathies, Tyler."

He took a step back. "You're angry. I get it. It's okay for you to—"

Was this guy for real? "Oh, thank you," I spat. "Thank you so much for your *generous* permission, *Doctor*."

"Not what I meant," he said gently. "Uhm, I know there's no good time to bring this up, especially considering the circumstances, but…about what happened at college. I'm very—"

I almost let out a sigh of relief when my phone rang, cutting him off, and I grabbed my cell so I could take the call before Tyler spoke again. "Hello?" I said, turning away.

"Hi, Frankie? This is Cleo from Jake's Cakes."

"Oh, hi." I wondered if she was going to give me a hard

time for getting Evan's details from her, but her tone sounded upbeat and friendly. "How are you?" I asked.

"Great, thanks. Guess what? I found your notebook."

"Really?" I whispered. "You sure?"

"Yeah, got it here, sunflower cover and all. A customer handed it in a little earlier. I must've somehow missed it when I searched the place."

I turned to see Tyler hovering, waiting for me to finish. I ignored him, said, "When can I pick it up?"

"Anytime before ten tonight, or tomorrow morning after seven. Whatever works for you. I'll keep it behind the counter."

"Thanks. I'll be there as soon as I can." I hung up and glared at Tyler, my eyes narrowing. "Shouldn't you be scrubbing your hands or something?"

"I'm going to the OR now, but…uh, can we talk about what happened sometime?"

"I don't want to discuss it," I said. "There's nothing to say."

When he opened his mouth to respond I didn't bother waiting to hear what lies or excuses or justifications he wanted to throw my way to assuage his guilt. He was a pediatric surgeon for fuck's sake. What was he going to do? Thank me for helping him move his career into a different oh-so-rewarding direction when we'd royally screwed mine?

"Do your job. Taking care of Azumi is all that matters," I said. "And once you're finished, get the hell out of our lives and don't come back."

CHAPTER ELEVEN

Dad left thirty minutes later to grab a change of clothes and a few other things for Noa and Rico, so they'd be as comfortable as possible at the hospital, but another thirty passed before my brother shooed me home. If it had been my choice, I'd have stayed all night, waiting for Azumi to come back from the operating room, but the nurse had stopped by twice already to tell me visiting hours were over. When she popped her head through the doorway a third time, Rico gave me a hug, said, "Go, get some sleep. Even if the operation's over soon, she'll be in recovery after."

"You're sure you don't want me to stay?"

"There's no sense," Noa answered, rubbing his hands over his face. The circles around his eyes looked like he'd drawn them on with charcoal, and his crumpled shirt had definitely seen better days. "Honestly, Frankie, we'll be okay. We'll try to get some rest while we wait."

"And if you stay, you'll look even worse in the morning," Rico added.

"*Even* worse?" I gave him a tentative grin, which didn't sit right given the circumstances and immediately slid off my face. "Thanks, but insults can't get rid of me so easily."

He tried a smile, too, but same as me, didn't seem able to keep it in place. "As soon as we get news, you'll be the first to know, I promise. Deal?"

"I don't want you going through this alone."

"Don't worry," Noa said gently. "Finn will be back soon, and I guess he'll stay awhile if they let him. But Rico has a point. Go home. You'll be of no use to any of us if you're exhausted."

I did as I was told and headed off. The selfish part of me was relieved to be getting out of the building for a bit, and I knew I wasn't the only one.

When Dad had insisted on picking up the stuff Rico and Noa said could wait, he'd told us it was also because he had to feed and walk his dog, something my brother and I knew his next-door neighbor would've done. From the look in Dad's eyes, I recognized our shared struggle with being in hospitals for any length of time since Mom's accident. No wonder. Her death had been a cataclysmic, life-altering event, cutting canyon-deep wounds into our hearts and souls, scars which had never properly healed. Not that we ever really shared any of this. Despite Dad saying Mom was the love of his life, he didn't cope well with talking about her, and neither did I. It hurt too much.

Legend had it they'd met at the grocery store when he'd helped her reach for a box of double chocolate cookies. "Our hands touched, our eyes met, and I was smitten," he'd once said with a sad smile. They'd adored each other, and Rico's and my childhood was filled with love and laughter.

My mother was the queen of April Fools' pranks, besting herself every year. One time she laminated a life-size photo of her face and put it in a water-filled mason jar she set in the fridge. Dad screamed and dropped his coffee when he discovered his wife's severed and perfectly preserved head next to the milk. She'd collapsed in a fit of giggles, gasping for air as she pressed her hands over her stomach, and my father had never come close to getting her back.

The other thing I remembered most from my childhood was the radio. As a sixth grade music teacher, Mom always listened to something, and we often found her dancing in the house, her eyes closed, utterly lost in the moment. When she spotted Rico or me, she'd grab our hands, try to convince us—generally unsuccessfully the older we got—to join her.

She'd listen to anything. Classical, alternative, grunge, hip-hop, rap, rock 'n' roll, and everything in between, often humming new tunes well before Rico and I discovered them. After her accident the house remained silent, the radio sitting on the shelf untouched for years.

It happened on an early summer Tuesday. Dad had an emergency call on one of the construction sites, so Mom, Rico, and I were cleaning the kitchen after eating homemade pizza and strawberry ice pops while listening to ABBA, one of her favorite bands.

"Who wants to come for a walk?" she said, wiggling her hips to "Dancing Queen."

I tried not to groan. Mom went for an hour-long post-dinner stroll with our dachshund, Dax, almost every evening, something else she always tried to convince us to do.

"Come on, lazybones," she said, doing a shimmy. "Let's get some exercise."

"I'm going to Josh's," Rico said. "We're building Star Wars Lego."

"Neat." She turned to me. "How about you, kiddo? We can chat."

I hated it when she called me kiddo. I was fourteen, not a child. "Can't. Headache."

"Oh, no. Is it bad? I can stay home."

"No, you go," I said.

Mom had no clue I'd been dumped by my first ever boy-friend she knew nothing about. I wanted to be alone; it would be nice to have the house to myself for a while, plus I had no intention of walking around the neighborhood with my mom at my age when it would provide school bully Chelsea Fischer with more ammo to dispatch my way.

"I'm fine," I said. "Honestly. I'll lie down."

"You're sure?" she said, and when I didn't answer she added, "I'll see you guys later. Maybe we can watch a movie if you're feeling better. What do you think?"

Already halfway out the kitchen door, I said, "Maybe."

Maybe was the last word I said to Mom. Not *I love you* or *thank you for being a great mother* or the two words that would've made the biggest difference of all: *Don't go.* If only I'd known half an hour later, I'd hear Dad's truck pull into the driveway, and not long after it would be his screams. Deep and guttural, not a cry of shock and surprise similar to when he'd found the picture of Mom's head in the fridge, but acute and bone-deep agony, almost otherworldly cries which would still haunt my nightmares close to two decades later. When I heard them, I raced to my bedroom window and looked down, a sudden and desperate knowing yank-ing on my stomach when I spotted the police cruiser, and saw Dad with two officers, one of them crouching next to my father, who'd collapsed in the middle of our driveway.

Much later, we found out Mom and Dax had been in the middle of the street on a pedestrian crossing when she'd been struck in a hit-and-run. Our Riverton neighborhood was quiet, many of the properties hidden behind leafy elms and maples. Nobody had seen or heard a thing. No witnesses came forward despite multiple appeals, and the accident happened years be-fore door cams became popular.

Dax had been unharmed, but Mom passed four days later

with Dad, Rico, and me by her side, after my father made the agonizing decision of turning off the life support machines because her brain had long gone.

For months afterward I lay awake at night, worrying if my father would die of a broken heart and leave us, too. We'd been a mess, not remotely equipped to deal with that level of tragedy. In an instant, Rico and I became half orphans, Dad lost the love of his life, we'd never got any sense of real closure, and none of us had properly recovered despite our efforts at pretending. My father had grappled with his grief as well as ours and had to keep running his company because life had a sneaky little way of continuing regardless of anyone's circumstances.

Losing a parent so young made Rico and me grow up real quick, whether we wanted to or not, so we pushed our pain down and plowed ahead. My relationship with Dad had never been of the *let's-sit-down-and-share-everything* variety and when I got into deep trouble a short while after Mom passed, things between us got worse. Talking about emotions went from intensely uncomfortable to near impossible, and I'd long recognized my inability to express my feelings to anyone.

An ex once called me *emotionally stunted* and said I had attachment issues. I'll admit to the assessment stinging a little, but I didn't seem capable or willing to do anything about it. It was easier and safer to guard them, hide them away. Rico wasn't as bad, but Dad was the exact same as me—anything to avoid expressing how he felt unless it was displeasure.

One time a few years ago, when I'd gone to his place for Sunday lunch, I'd discovered he had a new dog. It didn't make much sense considering Rico and I had bugged him about getting another pet for years after Dax died, but Dad had maintained animals were too much hassle and he didn't have time. When we'd insisted we'd take care of a puppy, his position remained steadfast. Now, the man who'd been adamant about never having another animal in the house was on his knees, stroking the tiny dachshund who couldn't seem to decide between nibbling Dad's fingers and attacking the tassels on my boots.

"Frankie, meet Chip," Dad said. "Isn't he great?"

I sat on the floor, held out my hand, giggled when the dog put his damp nose on my fingers, snuffling and panting. "He's cute. Why did you call him Chip?"

"'Cause he's a dachshund."

"Uh…I don't get it."

"A sausage dog." Dad rolled his eyes when I looked at him with an expectant expression. "Sausage. Wiener. Chipolata. *Chip*. Get it?"

I burst out laughing. "You said you never wanted a dog again. Why the change of heart?"

"I dunno. Fancied one. Can you set the table?"

End of discussion. I knew damn well he'd recently split with his on-again, off-again girlfriend. This time by the sound of things it was for good, and he was spending more time than usual at work to avoid being home alone. No wonder he wanted some companionship. But would he admit it to anyone? No chance.

I understood his rationale perfectly. I'd never been eager to bare my soul to anyone—except for my anger. That beast always found ways to escape. Over the years I'd figured out a large part of my rage stemmed from past trauma, which society either wanted me to talk about or deal with in a quiet and dignified fashion such as curling into a ball and silently sobbing. I wasn't supposed to lash out and break stuff like I had at work, but at times it felt as if there was a pressure relief valve in my head, and if I didn't let out at least part of my fury that way, my whole body would implode.

Now, with the uncertainty of Azumi's illness, our glued-together family was facing another of life's ultimate challenges. Would we find our way back together if another tragedy shattered what remained of us into a million pieces? How would we survive if somehow Azumi didn't?

I pushed the painful questions away as I neared Jake's Cakes. Getting my notebook back and closing off this peculiar incident was at least something I could do. As I contemplated whether I should apologize to Evan for accusing him of something he obviously hadn't done, my phone dinged with a string of incoming messages, and when I parked the truck, I saw they were from Sandy. My immediate thought was him still being pissed at me for giving him a hard time at work this morning but when I scanned his texts a sense of unease prickled the back of my neck.

Have you seen this video?

Is this really you?

They had to be spam. Perhaps someone had spoofed Sandy's account and sent a malicious link to all his contacts. I typed out a reply.

Did your phone get hacked?

Three dots appeared, and Sandy's reply was immediate.

No! But if your dad sees this he'll shit a brick. It's bad.

A knot of anxiety built in my stomach as I tapped on the link, and Facebook opened in my browser. I'd deleted the app ages ago, and it took me a few tries to remember my password. When I finally succeeded and the video started playing on the screen, my heart sank straight to my feet. Sandy was wrong. This wasn't bad. It was cataclysmic.

CHAPTER TWELVE

I let out a groan, whispered, "Oh, no. No, no, no, *no*." The person on the screen was me. *Me!* At the gas station earlier today, mouthing off, my tone curt and eyes wild. I had to admit I looked more than a little deranged. Above the video was a detailed and descriptive post from a certain Nicole Nelson, the blonde Range Rover woman with whom I'd had the argument. The settings were public, meaning the video was available for everyone on Facebook to see. As I began to read, dismay changed to anger, filling my veins with venom.

Trigger warning!

I had the most unbelievable experience this afternoon and I'm still badly shaken as I write this. While getting gas at a service station earlier today, this woman (I refuse to call her a lady, because a proper lady wouldn't behave this way) came INTO THE STORE (!!!) and told me to HURRY UP (!!!) because she was stuck behind me. She didn't ask politely, and when I wouldn't comply with her ridiculous demands, she was unbelievably rude. When she stormed off, she gave me the finger (two, actually). Can you believe that? How uncouth!

If only things had ended there, but they didn't. As I was leaving, she **DELIBERATELY RAN INTO THE BACK OF MY CAR!!!!!** I'm physically okay, thankfully, so please don't worry, but I'm shaken. This was an absolutely terrifying experience. Thankfully the gas station owner called the police who made quick work of this woman but what is the world coming to? I mean, can't you get gas nowadays without being accosted by some lunatic?

I'm tagging who I believe is her employer Morgan Construction because I want them to know how their staff treat folks. If you're her boss and you read this, I hope you **FIRE her!!!!!**

The message continued another few lines, but when I watched the video again and saw Nicole Nelson had filmed the side of my truck and taken a close-up of the company logo and phone number underneath, my stomach lurched so hard I thought I might hurl. Once I'd steadied myself, I flicked to the comments, of which there were over a hundred already, nearly all of them calling for my head on a spike.

She's mental!

Such a horrific and awful experience.

Thinking of you.

Glad you're okay after being attacked.

You're a survivor!

Morgan Construction needs to get rid of her a$$.

Never working with this company, for sure.

Here's their website! Take note.

What an evil witch.

Sending thoughts and prayers.

Holy motherfucker. I really didn't care what Nicole Nelson thought or said about me, but if Dad saw this, he'd have a fit. I tapped out a text to Sandy, my mind whizzing ahead, trying to determine how I could best manage the situation and start what I already knew would be some serious damage control.

Don't show this to my dad. I'll handle it. I'll talk to him. Before hitting Send I added, Apologies about this morning and happy birthday.

Sandy returned a thumbs-up. This thing was by no means contained, but I hoped I could shield my father from the online hassle my big mouth had caused, if only for the night. Unless one of his friends or another of our colleagues saw it and called him, of course, which was entirely possible. I crossed my fingers and hoped he'd be too busy to pay attention to his phone because of everything going on at the hospital.

But... *fuuuuuuuck*, I hadn't reacted well at the gas station, I knew that. Then again neither had Nicole Nelson, but she'd put her version of the story out there first, edited the content to suit *her* narrative. Like so often on social media these days, it didn't much matter what I said or did now—it was out there, damage done, the court of public opinion's verdict mercilessly rendered. Final ruling? I was a prick. Worse still, Morgan Construction employed pricks.

How would this affect the company? If, for example, Patrick Davies saw it, would it give him one more reason to cancel the project Dad had worked so hard to win? Our cash flow wouldn't survive. We'd have to get a loan from the bank, which was by no means a given. Because of me, everyone could be out of a job.

Heart and head pounding, I hurried to Jake's Cakes, my palms sweating so much I had to wipe them four times on my pants as I practically ran to the front door. Inside, the place heaved, crowded and noisy, a line of thirsty patrons snaking halfway down the store. There was no way I could put up with this, and I had no intention of waiting to get my hands on my notebook. I took a step.

"Hey, excuse me," a man with a tie covered in pink one-legged flamingos said as he pointed behind him. "The back of the line's over there."

I was about to tell him to mind his own business, but with Nicole Nelson's video still fresh, and the possibility of my face going viral twice in one day because everyone had a camera in their pocket, I slunk to the back and put my head down. It took ages to get to the front and finally recover my notebook. Cleo wasn't there, so I asked the barista to thank her for me and stuffed a twenty into the tip jar before buying the last cheese and spinach sandwich from the display case.

All was quiet in the hallway when I got home shortly after nine. I crept past Edith's apartment, from where I heard her squeaky violin playing a mutilated rendition of something sounding Chopin-esque, and when I reached my front door and looked down, I saw another bunch of sunflowers, bigger and brighter than the first. Same as last time, there was no note. No store logo. Who the hell had left them?

I grabbed the bouquet and headed for the trash chute, launching it inside and listening for the satisfying thud as it reached the bottom. As soon as I got to my apartment, I snatched the first bunch and expedited it down the garbage as well, wanting no reminder of the fact this was the second time someone had left an anonymous gift for me in a matter of days.

My nerves settled a little once I'd showered and had eaten the sandwich. Exhausted, I texted Rico, and when he responded saying Azumi was in recovery, I settled in bed, hoping for sleep.

Half an hour later I was back in my living room, going through Facebook. The mindless scrolling was one of the main reasons I'd stopped using the app in the first place, but now I seemed unable to put the thing down. A behemoth lack of judgment enticed me to read every single comment people had added to Nicole's post since I'd last checked, and I kept going back again and again so I could see the latest barb aimed at me.

By some miracle I managed to keep my fingertips under control and not type out a reply, but with every new comment, fresh hot anger filled my guts. I grabbed my sunflower notebook—which no longer made me happy either—flipped to the page with my list of names and was about to write Nicole Nelson in large capital letters when something in my brain clicked and whirred, telling me to stop.

What was I doing? Geraldina had been quite specific about this assignment. It was supposed to be a forgiveness list, and yet, before I'd written the first name, I'd already decided I wouldn't be pardoning anyone. Christ, I'd felt proud of it being the opposite.

As I sat on my sofa with old and new resentment whipping up my insides, Nicole Nelson's ugly post glaring at me, I stared at what I'd known from the beginning would be a *hate* list. The discomfort of what that said about me as a person— mean, spiteful, childish, *embarrassing*—made me want to dive under the sofa and hide for a month.

I looked at the names, eleven in total, including mine, wondered if Geraldina was right, if I'd feel better by somehow—and the *how* was the biggest obstacle—finding the courage and ability to forgive. I took a second, thought hard whether I might possess the power to let all the negativity I harbored against everyone on my list slip away. How would my life be if I did? If I chose to? Was it a choice? And if so, did I want to?

Until now, I'd considered forgiving people who'd hurt me so deeply a sign of weakness, of surrender, and not something Frankie Morgan would do. I put the pen and notebook down. I'd never been one to turn the proverbial cheek—had asked my mother when I was four why I'd let anyone hit me once let alone twice—and I wasn't about to start doing so. Still, for now I wouldn't add more names to my list, no matter how badly I wanted to.

Figuring out the Nicole Nelson fiasco would have to wait until morning, I decided, which would hopefully give me enough time to digest everything and come up with a sensible plan not involving getting into social media spats with her or her friends.

Flicking back to my Facebook feed, I wondered if the best thing would be to delete my account for good, so I wasn't tempted to log in and check what people were saying about the situation. Before I came to a decision or had a chance to navigate to the depths of my account settings, a new notification made me pause, my finger hovering above the screen. It was a post from a person I'd known in high school, who'd friended me a while back and I hadn't interacted with since. She was asking people to pray for her friend, Chelsea Fischer.

A shiver ran down my spine and I glanced at my open notebook on the coffee table. *Chelsea Fischer* was the fourth name I'd written on my list.

I opened the post and went through the details. Chelsea

had been in a road accident this morning when the back wheel of her car had come off, sending the vehicle straight into a ditch where it had smashed sideways into a tree. She'd been alone, no kids in the vehicle, thank goodness, but she was quite badly hurt. Lacerations to her face from the airbag deployment and windshield debris. Fractured shoulder and two broken arms, which necessitated a hospital stay.

Part of me had compassion for Chelsea. Another part, the one almost everyone has but won't admit to and buries in the depths of their soul, remained cold. Moments ago, I'd pondered forgiving those on my list, but the tinge of schadenfreude, which I'd never have confessed to anyone, made me realize it was near impossible to drum up more empathy for the woman who'd made my life a living hell for years.

Like Tyler, back in school everyone had known who Chelsea was. Long, glossy blond hair, big doe eyes, legs up to her armpits, as my mother once said when she saw Chelsea at a school play, all combined with an innocent charm with which she entranced the teachers. She had clear skin, a perfect nose, a body sparking envy and desire in equal measure.

Her immaculate looks were delivered in a beautiful package that also contained buckets of intellect and a quick wit, not to mention an obscene amount of attitude and self-confidence. Sometimes I'd wondered what she might have accomplished if she'd used her forces for good rather than evil, and I thanked the universe she and Tyler Vance never ended up together. If they had, we all would've been doomed.

I never knew exactly why Chelsea targeted me. I had my suspicions although in my experience, bullies didn't require a particular reason. All they needed was the knowledge you wouldn't put up a fight, meaning they could get away with whatever abuse they hurled your way. Your pain was their gain, your weakness became their source of strength, and destroying you was their superpower. This was all part of the unwritten bully manifesto, accompanied by a free pass to be as cruel as possible and see how far they could push you before you broke. It'd certainly been Chelsea's modus operandi.

She'd walked up to me one morning at the start of eighth grade when I'd been elbow deep in my locker, retrieving a math book. Mostly I'd kept my head down in school when it came to other students. I wasn't trendy enough for the cool kids, not sporty enough for the cheerleader gang, and too boring for the rest. Most thought my interest in crime fiction when they couldn't get enough of rom-coms and happily ever afters was plain strange. Consequently, I didn't have many friends, and Chelsea was about to make things a whole lot worse.

She snapped her gum as she twirled one of her French braids around her finger until I gave her my full attention. I wondered what she was doing. Worried she'd ask me to join her group for lunch at the cafeteria and immediately fretted about what I'd say when at a table with the most popular girls.

She wrinkled her nose, cocked her head to one side. "You're Frankie?"

"Uh, yeah?" I'd made it sound as if I didn't know who I was. Duh.

Chelsea snapped her gum again. "Did you hear the rumor about you that's going around?"

"N-no," I said as my bowels made a sudden and uncomfortable movement. "Wh-what?"

Chelsea bit her lip as she came closer, her breath minty fresh, the rest of her smelling of coconuts, like a sublime vacation at the beach. And then she hit me with, "You only shower and change your underwear once a week."

I gasped. "But that's not true. Who said that?"

She looked me over, leaned in again and sniffed the air before jumping back with a disgusted look on her face. "Me." She walked off, her laughter ringing in my ears as she glided down the hallway, her royal entourage tittering close behind.

That had only been the start. Other, more persistent lies circulated. They said I gave blowjobs in the back of the school bus in the morning, and in the second-floor bathroom at lunchtime, and my motto was *the bigger the better.* They insisted I'd beg for more, do *anything* a boy wanted and the only way I got As in all my classes was because I slept with every teacher I could. Not sure how many people believed it, but everyone ignored me after that. Nobody wanted to take the chance of their reputation being sullied by attaching it to mine.

This pattern continued for a year and stopped for a while after Mom was killed and my life derailed, but a few months later, when I thought Chelsea had taken pity on me and would leave me alone because she couldn't possibly be so cruel, someone asked me if it was true I'd run my own mother over and refused to confess. I confronted Chelsea. Told her I knew she'd started the crass lie. She laughed. I threatened her with going to the principal. She laughed harder.

"Go for it," she said, waving a hand. "But you know they'll never believe you."

I did nothing and couldn't leave the school either because I feared Chelsea would seize the opportunity to turn her viciousness against Rico as soon as he arrived. Not an option. Not when he was desperately trying to fit in and hide his true self, and I'd found those pills in his bag.

I'd kept my head down and ignored Chelsea as best I could. Being this angry felt new to me and I tried to stuff all the hatred for her down to the pit of my stomach and instead get my revenge by besting her in every class I could. It had worked for the most part. Top of my year, valedictorian, and

I got a full scholarship as a result, but that had ended badly because of my ill-advised decision to help Tyler, and I'd been thankful Chelsea hadn't been there to gloat at my fall from grace. Or so I'd thought.

We had a high school reunion five months ago, one of many I'd fully intended on sitting out, except Rico insisted it would be good for me. An opportunity to get some of the animosity I had for my school days out of my system now we were all older and hopefully wiser. "Trust me, you can slay your demons," he'd said, chiding me when I asked if he meant literally. In any case, he'd been wrong. Sometimes monsters past were best left alone, hidden in the deepest, darkest forests of our minds, tucked away behind the gnarliest trees.

When Chelsea walked in, her emerald silk cocktail dress flowing, face aglow, I could almost taste the collective awe. She regaled everyone with stories about her cherubic toddler and flourishing business designing a line of baby clothes which had recently been picked up by a high-end store. Not that she could possibly tell us which one, or when, she'd said, putting a perfect finger to her perfect lips. Those details were top secret, but the deal was *huge*, they'd said she was a rock star, and she'd share on social media as soon as possible for all to see. As she spoke, I wished her phone would shoot up her ass to stop her from posting anything ever again.

Later in the evening as I stood at the bar waiting for a drink because I badly needed one, she sauntered over, not saying a word as she gave me the once-over, openly scanning me from the top of my head to the tips of my toes, a condescending smirk pulling at her lips. This was the real Chelsea, the woman who'd evidently graduated from high school Mean Girl to suburban Mean Mom. I wanted to tell her exactly what I thought of her, and I knew precisely the kind of person she was, but she spoke first.

"I hear you work construction," she said, tilting her head to one side. "Oh, dear."

She pulled a sad face, patted my shoulder, and walked off. As did I. Except I strolled straight out of the venue and went home without as much as a backward glance. I hadn't seen Chelsea since and had no desire or intention of talking to her for the rest of my life. Yes, it was sad she'd had an accident, and while I didn't wish her any physical harm, nothing major anyway, I'd have been lying if I said I'd lose sleep over her condition.

I was about to shut my phone off and push my old rival to the depths of my brain where she belonged when I saw an update on the Facebook post, making instant nausea hit.

OMG! The wheel on the car may not have come off by accident! It could've been deliberate. I'll say more when I can. In the meantime, please, please pray for our beautiful, darling Chelsea.

My eyes dropped to the names I'd written down, and I clawed at the neck of my T-shirt, pulling it away as if I hadn't had a drop of water in weeks. With shaky fingers I tore the forgiveness list from my notebook and crushed it into a ball before flattening it out and ripping it to pieces instead.

Two people on my list had been hurt in the last two days. That had to be coincidence…didn't it?

CHAPTER THIRTEEN

I couldn't sleep. Geraldina's and Chelsea's accidents happening so close together had weirded me out, plus I kept worrying about my niece. Even after Rico sent an update saying Azumi was back in the room and they were all trying to get some rest, I found myself flip-flopping on my mattress, getting increasingly fidgety. Neither reading nor watching TV helped, and as I'd implemented a self-imposed social media ban until dawn to avoid reading more nasty comments about myself, I spent the next little while researching Tyler, trying to reassure myself he was the best person to treat Azumi, considering what I knew about his academic history.

The answer surprised me. No clue exactly how or when his journey had taken him from asshole to the new starlet of the pediatric surgery world, but his reputation as a skilled doctor was more than solid. Years after leaving Northwestern he'd graduated from Yale summa cum laude and been offered his pick of residencies, multiple hospitals fighting over his steady hands while dozens of patients revered his bedside manner, especially the kids. I wondered why he'd returned to Portland when by the looks of things, he could've gone anywhere, until I located an interview where he mentioned his father's terminal cancer diagnosis and wanting to be close to family. Apparently, Tyler Vance hadn't sold the remainder of his soul. Yet.

A few more swipes and taps, and I located his address, instantly making curiosity bloom in my belly. To hell with it, I couldn't sleep anyway and needed a distraction, so I drove to Bay Street, expecting a humongous and sprawling residence, complete with a fountain and statues of Tyler himself. Instead, it was a traditional two-story home with gray siding, a double garage, and an Adirondack chair on the front porch with a carved pumpkin on either side, making me wonder if he had a family although there'd been none mentioned in anything I'd read. I drove to the end of the road and turned back, crawled past Tyler's place again, craning my neck. When a light came on inside the house next to his, I decided to head off.

On the way to my apartment, I grabbed a few beers, quickly drank two of them when I got home, and finally collapsed in bed fully clothed. I must've fallen asleep straight away because the next time I looked at the clock it was 5:00 a.m. I grabbed my phone. No news from Rico, which I hoped meant all was still okay. I flopped back down, whispering a silent thank-you to the ceiling. Azumi was going to be all right, I told myself. She'd be *fine*. I sent my brother a text, asking him to call when he was awake.

Once I'd dragged myself out of bed, I made a vat of the strongest coffee I could stomach. It wasn't until I'd downed two and a half industrial-sized mugs that I saw the flaw in my plan. All the nervous energy left over from last night had multiplied and, mixed with the caffeine, was now pulsing through my veins, making me buzz around my little apartment like a wasp on steroids.

For the next half hour, my thoughts refused to be quietened, racing from everything that had happened since the beginning of the week. Azumi's illness was bad enough in itself, but I'd made things far worse for Dad by losing my temper at the service station. I'd drawn the wrath of Nicole Nelson, made myself look like an ass, and potentially put the company in more jeopardy than I had with the Patrick Davies fiasco.

That wasn't the only problem. My shoulders dipped as I pushed my mug away and touched my notebook. Getting it back was great, but it hadn't answered any of my other questions, such as where, when, and how I'd lost it, or whether Evan had actually stolen and returned it to the coffee shop to mess with me. Then there were the two bunches of flowers and the Uber driver. As much as I tried to insist he'd been legit, Barney the Dinosaur figurine and all, it still didn't seem right.

Another red flag vied for my attention, the one I'd wanted to ignore but which wouldn't let me. Two people on my now ripped to shreds forgiveness list had been hurt, one of them quite badly. Throughout the night I'd insisted to myself Geraldina and Chelsea having separate and unrelated accidents was a fluke and chastised myself for seeing a connection where there obviously was none. What was that line again? Something about once being an accident, twice a coincidence, three a pattern. Made sense, but never mind how much I reassured myself there was no relationship between the incidents, I hadn't quite got rid of the voice inside my head insisting it was odd and reminding me of the other names on the list, including Dad's and mine.

I let out a groan and rubbed my eyes. The day had barely begun, and I had to snap out of this funk if I was going to get through the rest of it without freaking out. With a shake of my head, I reached for the remnants of my now lukewarm coffee and drank the last mouthful as my phone rang.

"Rico?" I said. "How's Azumi?"

"Resting." He sounded as if he needed to do the same but knowing my brother, he'd hold vigil by his daughter's side and never shut his eyes. "Noa's sleeping next to her so I'm in the hallway, trying to get my head around what's going on. I should've called last night, but we were all exhausted."

"No problem. Did you see Tyler after the operation? What did he say?"

"It went okay, but she's not out of the woods yet. Apparently, there are still risks of infection, so she's being closely monitored. He said things can still turn so we have to be prepared. God, I can't believe this happened."

I pictured him slumped on the floor, his back to the wall, literally and figuratively. It made me want to jump in my truck, drive to the hospital, and throw my arms around him so I could protect him from whatever might come his way. "It'll be all right," I said.

"I'm scared," he said, his voice rising a little. "I'm terrified about the potential complications Tyler told us about and freaking out because of the costs. And just thinking about money makes me the worst dad in the history of all the universes."

"Stop. You and Noa are the best parents I've ever seen," I said in my best *don't-argue-with-me-I'm-your-big-sister* tone. "We'll figure out the money. You know Dad and I will do whatever we can to help." I meant every word, including continuing with the anger management sessions to keep the peace with Dad and seeing Evan there again, getting the company cash flow back on track so Dad and I could help Rico and Noa financially.

We chatted for a bit, and once we hung up, I knew there

was something else I had to do to keep the promise I'd made to my brother. After spending a little while longer planning my strategy and swallowing the massive lump of pride lodged in my throat, I headed to Messenger.

Finding Nicole Nelson's profile took seconds but drafting a note in which I offered a profuse apology for yesterday's behavior, explained my niece was sick and I'd been in a rush to get to the hospital to see her, took ages. I spent forever adding and deleting words, making the letter overly gushy before paring it back and finally hitting Send.

One long shower later, and Nicole hadn't replied. Depending how tech savvy she was, it might take a while for her to spot the message request. Then again, if she'd already seen it, she might choose to ignore me. Worse, and the thought made me shudder, she could take a screenshot and post it as a public claim of victory or lambast me for writing to her only because my job was under threat, and I wanted to save my ass.

It was shortly before seven, way too early for a hospital visit and Jeff wouldn't be up yet for me to offer to walk Terry. I didn't want to go to the office, either, hoped I could delay telling Dad about Nicole's Facebook post a little longer. Maybe if she deleted it, he'd never find out.

More nervous energy coursed through my veins, and I had to do something before my body spontaneously combusted. I peeked out the window, saw the signs of pinky dawn creeping across the clear skies, the first rain-free day this week.

With renewed enthusiasm I went to my bedroom closet. In no time I'd pulled on a pair of leggings and the Sex Pistols T-shirt my mother always wore whenever she cooked Sunday breakfast. I tied my hair back, stuffed my feet inside my trusty sneakers, grabbed a light jacket and car keys, and headed out.

Evergreen Cemetery was a few miles away, a quick drive

along Deering, Brighton, and then onto Stevens Avenue. It was often my place of choice whenever I needed to clear my head, and, as always, the first thing I did when I got there was visit Mom's grave.

I didn't stop by as much as I used to. Almost twenty years of her absence and the desperate need to drop in and tell her everything going on in my life, which I hadn't done when she was alive, had waned considerably. Over time, the intense and debilitating grief and guilt of her loss had transformed itself into a dull ache—something that would never leave, and which I'd learned to deal with enough to function.

I wished I could say the same about the anger I had for the person who'd run into her. That fury still burned hot as plasma. Whenever I thought about them—which I didn't allow myself to do often—the fact they still walked around unpunished, enjoying a life free from any consequences for their actions, threatened to rip me to shreds. This deeply entrenched resentment had fueled many runs over the past years.

At one point I'd tried boxing but got into trouble when I kept beating my opponent after she'd sunk to the floor and gone limp. As soon as our coach, a beast of a man from London, had ensured she was all right, he'd marched me to his office, slammed the paper-thin door and bellowed, "What the blinking hell were you thinking, Frankie? Were you trying to kill her or what?"

His comment had seriously messed with my head. If I killed someone, it would make me the same as the bastard who'd mowed down my mother. What scared me more was not knowing if I'd have stopped punching my opponent had the coach not stepped into the ring. It frightened me so much I never went back to the club, preferring to bury my frustrations deep or trying to release some of them during long runs alone.

Years had passed since Mom died but God, I missed her. I yearned for closure, wondered how I might react if the driver confessed after all this time. Then again, I wasn't sure I'd trust myself enough to sit in a courtroom during the trial, look them in the eyes knowing they'd left Mom for dead in the middle of the street after crushing her legs, ribs, and skull. Chances were astronomical I'd leap over a table and put my hands around their neck. I'd have been a liar if I denied fantasizing about it sometimes. Would I feel the same if they'd stayed at the scene? Could I have found space in my heart to forgive because they did the right thing? Moot point as no arrest would ever be made.

Pushing the thoughts away, I knelt next to her headstone, a simple black granite slab with four hearts representing Mom, Dad, Rico, and me.

"Hey, Mom," I said. "It's been a while."

I told her about Azumi first, asked her to watch over the granddaughter she'd never met, to give Rico and Noa strength to get through this because they needed her legendary optimistic outlook on life more than ever. Next, I gave her an update on how things were going with Dad, and the fact I'd landed in anger management sessions because my temper had got the better of me after an incident with a jerk of a client. Telling the story made me resent the fact I'd questioned what Davies may have done, so I pressed my lips together and stopped talking.

As the cold began to sneak its way into my legs, I plucked some weeds from her grave and tidied a little. Standing, I wiped my eyes, forcing the giant lump down to my belly. No matter how many times I'd done this before, saying goodbye was always the hardest part.

When I finally turned away, I made my feet find a steady rhythm as I ran down the path to the forest, and a little while later my head and heart became clearer, lighter. Running always did this to me. Rico—a self-confessed couch potato until he met Noa—used to shake his head and groan whenever I laced my shoes. He'd been known to hide them a few times when I'd threatened to make him come with me.

"What's wrong with walking?" he said once, settling on the sofa with a bowl of chips balanced on his enviable flat gut, whereas mine would forever have a tiny paunch and stretch marks I'd never get rid of, no matter what I tried. "Running is way too much work so face it, sis, I'm never, ever going to be sporty. Ever." True…until he met Noa, who loved working out, and the harder the better. Swimming, tennis, cycling, downhill or cross-country skiing. Kitesurfing, obstacle runs, archery, he'd try anything once and had completed three full marathons. Finally, his athleticism inspired Rico to get off his lazy butt, and now the two of them regularly cycled for miles, with Azumi sitting on the back of Noa's bike wearing her turquoise bunny helmet, clapping her hands, and squealing, "Fast, Daddy, fast."

I tried hard not to think of her lying in the hospital bed, of what might happen if Tyler didn't have as steady a hand last night as he professed. Operating on a child had to be one of the most dangerous things a doctor could do, they were so tiny and fragile. I hated the fact we were dependent on him, and in an instant of utter selfishness I'd almost considered urging Rico and Noa to find another surgeon. Thankfully I'd kept my churlishness in check.

A noise on the path behind me made me jump, pulling me out of my thoughts. I'd been so focused on them I hadn't heard someone else's footfalls. I looked over my shoulder, saw a tall, broad white guy not far away who was gaining speed.

I'm not sure what it was. Probably the combination of lack of sleep and all the stressful stuff that had happened over the past few days but seeing him coming behind me like a bullet train made a shiver zap through me. I glanced over my shoulder a second time, saw he was now under thirty yards away.

As the memory of the mystery rideshare trip flashed through my mind, and images of both Chelsea and Geraldina loomed large, panic took hold. I tried to calm down, but my brain switched into flight mode, yelling at me the trails were empty, with nobody else in sight if I needed help. If this dude was following me, if he attacked me, I didn't stand a chance.

My heart rate spiked, and within a nanosecond I'd evaluated my options: slow down and hope he passed without incident, try to fight him, or speed up and try to outrun him if he gave chase. As much as I wanted to believe I'd be a match for him if we engaged in battle, I went for the latter option. My truck was about eight minutes away. Four if I upped the pace to a full-on sprint. Another glance and he'd gained more ground, hardly difficult considering he was at least a head taller than me.

I took another step, not paying attention to where I put my foot, and without warning it landed on a rock in the middle of the path. My ankle rolled, and although I tried hard to catch myself, momentum and gravity sent me to the ground, palms and knees hitting the path, grit and dirt ripping into my skin.

"*Ow,*" I yelped. Turning my head, I saw the man approaching at full speed. I pushed myself up and tried taking a step but as I put weight on my ankle, I cried out again.

"Hey, are you okay?" the guy called over. "Holy moly, that was quite the tumble."

"I'm fine, I'm fine," I said, wincing. "Honestly, you go ahead, get back to your run."

"Are you sure?" He moved a little closer.

"Don't come near me." I growled the words through gritted teeth, making his eyebrows disappear into his hairline as a startled expression took over his face.

He more than likely had no idea how uncomfortable he was making me feel. Me, female and alone in the presence of a large man out in the middle of nowhere was bad enough but add a busted ankle to the mix and it made me beyond vulnerable.

Guys, those with honorable intentions at least, often had no idea how threatening they could be just by breathing. Men like this one had the luxury of rarely feeling threatened. When they went for a run or walked home late at night, the only thing they thought about was which route to take. For women, it was all about risk mitigation. With or without earbuds? Keys in our pocket or held tight between our fingers? Should we carry pepper spray? Was it too late in the evening to run, too early, too dark, our route too isolated? Was there someone we could go with instead of exercising solo? It was exhausting.

"I'm fine, thank you." I waved a hand, moved my foot around to demonstrate there was no harm done. "Go on ahead. My truck's not far."

After another round of *are you sure* and *yes, yes, I'm fine*, he headed off, leaving me to scold myself for my paranoia, although sometimes paranoia could be the difference between getting hurt and getting away.

By the time I spotted the parking lot in the distance, the pain in my ankle had reduced to a dull throb I could almost ignore. As I limped a few steps, digging around my pocket for my keys, I looked up, saw a black car parked next to mine. Something familiar about the vehicle lurked in the back of my memory, demanding attention, but I couldn't quite grasp what it was. I craned my neck to get a proper look, but the distance was too great. When I tried walking faster, my ankle throbbed again, making me do a clunky hobble, skip, hobble, skip. As I got closer, my memory finally clicked, fitting pieces together as if they were a jigsaw puzzle.

The car, a Mazda CX-3, seemed familiar because it *was* familiar. In fact, I was almost certain it was exactly like the rideshare one I'd clambered into Monday night.

CHAPTER FOURTEEN

I looked around, unease making me shiver in the cool breeze. Was someone following me? As I stood in the parking lot, I tried focusing on my memory, urging it to go back to Monday night and recall my driver's face, but nothing came out of the static, empty void. I circled the car, bent over so I could see inside. No purple Barney the Dinosaur hanging from the rearview mirror. Didn't mean anything as the owner could've removed it. I cupped my hands against the driver's window, tried to spot anything else useful.

"Can I help you?"

I spun around, saw a woman somewhere in her sixties dressed in a fire-engine red puffer jacket, matching the color on her lips. She came a step closer, lifting her sunglasses and resting them on top of her head. "What are you doing to my car?"

"Uh, only looking."

"Clearly. What for?"

I shrugged. "It's nice."

"This old piece of crap?"

"No, I mean the model. I've been looking into buying a Mazda. I was curious."

Her face shifted, the apprehension giving way a little. "It's a good choice. Reliable."

"I'm thinking of getting into the rideshare business," I said casually. "Maybe Uber."

"Never taken one myself. I was brought up not to trust strangers."

"I hear you," I said. "This is your car?"

"Yeah."

"And, uh, what do your partner and kids make of it?"

"Ha, I have neither. Nobody's driven this one but me, but I love it. Had it almost eight years, hardly any repairs. Anyway, I'd best be going. Nice chatting with you."

I gave her a wave and watched as she set off. This woman definitely wasn't the person who'd driven me home Monday night, and as much as I wanted to be certain I'd got a ride in a car identical to hers, I still couldn't be a hundred percent sure. I decided I had to accept I'd never know what had gone on. What mattered was from now on I paid more attention when I got a ride, so I never ended up in this situation again. I hadn't been harmed, whoever had driven me hadn't stolen my notebook. It was time to drop it and move on.

By the time I arrived at my apartment, I was looking forward to having a shower, during which I planned on giving myself a pep talk about how I'd tell Dad the details of the Nicole Nelson disaster. Things didn't work out as planned.

As soon as I unlocked my front door and my foot passed the threshold, every single hair on the back of my neck and arms stood up. A tingling sensation traveled down my rod-straight spine as I stood still, straining to listen. There was no noise coming from my apartment, not a single sound, but somehow the overbearing sense I wasn't alone swirled around me, making it hard to move.

"Hello?" I called out.

The air had become dense, thicker than winter fog, and it floated to my nostrils, bringing with it a scent I didn't recognize, something woodsy mixed with citrus. I took a step, gripped my truck key between my knuckles so it stuck out like a dagger. I leaned in, tried to peer into my kitchen and all the way to the bedroom, shouted, "Who's there?"

The question was ludicrous. If a serial killer happened to be hiding somewhere in my apartment, he or she was hardly going to step out, shake my hand, and make a formal introduction. I stayed where I was and listened, but other than my ragged breathing all remained quiet. Slightly bolder, I took a few slow steps, leaving the front door wide open behind me in case I needed to escape.

My gaze scanned the kitchen as I calculated the potential each object had to become a weapon. The butcher's knife seemed an obvious choice, except when it came down to it, I wasn't sure I'd have the courage to stab someone. Couldn't imagine piercing their skin and drawing blood, let alone shoving it deep enough to incapacitate them. I'd read somewhere initial stab wounds were often tentative because people didn't have the nerve to thrust the blade in deep.

I reached for a cast iron frying pan instead, closing my fingers around the handle as I inched my way through the living area. There was nobody there, and I soon established the bathroom was empty as well. Only the hallway, and my bedroom and closet remained. I inspected each space, but nothing was out of the ordinary there either.

As I lowered the pan, letting it dangle by my side, I told myself I really needed to get a hold of my newfound paranoia. I still jumped when my cell rang as I headed back through my apartment to shut the front door, freezing when I saw my father's name flash across the screen.

"Hey, Dad," I said.

"What did you do, Frankie?"

I had a sneaking suspicion about the reason for his call, but on the off chance I was wrong, I muttered, "What's up?"

"You know exactly what's up," he said. "Three friends sent a link to a Facebook post. I'm guessing you know the one?"

"Yeah. I can explain."

"Save it. I spent the last half hour trying to decide what to do. Have you seen the comments these people are making about you? About the company? It's like I've been dragged through the Battle of the Bastards and back."

"Ah, so you're finally watching *Game of Thrones*?"

"This is serious. What happened? What were you *thinking*?"

"I wasn't—"

"No, damn right you weren't," he said. "That's the problem. When will you understand your actions can carry consequences for people other than yourself? *Serious* consequences."

"For God's sake, Dad, I know."

"You know *nothing*, you—"

I forced a small laugh. "Neither did Jon Snow."

"Read the room, will you? Can't you tell I'm goddamn furious? You're hurting the company. If you want to fuck up your livelihood then go ahead, but as long as you work for me you get in line like everybody else and you stay there, do you understand?"

It took me a moment to register Dad had used the f-word. Despite his Irish roots, it wasn't something he let cross his lips often, not in the workplace, and he'd never directed it at me. I wanted to apologize. Say I regretted what had happened with Nicole, but the way he spoke to me made groveling impossible. Instead, I added another layer to the resentment between us, a thick coat of the stuff we both knew existed, but which we usually glossed over. Addressing it risked us never speaking to one another again. There was, however, another solution.

"You know what, Dad?" I said. "Maybe it's best if I find another job." Not the first time I'd thought about it or the first time I'd brought it up, but I'd never meant it until now.

"You might be right," he said, his voice cool. "Except I don't have time to sort out the logistics of hiring a new project manager. Not with what's going on with Azumi. She's what's most important. Noa and your brother need support. Don't be selfish."

"You mean the kind of support you didn't give Rico when he came out to you?" I said. "You may want to go look in the mirror for a while." I knew it was a low blow but couldn't help myself, not when the memories of Rico's devastation when Dad didn't speak to him for a week still stung. It might have been ten years ago, but those wounds ran deep.

"I'm not having this discussion with you again," Dad said. "I apologized to him, and you, for not being accepting. I educated myself, saw I was dead wrong. I changed. Realized it wasn't about me. Maybe you should try it sometime."

He hung up, leaving me standing in my apartment clutching the phone to my chest as if I'd been sucker punched in the gut. Dad would never have spoken to an employee the way he had to me, and his words burrowed deep under my skin.

I tried to push his voice from my head and focus on work, wanted to turn off my phone to make it more difficult for me to call him back and say things I might not regret, except I couldn't in case Rico tried to reach me. I stabbed at the screen and muted my dad's number instead, satisfied the gesture would keep him out of my face and ears if only temporarily.

I headed to the bathroom for a shower. Once done, I stuck two slices of bread in the toaster and pulled a yogurt from the fridge, ripping off the lid. When I went to stuff the foil top in the garbage, I frowned and pulled the bin out. Hadn't I dumped my forgiveness list in there last night? And if I had, why weren't the pieces there? I pushed the other trash aside to see if the bits of paper had slipped lower down. Nothing. The hair on the back of my neck stood sentry again. I had a habit of dispatching anything I no longer wanted—cards from a cheating ex, sunflowers from anonymous sources— down the garbage chute, but I didn't remember doing the same with my confettied list last night.

Had someone been in my apartment after all? I let out a ridicule-filled snort. For what? To go through my trash? My laptop was still on the coffee table, untouched. I had a clear glass jar with about two hundred bucks of emergency funds on a kitchen shelf. Either of those would've been of far more interest to a thief.

I remembered the beers I'd had in quick succession when I'd come back from my late-night drive past Tyler's place. I'd hoped the alcohol would make me sleep, not confuse the ass off me, and I definitely recalled dropping the cans into the recycling bin next to the trash chute in the hallway. I must've got rid of the shredded forgiveness list then, too, but why did I remember differently?

CHAPTER FIFTEEN

While insisting my lapse in memory of what I'd done with some garbage was because I'd downed two beers in record time, I got ready for work and drove to one of the building sites for a meeting with the electrician, after which I called Rico to agree I'd stop by the hospital as soon as I could. He didn't mention anything about Dad, so I assumed they hadn't spoken about the infamous Facebook video, but I couldn't be sure, and I wanted to be prepared in case my brother had a go at me when I saw him. I unmuted Dad, immediately wishing I hadn't bothered.

8:26 a.m. Dad: Did you order the lumber for the Benson project?

8:45 a.m. Dad: What's the scoop?

9:17 a.m. Dad: Can you answer?

9:34 a.m. Dad: Frankie!

Jaw clenched, I typed an answer, knowing the brevity of it would piss him off.

10:17 a.m. Me: Y

10:18 a.m. Dad: OK. Did they approve the extra skylight?

10:20 a.m. Dad: Did they?

10:23 a.m. Dad: Frankie!!!!

10:36 a.m. Me: Y

I couldn't be bothered with any more work, and after I'd made a few calls to rearrange my schedule, I drove to the hospital. It was glaringly obvious neither Rico nor Noa had slept much as they looked after Azumi, and I tried not to wince when I saw her lying in bed, her face pale, her Dalmatian stuffy tucked under her chin, another intravenous drip stuck in her arm.

"Frankie," she said, wiggling a few fingers in my direction. "My tummy hurts."

"I'm sorry, sweetie," I said, gently kissing her cheek, too afraid I'd cause her pain if I touched her elsewhere. "Are they taking good care of you?"

She nodded, let out a yawn and closed her eyes. "I'm tired."

"Go back to sleep, baby girl," Rico said. "We'll be here when you wake up."

"Has Tyler come by?" I asked quietly. "Any more updates or news?"

"So far, so good," Noa answered. "All we can do is wait for the antibiotics to do their job."

"Then I'm waiting with you." I took a seat and shoved my bag underneath the chair, settling in. An hour went by, and the conversation shifted from Azumi to work.

When Rico asked me when I was going to tell them about Facebook, and he and Noa spent ages advising me on what to do and how to handle my father, I let them have at it. At least my problems took their focus off their daughter's condition for a while, although I seriously doubted I'd have a heart-to-heart with my father as Noa suggested.

"Then I'll talk to him," Rico said. "I've helped you guys smooth things over before."

"Yeah," I said. "This time you'll need a few tons of heavy-duty crack filler."

"Nah." He winked. "Remember you once said I'm the superglue holding everything together?"

It was true, I had said that, but when Dad arrived a little while later and saw me in the room, the atmosphere immediately shifted, turning so frigid, I could've sworn frost appeared on the windows.

"I'd better get going," I said as I gathered my things, acutely aware running away made me meek and a coward, but I didn't want to get into another argument, didn't want Dad to ask me what I'd done to fix the situation I'd caused. I hadn't yet received a reply from Nicole Nelson, who was probably enjoying the attention her post bestowed on her.

Adding to my discomfort was the unease about not being able to precisely remember what I'd done with the shreds of my forgiveness list, no matter how often I told myself I was being silly. Still, when I got home, I went through each room again, checking through cupboards and drawers, the hall closet, and the bathroom to reassure myself nothing was missing or out of place.

Everything looked exactly as it had before I'd gone for my run at the cemetery. Clearly this week's events had me all wound up. I was hungry, too, and I decided instead of cooking or having food delivered, I'd grab something so I could stretch my legs and clear my head.

Ten minutes later I was at my favorite Thai place a few blocks away ordering shrimp panang with a spicy pumpkin and coconut soup. The rich aromas made my mouth water, but my good mood only lasted until I pushed the restaurant door open and walked straight into a guy dithering outside. The paper bag slipped from my grasp and when it hit the ground, one of the container lids came off, sending hot orange liquid flying.

"You owe me a soup," I yelled at the man who was already halfway down the street. The imbecile didn't turn around, but kept going, hoisting a bag over the shoulder of his plum-colored jacket. I wanted to run after him and demand an apology, but stopped myself before I ended up on another video.

I went home, gobbled down my food, and when Edith came asking for a contribution to another of her never-heard-of-before charities, I told her I had something on the stove and didn't have time before she got two sentences out.

I had a few hours to kill so I went for a drive, surprising myself when I landed at the church hall. According to my father, Geraldina ran two different anger management groups a week, the Monday one I'd attended, and another on Thursdays. As I sat in the parking lot, staring at the front door, I speculated if attending another session and seeing it through might help me deal with some of my issues. After all, my decade-long strategy of pretending to ignore them and pushing them aside wasn't working out too well. Something else was worth a try.

As I walked into the room shortly after seven, most of the attendees had already settled in their seats, cups of coffee and a muffin or donut in hand. Geraldina stood at the front, her bright orange scarf wrapped around her neck, a white plaster cast covering her nose. The skin around both eyes appeared swollen and tender, and a shade I'd only ever seen in sangria or fruit at the grocery store. I tried not to wince when I greeted her, tried harder to push away the fact I'd written her name on my forgiveness list.

The way Geraldina rolled her eyes looked as if it should hurt, but it didn't stop her from smiling wide. "You should see the other guy," she joked, which would've been funny if I didn't somehow feel responsible for her predicament.

"Are you all right?" I said with genuine concern. "I'm sorry about what happened."

She waved a hand. "Not your fault. I'm fine, thanks. It's not as bad as it looks."

"Really?"

"Really."

"Your sister said the handrail on your outdoor steps came loose?"

"It did," she said. "I guess a screw came out or something, and my top step has always been a bit slippery, so my feet shot right out from underneath me."

I put my hand on her arm. "That must've been horrible."

"I honestly thought I was going to break my neck. Thankfully Oksana heard the commotion, because I passed out from all the blood so she called the ambulance. Thank goodness she'd stayed overnight."

"Did the cops come, too?"

"Briefly, but there wasn't much they could do."

"They didn't find anything?"

She raised her eyebrows, gave me a quizzical expression. "Like what? The handrail came off the wall. I don't think we need Sherlock Holmes on the case." She touched the strip of blood-tinged gauze underneath her nostrils as she leaned in. "I always wanted a nose job. Would've preferred it being on my terms, though."

I shifted from one foot to the other, still not quite satisfied this was purely an accident. "Do you have any security cameras outside?"

"Why do you ask?"

"Uh, well, your, uhm, accident reminds me of a story I read once. Some school kids had loosened the, ah, front step and the homeowner took a tumble. I'm not saying that's what happened to you, but if you have a camera…"

"Actually, I was talking to Finn about them last week. There's been a slew of break-ins around the neighborhood, so he's coming over soon to install a door cam and fancy lighting with motion detectors. Something I should've done ages ago but kept putting off."

"That's great," I said, disappointed there was no footage to comb through, and surprised by the surge of protective affection I suddenly had for Geraldina. I was glad my father would help with security upgrades. "For the record, I think you're a trouper for being here."

"Thank you. Anyway, how are you holding up? Finn told me about Azumi."

"It makes me…angry." I tried a smile, probably looked a whole lot deranged. "Did Dad tell you about the Facebook video?"

She reached for my arm. "Yes, he did… Frankie, I know this isn't officially your group tonight, but you will stay, won't you? We can add an extra chair, and the two of us can talk more later if you have time."

Before I had a chance to answer, the church hall doors opened behind us. When Evan walked in, the mere sight of him made me grit my teeth. Once again, he looked as if he'd stepped away from a photo shoot. His trademark slouchy beanie, a pair of ripped jeans—blue this time—a red sweater skimming his trim middle, his brown hair swept to one side. Cool, suave, sexy—but it all left me cold. He was back on my list of notebook-stealing suspects. In fact, he was my *only* suspect. How else would it have turned up at the café we'd visited together after Cleo had searched it? No way was *that* a coincidence. What was he doing here? He had to know as well as I did this wasn't the night for our session.

Was *he* following me?

I looked at Geraldina and lowered my voice. "I was hoping there might be a possibility I could switch groups permanently and come every Thursday instead."

"Ah, well, the trouble is, this is already the fifth session for this group."

"Could I join when the next one starts?"

Geraldina grimaced. "Uh, I think you'd have to discuss that with Finn."

"My father doesn't get to control me," I said, trying not to raise my voice. "I'm here as a favor. Maybe I should find another counselor who's more helpful."

"Frankie," she said, tilting her head to one side. "Is it possible your anger is because you want to get out of the commitment you made?"

"*No.*"

"Because you and Finn have an agreement. Six sessions, starting last Monday. I'll happily count this one as your second, but you'll have to stick to Mondays after this, I'm afraid."

I didn't want to beg or tell her about the argument I'd had with Evan, not when I couldn't be sure if she'd repeat it to my father, ethics be damned. "Thanks anyway," I said.

Trudging to the seats arranged in a circle, I chose the one as far away from Evan as possible and pulled out my phone as I sat. I had a new message, and my heart flip-flopped when

I saw it was from Nicole Nelson. Bracing myself for what I might read, my shoulders dropped when I scanned her words.

Dear Frankie,

Thank you for contacting me and being so forthcoming with an apology. I'm so sad to hear about your niece's condition and wish her a swift and full recovery.

It seems we were both having a terrible day. Without going into detail, I wasn't quite myself for, shall we say, "marital" reasons. Nevertheless, it was wrong to lash out at you, and I shouldn't have tagged your father's company. It was unfair and I apologize. After due consideration, I removed my post completely.

I hope there are no hard feelings between us. I'm beginning to realize life is too short to make enemies. What the world needs is more kindness and compassion, not animosity, and we can all do our part.

Wishing the absolute best to you and your family,
Nicole Nelson

Relief flooded me, increasing when I flicked to her Facebook profile and saw she was as good as her word. The post—and all the vile comments her friends had made—had vanished. Hopefully our disagreement was already old news, and I crossed my fingers the incident would soon be erased from people's memories, replaced by more sensational social media stories.

"You look happy," Evan said, making me jump as he plopped himself in the empty seat on my left, dropping his Nike backpack on the floor.

I looked at him, and then at Geraldina, who was deep in

conversation with another of the group members, not yet ready to start the session. Evan pointed at my open bag on the floor, from which the top of my notebook stuck out, sunflowers on prominent display.

"You found it."

"No surprise to you."

"What's that supposed to mean?"

"Don't act like you don't know. You returned it to Jake's Cakes. You stole it, read it, and handed it in."

"Okay…" He drew out the word as he raised an eyebrow. "Can you tell me why I'd do something weird like that?"

"Same reason you went through my bag in the first place. Because you *are* weird."

"I swear I didn't take your stuff."

"Ha. And I suppose you didn't send flowers."

"No, I didn't." Evan narrowed his eyes. "Look, I just told Geraldina I wanted to come here tonight for some advice, but actually it was because I spotted your truck outside, and—"

"What the hell? You *are* stalking me!"

He gestured for me to lower my voice, which made me want to shout at him. "I'm not stalking you," he said. "I drove past, stopped, and came to try to apologize again but obviously trying to have any kind of conversation is a complete waste of time."

"I don't want to talk to you, or hear your apology. What I want is for you to stay away from me, preferably as far as possible. In fact, why don't you go home? No, scratch that. I will."

"Wait—"

"Go ask Geraldina for advice on how not to be such a dick. And I'd better not see you behind me when I turn around." I jumped out of my seat and grabbed my bag, double-checking the floor and under my chair to make sure I hadn't dropped anything Evan could steal again.

"Frankie—"

"Nope, not interested," I snapped, heading for the door. Storming off wasn't the best decision, and sure enough, my father called me a little over an hour later, demanding to know why I'd been trying to get out of therapy.

"I wasn't," I said. "And why is Geraldina giving you a play-by-play?"

"She isn't."

"Sounds like it to me."

"She was worried about you. Said you left again tonight. Why?"

"None of your business."

"Except it *is*. It's all about *my* business. What's going on? Is this about a boy again?"

"A *boy*?" I scoffed. "I'm not fourteen."

"No, but we both know what happened back then."

"Meaning?"

Pause. "Nothing, forget it. I shouldn't have said—"

"No, you shouldn't. And you don't get to leave that hanging. Tell me what you mean."

A longer pause. "It wouldn't be the first time you messed up because of a guy."

We never spoke about that piece of my history, and his words hit me in the gut, hard. "Go to hell, Dad," I whispered, unable to hold it in any longer. "Go. To. *Hell.*"

I hung up, shoulders shaking. This time things had gone too far. The cracks and fissures had turned into valleys we'd never be able to bridge. Nothing, not even Rico's superglue powers, could help us. As I dropped my phone in my lap, I wasn't sure I wanted them to.

CHAPTER SIXTEEN

I'd spent the rest of the workweek and all weekend either ignoring or avoiding Dad as much as possible. It was already Sunday evening, and although I'd used the notes from my recovered book to prepare a fantastic quote for the potential new client, and sent Nicole Nelson's reconciliatory message to my father, things remained icy between us. As a result, we'd barely exchanged more than a word when we ran into each other on Friday and had since only communicated via short texts when strictly necessary.

"Things still shitty between you and Dad?" Rico asked as we sat in the hospital cafeteria.

"Yup." I took a sip of coffee, glanced around the room, my eyes landing on a pregnant woman sitting in the corner, rubbing her swollen belly. My hand instinctively moved to mine before I let it drop, shaking my head and refocusing on Rico. "What's the latest update from Tyler?"

"He thinks Azumi might go home tomorrow or Tuesday, depending on how she does."

"Really? Fantastic news. She certainly seems to be getting back to her chirpy self."

"She asked for a real puppy like Spotty again today. I'm thinking it's a good sign."

"Definitely. What about Noa? He was a bit quiet upstairs."

"Honestly, he's a mess," Rico said. "Ten times worse than when his sister died last year."

"I still can't believe she had a heart condition nobody knew about."

"Yeah, I know. And don't forget their parents passed away not long before. He's gone through enough to make my head explode."

"You did an amazing thing, adopting Azumi. I bet Noa's sister's looking down at you and is incredibly grateful."

"I can't imagine life without my baby girl. She's our world," Rico said. "If you'd told me a year ago I was about to be a dad, I'd have laughed in your face."

"I'd have laughed with you. I mean, you always said you wanted kids, but you hadn't been together twelve months."

"True, but I knew from day one Noa's the love of my life and bio-dad didn't want anything to do with Azumi. Who knows where she'd have ended up if we'd decided it didn't fit our timing." He looked at me, blinked a few times. "Oh, wow. I'm sorry, that was really—"

"Forget about it. It's fine."

I hoped Rico would move on, but I saw him hesitate as he threw a glance over to where the pregnant woman was sitting. Avoiding eye contact he said, "Do you ever think about...what happened back then?"

I waited until he looked at me, said, "I try very hard not to." I hoped the words were clear enough for him to understand I was about to steer the conversation away from my past, that I didn't want to go back there, not with him or anybody else. "Anyway, you did a great thing, adopting Azumi. And you're both awesome dads."

He looked at me for a few beats before seemingly accepting defeat. "I made the mistake of speaking to the hospital's billing department today." He closed his eyes, shook his head. "I can't believe how much they're already charging us. It's obscene."

"I'll do whatever I can to help," I said. "Dad will as well."

"Thanks, but I'm worried, and I know Noa is, too. He's the one with the steadier income. We've already agreed I'll cut back on my projects until she's fully recovered."

"Is that even feasible?"

"What choice do we have? When I told Noa the numbers, he looked like he might throw up, and the insurance company has already called him three times to—" he made air quotes "—discuss things."

"You mean wriggle out of paying what they owe," I snarled. "Bastards."

"Exactly. God, she's a kid. She's still in the hospital. The system's so screwed up. It's going to bankrupt us. Don't they have any empathy at all?"

"I'm not sure it's part of the job description. Want me to call them?"

"No, but thanks. I told Noa they should only contact me. I'll deal with them. Anyway, I'm thankful Tyler was here when we brought Azumi in. He's amazing."

My back stiffened some more. "Uh-huh."

"Honestly, he's been fantastic," Rico continued. "Compassionate, doesn't dodge questions. Not your stereotypical bedside manner, that's for sure. You remember him from high school?"

"Vaguely."

Rico let out a snort. "Same. I mean, we didn't move in the same rich-club circles and from what I remember he was a bit of an ass. He's changed."

"People like him never change."

"They can if you give them a chance," he said with a shrug. "He said you went to college together? I don't remember you mentioning that."

I sipped my coffee. "Slipped my mind. You said it, different circles and all."

"Makes sense." Rico sat back in his chair and folded his arms. "Okay, time for you to tell me how I can help fix things with Dad."

"Nope."

He shook his head, let out another sigh. "Then entertain me some other way. Let's pretend everything's normal. What's new with you? Met anyone interesting? And I'm talking about someone you've seen more than once, *and* fully clothed."

I grinned, happy to play pretend for a while. "Less of the sass, asswipe. And lower your voice. The people on the next floor heard you."

"You didn't answer my question."

"No, I haven't met anyone."

"And they say married life's boring. How's anger management?"

"Countereffective."

"Hmm…well, for what it's worth, you know I believe Davies grabbed your ass."

"Thanks."

"And I think it's admirable you agreed to the sessions to keep the peace with Dad." He looked at me again, waggled an eyebrow. "Any cute guys there?" When I let out a grunt he leaned in, elbows on the table, curiosity piqued. "Ooh, I know that sound. Who did you meet? What's he like? Are his intentions completely dishonorable? Tell me everything."

"I didn't meet anyone."

"*Bullshit.* I know that look, too."

I could already tell Rico wouldn't let this go. He'd press me like a lemon for details. The lesser of two evils was to give him a few drops so he'd quit and leave me alone. "All right, fine. There was one guy who seemed cool."

"Cool and hot, knowing you."

"Pfft, am I so incredibly shallow?"

"I plead the fifth."

"Jerk. Yes, he was exceedingly hot, but turned out to be a jackass. The end."

"That's it? That's all you got?"

"Yup."

"Pathetic story. And I wish you'd meet someone."

"News flash, this isn't the fifties. And even if it were, I don't *need* a guy to be happy."

"Duh, I *know*. All I'm saying is it wouldn't do you any harm to let someone in." He pointed at my head. "In there, and into your heart. Someone who knows you're a loveable sweetheart with a bit of a temper."

I pulled a face and stuck out my tongue, pretending to gag. "Pass me the barf bucket."

"There she goes again, ladies and gentlemen." My brother spread out his arms as if he were holding court in the middle of the cafeteria. "Using her so-called sense of humor to deflect her true feelings."

"Screw off," I said, but not without a grin. Before I could add another insult, Rico's phone beeped, and he looked at the screen.

"Dad's here. If you come upstairs, I'll help you bury the hatchet in no time. Again."

I downed the rest of my coffee and stood. "You're gonna need a bigger shovel."

"Frankie…"

"I need a bit of time, is all. I'm still here for you, you know that. Message me if anything happens and I'll come straight over. Otherwise, I'll see you tomorrow."

He crossed his arms, and shook his head, looking exactly like our father. "You work together. You guys will have to face this sooner or later."

"Then let it be later." I hugged him and instructed him to give Noa and Azumi a squeeze, and we made our way out of the cafeteria where we headed in different directions.

It was already dark outside, clouds absorbing most of the moonlight and heavy with the threat of more rain. Although a couple of people took the parking garage elevator with me from the lobby, by the time I reached the sixth level where I'd left my truck, I was alone. Fluorescent lightbulbs flickered overhead, and when I heard the heavy metal clunk of a door slamming somewhere in the distance, I moved faster.

Gripping my bag by my side, I listened for the sound of someone else's footfalls, trying to determine if I was still alone. Relieved when I heard none, I took another few steps until I saw movement to the left of me, except when I looked, there was nothing but concrete pillars and shadows. The feeling I was being watched slid down my spine, a treacherous river I couldn't stop, and I sped up. The truck was twenty yards away now, one of the only vehicles left on the entire floor, and as I half walked, half jogged toward it, the echo of another door slamming bounced off the walls.

As soon as my fingers closed over the truck's handle, I yanked the door open, practically hurling myself inside. I slammed and locked the door, sank into my seat. The relief only lasted until I looked at the windshield and saw what someone had left for me, clamped underneath the wiper blade.

A sunflower.

CHAPTER SEVENTEEN

"What the...?" I whispered, leaning in, my nose almost touching the glass. The single flower was wrapped in clear plastic cellophane, and like the bouquets at my front door, there was no indication where or whom it was from.

Surprise switched to irritation, which quickly shifted and morphed, transforming into something unpleasant and gnarly, close to fury. Was this some kind of recurring bad joke? Another of Evan's pathetic-ass apologies for that bullshit at Geraldina's session Thursday evening? If so, how would he have known where I was? He couldn't have. Not unless he really was stalking me, following me around, first to my home and now here, to Maine Medical.

It didn't make sense. Over the last few days, with the benefit of distance and hindsight, I'd conceded perhaps I'd got it wrong. Maybe Evan's initial apology really had been genuine... at least until he'd doused me with water, but to be fair I'd been more than a little annoying that night, playing a symphony on his doorbell. He'd been so adamant he hadn't taken my notebook, and practically indignant at the suggestion of him leaving flowers. The more I'd thought about it, the more I understood it'd been convenient to believe Evan had done both, because if not him, then who?

The skin on my arms prickled when I couldn't come up with an answer fast enough, and I had no intention of sitting in the dark waiting for one to arrive, not when there was a chance of my still being watched. I needed answers, and there was a way of finding out here and now.

I drove to the main floor where I chose a well-lit, busy area with plenty of other vehicles I could park next to and waited until I saw a couple with a kid heading for the hospital's main doors. Quickly stepping out of my truck and locking it behind me, I grabbed the sunflower and crushed it into a mangled ball which I threw in the trash as I followed the trio of people back to Maine Medical's entrance, where I marched to the front desk.

The woman behind the counter whose name badge read Philippa, looked at me and smiled as she put aside a copy of *Cruising World*. For a split second I wished I could board a ship and sail off into a glorious Caribbean sunset, have the opportunity to forget all about mysterious gifts, missing notebooks, fights with my father, and people on my forgiveness list getting hurt. But I couldn't cut and run. Rico, Noa, and Azumi needed me, and I needed to figure stuff out immediately so I could support them in the way they deserved.

"Good evening," Philippa said, her smile broadening. "How may I help you?"

"I need to see someone from security, please. It's urgent."

Her eyes widened. "Security? Oh, dear. Can I ask why?"

"I need to know if the parking garage has cameras, you know, video surveillance."

Philippa tapped her pink lips with her index finger. "Hmm…I believe so but let's find out for sure." She raised her hand and waved at the gray-haired security guard standing by the entrance, who had to be at least six foot four but so slim, he looked as if he might need a set of crampons on his shoes to stay upright in a slight breeze.

"Everything all right, Ms. Burns?" he said to Philippa, his voice deep and raspy.

"Yes, thank you, Eugene. But this young lady, Miss…" She glanced at me with her eyebrows raised and another toothy smile.

"Oh, I'm Frankie," I said quickly, putting a hand to my chest.

Philippa gestured to me and looked back at Eugene. "Frankie was wondering if there's video surveillance in the parking garage. We have cameras of some sort, don't we?"

"You got it," Eugene said. "A few on each floor, more by the elevators." He turned to me. "Was there an incident? Did something happen?"

"Someone put a sunflower on my windshield." As soon as the words left my mouth, I knew how ridiculous I sounded. Sure enough, Philippa clapped her hands.

"How adorable. I love sunflowers. Lucky you."

"Yes, well, I don't know who left it," I said. "And just because it's flowers doesn't mean the gesture's innocuous. Actually, it's downright creepy." This was the problem, wasn't it? If a stalker wasn't actually harming their target, we were told to deal with it, brush it off, move on. Or, worse, almost expected to be *flattered* by the attention.

"There wasn't a card?" Eugene said. "A note or something?"

"No."

"Maybe it fell off?" Philippa asked. "Did you check the ground? Under your car?"

"Might've been from another patient or family member," Eugene offered with a small shrug. "Happens all the time."

When Philippa caught my quizzical look, she came to the rescue with an expression of absolute joy, her voice full of sparkling excitement. "So true. Sometimes, if a patient or their family has too many bouquets or whatever, they leave them for other people to enjoy rather than throwing them in the trash. Maybe someone was brightening your evening. You know, like those random acts of kindness days."

"I don't think—"

"I love those," Eugene jumped in, practically swooning. "Last time I got three cups of coffee during my morning shift alone. And a donut. Chocolate." He patted his concave stomach and tapped his nose. "My favorite."

Sure, I knew those random days were a thing. I'd paid the drive-through order for three people behind me on one of them, but I knew this wasn't why the flower had appeared on my truck, and I wasn't here for the warm and fuzzies. I needed facts. I wanted answers. When Philippa opened her mouth, I held up a hand before she could jump in and regale us with a story of her own.

"My truck was parked on the sixth floor," I said. "Can we look at the footage?"

Eugene sucked in a long stream of air. "Oh, no. I'm afraid that won't be possible, young lady."

I ignored his school principal tone and clambered right back out of the box in which he thought I belonged. I straightened my back, trying to gain some height. "Why?"

"Well, because—" he grimaced, leaned in as if he were about to reveal a secret buried in Area 51 "—*privacy.*"

"What about *my* privacy?" I let out a small cough to disguise the fact my voice had risen a level. They didn't know about the other bouquets. As far as they were concerned, I was being petty and overreacting about someone leaving me a gift, something they only saw as a kindness. Counting to five, very, *very* slowly, I reminded myself I needed Eugene and Philippa on my side if I was to get what I'd come for. "Please? I need your help."

"Was your vehicle damaged?" Philippa said.

"I don't believe so. I didn't check."

"Even if it was, I must inform you the hospital assumes no responsibility for—"

"I don't care about my truck. That's not the point." I turned to Eugene, gave what I hoped was a charming and disarming enough smile to win him over. "Could I please speak with your boss? Maybe we can ask them? I really need to see the footage and see who left the sunflower. *Please?* It's important."

Eugene looked at Philippa, who sighed and picked up the phone in front of her, pressing a button before passing him the receiver. The conversation lasted all of twenty seconds before Eugene hung up and turned to me with an apologetic shrug.

"It's as I said, privacy. The only way we can give access is if you have a warrant, which means unless you're a cop..." He held up his bony hands and wiggled them around in the air. "These are tied."

Defeated, for now at least, I thanked them for their time and headed out to my truck, was about to climb in when a thought hit me. If I was being followed, was someone tracking my car? I whipped out my phone, Googled *tracking devices for cars*, and spent the next thirty minutes trying to find one on my vehicle. Nothing.

Although I wasn't massively hungry, once I'd left the hospital, I decided on Thai food again, something I could wolf down as I processed what was going on. The flower on my windshield was something else to add to my ever-growing list of things leaving me rattled. I wanted to be able to focus on Rico, Noa, and Azumi, and now I was skulking around the hospital and dodging my father. My brother was right, I'd have to sort things out with Dad soon, paper over the cracks again and hope the temporary repairs would hold.

The restaurant was packed, and when I stepped inside, I caught sight of the guy I'd bumped into last time I was here, the one who'd made me drop my soup. I was too tired to say anything to him. Even if I'd wanted to, the chance wouldn't have presented itself, because as soon as he saw me, he ducked into the kitchen. Poor guy. He was probably worried I'd open my mouth and get him fired.

I got my jasmine rice and golden curry, and headed out, and as I drove the short distance home, my thoughts went back to all the unfinished business between me and Dad. For a long time now, I'd wondered if he held me partially responsible for Mom's death. He'd never actually said it out loud, but I swore I sensed it all the same. I didn't blame him for thinking that way. How could I when I blamed myself more? I'd lost count of how many times I'd wished I could go back in time and tell Mom to stay home, or I'd delayed her walk for a few minutes by saying I'd go with her instead of scurrying to my bedroom on a lie about a headache. I knew it wasn't necessarily rational, but if I had, everything would've been so different for so many of us.

But Mom had passed, and with all that happened in the aftermath, the relationship with my father had changed dramatically. A distance grew between us, something invisible yet immovable, magnets repelling one another. I'd walk into a room, and shortly afterward he often left unless our human buffer, aka Rico, was there. Dad also favored spending time with my brother, taking an interest in his hobbies and schoolwork whereas he barely mentioned mine. I'd told myself the indifference had been because I was doing the same to my father and, despite everything, I'd remained an A student whereas Rico had lost focus and needed help. Perhaps it was Dad's subconscious physically removing him from one of the sources of his despair—a form of self-preservation, not a deliberate act on his behalf—or maybe because I looked a lot like Mom, which must've been hard for him to deal with, but there was no question the love he'd had for me became tainted. In my darkest moments I wondered if it had disappeared completely, and what remained was out of a sense of obligation. After all, weren't parents supposed to love their children no matter what?

When I got home, I pushed the thoughts aside and settled on the sofa with the food in my lap. Once again, my intention was to work my way through Netflix for a bit before heading to bed to read until I was tired enough to sleep through the night. My plan faltered immediately when I switched on the TV, and it landed on the local news station.

The image of a female reporter talking into a handheld microphone filled my screen, and although the volume was too low, I instantly knew who it was—Danika Danforth, an investigative reporter and Portland treasure who'd been in the business forever. She wore a red wool coat with matching lipstick, her brown eyes captivating, hair styled in her trademark complicated chignon. It was a well-known fact Danika didn't do hats when on camera, not in the dead of winter, and therefore definitely not on moderately chilly nights such as this one.

She stood in a street somewhere, flanked by houses on either side, and despite the fire trucks and cop cars parked thirty yards away with their lights flashing, she conveyed a sense of calm, oozing effortless glamor and elegance I could never hope to achieve. I was about to switch channels when the words on the bottom of the screen caught my eye.

Man critically injured in Portland house fire.

As I turned up the volume, Danika's familiar voice filled my living room, her tone low and serious. "The police have not confirmed whether they're treating the fire as suspicious. However, the house belongs to well-known local business-man and owner of the Tasty Tomato restaurant chain, Patrick Davies, who, according to a source, was home at the time."

It was as if my entire body had gone numb, and my ears didn't seem to work either. I could no longer hear what Danika was saying because the Patrick Davies I knew, with his wandering hands and desire to get me fired, owned that restaurant chain. My head filled with white noise, distorting all sound, and I was only jolted back into action when my curry-filled fork slipped through my fingers and landed in my lap with a splat.

I shoved the bowl of food away. Grabbing the remote, I hit the rewind button and leaned in, hoping doing so would miraculously transform what I'd heard into something else. Oblivious to the turmoil she was creating inside my apart-ment, not to mention my head, Danika Danforth repeated her words, and continued with, "According to emergency services on the scene, a man of Mr. Davies's approximate age and description was rushed to the hospital in serious but stable condition."

What. The. Actual. Fuck?

I'd almost convinced myself two people on my forgiveness list getting hurt was a coincidence. Insisted it would require another for it to mean anything more.

Patrick Davies was number three.

CHAPTER EIGHTEEN

I wanted to stick my fingers through my ears and into my brain so I could remove the absurd yet undeniable idea the three incidents involving Geraldina, Chelsea, and now Patrick Davies were linked. If I could, I'd have dumped the thought into the take-out box and stuffed it all in the hallway trash chute, never to be seen or heard from again. With a herculean effort I refocused my attention on Danika, and when she mentioned the name of the street from where she was reporting, I grabbed my coat and keys, and bolted out of the door.

Chadwick Street in the West End was only a short drive away. Red and blue flashing lights greeted me, the smell of smoke and char heavy in the air when I parked the truck and got out. Yellow tape ran from one side of the road to the other, wrapped around street signs and trees, keeping nosy onlookers such as myself away.

By the looks of things, Patrick Davies's house had been a grand Victorian affair with red brick, a large balcony, a conical turret, and what might have been a sunroom. The windows of the latter lay in shards on the lawn, the roof of the main structure had a gaping hole, and the whole place threatened to collapse into itself. From what I could tell, the flames looked to be extinguished, the immediate threat alleviated because the firefighters had their protective equipment and heavy jackets slung over their shoulders as they stood around the two trucks.

"Excuse me," I called out to one of them, ducking underneath the tape. I only made it a few steps before a police officer planted herself in front of me. As she held up her hand, I noticed the intricate black-and-white adinkra symbol of a fern tattooed on the inside of her wrist, the word *Persevere* underneath.

"Woah, stop right there," she said. "We put the tape up for a reason."

One look into her brown, amber-flecked eyes and I knew the inscription on her arm wasn't to be taken literally. This lady's bullshit-o-meter would immediately activate when I opened my mouth, meaning there was no point trying to fabricate a story she'd see coming from three blocks away. Shuffling backward but keeping my gaze on hers so she didn't yet turn her attention elsewhere, I moved behind the tape, deciding honesty was the best way to get info.

"Can you tell me what happened?" I said.

"House fire."

"Yes, yes. But do you know what started it?"

"That's for the fire marshal to determine. Make sure you stay behind the tape, please. We don't want anyone else getting hurt."

"Who did they take to the hospital?"

Her radio screeched, and she waved me away, signaling the end of our interaction. I turned and looked around, searching for another option. An older man in a pair of green-and-yellow pajamas stood on the steps of the house directly opposite Davies's, and I hurried over.

"Excuse me, sir. Do you know what happened?"

He rubbed a hand over his shiny scalp. "Hadn't a clue it was burning until I heard the sirens," he said. "I was at the back, watching TV, but when I looked out the front window, I saw flames coming out of the roof. Can't believe how fast it went up. Never seen anything like it."

"Are they sure Mr. Davies was inside?"

"Yup, that's what I told them. Saw him come home earlier. Good job he got divorced, I guess, or the wife might've been home, too. Bet he wished he hadn't got the house in the settlement now." He scratched his ear, looked over my shoulder. "I wonder if it was an electrical fault."

My heart leaped. "Is that what they told you?"

"No, dear, they haven't said anything. I'm speculating because it happened to a friend last year. But, oh my, this is going to be a nightmare. With the cleanup and reconstruction, I won't get a quiet afternoon for months." He craned his neck as he stood his tiptoes. "I hope the darn vultures leave soon."

"The what?"

"Reporters." He waved a hand. "Tragedy sells, I suppose."

His comment sparked an idea. "Well, the best of luck to you," I said, before heading down the street to the news vans, my eyes scanning them in search of a specific logo. As soon as I saw the familiar green-and-white WPRM emblem I picked up the pace, sprinting toward Danika Danforth, the woman I'd seen on my TV screen, who now stood talking to a guy loading equipment inside the rear of the van.

When I approached and she turned, I was suddenly in the presence of a mystical and ridiculously beautiful creature. I'd never seen Danika in real life, and she was considerably taller than I'd imagined, towering over me in her heels. She smiled, the gesture an effortless combination of professionalism and warmth. No wonder she had a reputation for getting the best interviews. She was always calm, polite, coaxing. I already wanted to confess my darkest secrets to her.

"Excuse me, Ms. Danforth," I said. "Uhm, do you have a second?"

"And with whom do I have the pleasure of speaking?" she said, her voice soft, disarming.

"Frankie Morgan."

Uh-oh, I'd answered too quickly. Wishing I could pluck my name from the air, I scolded myself for not having the ingenuity to invent a fake identity. While I didn't torch Davies's place, I'd recently had a public disagreement with him. If Danika looked into my background and somehow found out about our argument, she'd definitely be suspicious of my being here. The voice in my head shouted it would've been better if the seasoned journalist had no clue who I was—same for the cops—especially when it would take little digging for them to uncover I'd landed in anger management sessions after Patrick Davies had left our office and I'd shoved my foot through the wall.

"It's nice to meet you, Frankie," Danika said, giving a gracious nod.

"You, too." The internal whispers increased in volume, stamping their feet like petulant children, yelling at me to leave. I told them to shut up. When examined rationally, my anxiety made no sense. I hadn't done anything wrong. Hadn't harmed anyone, deliberately or otherwise, and yet… the knowledge three people on a list I'd written had been hurt in an equal number of incidents arguably gave me something to hide.

Danika cleared her throat, forcing me to snap my attention back to her. She glanced at her colleague who was busy sorting out cables, and leaned in, her voice a conspiratorial whisper, one woman sharing a secret with another. "Is there something you want to tell me, Frankie?"

For a split second I wondered if I'd somehow set fire to Patrick Davies's house. Had an out-of-body experience, was suffering from amnesia, or had too much booze like some of the antagonists in my crime novels who woke up hungover and discovered they'd hurt someone. But I'd only had two beers a few nights ago. I shook my head, probably way too hard for Danika to believe what came out of my mouth next.

"Absolutely not. No, nothing at all." As I fought to get my face to form something close enough to a smile, I hoped the shadows would hide its insincerity. "I, uh, I know the man they think was injured. Patrick Davies."

Her expression turned to compassion, but unlike my pathetic acting effort, I couldn't tell if she was being genuine. She took a step, put a hand on my arm. "You poor thing."

"So he *was* hurt?"

Danika blinked, slowly. "How long have you known him? Were you close?" As she tilted her head to one side, I could tell she was determining if she'd caught the whiff of a story. Didn't matter how good a reporter she was, I couldn't let her into my head.

"Not long," I said. "I barely know him, really, but I live nearby so when I heard the news, I came to see what happened." Danika didn't say anything, so I rushed to fill the uncomfortable silence. "Cops don't seem to know much. Any idea about his injuries or what caused the fire?"

"For someone who says she barely knows the *alleged* victim, you seem very...interested. I'm intrigued as to why that might be." She continued staring at me, her eyes drilling into mine.

A blush snaked its way up my neck, and I looked away. "Just being a good neighbor."

"Of course. Well, I'm afraid I can't share more information than you already seem to have. Yes, your neighbor's in the hospital, there was nobody else inside, and they won't be able to tell what happened until they've secured the house and examined what's left of the building. Speaking from experience, it's going to take a while."

Her colleague turned around. "It's strange, though. Houses don't typically burn so quick." Danika shot him a glance, but he didn't seem to notice. "All that damage in so little time."

"Eddie," Danika cut in. "It's far too early to speculate."

"What are you saying?" I said, my voice a little higher pitched than I'd have liked, but I couldn't help it. "You think it was deliberate? Are you talking about arson?"

Eddie glanced at Danika, who gave her head the slightest of shakes, looking as if she might slice his jugular with one of her spiky heels if he uttered another word. He turned, busying himself with stashing away more materials in plastic bins, snapping the lids shut.

I moved closer to Danika. "Do *you* think the fire was deliberate? I'm just curious."

"What makes you so interested in Mr. Davies, I wonder," she said. "*I'm* curious."

"I already told you, I'm doing—"

"The neighborly thing, yes…" She put her head to one side.

This wasn't getting me anywhere, plus I was now firmly in Danika's sights, and she had my name. I needed to retreat. "Thanks, anyway," I said, trying not to run.

As I got to my truck and drove off, I wanted to rationalize what had happened to Geraldina, Chelsea, and now Patrick. People often fell at home. Wheels came off vehicles. As for house fires, well, like the old neighbor had said, electrical stuff malfunctioned… Except I couldn't forget someone might have loosened Geraldina's handrail, the police were apparently treating Chelsea's accident as suspicious, and according to Danika's tech guy, Patrick Davies's house may have deliberately been torched.

Three names on my list. Three apparent *accidents*.

There had to be a straightforward explanation. Maybe Geraldina simply wasn't great with the upkeep on her property. Perhaps Chelsea had a hefty life insurance policy, and her husband wanted the money. Despite the lavish lifestyle she projected, they wouldn't have been the first to be snobby nose deep in debt with no way out. As for Patrick Davies, Noa had once told me he'd heard Patrick had screwed over many of his employees during the pandemic in order to save himself. Most likely his staff members weren't his only enemies, and from the encounter I'd had with him, I doubted he'd ever win a Gentleman of the Year award. The guy was a known douchebag, so it was possible somebody had decided to burn his house down with or without him inside. Maybe it was his ex-wife.

I parked the truck in front of my apartment building and switched off the engine, sitting in the dark as I drummed my fingers on the steering wheel, thinking some more. Before I'd heard about Patrick's house fire, I'd told myself if another person on my forgiveness list got hurt, I'd have to *do* something, and here we were…but what could I do? Go to the cops? I imagined the conversation, pictured myself sitting in a bland interrogation room, explaining—*confessing*—I'd been in anger management therapy, had written a list of all the individuals I loathed, and now people on said list were getting hurt. At whom, exactly, would they point their fingers? Me. Times three. Even if I insisted I'd included my name, I couldn't prove it.

Jaw clenched, I got out of the truck, my mood darkening when I went home and found another colorful bouquet propped against my front door. Sunflowers, exactly like the others, and that wasn't all—this time there was also a box of assorted truffles tucked to the side.

Heart pounding, I picked up the candy and shoved the bouquet under one arm as I unlocked the door, flicked on the lights, and went inside. A quick scan of the room told me nothing had been moved. Ever since I'd returned from my run at the cemetery and thought someone had been inside my apartment, I double- and triple-checked everything was locked properly before I went out, but whenever I returned, I still felt anxious.

I dumped my bag on the table and forced myself to examine the flowers and chocolates for clues. The bouquet was a similar arrangement to the first, wrapped in the same clear cellophane. No note, no card, no store sticker. The truffles looked like they'd melt in my mouth, but as tempting as it was to tear into the cerulean box, I wasn't about to touch them.

Unease, far greater than what I'd experienced up to this point, pushed its way into my core where it spread like poison ivy, winding itself around my belly, squeezing hard. I snatched up the flowers and chocolates, stormed into the hallway and shoved everything into the trash chute. On my way back, I knocked on Edith's door. When she opened up, dressed in a kitten print housecoat, holding Penelope in her arms, her eyes narrowed. As did the cat's.

"Francesca, do you know how late it is?"

I didn't have time for her attitude. "I got another delivery," I said, my voice curt, none of the sugary crap I used to keep the peace. I was done. "I bet you saw who left it."

She opened her mouth, looking like she might breathe out

fire, but then she closed it again before saying, "As a matter of fact, I did."

"Great. Who?"

She clicked her tongue, pursed her lips and as she stroked Penelope's back, she resembled an evil Bond villain. "Didn't your mother teach you any manners?"

"Edith, my mother died in a hit-and-run when I was fourteen. It's been a while."

Her mouth fell open this time, her features rearranging themselves. It was the first time since we'd met that she actually looked as if she might possess an ounce of compassion. "My goodness, Frankie," she said. "I had no idea."

For a split second I considered making her more uncomfortable and ashamed than she already appeared, but what was the point? Plus...had she called me Frankie? "It's fine," I said gently. "And I don't want an argument or anything. All I need is for you to please tell me about the person who made the delivery."

She gave a small shrug. "I can't say much, really. I couldn't see well through the peephole, and I didn't have my glasses on."

"But if you opened the door..."

"I didn't when I saw it wasn't you."

"Okay, but was it a man or a woman?"

"Hard to tell." She indicated to her head. "They wore a hat, one of those woolly baggy ones. What do you kids call them...a beanbag thing?"

"A beanie?"

"Yes. Can't tell you the color. Black, or gray, maybe." She waited a beat, and when she spoke again, she almost sounded maternal. "I really am sorry about your mom. I, uh, lost mine to cancer when I was twenty. It was hard. Still is. It's not something I talk about often."

"Yeah. Me neither." My hostility dissipated a little. Someone had once told me we were all the sum of our experiences, that our past almost inevitably shaped our present and future unless we made a conscious effort to stop it from doing so. I'd wondered how Edith had ended up so bitter, thought we were very different when we seemed to have two glaring things in common—we'd both lost a parent young, and we both pushed people away. The sudden realization I might be treading a path leading to an existence as lonely as hers gave me the shivers.

"Well, good night then," she said.

As she was about to close her door, I softly put my hand against it, said, "If you ever need help with anything, you know, picking up groceries or whatever, let me know?"

Her eyes widened. "Goodness, uh, how kind of you. Thank you."

"You're welcome," I said. "It's what neighbors are for."

She was about to close her door when she said, "Oh, I remember something. Whoever dropped those things off had a backpack with a logo on it. The swoosh thing, I think. Does that help at all?"

It sure as hell did. Slouchy beanie and a Nike backpack? I knew exactly who it was.

Evan.

CHAPTER NINETEEN

I was back in my apartment, trying to calm down. Evan had stolen my notebook, no question. He'd left me gifts both at home and on my truck when I was at the hospital, which meant he'd followed me. I contemplated calling the cops, but I still had no proof, he hadn't hurt me, and as he'd deny everything anyway, there wasn't much point. The police would probably have the same reaction as Philippa and Eugene at Maine Medical and wonder why I was making a fuss over some flowers and candy.

As I thought about what Evan had done, I wanted to drive to his place on Forest Street and confront him immediately, but aside from the fact I might not get inside the building at ten o'clock on a Sunday night, being impulsive probably wasn't my best move. I needed to think this through, catch him off guard, which couldn't be at his cushy apartment where we might be alone. No, my best bet was to wait until morning and challenge him somewhere public.

I faced another night of tossing and turning as I grappled with what I'd learned. Unsurprisingly, the dreams I had during the little sleep I managed to get were stuffed with people following me, hands reaching out to grab my limbs, and gigantic sunflowers complete with open mouths filled with endless rows of razor-sharp teeth.

Come morning, I expected to be a wreck, but when my alarm rang shortly after six, I bounced out of bed and made myself a strong coffee. Whoever perceived anger as a negative thing was wrong. For me, it was fuel, and I had a ton of it.

Once dressed, I made my final plans to confront Evan. Although he'd denied sending flowers or taking my notebook, after Edith's comments about the beanie-wearing, Nike backpack–carrying person she'd spotted outside my apartment, there was no way I believed him.

He was a compulsive liar who got his kicks from manipulating people. I didn't give two shits about the flowers and chocolates—at this point the importance of him following me had waned a little. The vital question now was whether he'd used the forgiveness list in my notebook to hurt people. The second was why. The third was if the rest of us were in danger. Was that even a question?

I thought about how stealing someone's forgiveness list from an anger management session was the perfect cover if one wanted to perpetrate acts of violence for the hell of it. It was genius, really—a brilliant opportunity to find a curated list of potential victims not directly linked to oneself. There had to be something desperately wrong if you acted like that.

I shifted in my seat, trying to slide into the mindset of a criminal, see things from such a warped angle. As I took another sip of coffee my throat tightened, and I put the mug down.

What if Evan's endgame was to hurt people on my list and frame me for it, thereby ensuring he never had any consequences for his actions? Was that why he'd returned my notebook, complete with my list, via the coffee shop?

"Stop it," I whispered, insisting I was in danger of veering into *Dateline* or Hollywood blockbuster territory, but the thought wouldn't let go. I'd barely met Evan. For all I knew, he had psychopathic tendencies. I'd watched and listened to a ton of true crime, read a lot about people like that in novels, gathered they could be slick and charming, fooling everyone around them about who they really were, including their families and closest friends. They were often highly organized, and meticulously planned every detail of their actions. They mimicked other people's emotions, too, like empathy because they were incapable of it.

Had Evan done this before? Maybe he joined groups all over the city and beyond, inviting his chosen targets for a coffee to steal and use their therapy assignment if making forgiveness lists was standard practice.

The thought made me stop. I'd fixated on Evan, but truth was I hadn't known anyone at the session, which meant tattoo guy, bug lady, and killer heels, hell, even Geraldina might have taken my notebook while I was standing at the church hall table flirting with Evan over gross coffee.

Maybe I had it all wrong. Could my counselor—Dad's presumed girlfriend—be the one behind people getting hurt? Yes, she'd been injured but she could've staged her accident, making it look like she was the victim, ensuring nobody suspected her. No, the theory didn't fit. My notebook had turned up at Jake's Cakes—Evan was the only person I'd been there with, and he'd been the one rummaging around my wallet to find my address. The slouchy beanie and Nike backpack Edith had seen were more confirmation it was him, and the sneaky bastard was gaslighting me.

My temper surged, and as I let out a frustrated yell I swept my arm across the kitchen table, sending my mug tumbling to the floor. The cup shattered, shards of porcelain and the remains of my coffee bouncing and splashing against the wall.

Everything in my head was so jumbled, so confused. I didn't know what was going on—if there *was* anything going on—as I had no tangible evidence. One thing was certain: if Evan was messing with me, if he was hurting people, I needed to make him stop, and the only way I could do that was by seeing him face-to-face, call him out on all of it.

It was Monday and going to the group session this evening was a bad idea if I didn't speak to Evan beforehand. First, I didn't think I'd be able to wait so long to confront him without exploding. Second, if someone else in the group was involved either on their own, or in collaboration with Evan—holy hell, was he working with someone?—provoking them there was a bad move. I needed to act now.

I pulled out my phone. While Evan's Instagram and Facebook profiles hadn't revealed much, LinkedIn had a ton of information, which I only combed through once I'd changed my own privacy settings so he wouldn't know I'd looked. Apparently, he worked as a project coordinator for a non-profit called DoNation, which helped underprivileged kids and was located on Milk Street.

I'd expected him to be employed by a bank or a tech company—someplace very much in the *for*-profit sector paying a salary with which he could afford his plush apartment. I headed to the job boards, found some old postings. No way could he have a place like the one he was living in on the salaries DoNation offered.

Something flickered in the back of my brain. What if Evan's ruse was to steal forgiveness lists, hurt a few people on them and extort the owner, aka me, saying he'd hand a copy of the list, and thereby motive, to the cops if he wasn't paid off? Anyone desperate enough, someone who'd already been in trouble with the law and had court-mandated anger management therapy, for example, might comply. Jesus, he really was a cunning bastard. I had to stop him.

I glanced at the time. It was still too early to leave my apartment no matter how riled I was, so I tried occupying myself by cleaning up the mess I'd made. Once done, I forced myself to answer a few emails and searched the news for an update on Patrick Davies's condition but other than the confirmation of him definitely being the victim of last night's house fire, neither Danika Danforth nor anyone else had provided further details.

More time was used up by scrolling through Chelsea Fischer's Facebook profile. Aside from messages of support and well wishes, there was little else new there either. When I came across a picture of her daughter smiling into the camera, my fingers stopped moving. Chelsea may have been horrendous to me in school, and there had been times when I'd wished she'd be struck by lightning in the middle of class or a sinkhole would open beneath her feet, but I'd never wished her dead for real, and I didn't now either. I knew only too well what her daughter would go through if Chelsea died, how she'd suffer from the loss of her mom.

I closed the app. A half hour had gone by; I couldn't wait any longer, and not only because Dad had sent a few texts asking where I was, to which I'd replied saying running late. I dialed the number for DoNation, asked if Evan Randell was available.

"You betcha," the man said. "The team's always here bright and early. I'll put you through."

I hung up. Five minutes later I was in my truck, vowing I wouldn't let Evan brush me off again, trying not to think too much about the fact he might actually be mentally ill, and what could happen if I pushed too hard. At least we'd be in a public space, and with the person who'd answered the phone, there'd be someone else around. *You'll be fine*, I insisted, a mantra I repeated until I stood in front of the entrance of DoNation. Showtime.

The reception area was tiny, with a few bright orange plastic chairs and a royal blue feature wall, half covered in distressed wooden paneling, the charity's name and logo mounted in silver letters similar to those at Jake's Cakes. I presumed Evan had made these, too, winding everyone around his little finger one trendy piece of artwork at a time.

"Good morning," the man behind the desk said. I recognized his chipper voice as the one belonging to the person who'd answered the phone earlier but although it was on the deeper side, it didn't seem to fit his body, which was barely bigger than mine. If things with Evan went awry, I might be on my own to deal with them. "What can I do for you?" he continued, his voice chirpier.

"I'm here to see Evan Randell."

"Of course. May I have your name, please?"

"Tell him it's Frankie."

"Yes, ma'am." He gestured to the chairs. "You can take a seat."

"I'll stand."

He talked into his phone before throwing a glance my way, his eyes narrowing as he spoke. When he hung up, he lifted his chin, said, "I'm afraid you don't have an appointment. Mr. Randell's busy. He can't see you."

"Is that so?" I crossed my arms, readying myself for battle. "I suggest you call him back. Tell him I'm not leaving until he does."

"Yes, uhm…" He grimaced, squirming in his seat. "He, uh, he thought you might react this way, and asked me to tell you, and I quote, you'll have a long wait."

I hoped he was the kind of guy who detested confrontation and would do everything he could to avoid it. Glancing at the only hallway to our right, I gathered it wasn't a huge office. Maybe five or six separate rooms. Decision made, and before he could stop me, I headed for the first door.

"Evan," I shouted. "Evan Randell, get your ass out here."

The receptionist was already on my tail, walking so close behind me I could almost sense his breath on my neck. "Excuse me, ma'am."

"Don't call me ma'am."

"Oh, uh, *miss*. You can't barge in here. Please leave."

"Not until I've spoken to Evan."

"I told you, he's—"

"Busy. Whatever. *Evan!*" I threw the door open, startling the two women and one man who sat at their desks midconversation. "Nope," I said, backing out and closing the door, bumping into the receptionist who jumped to one side.

"You need to go."

"Evan!" I shouted again, taking another few steps down the hallway. As I was about to open a second door, my opponent appeared at the end of the corridor, his face darker than a hurricane.

"What are you doing?" Evan said. "What's going on?"

"I want to talk to you."

His eyes widened, his expression almost fearful, making me want to point at him and shout *gotcha!* "A-about what?" he muttered.

"What do I do?" the receptionist butted in before I could answer, wringing his hands. "Should I call—"

"Relax, there's no need to call anyone." I threw the words over my shoulder. "This shouldn't take long."

"It's okay, Blake," Evan replied, a slight tremor in his voice. "Frankie's leaving."

"The hell I am." I pulled my arm away as he reached for

me. "*Don't.* Either we talk somewhere private, or I'll say what I've come to say right here in the hallway."

Evan clenched his jaw, the vein in his temple pulsating hard. "Conference room," he said quietly, opening a door and gesturing for me to go inside.

Before I'd moved an inch, I looked back and caught him whispering something to Blake, but I wasn't close enough to make out what it was. I ignored them and walked into the conference room, a tiny space with a glass partition separating it from its twin. An egg-shaped wooden table and a mix of different styles of office chairs filled most of the area, something I could perhaps dodge behind if our conversation turned ugly.

"How did you find me?" Evan said, moving into the room and away from the still open door, but when I opened my mouth to answer he waved a hand, quick and dismissive. "Never mind. Say whatever it is you came to say."

"I want you to stop stalking me."

His expression shifted, going from what might've been concern to something close to disbelief. "What are you talking about?"

"I know you've been following me. I'm here to tell you to stop. *Now.*"

He laughed, a full-on chortle that made me want to put my hands around his thick neck and strangle him. "No, I haven't."

"My neighbor saw you."

"Saw me where?"

Damn it, I couldn't tell if he was faking it, reminded myself I might be dealing with someone who would lie to anyone, anytime, if it suited his purpose, and he was obviously good at distorting the truth. "Outside my apartment."

"I haven't been anywhere near your place," he said, crossing his arms, now standing with his back to the glass partition. "I wouldn't dream of it. In fact, I'd be ecstatic if this was the very, *very* last time we saw each other, ever, because cross my heart and hope to die, I want nothing to do with you. I don't care about you, Frankie."

A flash of something darted across his face, and when he looked away, it disappeared. But the way he stood there, making it seem as if I were in the wrong, was like a flamethrower to a pile of tinder. My teeth clenched so hard, my next words barely made it through.

"Stop gaslighting me."

"I'm not—"

"Then how come ever since we met, weird stuff is happening to me?"

Instead of answering, he pinched the top of his nose between his thumb and index finger and closed his eyes, his mouth moving in silence.

"What the hell are you doing?" I said.

He held up a hand and another few beats passed. "Breathing exercise," he said as he finally looked at me again. "Something Geraldina taught us on Thursday when I dropped in. You'd know if you hadn't stormed off."

"I didn't—" This time I was the one who stopped talking. He was deflecting, changing the subject. I decided to give one last push at uncovering the truth. Everybody had a weak spot, maybe I'd find his. I planted my feet, squared my hips, and whispered, "Are you hurting people?"

His jaw dropped so far, I thought it might hit the floor. "What did you say?"

"Have you been hurting people I know?"

"I swear to God, I've no clue what you mean."

I took a step. "You didn't go to Geraldina's house?"

"Why would I—"

"What about Chelsea?"

"Who?"

"Did you touch her car?" Another step. "And Davies? Was it you? Do you enjoy playing with fire, Evan?"

"What are you talking about? Chelsea and David—"

"Davies," I shouted. "His house burned down. They're both in the hospital."

"Which has nothing to do with me," Evan yelled back.

"You're lying. You stole my notebook, and now you're hurting people."

"Okay, we're done."

"Why are you doing this? It's sick. Stop or I'll call the cops."

"Be my guest. But you'll do it outside because you're leaving."

I'd hit a nerve. His face had shifted when I mentioned the cops, the nonchalance in his words not matching his expression. He was hiding something. "I'm not going anywhere," I said. "Not until you tell me the truth."

"Get out. Now. I won't talk to you when you're like this."

"No!" I screamed, as all the frustration from the past week rose from within, turning into an uncontrollable bundle of energy I didn't know what to do with.

Without thinking, I shoved Evan with everything I had, sending him flying. He fell sideways, and as he put his foot down, he stumbled on one of the chair legs, his body careening toward the partition. By the time I knew what I'd done—and regretted it—it was too late. A loud crack filled the air when Evan collided with the glass full force and the pane imploded.

CHAPTER TWENTY

"Goddamn it, Frankie," Evan shouted, scrambling from the floor, brushing what had to be a thousand shards from his clothes. "What the hell's the matter with you?"

I couldn't answer. My mouth was open, but no words came out. Evan stood six feet away, on the other side of the broken partition, his left hand pressed against his forehead. When he pulled his fingers away, a steady gush of blood flowed from a cut above his eyebrow, dripping onto his shirt. His sleeve was torn, a dark patch of crimson spreading down from the elbow.

"Oh my God," I said, moving over to him, but he backed away, putting up his hands, making me stop. "Evan, wait. I didn't mean to—"

"Jesus Christ, you really have lost your mind." He swiped a few tissues from a box on the table and pressed them to his temple. They did little to stem the blood flow, and within no time they'd already turned scarlet.

"Let me help."

"Get the fuck away from me," he growled, grabbing some more tissues. When he noticed the state of his shirt, he let out another string of expletives, cursing me to the end of the world.

Before I could say anything else, two police officers, one male, one female, burst into the room and I suppressed a small groan. I'd met the woman at the scene of Patrick Davies's house fire last night. She had the adinkra fern tattoo and had insisted I stay behind the yellow tape. I crossed my fingers behind my back, hoping she wouldn't recognize me. Meanwhile, Blake looked triumphant.

"I'm Officer Kemp," the policeman said. "This is Officer Armstrong, and—"

"That's what you two were whispering about," I said to Evan, failing to keep myself in check despite the authorities arriving, and pointing at Blake. "You were talking about calling the cops."

Blake gestured to the glass. "Evidently, a good decision."

"Sir," Kemp said to Evan. "You're bleeding."

"I'm fine."

"Want to tell us what happened here?" Armstrong said.

"Officer, this woman wouldn't leave," Blake jumped in. "She came looking for my colleague, Mr. Randell, and when he wouldn't see her, she stormed in, trying to find him, and caused an absolute ruckus, ranting and raving, and—"

"Don't you dare paint me as the hysterical woman," I said. "I told you I needed to speak with Evan."

"*Speak* with him?" Blake huffed. "You went ballistic. You damaged our property."

"Name?" Armstrong looked at me as she pulled a small notebook and pencil from her vest.

I swallowed. "Frankie Morgan."

"Frankie short for anything?"

"Francesca."

She wrote it down and turned to Blake. "Please continue, sir."

"Evan, uh, Mr. Randell, asked me to stay by the door, and when I heard Ms. Morgan shouting, I called 911 because things were escalating. Then the glass broke and—" he ran a hand over his face, shaking his head "—my God, Evan. We can't afford to replace it. You know how much the previous tenants paid."

"It's fine, don't worry," Evan said. "We'll work something out."

"I'll take a statement from you separately, Mr. Randell," Kemp said. "But first we need to get your injuries taken care of."

"Really, I'm fine."

Kemp pointed to Evan's forehead. "Looks pretty deep to me, sir. Let's be safe, okay?" When Evan nodded, Kemp turned to Armstrong. "I'll take Blake and Mr. Randell to reception and have the EMTs treat him. You good getting a statement from Ms. Morgan?"

"Sure thing," Armstrong said, and when she looked at me, there may have been a flicker of recognition passing across her face. Balls. As I watched the three others leave, I turned to her, speaking quickly. "I didn't mean to hurt him. It was an accident."

"Uh-huh. Tell me what happened."

I looked at the floor, shuffled my feet. "I needed to speak to him."

"So you've said. What about?"

Although I knew I was under no obligation to voice a single word about any of my suspicions, a virtual crossroads appeared in my head, one I didn't want to ignore. Go left, and it meant telling her about everything that was going on, including the forgiveness list, which I'd destroyed. Go right, and I could mention what I knew to be true without sounding bonkers, things Evan would have trouble disputing.

"Evan and I went for a coffee a week ago, at a place called Jake's Cakes."

"Uh-huh." She sounded impatient.

"Yes, well, when I came out of the washroom, I caught him going through my bag, and when I got home, I noticed my notebook had disappeared."

"You're saying he took your computer?"

"No." I gestured to the pad in her hand. "A paper one like yours, only bigger."

She frowned. "I see, and you're alleging he stole your property?"

"Yes, well, no."

"Which is it? Yes, or no?"

"I don't know," I snapped, mimicking her tone, which made Armstrong raise an eyebrow. "It showed up at the coffee shop two days later."

"You mislaid it?"

"No. He took it. Then he handed it back in and acted all innocent. I came here to confront, I mean *talk* to him, and I shouldn't have shoved him, but he's lying, he's not being honest about *something*." The words tumbled out, the volume of my voice increasing with each syllable. As I imagined Evan at reception laughing his ass off with the two other guys, talking about me as if I was some hysterical bitch, I could hardly contain myself. No doubt getting me into trouble with the cops had been his plan from the moment I stepped into the office, and I'd imagined any discomfort I thought I saw on his face. He was probably out there congratulating himself on a job well done. "He's the one in the wrong here," I said, my voice rising again. "He's the one you need to talk to, not *me*."

"Calm down, Frankie, or—"

"Oh, what a surprise," I scoffed. "He's got everyone fooled, *damn it!*" I kicked a chair, hard, forgot it had wheels, and sent it flying. When it smashed into the wall with a loud thud, leaving a sizeable dent, I knew I'd gone way, way too far.

"Put your hands against the wall," Armstrong said.

"Wait—"

"Do it now."

When I saw her reach for her weapon, I complied. "I can explain."

"We'll talk at the station. Let's ensure you don't cause any more damage."

"But—"

"Francesca Morgan," Armstrong said as she put my arms behind my back and the cool steel of the handcuffs slid around my wrists with a decisive *click.* "I'm arresting you on the grounds of aggravated criminal mischief and assault—"

"No. Wait, you don't understand," I said, trying to shake her off but she held firm.

"You have the right to remain silent." Armstrong continued with the Miranda rights. Her words didn't register, not when she marched me out of the conference room and down the hallway, not when we stood by the reception where she had a brief exchange with Kemp, and not when she led me to the patrol car parked outside. All I could hear was the ba-*boom* of my heart and the whoosh of blood thundering in my ears. I finally snapped back to reality when she closed the car door.

Apart from the gas station incident, I'd never had a run-in with the cops, not even when I'd screamed for hours during the Women's March in 2017. I'd never done anything to get myself arrested, had no experience as to what would happen next or what I should do. All my knowledge came from novels and TV shows. Would they throw me into a cell for the night, tell me to cool off, and let me go? Should I ask for a lawyer? Demand a phone call? And if they took my cell, which I presumed they would, how would I remember anyone's number?

People walking by gawked as I sat in the back of the cruiser, no doubt wondering what I'd done to end up there. Judging. I tried to plead with Armstrong and Kemp as they got in the car, but when she glanced over her shoulder, it made me shut up, and I gulped down the anger trying to shoot out of me. Blake had already insinuated I was borderline hysterical. No way could I prove him right.

I dug deep. Evan, dick that he was, had mentioned a breathing exercise. I'd once seen a meditation video on YouTube. Square or box or something. Inhale for four, hold for four, exhale for four. I tried again. And again. But all it did was make me more upset and gave me the urge to hyperventilate. Why wasn't it working? My insides were about to explode, ripping me, Armstrong, Kemp, and the cruiser all to pieces.

I went into planning mode. Made myself think about what I'd tell them when asked to go over what had happened at DoNation. Then I thought about what Evan might have told them and it got me all furious again. I could only imagine how being in anger management therapy would work against me, particularly with what I'd said and done in the conference room. I'd accused him of hurting people. Had he mentioned that to them? And if he had, and they confronted me, was it wise to tell them about the forgiveness list, after all? Would they believe me? I imagined the conversation with the cops.

Them: You say you wrote a forgiveness list in a notebook.
Me: Yes, as a therapy exercise.
Them: And now people on your list are getting hurt.

Me: Yes. Geraldina Hoyos. Chelsea Fischer. Patrick Davies.
Them: People whom you bear a grudge against. Correct?
Me: Yes, but my name is on it, too. I might be in danger.
Them: Where's the list now?
Me: I destroyed it.
Them: How convenient… You have temper issues, don't you,
Frankie?

I shuddered. What if Armstrong remembered seeing me at Patrick Davies's house last night? If I told her his name was on my list, would she question whether I set the fire? I knew arsonists often returned to the scene of their crimes to admire their handiwork and bask in the glory of their deviousness. If the cops dug a little deeper, asked people at work, they'd uncover Davies and I had an argument, I'd embarrassed him, put my boot through a wall, and ended up in anger management because of it. Wouldn't be much of a stretch for them to conclude I'd torched his house to get revenge. Same went for Chelsea's accident. Once they found out about my history with her, it would give me motive for her alleged accident. No evidence I'd done anything, unless—and the thought made me shudder—someone, Evan, for example, had planted some. God, this was such a mess.

I pressed my lips firmly together. No, I wouldn't share anything about what I knew, or thought I knew. No way would I implicate myself by mentioning a list which no longer existed, not when there was a chance they'd turn it all against me.

For once, Frankie Morgan would keep her mouth shut.

CHAPTER TWENTY-ONE

It was late afternoon when I was finally released from Cumberland County Jail, where I'd sat all day after being booked. I'd had my picture and prints taken, and an arrest report was filed. I'd sat in a cell waiting until the powers that be called the bail commissioner. With the amount set at three grand, the other conditions of my release included not setting foot in DoNation's offices, and I'd been told to expect a follow-up from a Detective Willows.

Rico had not been impressed when I called for help. "What the...what do you mean you were *arrested*. What happened? What did you *do*?"

"It was a misunderstanding," I said quickly. "Can you help me find a lawyer?"

He couldn't but thought Noa would be able to. Sure enough, about an hour and a half later a stout, balding man arrived, and introduced himself as George Cumberbatch, exclaiming, "Alas, no relation, har, har."

He carried a battered brown briefcase, wore round tortoiseshell spectacles, and reassured me he'd get everything straightened out. When he told me Rico would post bail for me, I almost cried. Not only had I snatched my brother's time away from his sick daughter, but now I was about to take a thousand bucks from the funds he desperately needed to pay for Azumi's care, because I only had two grand in my savings account. I was selfish, and surely Rico thought the same about me because when I was allowed to call him back and asked him to bring the money, he said, "We're waiting for an update from Tyler and I'm not leaving until I've seen him. I'll get there when I get there." I hadn't argued, didn't say much of anything at first when he arrived.

"I'm sorry," I finally whispered to Rico when we were alone and walking out of the building after I'd thanked George, but my brother didn't respond. Instead, he unlocked the car door and I scooted inside, buckled myself in, and sat hanging my head.

"I'll pay you back," I said as soon as he settled in the driver's seat. "I promise. Every cent."

Rico put both hands on the steering wheel, his knuckles turning white. I expected him to turn around, demand to know what had happened, chastise me for losing my temper by finally losing his, saying *I told you so* about my anger being a problem. But he didn't. He took a deep breath, switched on the ignition, and drove without a word.

His silence wrapped itself around my throat, squeezing tight. I wanted him to rant and rave, shout and scream. Rico not talking to me, not uttering a single syllable as we pulled away from the police station, was worse. The air between us filled with thick disappointment, the exact kind I saw in Dad's eyes whenever I looked in them too long.

I couldn't stand it. Part of me wanted to rip off my seatbelt, throw open the door, and hurl myself onto the road, regardless of who or what was behind us, hoping it might be a truck large enough to… The thought only lasted a millisecond before it morphed into an image of my mother lying in the street. I shuddered, pressing my backside into my seat, and hung my head again.

"I'm sorry." I wasn't sure the words had come out loud enough, so I repeated them, hoping they'd have an effect. "I'm sorry, Rico. I'm really, really sorry."

"Where's your truck?"

I gave him directions to Evan's office, thankful my brother was talking to me again, before remembering I wasn't allowed to go anywhere near the place. "Uh, maybe park on the top of Silver. If I give you the keys, can you drive my truck around? I can't be anywhere near the place where I got in trouble."

Rico grunted and the silence descended upon us again, making me wonder if I might suffocate from it. I cracked open the window, closed my eyes as the cold breeze hit my forehead. I tried again. "Listen, I'm—"

"Stop apologizing," he said. "It isn't helping. This time, it's not enough."

This time. I didn't have the energy to challenge or explore what he meant, if he blamed me for what had happened to our mother the way I suspected Dad did, or if it was something else. "I know. I'm…" I swallowed the apology before it managed to slip out. "I can explain."

He turned to look at me for so long I almost yelped when I thought he'd rear-end the bright yellow delivery van in front of us stopped at a red light. Maybe he was considering it because he needed a place for his anger to go, and I understood him all too well. Rico slammed on the brakes, bringing us to a halt inches from the van's rear bumper. Nostrils flared, teeth clenched, he turned to me, his voice low, calm, and cold. "What the hell, Frankie? Aggravated assault? That's a class B crime."

"Uhm…"

"In case you weren't listening when George mentioned it, that's ten years of jail time and ten grand in fines."

"Those are the maximum. He doesn't think they'd ever—"

"Do you have any idea what you're doing to us? To my family?"

"I'm—"

"We needed the bail money, Frankie. Azumi is *sick*."

"I know."

"She needs care."

"I *know*. I said I'll pay you back."

"How? You told me last week you're broke. And it's not just bail. Never mind the conviction, you're going to court. Even if they don't throw you in prison, your legal fees are going to be way more, and I can't cover them, do you understand?"

"I—"

"I don't want to hear it. For once in your life, can you not be an inconsiderate bitch and think about consequences before you do shit? Why is that so impossible for you? *Fuck!*"

The words stung as if he'd slapped me twenty times across my face. He'd called me names before. We'd teased each other all our lives, mouthing *fart breath* or *poop face* across the dinner table when we were kids, collapsing in giggles whenever Mom and Dad asked us what we'd said. But we'd never meant it. We wanted to see what we could get away with and hadn't gone through the typical teenage stage where we hated each other. We'd been too busy picking up the pieces after Mom died, and I'd already been at odds with my father, so I couldn't bear losing Rico, too.

Now, the thought of our relationship deteriorating because of my impulsiveness filled me with shame. He needed me. His daughter and husband needed *him*. As I sat there, avoiding his gaze, I made a silent promise to fix things between us, no matter what.

"Did you tell Dad?" I said.

"No."

"Thank you. I'll tell him I was sick or—"

"Noa did."

"What?"

"Dad called when I was on the phone with you. He asked about Azumi and then mentioned you hadn't shown up for work. He was worried."

"And Noa told him I'd been *arrested*?"

"You're the one who got into trouble, Frankie, so don't go blaming Noa. Anyway, what difference does it make? You can't be thinking about going to work when—"

"I have to. My projects—"

Rico snorted. "Dad doesn't want you anywhere near them. Or him."

"You think he's going to fire me?"

Rico stared at me. "Wouldn't you?"

I looked at my hands again for the rest of the drive, picked at the skin around my nails before remembering I hadn't washed them for hours, and shoved them under my thighs.

Rico parked on Silver, fed the meter, and left in silence. I watched him walk away, my heart so heavy it ached. Trying not to think about landing in prison, I turned on the radio to distract myself but quickly got antsy as I flipped through the stations and gave up. I snatched a box of spearmint gum, unwrapped two pieces and shoved them in my mouth before stuffing the garbage into the door pocket. As I looked down, I noticed a crumpled coffee cup, immediately recognizing the Jake's Cakes logo, making me frown.

I told myself to knock it off. It was obviously a popular place, slammed on the two occasions I'd been there. The fact it wasn't anywhere near where Rico or Noa lived or worked didn't mean anything, did it…? Jesus, I was becoming more and more paranoid. I thought people in fake Ubers were out to get me, a man was about to attack me at the cemetery, and someone had been in my apartment to steal what? My garbage? Now I was sitting in my brother's car, the person whom I loved most in the world, wondering if a coffee cup meant something nefarious. Evan's antics—because they had to be his—were seriously messing with my judgment. I tried to distract myself by people watching until Rico came back.

When he opened the door, he bent over and threw me my keys. "It's not there."

"Huh?"

"There's construction going on. Big temporary no parking sign, valid as of noon today. Didn't you see it? I think you got towed."

"Are you kidding me?" I yelled, immediately lowering my voice. "I mean, that sucks."

"I have to get back to the hospital. Call the cops and find out where your truck is. I don't have time to taxi you around so take an Uber or something if it's far."

Not likely. "Sure," I said, and, unable to help myself, added, "Is the coffee at Jake's Cakes worth the hype?" When Rico threw me a quizzical look, I pointed to the cup in the door.

"Not mine. Think Noa was there last week sometime."

"Oh? Which day?"

"I don't know. Monday? Why?"

My gut clenched, and I tried hard to keep my voice light. "No reason. I heard it's great is all. Fantastic pastries, apparently."

"You're not going to have the funds to splurge for a while,

are you?" he said before letting out a sigh. "That was uncalled for. I'm sor—"

"Don't. I deserve everything you've got and then some." I got out of the car and walked over to Rico to hug him. He only half reciprocated, making it seem as if I'd put my arms around a lump of stone. "Thank you," I said, taking a step back. "And I promise I'll figure things out."

I willed him to answer, say everything would be fine, we'd get through this because we always had, but he hopped into his car and left. As he drove off, taking the empty Jake's Cakes cup with him, I felt more confused and alone than ever.

CHAPTER TWENTY-TWO

By the time I'd located my truck and sorted everything out at the impound, I was over a hundred bucks lighter, and another hour had gone by. When I finally made it back to my apartment, it was almost 6:00 p.m., and with the mood I was in I decided I'd best not go to anger management. I had a shower and changed my clothes before wolfing down a bowl of cereal because I couldn't be bothered to cook.

I washed and dried the dishes, cleaned the kitchen, and popped down to Jeff's, where I offered to take Terry for a walk, taking a ridiculous amount of time with each task as I attempted to put off the inevitable confrontation with my father.

There was no sense trying to have this conversation over the phone, but I didn't want to wait until morning. I needed to see him in person and explain what had happened without him being able to put the phone down on me.

No matter the frostiness between us, I also didn't want him thinking I was the kind of person who felt indifferent and selfish toward Azumi. Except I *was* selfish. Even Rico thought so.

When I arrived in Riverton, my father wasn't home. I texted my brother, who told me Dad had left the hospital a short while ago and had gone out for something to eat. Damn. Our conversation would have to wait until tomorrow after all. Can I come over? I asked Rico. His response was swift. Leave it for now. I dropped my phone in my bag and started up my truck knowing this would be one hell of a long night.

By the time morning came, I'd barely slept. If I remembered this week's work schedule properly, and providing things hadn't changed, Dad would be on site in Deering all day, where Morgan Construction had been charged with the full gut and reno of an older two-story home. I headed off, my mind working through how I could best word an apology while trying to avoid losing my temper if he didn't listen.

All that changed when I turned onto Alba Street, and the first thing I saw was an ambulance and a cop car in the distance, parked outside the house we were renovating. In a flash, I pictured all the possible reasons for the police and EMTs to be there. I dumped my truck next to my father's and leaped out, raced up the pathway and burst through the open front door.

"Dad?" I shouted. "*Dad!* Are you here?"

I heard noises, muffled voices coming from the basement. I bolted down the temporary wooden stairs we'd installed, kicking up dust with each step, my heart pounding so fast I thought it might explode, head filling with the terror of what I'd find.

I'd seen a few jobsite accidents since I'd worked with my father, most minor, resulting in lacerations and the odd broken bone. Only one in the history of the company had been more serious, and while it had required an ambulance, it hadn't been fatal. Would it be the same this time with a quick trip to the emergency department and a few days of rest? What if it was worse? What if my father was—I could barely finish the thought—*dead*—because of the list I'd written.

Part of me wanted to turn and run back up the stairs two at a time, head out the door and directly to my truck but my feet wouldn't cooperate, my brain shutting down flight instincts as it forced me to take another step. If Dad was hurt, I couldn't, I *wouldn't* leave.

As I reached the bottom of the staircase, I saw two paramedics kneeling next to someone lying on the ground. The temporary lights the electricians had installed only illuminated the basement enough for me to make out dusty brown work boots and the bottom of a pair of jeans, both of which matched Dad's typical daily uniform.

Before I had a chance to ask what was going on, I spotted two other people in the corner. Officer Armstrong and my father. I lunged and flung my arms around Dad, for once not caring about my display of affection.

"I—I thought you…" I stammered. "I thought you'd… you'd…"

"It's okay," he whispered, hugging me back. "I'm fine. It's…"

Dad didn't seem able to finish the sentence, and as my eyes adjusted to the relative darkness and I looked down, I could make out Sandy's face. His eyes were closed, his body completely still, the only movement caused by the paramedics who were gently and efficiently moving him onto a spinal board.

"What happened to him?" I whispered, my gut clenching as images of Sandy's toddlers and pregnant wife appeared in my head. Zoe was a fabulous woman who often sent her husband to work with lemon zucchini muffins for the crew and snuck cute handwritten love notes she and the twins had made into his lunch box on a regular basis. Whenever he found one, he held it up and showed me, his face set in the biggest grin. Sandy's family meant everything to him and vice versa. Did Zoe know he was hurt? Had Dad already told her?

"Hey, you okay?" my father said, snapping my attention back to him.

"Huh?"

"Mr. Morgan was explaining what happened here," Armstrong said before pausing and looking at me, eyes narrowed. "How are you, Frankie?"

Dad frowned. "I see you know each other."

"Uh…" I tried to find a good way of explaining she was the one who'd arrested me twenty-four hours ago but didn't think that particular detail would help the situation. Lucky for me, Dad didn't seem to be looking for confirmation.

"Never mind." He waved a hand, focusing on Armstrong again. "As I was saying, officer, I don't know what happened. Sandy and I agreed to meet here this morning as he had some questions about the specs for the first-floor stairs, but I was delayed."

"Why?" she asked.

"Because I thought someone had broken into the office, then I got a call from one of the crew telling me a generator had been swiped from a site downtown. I had to arrange another."

"Wait." I gestured with my hand. "Back up. The office got robbed?"

"No, I said I *thought* it did. Nothing was missing, not the petty cash box or any of the computers, but the door was unlocked. I was the last person out yesterday and I'm sure I didn't leave it open. Unless you went there last night?"

"Me?" I said, digesting the accusation of being inattentive. "No."

"Then I must've forgotten. Anyway, once I'd dispatched a spare generator I was running late. I arrived here, saw Sandy's van and when I got in the house I…" He rubbed a hand over his face. "God, there's an image I'll never forget."

I put my hand on his arm, was about to speak but Armstrong got there first. "Do you think he fell down the stairs?"

"I don't believe so," Dad said, his face pale as he pointed upward. "Look."

As I tilted my head back, I knew what he meant. I could see right up to the rafters.

"I don't understand," Armstrong said. "What am I not seeing?"

"We always put wooden planks across the opening where the stairs will go." I gestured at the boards scattered around the basement floor.

"Jeez, you think he fell from all the way up there?" Armstrong said.

Dad nodded. "Yeah. Looks that way."

"But...but how?" I said. "We're always so careful. Since I was a kid, you always told me to ensure the boards are positioned properly. It's something we check multiple times a day because they can move."

"I know." Dad's upper lip trembled as he blinked back tears, but before he could add anything else, one of the paramedics got up.

"He's ready to be loaded into the ambulance," she said.

"Will Sandy be all right?" I asked.

"We'll do everything we can, I promise."

I recognized the canned answer, almost identical to the one Tyler had given us about Azumi. Words which served to reassure and placate but remained noncommittal. It was something the doctors had said after Mom's hit-and-run, and while they truly had done everything they could, it hadn't been enough.

From the way Dad stood with his shoulders hunched, jaw clenched, I wondered if he'd remembered their words, too, and I wasn't sure how to help him. One of the most important things for my father was his employees' safety. He never cut corners, always insisted people respect all site safety protocols, and made sure everyone he hired knew their job was in jeopardy if they didn't. Hell, during the pandemic he'd fired a guy who wouldn't wear a mask, and he refused to work with a few of the subs until they took the restrictions seriously. More recently, Dad had cut a young kid loose on his third day at a site because he'd accidentally bumped a ladder one of the other crew members was working on, sending him flying and almost out the window. It had resulted in one dislocated shoulder, and Dad reading the kid the riot act.

"As an employer I have a responsibility," Dad told me when I got hired way back.

"Yeah, yeah," I'd said, rolling my eyes. "My safety comes first. I know."

"Not only *yours*. Everyone else's, too. I don't want to be the reason someone doesn't go home one night. Understood?"

My father had always been concerned about safety—wearing seatbelts, bicycle helmets, checking smoke detectors, which all make perfect sense—but it had increased tenfold since Mom had been killed, and expanded far beyond his biological family. Sandy's accident was cutting him deep.

"This will be viewed as an industrial accident, Mr. Morgan," Armstrong said. "I'll be filling in a casualty report, and we'll speak to Sandy once he's regained consciousness."

"Of course, thank you. I'll follow the ambulance," Dad said. "Call his wife on the way there."

"I'll go with you," I said. "And, uh—" I threw Armstrong a glance, lowered my voice hoping only Dad would hear "—maybe we can talk about what happened, you know... with me? I know I missed the session with Geraldina last night as well."

My father's face hardened more than I'd hoped. "I can't deal with all that now. One mess at a time, okay?"

"But I want to explain."

"No. I mean it."

Armstrong coughed, said, "I'm going upstairs to check on the EMTs."

Both Dad and I watched her leave, and once she was out of sight he turned to me, said, "That was my polite way of saying I don't want to be around you right now. In fact, I want you to take a leave of absence."

"That's ridiculous."

"It's for the best."

"But what about all the projects? How will you manage?"

"I made a few calls yesterday and early this morning. An old buddy will help out."

"Are you *firing* me?"

Dad's jaw made tiny sinewy movements, and he took his time before saying, "I haven't decided."

"Then maybe I'll decide for you. Maybe I'll—"

"Quit? Okay, listen, you may as well know I'm thinking of selling the company."

"What?"

"It's something I talked with Rico and Noa about a while ago." He held up a hand when I tried to interrupt and ask why the hell he'd discussed this with my brother and not me, considering I was the one who worked with him. "I've been thinking about it for months and had planned on an exit by the end of next year, but if I do it now, I can help Rico and Noa with the medical bills."

"But you love this company. What if I ran it? You could take a back seat. You could consult. We could get a loan or something."

"Pah. We both know you took the job as a stopgap. A very long one. No, you need to work out what will make you happy, because this isn't it." He stopped talking, and I could tell he was choosing his next words carefully. "Until you've fixed what's going on in your life, I think you should keep your distance from Rico. Let him focus on his daughter, not your bullshit."

I gasped. "Did he ask you to say that?"

"No, but you know it's true. Sort your head out."

I opened and closed my mouth a few times, felt my anger turn and shift into something unexpected—vulnerability. I wanted to tell Dad I needed help, that I didn't understand what was going on, like the forgiveness list I'd written and people on it getting hurt, but I couldn't. Our relationship was hanging by a thread and if I uttered a word, he might never speak to me again, and neither would Rico. As brittle as my relationship with Dad was at times, I didn't want to lose him. And so, I remained silent as he walked away, carefully stepping around the broken boards that had tumbled to the basement with Sandy.

Five minutes later I heard footsteps, and when I moved to the stairs, I saw Officer Armstrong at the top. "Didn't expect to see you again so soon," she said. "You sticking around here?"

"Yeah," I said. "For a while."

"Mr. Morgan asked me to tell you to lock up. Can he trust you?"

I tried not to roll my eyes. "Sure."

"You won't cause more trouble, will you?"

"No, ma'am," I said, wanting to remind her I hadn't caused Sandy's accident, but kept my mouth shut. I stood there for a long time after she left, the smell of concrete and sawdust filling my nostrils. Dad was giving me a leave of absence, possibly letting me go, thinking about selling the company. I waited for a hefty shot of anger to consume me, but it didn't come. Instead, I felt hollow and empty, as if my insides had been scooped out and dumped on the floor.

No use sulking in the basement, but when I moved across the room to turn off the lights, I changed my mind. I picked up one of the broken boards and hauled it to the light, turning it over, gently running my fingers down the wood. Nothing. I examined the second one and then the third. My heart thumped. The plank was fractured and split, and a crack that size across the middle would've been enough for the board to give way under a person's weight. I might've got away with walking across, but Dad and Sandy were taller and heavier, and with extra pounds of tools and materials, it was no wonder he'd fallen.

Impossible to tell for sure if it had been deliberately damaged before the accident, or if it had happened when they'd smacked into the ground. It was possible the boards had moved during construction, someone accidentally kicking one of them too close to the edge of the gap it was supposed to cover. I tried to make my analysis sit well in my stomach, but it warped and twisted, refusing to comply.

"Sandy wasn't on my list," I whispered, the words echoing around the basement. Except it meant nothing. Because the second name I'd penned was Dad's.

I connected the trail of breadcrumbs back to my father mentioning the office door had been unlocked, something he'd never do. What if the only thing whoever had snuck in there had wanted was to know where my father would be working today? It wasn't tricky. The whiteboard in the main office had the schedule with all the details displayed for anyone to see. All they'd needed to do was look. But who was *they*? Evan, the person I suspected of being behind all these pseudo-accidents? How would he have known where to find the details?

The image of the Jake's Cakes cup in my brother's car jostled for attention. Dad had told Rico and Noa he was thinking of selling the company, and Noa had worked in various start-ups before he'd met my brother, gone through a couple companies being sold. He'd told me off-loading a business was complicated. Finding the right buyer and going through the due diligence process could take forever.

"It's never a done deal until the ink on the contract is dry," he'd said, recounting a sale which had turned nasty during the final meeting, and both parties had walked away with nothing but a pile of legal bills.

They needed money for Azumi's care, and Rico had mentioned how worried he was multiple times already. If they hoped to get cash from Dad soon, they both had to know it was unlikely, but if my father was hurt in an accident, there would be a hefty payout from his disability insurance, and with the life insurance he had if he died... And Rico had a spare set of keys to the office, something Dad had given him in case his ever went missing.

I let out a ridicule-filled laugh dripping with self-loathing. No. *No.* It was absurd. They'd never hurt Dad. No way. Guilt filled my soul for the minuscule flicker of a thought that my brother or his husband would harm my father for money, no matter how sick their daughter was. No, this was someone else's doing. The person behind these attacks was picking the people on my list off one by one. Except—I shuddered as a thought hurtled into my brain like a semitrailer—Dad *hadn't* been hurt. Sandy had. Did it mean they'd go after my father again? What about everyone who was left? And why were they doing this?

I flicked through the rest of the list in my head. Six names remained, including my own, and the person because of whom I'd assigned myself the number one spot, the reason why I'd never forgive myself for what I'd done and choices I'd made in the past. The person my family never mentioned.

Shay Callan Morgan. My son.

CHAPTER TWENTY-THREE

"*Shay.*" Because I never allowed myself to say the word out loud it sounded unfamiliar on my tongue, almost forbidden. We—Rico, Dad, and me—barely spoke about him. It was an aspect of my past we hardly discussed. After all these years, with lots and lots of practice and if I worked hard enough, I could almost pretend it had never happened, and I'd never been pregnant or given birth to a healthy baby boy a little over eighteen and a half years ago.

Compartmentalizing made it easier, at least on the surface, and so I kept the emotions about Shay hidden deep inside, stuffed into a tiny box I nailed shut, and wrapped in chains. My performance was so convincing, Rico and Dad probably believed I'd moved on years ago. They never mentioned Shay, possibly because they thought it was what I wanted, and in a way, they were right because the pain threatened to tear me in half if I dwelled too much or too often. But I'd never forgotten him.

When I was fourteen, not long before Mom died, neither of my parents had any idea I'd been seeing a boy in secret for a few weeks. Nobody knew. Ever since Chelsea Fischer had turned me into her daily spite-filled target practice, I had no long-term girlfriends to share my news with, and I'd chosen not to tell Rico. I loved my goofy brother, but he was twelve. To him the most hilarious things in the world were fart jokes and cartoon drawings of balls, and he'd have made fun of me. I wanted to keep my first boyfriend all to myself. I had no idea it would be a defining relationship, one which would shape me, my attitude, and my future, all for the worse.

Adrian Costas. Three grades ahead. Tall, shoulder-length dark brown hair, hazel eyes, and pillow-lips I wanted to press mine against. His only flaw, if you could call it that, was a slightly crooked nose—a trophy from a wrestling match he'd won. I thought it gave him an edge, making him more perfect by not being completely perfect. Confident but not arrogant, Adrian was a deadly combination of smart and cool. A+ grades across all subjects, and while he always had a book in his hands, he never got teased. He was an anomaly, an outlier, and although middle schoolers and high schoolers attended classes in the same building, as far as I knew, he had no idea I existed.

We only had a few days of school left, and during one lunch break in early June, I'd snuck to my favorite reading spot under a weeping willow, which provided much needed relief both from Chelsea's taunts and the unusually high temperatures. As I took a bite of my sandwich, a shadow fell across the pages of my book. I looked up, saw Adrian towering over me, and tried not to gape.

"Hey, Frankie."

His gravelly voice made an instant pool of sweat collect under my armpits. I wondered if he'd mistaken me for someone else, covered my mouth with one hand as I tried to swallow a bite of food, which now resembled wallpaper paste. How did he know who I was? More importantly, why was he talking to me?

"What are you reading?" he said, a smile so charming spreading across his face it made my heart sing. Afraid he might hear it, I feigned a cough. When the chunk of bread and cheese still hadn't gone down, I held out the book.

"*The Darkness Gathers* by Lisa Miscione," he said. "Any good?"

"Yeah," I croaked.

"Cool."

I thought that would be the end of our conversation, either because he'd realized I wasn't who he thought I was, or because he'd determined I couldn't hold a conversation and was the most boring person on the planet. Expecting him to turn and walk away, I buried my head in my book, jumping when he plunked himself on the grass in front of me, our feet almost touching.

"What's it about?" he said.

I looked up. "Huh?"

He grinned and my insides melted. "What's the book about? I might want to read it."

"Really? Uh, well, there's a woman whose mother was murdered and now she's obsessed with bringing killers to justice. It's a revenge thing. It's great." God, what a pathetic explanation, it didn't do the novel any kind of justice. Lisa Miscione's writing was perfection.

Adrian plucked a blade of grass and twisted it around his long fingers. The gesture was mesmerizing, hypnotic. *Erotic.* "You enjoy crime fiction, Frankie?"

The way he said my name, soft and intimate, made my cheeks burn again. "It's my favorite." Feeling braver I added, "I wish it's what we read in class instead of the classics."

"Oh, hell, yeah, I'm on board." He leaned on his elbow

and smiled again, and this time I dared myself to not look away. Books were my thing. If I focused on them, maybe I could hold an entire conversation without sounding silly.

"What do you love most?" he said. "Solving the mystery? Figuring out whodunnit?"

"No. I mean, sure, it's fun, but I'm more into the whydunnit."

"Oh?"

"Uh-huh, it's way more intriguing. I love digging into the criminal's head. Understanding what drives them to commit heinous acts." I wondered if I sounded like an English teacher or something, decided I didn't care because what I'd said was my truth.

"Hmm…I'd never thought about it that way."

"You should. It's interesting. Sometimes there's no real answer, though." I giggled. "Some characters are just utter dickheads."

He put his head back and laughed. "Fair enough. Tell me about the main character in this one then. What's she like?"

Hours later when I'd been at home in my bedroom, I recalled our conversation word for word. It had been magical, as if we'd been sprinkled with fairy dust and transported into a fantastical world of books where only the two of us existed.

We'd spent the rest of break chatting about authors and novels we loved, which releases we couldn't wait for, and what we hoped would make it to the screen. Neither of us reacted when the bell rang. I knew the math teacher would reprimand me for being late, even if I'd got a hundred percent on my last three tests, and usually arrived early. Mr. Johansson didn't make exceptions for tardiness no matter what, and typically the thought alone would've made me break out in hives. Except now I didn't care. Seconds passed, almost a full minute, and still, we didn't move.

"I suppose I should get to class," Adrian finally said after the second bell rang. When he held out his hand to help me up and our fingers touched, I thought my legs might collapse.

"This was fun," he said. "Want to chat about books again?"

"Oh my gosh, yes." The answer came out breathless and excited, way too enthusiastic. "I mean, being in a book club would be great." I didn't mention I'd thought about starting one at school but feared Chelsea would show up and ruin it. That wouldn't happen with Adrian there.

He gave me a sly grin and winked. "I was thinking it could be the two of us."

I gawped at him, wanted to jump up and down, clap my hands and shout it was both the most incredible and ridiculous thing I'd ever heard. Incredible because I wanted to spend time with him. Ridiculous because why on earth would he want to spend time with me?

"I'd love to," I whispered, and when he reached for my hand and gave it a squeeze, a million fireworks exploded in my body, lighting me up from the tips of my toes and all the way to my crown.

"Bye, Frankie," he said, giving me a wave.

I stood rooted to the spot with my heart pounding, unable to move as I watched Adrian from between the waving willow leaves as he jogged up the front steps and disappeared into the school. Just like that, he'd cast his spell, bewitching me completely.

Over the next two weeks I fell hard, became one of the wide-eyed, lovesick girls I'd rolled my eyes at. Butterflies invaded my stomach whenever I thought of Adrian. When we kissed, out of sight and always in secret, it was as if his soul was etching itself onto mine. Until school finished, we met in the evenings, and always at his parents' home. They both worked late, and as Adrian had no siblings, it meant we could hang out undisturbed, which suited me fine. Rico wouldn't have lasted more than a heartbeat without making kissing noises if he'd seen us together, and I was sure Dad would've had a fit if I'd brought a boy home. Mom was more relaxed on the surface, but she'd have checked in every ten seconds to see what we were up to.

As soon as school ended, and whenever I was done with my chores and didn't have to work at the grocery store where Mom had found me a summer job, I headed to Adrian's. One balmy Friday evening we were stretched out on a plaid blanket in his backyard. He'd laid it down before I'd arrived, added a tray of sandwiches and lemonade, and cans of beer he'd lifted from his parents' stash. I'd never tasted beer before, and the more I drank, the more I liked it, enjoying how it softened everything around the edges.

The warm air filled with the scent of lavender and honeysuckle, and I inhaled deeply before letting out a contented sigh. School was done, which meant a break from Chelsea. Over the next two months I'd work four shifts a week and spend my free time with Adrian. We'd go swimming, fishing, maybe take off somewhere if I could convince Mom and Dad I was with my barely existent girlfriends. This summer would be perfect.

I leaned over and pressed my lips against his, couldn't wait to see the looks on people's faces, especially Chelsea's, when we made our coupledom official. Because that's what we were, a couple, however, when I shared my thoughts with Adrian, he wasn't impressed.

"Let's not tell anyone," he whispered, his hand resting on my hip, lips nibbling the length of my neck. I arched my back and pushed my body against his, trying to dissolve into him. "I don't want to spoil what we have," he continued, his voice low. "You know what happens when other people are around. It ruins things."

My arms went around his neck, pulling him closer still as his hands traveled up my buttoned shirt. I'd kissed a boy before, but never gone further, and although it had only been a few weeks, I knew I already loved this gorgeous man. I kissed him harder, willed him to slip his fingers beneath my shirt, my bra, and cover a breast with his hand. Instead, his arm snaked around my waist, making me let out a small moan.

"Did I hurt you?" he said, moving away, creating distance I didn't want between us.

"No."

He kissed me again. "You're beautiful, Frankie. So, so beautiful."

Nobody had said that before, no one other than my parents, who didn't count. Adrian's words sent a thousand fireflies fluttering around my stomach, making me glow from the inside out.

He leaned back, touched the tip of my nose with his, the scent of beer on his breath. "I want to take your picture," he said, pulling out his new phone. His dad, who worked for some tech company and was on a business trip at least every other week, had given it to him. The device was brand-new, had a built-in camera, and wasn't on the market yet. Adrian had proudly showed it to me a few days ago and we'd spent the evening taking pictures, heads smooshed together in the frame, making faces, and sticking out our tongues. "What do you think?"

"I think I'd like that."

He got up, stood over me as he snapped a few shots, repeating how gorgeous I looked. It was the first time in my life I'd not only felt desire, but how powerful being desired could be. When I shimmied out of my shorts so he could take a picture of my toned, tanned legs, it was the most natural thing in the world. Crouching down, he instructed me to roll on my side, arch my back, and I did as he asked, the heat growing between my legs. The way he looked at me was intoxicating. Addictive.

I glanced around. The backyard was secluded, high trees and dense bushes on all sides. Nobody could see in. Gazing deep into his eyes, I undid the buttons of my shirt one by one and slid it off my shoulders. I'd seen strippers in movies, and a rush of confidence took over. I smiled, slowly, watched Adrian's mouth fall open as I reached behind my back and undid my bra. The bulge in his pants was visible, and the control I had over him turned me on so much it made me more daring. Adrian took picture after picture, and at some point—I don't recall how or when, only that I'd made the decision—my panties were in a discarded heap with the rest of my clothes.

We were kissing again, his hands wandering over my naked body, my fingers on the zipper of his jeans when the light in his house came on. I scrambled to get dressed, both of us near dissolving with laughter when I put my shorts on the wrong way around. Adrian straightened out the blanket, slid the empty beer cans underneath, and arranged our plates on top, setting a perfectly innocent stage. Seconds later his mother appeared with a fresh jug of lemonade. If it bothered her that her almost seventeen-year-old son had brought a date home to an empty house, she didn't say, instantly garnering Coolest Mom Ever status from me.

By the next morning, the alcohol had cleared from my system, and I knew letting Adrian take naked pictures of me had been reckless. Embarrassed, I asked him to delete the photos, and after putting up a fight and insisting they were art and nothing to be ashamed of, he promised he would.

The next few times we met, he wanted us to go further, pressed me to have sex. I said I wasn't ready. He called me a tease. Things turned bitter. After I told him no again, his calls dwindled. When I phoned his cell, he didn't pick up, and when I tried the house either nobody answered, or his mother said he was busy.

Mom sensed something was wrong, but like I'd refused to tell her about how Chelsea was treating me at school because I was afraid my mother would make a fuss, I didn't say anything about Adrian, making up a fake argument with a girl instead. Not long after, when I was on my way to work, I saw him with Chelsea. The two of them stood in front of Dairy Queen, fingers entwined, his lips on her neck. After my shift I went to his house to confront him.

"We broke up ages ago, didn't you get the hint?" he said, adding I was too jealous, too boring, repeating I was a tease, not at all like Chelsea, because she was supercool. I didn't think my heart would withstand being crushed so bad, but seventy-two hours later Mom died, and it imploded even harder.

A week after, I'd needed to get out of the house. I couldn't stand the raw grief, the sickly-sweet smell of flowers people had sent, now wilting on the counter because none of us had the strength to do anything about them, or the sight of a fridge stuffed full of casseroles well-intentioned neighbors had delivered. Why did they do that, I wondered. Feed the grieving when we couldn't eat a single bite without the instant need to bring it all up again.

Grief, flowers, and food weren't the only problem. The house felt claustrophobic. Dad tried his best to hide it, but I knew he couldn't stop crying at night, sometimes during the day when he thought I couldn't hear. Rico was either at his friend Josh's or holed up in his room where he stomped around, slamming doors whenever he emerged.

For all these reasons, and to get away from my own sorrow and guilt, I wanted to escape. I climbed out my bedroom window one night and phoned Adrian on his cell from a pay phone, not knowing whom else to call. We met in his yard, went to the back where we couldn't be seen from the house. He laid out the same plaid blanket, and when I cried, he held me, told me everything would be all right.

I'm not sure who seduced whom, but we ended up having sex. Fast, clumsy, and unprotected. Carried away by the need to feel something, *anything*, other than misery, I didn't mention contraception. It happened once. We didn't get back together, we barely spoke thereafter, and I didn't care. My mother's death had made our short relationship and the demise thereof insignificant, something trivial I assumed would soon be forgotten. I was wrong.

I didn't notice anything at first. My periods had always been erratic, cycles ranging anywhere from three to ten weeks. Almost four months late and I still didn't worry. I'd dropped a fair amount of weight after losing Mom and never threw up like the pregnant women in books and movies. When my belly began to round out, I refused to leave the land of denial for fear of what I'd discover.

More weeks passed before I found the courage to cycle five miles to a drugstore where I could buy a pregnancy test without being recognized. When it was positive, I got another three packs, unable to believe it when each result came up the same.

I went to Adrian's house. He first insisted I couldn't be pregnant, then denied the baby was his, accused me of sleeping around, making it clear he wanted nothing to do with me.

"But it's yours," I said. "I need your help."

"If you tell anyone it was me, I'll print those photos. I'll email them to everyone at school."

"You said you deleted them. You *promised*."

"I promise you this—tell anyone we slept together, and everyone will see them, including Rico, your dad, the teachers… and Chelsea."

"But—"

"I'll leave a stack of them in the cafeteria."

"N-no. Don't. Please don't. *Please*, I—"

"I think I'll choose the one where you're spreading your legs. Let's show everyone what a dirty little slut you really are."

I bolted. Locked myself in my bedroom and refused to come out, figuring Dad would think my tears were because of Mom. The next afternoon my gym teacher found me sitting in the changing room alone after the last class of the day. I refused to tell her anything at first, but she guessed, sitting with me on the cold hard bench until the building had gone quiet and we heard the gentle hum of the janitor's vacuum cleaner somewhere down the hall.

She convinced me to call a doctor, helped me find the number for the pediatrician who'd seen me and Rico since we were babies, a wonderful woman named Dr. Ali who always gave us sugar-free gummy bears and a comic book whenever we visited. Rico swore it was because of her that he'd made a career out of drawing his own.

Dr. Ali's office was more like a home, with a chalkboard hung low on the wall so kids could draw on it, and a rocking chair parents could sit in with their kids. She wore slacks and a variety of red shirts instead of clinical scrubs, her long brown hair tumbling over her shoulders in waves, partially obscuring her purple stethoscope she'd decorated with a panda sticker.

"How can I help you today, Frankie?" she said. "What seems to be the trouble?"

I focused on the panda for as long as I could, trying not to cry. When the tears came, Dr. Ali held me in her arms and waited until I caught my breath long enough to blurt out, "I'm pregnant."

I expected judgment in her eyes but there was none, her face filled only with compassion and understanding. We talked about options. She said she'd refer me to the best obstetrician she knew. Up to that point I hadn't heard of an ob-gyn, and another part of my childhood innocence fell away. When I asked if she'd help me speak to my father so we could tell him together at her clinic, she didn't hesitate.

"You can count on me," Dr. Ali whispered. "You can always count on me."

I wished Dad had said the same. The expression on his face when he heard his not yet fifteen-year-old daughter was five months pregnant wasn't something I'd ever forget. He asked who the father was. I lied, insisted I didn't know because I'd snuck out and gone to a college party where I'd had too much to drink and slept with a guy I couldn't remember. I watched his face contort as he did the math.

"But your mom died five months ago," he said. "We'd only just lost your mother and you...you...went to a *party*?"

I broke down. Weeping for so many things. Because I couldn't tell him the truth. Because I was carrying a child I didn't want. Because my mother wasn't there. And because I knew things between Dad and me would never be the same.

On Good Friday a few months later, I gave birth to a beautiful baby boy with Dad by my side, holding my hand, gently telling me everything would be all right, that I could do this no matter how often I cried that I couldn't. Once it was all over, I held my son for an hour before kissing him goodbye and handing him to the adoption agency counselor. As soon as we'd come home from the hospital, me with a wobbly belly but no child in my arms, it seemed Dad had done whatever he could to move on. Pretending I'd never had a baby was his way of dealing with it, I supposed, and because I didn't want to talk about it with anyone, in time it somehow became mine.

I'd done a fantastic job of pretending I was fine with my decision of placing Shay for adoption, and to some extent I still was. What other choice did I have? I'd been too young to care for a child, a sentiment Dad echoed, telling me I couldn't be expected to take care of a kid when I was still one myself. But the anger I felt toward him, toward *me*, for not fighting for Shay simmered beneath the surface, the self-loathing bubbling away ever since.

Now, eighteen and a half years later, I didn't know what had become of Shay. No clue what he looked like or if he'd kept the name I'd chosen for him. Over the years I'd catch myself thinking how extraordinary it was—somewhere out there was a baby, then a toddler, a boy, and now a young man, a life I'd created by accident yet had no part of. That was when I pushed the thoughts away again. It hurt too much to imagine he never thought of me and didn't care.

According to the adoption agreement, he'd been given the opportunity to find out who his birth mother was on his eighteenth birthday. As the date had approached, I'd had fantasies of a sweet, tearful reunion, of developing a relationship closer to siblings than mother and son because of the small age difference between us. And yet, his birthday had come and gone, and I hadn't heard from him. I hid my disappointment, told myself it was for the best. This was his decision, and my duty was to respect it.

As I resurfaced from the memories, glad to leave the pain they caused behind, I refocused on the present. Writing Shay's name on my forgiveness list had been irrational. I had nothing to forgive him for, but I'd been angry, disappointed, and hurt he hadn't yet made contact. All those emotions had been replaced by desperation. I'd put Shay on my list, and although I hadn't included his last name, there might be a chance whoever was taunting me would hurt him, too. It wasn't a risk I could take.

Now more than ever, I had to find my son.

CHAPTER TWENTY-FOUR

Making sure I locked the building site properly, I hopped in my truck, thinking about how I'd go about finding Shay, when my phone rang. It was a number I didn't recognize, and I almost didn't answer, regretted it instantly when I heard George, my new lawyer, say, "We need to meet."

"Oh, God, how bad is it?" I said, wiping the sweat from my palms on my pants.

"It's not bad, not bad at all."

"You could've led with that."

George chuckled. I didn't. "Point taken. Anyway, I can arrange for us to meet with Judge Orr, Mr. Geller, he's the assistant district attorney, and a—" I heard him rustling papers "—Detective Willows. Between the five of us we're going to put all this to bed. How soon can you be at the courthouse?"

"Today?"

"You heard me say this was to put everything behind you, right?"

A short while later I stood in Judge Orr's courtroom with George by my side, the detective and assistant DA to the right of us. Detective Willows resembled her name, tall and thin, but her green eyes had a kindness about them, almost putting me at ease. The assistant DA, Adam Geller, looked a little older and much heavier than Willows. He wore a pair of bright blue glasses and a Minions tie which, or so I hoped, implied a sense of humor. I crossed my fingers George was right, and this meeting would bring good news. Most of all, I hoped it would be short so I could get back to figuring out how to find Shay.

"It seems you got into a spot of bother, Ms. Morgan," Judge Orr said. His British accent made the words sound posh although his tone remained matter-of-fact, not in the least belittling, which came as a bit of a surprise and made me drop my guard a little more. "From what I understand there was trouble with a Mr. Evan Randell at DoNation's offices on Milk Street. Correct?"

"Yes," I said. "It was silly. I got a little angry and I…I pushed him." No sense denying it. He'd probably read through everything on file anyway.

"Shoving someone through a glass partition is a whole lot more than silly," Willows said. So much for the kindness in her eyes.

"She didn't mean for Mr. Randell to go through the pane or get hurt," George said. "It was an accident."

"And what do you make of this assessment, Mr. Geller?" the judge said.

"Ms. Morgan has never been in trouble with the law before," Geller said, tapping a stack of papers in front of him. "A few parking tickets, a small altercation at a gas station more recently, but nothing else. Almost a model citizen, one might say, until now."

"She's in anger management therapy," Willows said.

George jumped back in. "Not court mandated but Ms. Morgan's own initiative. She's dealing with some stress and wanted to get a better handle on her emotions."

"What kind of stress?" Judge Orr said.

"Work, mainly," I answered when George gave me a nod. "My dad's also my boss."

"Families can be difficult," the judge said. "Goodness knows I see it often enough."

"Yes, sir," I said, hoping Willows wouldn't jump in with another snarky comment.

"And her little niece is sick," George added. "She's in the hospital recovering from acute appendicitis. She's only two."

"Oh my goodness," Judge Orr said. "Will she be all right?"

"I think so," I whispered.

"My son was in the hospital last year," he said. "I understand the emotions generated by such events, emotions which evidently got away from you yesterday morning." He raised his eyebrows and looked at me over the top of his glasses. "But we can't have you going around pushing people through glass walls."

"No, sir," I said, unsure if I should add anything because on the phone, George had instructed me to let him do most of the talking and I'd best keep my answers short.

"Detective Willows, what's your take on this?" the judge said.

"I spoke with the victim, Mr. Randell," Willows said. "No lasting injuries, and he's back at work. For whatever reason he insisted it was all a *misunderstanding.*"

"Really?" I said.

"Would you prefer he claimed otherwise?" Judge Orr said with a slight smile, and I bent my head, cursing my big mouth. "Please, carry on, Detective Willows."

"Mr. Randell doesn't believe it was Ms. Morgan's intention to harm him," she said, her delivery telling me, and everybody else, she wasn't buying it. "And because he also insists it was an accident and their insurance will cover the glass breakages, he's not pressing charges."

"What?" I whispered, unable to help myself. "You mean… I'm not being indicted?"

"You got it." Judge Orr leaned forward, his wooden chair creaking beneath his weight. "But wait, there's more… While I'm of the opinion the officers overcharged in this case as no weapon was used, nor was there serious bodily injury, you do understand we can't simply brush this away and pretend nothing happened."

I nodded. George made wide eyes at me, urging me to speak. "Uhm, yes, your honor."

"Good," Judge Orr said. "In that case, here's the deal, Ms. Morgan. This case will stay on file for twelve months. I strongly advise you *not* to get into any trouble, at all, for at least a year. Preferably not ever. Do you think you can do that?"

"Definitely," I said. "I promise. Thank you."

"You should be thanking Mr. Randell," he said. "He was the one who advocated for you. But perhaps do it over the phone. Or stay off his radar entirely, just in case."

"Yes, sir. Thank you. And…uh, what about the bail money?"

"We'll get the paperwork in order," George said. "Rico paid for you, so he'll be the one authorized to get it all back."

I couldn't believe it, practically floated to the ceiling, feeling about a billion pounds lighter. Rico was getting his money. Evan wasn't pressing charges. As I thanked everyone profusely, even Willows, and hightailed it out of the courthouse, never to return, I couldn't help wondering why Evan had been so generous. Was it because I'd misjudged him and he was actually, genuinely a great guy who hadn't stolen my notebook or hurt the people on my list, or was this another strategic move? Sure, by not pressing charges he was doing me a massive favor, but he'd also helped himself, showing the cops and the judge how reasonable and kind he was. Damn it, if that was his play, he'd outmaneuvered me.

Part of me wanted to send a message on LinkedIn or Instagram and thank him. Another part wanted to ask what the hell he was doing. As I climbed back in my truck, I decided doing nothing was probably a safer bet, and instead I called my brother to fill him in on the good news.

"Hey, Rico," I said as soon as he picked up. "I need to tell you—"

"Can't talk now." His voice was small, terrified. I hadn't heard him sound this afraid since he'd snuck into my bedroom when Mom was lying battered and bruised in a hospital bed, hooked up to countless beeping machines, and we'd been told the chances of her making it were fading by the hour.

"What's going on?" I pressed a hand against my stomach to try to stop the nausea from traveling north. "Is it Azumi? Has something happened?"

"Yes…she's…she's…" A stifled sob. A few garbled words.

"Are you still at the hospital?" Silence. "Rico? *Rico!* Talk to me."

Rustling, muffled voices. The sound of the phone being shoved around. Finally, Noa came on the line. "Azumi's going back into surgery."

"Why? What for?"

From the lengthy pause and his tense breathing I could tell my brother-in-law was doing everything he could to maintain his composure. I clamped my mouth shut to give him enough time to find the words he needed, hoping they weren't as bad as I imagined.

"She developed an abscess. They need to get in there and stop the infection from spreading."

"How bad is it?" Another long pause. "*Noa*. How bad?"

"Bad," he whispered. "They've mentioned sepsis. They're prepping her now."

"Have you spoken to Tyler? What did he—"

"He's not available—"

"Why? He can't abandon—"

"He didn't abandon anyone," Noa cut me off, his voice rising well above mine. "Dr. Vance was hurt this morning. Someone attacked him at his house."

The words bounced off the outside of my skull like rubber balls, taking forever to get inside where they continued to leap around in a nonsensical mess, refusing to stay still long enough to be decoded. Nothing made sense. I must've misheard because it sounded as if Noa said Tyler had been attacked. It couldn't be true...except the sinking sensation in my stomach told me it was. Because Tyler Vance was another name on my forgiveness list.

"Is...is he all right?" I said.

"We're not sure, all we know is it happened at his home this morning, in his garage. And no, he's not okay." Noa took a breath. "He's in a bad way. Word is he's in an induced coma."

"A *coma*? But...but what about Azumi? Her operation?"

"We're working with another doctor. Oh, she's here. Gotta go."

"*Wait*. Can I come to the hospital?"

"We'll call you once she's out of surgery." With a small, tentative smile in his voice he added, "Stay out of trouble, Frankie. We need you."

I sat in the truck, clutching my phone to my chest, the air from the heating vents blasting into my face as I digested what Noa had told me. Tyler had been assaulted, seriously hurt. Put in a coma. My brain did its usual stunt of reaching for rationalization. Vance was an arrogant prick. He was bound to have pissed off more than his fair share of people.

Noa said Tyler had been attacked at home. Could've been a burglary gone wrong. Although Tyler might not be as flashy now as he was in high school and at university, where he'd loved showing off his cash, designer wardrobe, Swiss watches, expensive car, it didn't matter. Sometimes all an assailant hoped to find was a few bucks in their victim's wallet.

But reasoning wouldn't work this time. Tyler Vance had been on my list and the attacks were escalating, fast. First Geraldina's handrail mishap. The wheel coming off Chelsea's car. The fire, which had sent Davies to the hospital. Sandy's accident at the building site, which I suspected had been intended for Dad. Now Tyler. Where would this end?

I'd confronted Evan, and it hadn't gone well for me, even if I had got off with a stern warning from Judge Orr. Fact was Evan had the means and opportunity to take my notebook although his motive of why he was harming people remained unclear. Unless he really was the kind of person who didn't need a reason other than *because I can.*

I thought back to the Uber driver mix-up. As I'd done multiple times over the past week, I tried to remember if I'd told the driver my name and for whatever reason recited my address, but I couldn't remember. I'd been too mad at Evan for going through my things and cursed myself again for not paying attention to those details. I supposed it was possible my notebook had landed in his car, but it had shown up at Jake's Cakes again, and the only person I'd been there with was Evan. *Noa was there too that night.* I batted the thought away. No. Noa had nothing to do with any of this. He *didn't.*

With the progression of violence, I had to go to the cops, explain what was going on and hope they'd believe me. I needed to drive to the station and demand to see Officer Armstrong or Detective Willows and tell them…what, exactly? If I said anything about my forgiveness list, I'd have to explain why I'd added each name in the first place. It meant describing what had happened in school with Chelsea, at university with Tyler, and at work with Patrick Davies. I'd have to share my fraught relationship with my father. Basically, I'd hand them motive for almost every single person who'd been hurt because I *did* have motive. They wouldn't care if I said I'd included my name, why would they, particularly Willows, believe me?

I'd insist it would be ridiculous of me to come forward if I'd hurt anyone, which they could deftly turn around and argue was exactly what a criminal might say. Another encounter with Armstrong could jog her memory back to my being at the Davies fire. Then there was the recent video of me losing my shit on Facebook. Nicole Nelson had removed it, but there had to be a copy somewhere, and it would only be used as evidence of my temper.

I let my hands drop into my lap. No way could I incriminate myself and take the risk of being thrown back into a jail cell, not when I had to locate everyone left on my list, especially Shay, so I could warn them they might be in danger. And while I was doing that, I couldn't forget to watch my back.

CHAPTER TWENTY-FIVE

I had to speak to Dad. He was the one person who could give me information and help find Shay. This time it wasn't anger but nerves fluttering in my stomach when I thought about the conversation, especially as I knew it had to be face-to-face. I texted, told him the news about not being charged and asked to see him, but our exchange remained curt.

Him: At the hospital with Zoe and Sandy. Can it wait?

Me: No. Need to talk. Urgent.

Him: What about?

Me: Can't say. It's important.

Three bouncing dots appeared, disappeared, reappeared, and disappeared again.

Me: Dad!

Him: Fine. Cafeteria in 1 hour. Don't be late. Seeing Rico & Noa again after.

I didn't ask if he wanted me to go with him. Instead, my insides squirmed as I thought about mentioning Shay, and recalled how bad things had been between Dad and me when he'd found out I was pregnant. Although it was almost nineteen years ago, the memories of having a baby while in school were as fresh and painful as ever.

When I'd grown too big to hide my belly underneath baggy shirts and behind excuses of too many muffins, I quickly found out getting pregnant at fourteen turned me into even more of an outcast. Slut, whore, trailer trash—rare were the days when my cohort referred to me by my given name. Kids could be mean and judgmental—something that didn't seem to change much no matter the generation. I developed skin thicker than an elephant's as fast as possible to deflect the taunts, most of which I suspected had been instigated by Chelsea. Almost everyone but the teachers and staff stopped talking to me entirely, and kids avoided me in class and the hallways as much as they did on the bus.

Despite them keeping their distance, I heard the whispers. Rumors about who the father was or wasn't, that he was some forty-year-old married man I'd been involved with, or a colleague at the grocery store I'd boned behind the dumpsters during the summer.

Because nobody had ever seen Adrian and me together, his name never came up, and the abject terror of him making good on his threat to distribute those naked pictures made me do whatever I could to ensure it stayed that way. I never looked at him, never spoke to him. If I saw him coming down the hallway, I pretended to search for something in my bag or turned and walked away, darting into the bathroom.

The power he held disgusted me, but other than avoiding him, head down and mouth shut, I didn't know how to engineer his downfall without causing my total destruction. He held all the cards, the entire deck.

The silent animosity it caused dug in deep, the real roots of all my ensuing anger growing with every passing day. I hated myself for not having the guts to do anything but stay compliant, detested my silence and weakness, chastised myself for having urged him to take the naked photos in the first place, and, of course, regretted the one time we'd been intimate. I loathed how he could walk away from the situation and continue living his life without facing a single consequence. It wasn't right, it wasn't fair.

Rico looked at me differently, too, which broke my heart. As much as my stomach expanded, what remained of his wide-eyed innocence faded to nothing. He knew about sex, of course, and as most twelve-year-old boys did, thought it both fascinating and gross, but he was still a kid. He barely knew what to say when I clomped around the house in a bad mood because of another argument I'd had with Dad. When my brother heard me crying one night, he crept into my bedroom, sat on the end of the mattress, his shoulders hunched as he patted my feet. "Poor you," he said. "Poor, poor you."

His words made me feel worse because my situation was robbing him of time to deal with the grief of losing Mom, and I sobbed for the both of us because I knew I'd soon lose someone else when I placed the baby for adoption. Of course, it was the most logical choice, but I still fought with Dad about it, directing my anger at him because he was the easiest target.

"How will you support yourself and a child, Frankie?" he'd said, voice trembling when I'd challenged him again about the decision we'd made.

"I'll get a job. I'll work at the grocery store. They'll hire me full-time."

"And you'll do what, not finish school and take the baby on shifts with you?"

"Some employers have nurseries."

"On minimum wage? No, no, no. I won't let this mistake—"

"It's a person, Dad." I put my hands on my stomach. "And a person isn't a *mistake*."

"Listen to me. You have to stay in school, get an education, and a good job. Eventually you'll settle down. Have a family when you're ready. Not now."

"But this baby *is* family."

He shook his head, swallowed twice. "Can you, hand on heart, tell me you can offer this child the best future? Because I can't. Don't you think he or she would be better off with people who can give it everything it needs? Because I do."

I stared him down, challenging him. "If Mom were here—"

"But she's not, is she?" He shut his eyes, left the heaviness of the words hanging as my mind filled in the blanks about what he was probably thinking. *She's not here because you didn't tell her to stay home* or *because you refused to go with her and a two-minute delay while you found your shoes would've changed everything.* I wished I'd never told him I hadn't wanted to go out with her that evening. Some secrets were never meant to be shared.

He looked away, lowered his voice. "Your mother isn't here. We have no other family here anymore, no support. We can't do this, we *can't*. And we both know it."

I did know it, but it still hurt like hell. This baby would've given me comfort, something to focus on, to distract me from the loss of my mother, from Chelsea, from Adrian. But Dad was right—this child needed more, and it was selfish of me to think otherwise.

It was Dr. Ali who made the introduction to the Belrose Adoption Agency, which she assured us was the best in the area. "They'll be with you every step of the way," she said, and I was grateful because I hadn't appreciated how much help I'd need.

Holly, the assigned adoption counselor had so many questions over the course of our meetings. The reasons for placing the baby for adoption, if it was truly what I wanted, the kind of family I'd consider, whether I wanted them present for the birth, if I wanted time with the baby afterward, and if so, how long.

We discussed open adoption, meaning both parties knew each other's full names, and potentially developed a relationship including access to the baby for the birth mom. Next came semi-open, where a few nonidentifying details were shared. The final possibility was called *closed*, which sounded so drastic, so final, because no information about the identities of the individuals involved would ever be exchanged. As with everything else, I couldn't seem to decide what to do.

During one of the visits Holly gave me a portfolio of potential families to look through, but it sat on the kitchen table for over a week. "Want me to have a peek?" Dad asked one evening as we washed and dried the dishes, just the two of us as Rico was at a new anime drawing club, disappearing into an imaginary world of superheroes who could make things right. "I can go through the folder and make a note of the ones I think might suit best."

As Dad was about to turn away, I grabbed his arm, the first time I'd been that close to my father in weeks. "Would you…would you choose for me?"

"Frankie, I don't think—"

"Please? I'm terrified I'll make the wrong decision. What if I pick a bad family?"

"Remember what Holly said about vetting them? How much scrutiny there is?"

"Yes, but please? I don't want the responsibility. I can't mess this up as well."

He did as I asked, tried to convince me I should have a closed adoption to give the baby and me an entirely fresh start, allowing myself to leave the past behind. I refused, deciding for semi-open where we knew a few more details about the family, including the initials of their first names, S. and L., and the fact they lived in the Portland area. They'd also send us a photo via the adoption agency once a year.

With Dr. Ali and Holly's help, I wrote a good faith post-adoption agreement, in which I stated the baby had the right to my full name and contact details when he or she was eighteen. As I signed my name at the bottom, I didn't know if I'd be ready or willing to meet my child after so many years, but when I kissed Shay goodbye at the hospital and handed him to Holly, my heart shattering into a million pieces, I knew I'd made the right decision. All I had to do was wait, and it had given me a tiny spark of hope I cradled in my heart and refused to let go of.

Ever since, it seemed to Rico and Dad, Shay's birthday was like any other day, but I always took a moment to sit quietly, light a candle, and think about the boy I'd given up, imagine how much he'd grown and changed over the past year. I pictured him often, and as time passed, I'd linger at playgrounds trying to see if I could spot him, if I'd instinctively recognize my son among the children, but I never had.

As more years went by, I worried about how he'd react if and when his parents revealed they weren't his birth family. Would he hate me? Despise me for what I'd done? I tried to put myself in his situation but found it impossible. If I'd discovered I was adopted, I wanted to believe I'd have loved my mother, father, and Rico the same but without the experience there was no way to know for sure. Perhaps I'd have wanted to find my birth family. Maybe I'd have decided I didn't need anyone else in my life to make it more crowded and complicated, especially not someone who—at first glance—hadn't wanted me. I didn't have the answers, but as Shay's eighteenth birthday approached, I'd yearned for him to call me, come to a building site or my apartment and say, "Hey, Mom."

The memories shattered around me when my stomach let out a deafening squeal, reminding me how hungry I was. I still had over thirty minutes before meeting Dad at the hospital cafeteria and didn't want to waste any time by eating lunch there, so I drove to my favorite Italian deli on Park Avenue for a sandwich I could shovel down fast. As I walked to the door, I pulled up my collar and wrapped my arms around my middle. The wind lashed my face and the skies had filled with clouds again, dark and menacing. Somewhat like my mood.

"Hey, Lonny," I said to the old man behind the counter when I walked in. "How are you?"

He grinned, the creases appearing in his cheeks rivaling the depths of the Grand Canyon. "Oh, you know me," he wheezed. "Still giving the Grim Reaper the finger."

Despite the whole bizarre situation in which I found myself, I chuckled. He always did that to me—made me giggle when I was in the shittiest of moods.

Local folklore had it *Old Lonny* had worked at the store for over fifty years and could cite the price of everything he sold by heart, as well as how much it cost way back when. He scrunched his nose, indicating outside with his head. "How bad is it out there?"

"Winds have picked up. Wouldn't surprise me if it rains again."

"Ah, well. You know what Annie says about it being sunny tomorrow."

Along with his friendliness and impeccable memory, Lonny was also known for his eternal optimism. A wise old *nonno* who not only made the tastiest capicola and pickle sandwiches, but he also saw the best of every situation. He once told me it was the only way he knew how to be. I, however, less than half his years and cynical for all of them, made a face.

"You've jinxed it now. It'll probably snow."

Lonny laughed again. "I'll save you a place on my sled. Want the usual?"

"Please. I'll grab a few more things."

I roamed the aisles for a bit, choosing an apple, a bar of chocolate and a box of cookies. I was about to shove a Coke Zero in my basket as the bell on the door rang, making me turn around. A young man wearing a mulberry sweater strode in, and I saw he'd pulled the hood up so far it practically covered half of his face. Lonny would give him crap if the kid didn't watch it, especially if he wandered around with his hands in his pockets. I lost sight of him when he went down a different aisle, and I grabbed my Coke.

"Got everything you need?" Lonny said as he placed the foot-long, paper-wrapped sandwich on the counter, and the smell of it made me want to tear into the wrapper like an animal. "Haven't seen you in a week, kid. How are you doing?"

I looked at him, and the friendliness in Lonny's eyes made any flip reply I'd had turn to dust. How was I doing? It was self-indulgent to ponder the question when my niece was in the hospital, my brother and Noa were beside themselves with worry, I'd pissed my father off so much he was going to fire me, and multiple people had been hurt because of something I'd written. I lowered my head, the heat of intense shame rushing to my cheeks. How was I doing? Not well. Not well at all.

"Hey, Frankie, are you all right?" Lonny's frown made his entire face crinkle, and the concern in his voice was the ultimate thing to crack my infallible heavy-duty armor. Six gentle words from a kind old man I knew only from exchanging pleasantries and trivia over heavenly sandwiches.

Fat, heavy tears sprang from my eyes and rolled down my face. Not a full-on ugly cry but enough to make my shoulders heave, and I felt ridiculous. There I was, a grown-ass woman bawling in the local deli. "I—I'm f-fine," I said. "It's nothing."

"Doesn't seem nothing," Lonny answered softly.

"No, really. I'm dealing with a few things, is all."

"Mmm-hmm..." Lonny crossed his arms, scratched his stubbly chin as he leaned toward me. "I may be old, but I can see when someone's in pain. Maybe I can help."

I glanced over my shoulder. The man in the sweater was at the end of the store, his back turned and although I believed he was out of earshot, I whispered, "Family issues with my brother, and I upset my dad. I have to talk to him but I'm... I'm actually scared."

"Ah, classic. Well, I may be talking out of my butt here, and by all means ignore this advice, but I had issues with my father. Didn't speak for ten years and when I finally wanted to, he had a heart attack and died."

"Oh, Lonny, how awful."

"It's okay." He waved a hand. "Happened a long, long time ago, but I've regretted not picking up the phone almost every day since. Don't do what I did, kid. Leave it until it's too late." He looked behind, called out, "Anything I can help you with, sir?" before turning to me again. "Damn lurkers.

If it's not Edith, it's someone else. The woman will be the death of me, I swear."

"Has she been giving you a hard time again?"

"You're putting it mildly. *Dio mio*, every time she comes here, she asks for things she dang well knows I don't have, and if I ordered them for her, she'd turn her nose up. Come to think of it, I haven't seen her in a day or two. I've enjoyed the peace and quiet, for sure."

"But…I thought she came here for fresh rolls every morning?"

Lonny shook his head. "Not since Saturday."

I couldn't remember the last time I'd seen Edith either. We'd had a brief flash of kindred spirits when she'd told me about her mom dying. When had it been? Not yesterday. The day before? Saturday? Time had started to blend, rolling the hours together. She hadn't knocked on my door for money, nor had she burst into the hallway to yell at me when I'd walked past the last few times, which was another anomaly. The realization I should've thought of this sooner made a sense of dread crawl up my back. If something happened to her, it would be my fault for not doing anything to prevent it.

"I'd better go," I said, tossing bills on the counter.

"Good luck, Frankie," Lonny said. "I hope things work out with your pop. Perhaps the worst part is already behind you."

"Perhaps," I said, but couldn't help thinking he was wrong.

CHAPTER TWENTY-SIX

In the brief time I'd spent in the deli, the weather had got worse. Slushy sleet fell from the skies, and the howling winds pricked my face like tiny sets of needles. People had hurried indoors, and there weren't many pedestrians around, but as I got about ten yards from my truck, and despite the fact I was in a hurry, I had that odd sensation of being watched.

I turned around, fast, saw three people. A woman on the other side of the street, her tiny pink-and-white-polka-dot jacket–clad dog yapping as they went, a man carrying a briefcase, and who stepped around me with a friendly, "Excuse me," and the guy from Lonny's store, already heading in the opposite direction.

I thought about going after any one of them, took three steps before stopping again. What would I say, exactly? Demand to know who they were? Accuse them of following me? I'd never seen them before. Clearly, the woman was just walking down the street with her pet, one of the men perhaps on his way to his office, while the other had stepped into Lonny's store to buy some snacks. I was being irrational, and I had to get moving because my priority was to check on my neighbor, not an argument with strangers.

I made it to my truck in double time, thinking about Edith. All I had to do was knock on her door and make sure she was okay, but then what? How could I warn her about potentially being in danger? Should I make an anonymous call to the cops? Leave her a note?

As soon as I got back to my apartment building, I walked to her door, still unsure of what I'd say when she answered. *If* she answered. I gave a sharp knock and waited. When nothing happened, I knocked again.

"Edith?" I looked at my watch. Shortly after one, the time she watched one of her soap operas full blast. Pressing my ear against the door, I hoped to hear the TV or Edith's slow footsteps shuffling over, but there was nothing, not until I heard a cat mewing. *Penelope.*

Was I too late? Had something happened to her already? I tried the handle, but it didn't budge. I remembered how I'd been so certain someone had been in my apartment after my run at the cemetery. My front door had been locked then, too. I banged again, using my palm and making as much noise as I could, but Edith still didn't fling the door open, her usual biting words at the ready.

I wondered if I could break down the door before telling myself not to be impulsive. Mrs. Clayton, the superintendent, lived in one of the apartments on the ground floor. She probably had a key. I raced downstairs, feet thundering on each step, and banged on her door. Mrs. Clayton, a petite woman in her sixties who loved baking double chocolate chip cookies, always had sugar on tap if you ran out, and had once given each tenant in the building two rolls of toilet paper when the shelves at the stores were bare, widened her eyes when she saw me.

"Is everything okay? What's the matter, dear?"

"Edith," I said.

"Oh, no. You haven't got into another argument, have you?"

"No," I said, deciding to improvise and exaggerate a little to get what I wanted. "I haven't seen or heard from her in days, she hasn't played her violin, and she's not answering her door. I've knocked multiple times."

"Well…she did mention something about going on vacation."

"But the cat's up there. I heard it."

"Oh, my. That's not good. She definitely wouldn't leave Penelope behind."

"Exactly. I think we should go inside. Please?"

"I'll grab my keys."

We raced up the stairs, Mrs. Clayton taking them two at a time. "Stay there," she said over her shoulder when she slid the key in the lock. "I'll go in alone."

Although I didn't want to discover my neighbor's corpse decomposing into the carpet, I couldn't let Mrs. Clayton get her way, not when somebody else might still be in there. I followed close behind, my head on a swivel as soon as we switched on the lights. Penelope scowled at us from her spot on the sofa, and if the thing could've talked, I bet it would've told us to get lost.

With Mrs. Clayton a step ahead, we walked through the apartment, inspecting the kitchen, bathroom, and two bedrooms. I'd expected the place to be filled with clutter and a musty smell of potpourri, but the decor was surprisingly sparse. It almost looked as if Edith had recently moved in, not been a tenant for nearly ten years.

"False alarm," Mrs. Clayton said when we were in the living room. "Maybe the cat—"

"Who on earth are you, and what are you doing in this apartment?"

An almost identical copy of Edith, except she seemed a

little older, had much curlier hair, and was carrying a fluorescent green cane, watched us with an enraged expression from the front door. She came over, limping slightly, but one look at her face and I had no doubt she'd clock me over the head with her stick if I didn't answer.

"I'm Frankie, Edith's neighbor. This is Mrs. Clayton, the building's super."

The woman held out a hand, her grip firm. "I'm Mrs. Winchester."

"Are you…?" Mrs. Clayton said.

"Edith's sister," Mrs. Winchester said, immediately laughing at our confused faces. "Ah, I see she's never mentioned me. Not surprising. We never did get along. Anyway, what seems to be the problem?"

"I hadn't seen Edith in a while," I said. "When I came to check on her, I only heard Penelope and thought something was wrong."

"She's on a trip," Mrs. Winchester said, waving a hand. "Vermont, I think."

"Doesn't she take Penelope wherever she goes?" Mrs. Clayton said.

"Couldn't this time. Edith had organized a sitter but apparently, they bailed. My sister texted earlier, telling me to come get the cat." She clicked her tongue. "And I mean *telling*. Honestly, I don't hear from her in almost a year, and she's giving me orders about what to do with Penny."

"Penelope," I said without thinking.

"Whoops." Mrs. Winchester rolled her eyes, pulling up a sleeve to reveal three deep scratches on her forearm. "Should've named the damn thing Lucifer."

I laughed, making Mrs. Winchester chuckle as Mrs. Clayton said if there was anything else she could do, we should let her know because she had to get downstairs and check on the peach and blueberry cobbler she'd left in the oven.

"How long will Edith be away?" I asked Mrs. Winchester.

"Three or four weeks. Not sure I can stand having the devil incarnate living with me for so long. One of us may not make it out alive—" she lowered her voice to a stage whisper "—and I promise you, I'll be the one who survives."

Oh, how I wished she was my neighbor instead of her sister. "Thank you," I said, and I meant it for multiple reasons. Edith was unharmed, and gone for almost a month, leaving me to handle the other names on my list before she returned.

The old woman smiled. "You're a good neighbor, Frankie. I can't imagine it's easy living next to Edith. Anyway, I'd best take the monster home before she tries to eat my head. Have a good evening."

One potential crisis averted, I drove to the hospital, couldn't stop myself from regularly checking my rearview mirror to ensure nobody was following. After I'd parked on a busy floor, I went to the cafeteria, planning on sneaking a seat somewhere at the back where I could eat Lonny's delicious sandwich in peace and wait for Dad.

Change of plan as he was already there, except he didn't see me arrive because he wasn't alone. My father sat at a table with Geraldina by his side, empty plates and coffee cups in front of them. Their hands were entwined, and he pressed her fingers to his lips. I took a few steps back, making sure I stayed out of view, feeling creepy for spying on my father and his girlfriend. They chatted for a while before Geraldina glanced at her watch, leaned over, and kissed him on the lips before collecting her bag and walking away, turning around to give him a wave.

How long had they been seeing each other? Were they *seeing* each other, or was this—God, the thought grossed me out—a casual *fling*? I waited until I was certain she'd left the building before I walked to Dad's table. I needed to speak to him, and it couldn't wait any longer, secret girlfriends and trepidation be damned.

"Hey, Dad," I said as casually as I could. "Been here long?"

"Not at all," he said. When my gaze fell to the empty coffee cups, he didn't attempt to explain them, but leaned back in his chair.

"How's Sandy?" I said as I sat.

"Very lucky. He woke up in the ambulance."

"Oh, wow, that's great. Any injuries?"

"A broken leg and a fractured arm. He should be home by tomorrow."

I fidgeted in my seat, couldn't sit still as the guilt spread within me again. "That's such a relief. Did he say how it happened?"

"Like we suspected, one of the boards on the first floor gave way. He said he remembers grabbing hold of some scaffolding on his way down and holding on before slipping off. Thankfully that broke his fall because it could've been a whole lot worse. I'll speak to the crew about safety measures again."

"Good idea. And what's the latest on Azumi?"

"She's in surgery now. Rico said he'd text as soon as there's news. You know about Dr. Vance's assault?"

"Yeah."

He ran a hand over his face. "What a mess."

I leaned forward, almost changing my mind and bailing as I met his cool gaze. "I need to talk to you about something. It's really important and I don't want you to freak out."

"What kind of trouble are you in this time?"

I decided to let his assumption I'd done more bad stuff go unchallenged and dived in. "I need you to be careful."

"At work?"

"Everywhere."

He looked at me and I squirmed in my seat trying to maintain eye contact. "Is this because of what happened to Sandy? You're worried I'll have an accident, too?"

"Yes, because…" I closed my mouth and opened it again, getting ready to tell him about my forgiveness list, but I couldn't find the words. He'd hate me, disown me if he knew.

"What is it?" he said.

"I, uh, I need to find Shay," I blurted.

He stared at me. Blinked a few times, finally said, "Why?"

"I can't say."

"Frankie—"

I held up a hand. "It's important. I have to find him."

"Again, why?"

I shifted my feet under the table, pulled at the collar of my jacket. Had they turned the heat up in this place since I'd arrived? "What reason do I need other than he's my son?"

"I wondered if he had something to do with all this," Dad said.

"All *what*?"

"Everything that's been going on with you lately. I know his eighteenth birthday was a few months ago."

"You remembered?"

"Of course I did. It's not the kind of thing I'd forget."

"You've never mentioned it."

"Neither did you, which made me think you didn't want to talk about it. I guess you expected to hear from him?"

"Yes," I whispered. "But I haven't. And now it's urgent."

"Sweetheart…" Dad's expression softened, and the use of a term of endearment surprised me, it wasn't something he did all that often. "If he hasn't been in touch, it probably means he doesn't want to be." When he saw my face, he quickly added, "*Yet*. He's probably not ready, and you know it's his choice. You can't force this."

"Dad, I need to find him."

"This is exactly what I was worried about when you insisted on having a semi-open adoption." He tapped his index finger on the table. "This, right here. I didn't want you to go through the heartache of him not contacting you, of you ultimately being disappointed."

I let out a cold, sharp laugh as I crossed my arms. "Well, you certainly know what being disappointed by your child is like, don't you, Dad?"

"Why do you do that?" he said quietly. "Put yourself down and make me the bad guy?"

I sidestepped his questions. "Do you still have the file and the photos Belrose sent?"

"Yes, of course."

"I want them."

He didn't speak, just stared at me for ten seconds straight before lowering his eyes, shaking his head, and quietly saying, "No, I don't think it's a good idea."

"What? Dad, they're *mine*."

"Yes, but I have an idea what you'll do with them. You'll try to use them to look for clues on how to find him. I can't let you do that. We're talking about you trying to disrupt a young man's life."

"Disrupt?"

"You need to leave him be until he's ready. That was the agreement, wasn't it? The one you wrote. You said he could contact you *if* he wanted to."

I pinched the bridge of my nose with two fingers. "Dad, you don't understand—"

"No. Leave it alone. I won't help you. Not now, anyway.

You're a mess, and it pains me to say this but you're spiraling. It wouldn't be fair for you to barge into his life in your state."

"Oh my God, you're making it sound like I'm disturbed."

"You were arrested, for goodness' sake."

"They dropped all the charges."

"Great, but you still pushed a guy through a glass wall." He paused. "Tell me why you have this sudden need to find...your son?"

"His name was Shay, Dad. You can't even say it, can you? What kind of a messed-up family are we if we're incapable of uttering my child's name?"

"Fine, you don't want to tell me, but you need to talk to someone to get your head straight. What about Geraldina? Maybe she can help with your issues."

"Was she helping with *your* issues over lunch?" I snarled, reveling in the surprise on his face. "Seems I'm not the only one who doesn't want to share everything. When were you going to tell us about the two of you?"

"I don't believe it's any of your concern."

"And my wanting to talk to my son isn't any of *yours*. I'm an adult, Dad."

"Then act like one." He got up. "Forcing your way into his life when he may not want you in it is a bad move, for both of you."

I stood, bumping the table with my thighs, considered flipping the damn thing and sending everything on it flying, but then I'd appear exactly what Dad was making me out to be—the out-of-control, angry woman who couldn't get a handle on herself or her emotions. I put my hands on the table and leaned over him, lowering my voice. "You don't get to tell me—"

"That's exactly what I'm doing," he said. "It's for your own good."

"Are you *kidding* me? Would you say the same to Rico?"

"This isn't about your brother, but thanks for the reminder. I'm going upstairs to see him and Noa for the next hour and I'd be grateful if you didn't visit until I've left."

"Want to continue this lovely conversation at the office?" I said in a biting, singsong voice I laced with as much disdain as I could find. When he didn't respond I let out a snort. "I'm definitely unemployed? Thanks for letting me know."

"Goodbye, Frankie." My father hesitated, looked as if he might say something else but must've decided otherwise because he turned and left, shaking his head as he went, leaving me ready to boil over right there in the hospital cafeteria.

CHAPTER TWENTY-SEVEN

With no job to go to or projects to worry about, Dad had unwittingly granted me freedom and with it the gift of time—and if he wouldn't hand over Shay's photos, I'd find another way. To be honest, I wasn't sure they'd be of much use anyway. As agreed, we'd received an annual picture from Shay's adoptive parents, but when Dad had found me sobbing in my bedroom clutching a drawing Shay had made when he was three, he asked the agency to stop sending them. I hadn't objected, at all, which now made me want to curl up on the floor of Maine Medical's cafeteria and die. Did Shay know? If so, maybe it was enough for him to never want to contact me. I'd abandoned him, twice. Why would he ever want to see my face?

Back in my truck I pulled out my phone, searched for Belrose Adoption Agency. Nothing. I delved a little deeper, and deeper still, flicking through page after page before finally locating a news snippet from five years earlier about how Belrose had been taken over by a larger group called Abbot & Dean. There was no mention of a woman called Holly on the new website, but I wondered if my case worker might still be there, and whether she'd give me access to the adoption files if I explained Shay might be in danger. A long shot, but anything was worth a try. I had to start somewhere, and so, I dialed.

"Abbot and Dean, Trish speaking," a woman said when she answered the phone. "How may I redirect your call?"

"Hi, my name's Fr…ancine," I said, not entirely sure why I'd lied but deciding it was necessary in case I needed to change tack. "I'm looking for Holly, please."

"Holly Nierling?"

"Uh, sure? She was with the agency years ago when it was Belrose."

"Oh, yes, that was our Holly."

"Was? She doesn't work there anymore?"

"Oh, dear." Trish's voice fell. "I'm afraid Holly passed away from cancer a year ago."

"That's awful. She was so kind to me."

"Yes, she was such a lovely person, wasn't she? Always brightened the room, and her karaoke renditions were legendary. Did you ever catch one of her performances at the Beehive? They truly were spectacular."

"No, I'm afraid I didn't."

"That's a shame. We still have a regular drink in her honor. That's how much we miss her… Oh, dear. Apologies for the trip down memory lane there."

"Not at all. It's fine, honestly."

"Thank you, but let's see if I can find someone to help you. Was there something specific you needed, or do you have a more general question I might be able to answer?"

"Uhm…I'm looking for details on an adoption Belrose handled almost twenty years ago."

"Oh, wow, that's quite a while. Were you adopted?"

"No, I, uh, placed my son for adoption. It was semi-open.

He can contact me, but I haven't heard anything and I'm trying to find him."

"Yikes, I'm afraid we can't help you. It wouldn't be allowed."

"But I need to find him. It's important. He might…he might be in danger."

"I don't follow. How would you know he's in danger if you haven't had contact for this long?"

"It's complicated, I, uh…" I thought back to a thriller I'd read recently, *Find You First* by Linwood Barclay. The protagonist had a terminal illness called… *"Huntington's,"* I blurted.

"Pardon?"

"I've been diagnosed with Huntington's disease," I said, thinking I was surely going to hell for telling such a horrible lie, but it was too late to stop. In for a penny and all that. "It's hereditary, and fatal. My son needs to know so he can get tested early."

"How terrible, I'm so sorry," she said. "And I regret having to say this, Francine, I truly do, but I'm still not allowed to give you any information. You could write us a letter, and we could forward it to your son."

I was losing her; I could tell from the conclusory tone in her voice. "All I need are the adoptive parents' names," I whispered. "That's it. Can you please take a quick peek in your system? I'll never tell anyone about this conversation, I promise. *Please.*" I willed her to say yes, hoped I'd done enough to make her type a few keystrokes.

"I really can't—I could lose my job," Trish said, making my shoulders sag. "Even if I looked, the information wouldn't be in the system. The Belrose records from that far back are in archive boxes, they haven't been digitized."

"Oh…"

Her voice shifted again, filling with empathy. "Have you

tried Vital Records? They might be able to do something for you. Oh, I have another call. Goodbye and best of luck."

Another call, my ass, she wanted to get rid of me. I Googled Vital Records, and found out they were in Augusta, an hour's drive away. When a man answered my call and I explained what I needed, I hoped progress would be swift.

"Can I get my son's new birth certificate with his adoptive parents' name?" I asked.

"Oh." The man went quiet before gently saying, "Uh, no. Apologies, I misunderstood and thought you were looking for your own. We're not authorized to give you your child's new record without a release from the adoptive parents or your son if he's an adult."

"Seriously?" I said, anger nipping at my insides. "I'm trying to find him and every way I turn there's a roadblock."

"Are you already in our Adoption Reunion Registry Program?"

"No, what's that?"

"Well, you register as a birth parent. If your son registers, too, there's a match and you'll both be notified."

"How fast?"

"Immediately. You'll receive an email with each other's contact details, and you can decide how to proceed with getting in touch, if it's still what you both want."

"Then…he might already be in the registry?"

"Potentially. If he's over eighteen he could've registered directly, or his adoptive parents might have done so on his behalf if they wanted to find you."

Unlikely. If they wanted to find me in the last six months, they'd have had ample opportunity and could've done so via Abbot & Dean. So could Shay, unless he had no idea they weren't his biological parents. Yes, we'd agreed to a semi-open adoption. Yes, I'd said I wanted Shay to be given my information when he turned eighteen, but it was a good faith agreement and there was no guarantee it had happened, especially after we'd told Belrose no more updates should be mailed to us. Maybe his parents had decided he was better off without knowing me…but I had to follow every trail available and hope it took me somewhere.

"How fast can I get on the registry?"

"As soon as we have your paperwork and you've paid the registration fee. You can send everything to us here in Augusta. The address is—"

"What if I stop by?"

"Then it's almost instant. We can schedule a meeting for Thursday or Friday."

"Could you do it today?" When he didn't answer straight away, I added, "Please?"

"Oh, what the heck. This is obviously important, so I'll move things around. Stop by as quick as you can and ask for Jamie."

"Thanks. I'll see you in an hour."

"The notary leaves at three."

I looked at my watch. One forty-five. "I'll drive faster."

True to his word, Jamie helped me as soon as I rushed into the squat brown two-story building with about twenty-five minutes to spare. I'd gunned it up the Maine Turnpike, hoping the cops wouldn't see me because if they did, I decided they'd have to follow me with their lights flashing all the way to Augusta before I'd stop.

After I'd filled in the form Jamie gave me, I handed him my credit card and driver's license, silently urging him to work his administrative magic.

"You're all set and registered," he said a little while later. "As I mentioned on the phone, if there's a match, you'll get an email. If you want to withdraw from the registry—"

"That won't be necessary."

"Then I wish you the best of luck, miss."

Before I walked out the main door, my phone was already in my hand, fingers refreshing email over and over, hoping for an alert. Nothing. But I did get a text from Rico.

Dad left ages ago. Where are you?

I dialed his number. "How's Azumi?" I said when he answered.

"In recovery. Dad said you were at the hospital. Why didn't you come by?"

"Needed to take off for a bit." I didn't want to lie more than I already had, but the less he knew the better. "I went for a drive."

He fell quiet for a few beats. "Does this have anything to do with Shay? Dad said you're freaking out about him turning eighteen and not hearing from him. Is it true?"

Why couldn't Dad keep his mouth shut? "Something like that."

"Frankie…"

"Listen, do you still have a key to Dad's?"

"He warned me you'd ask for it. Said I shouldn't give it to you… He also mentioned he's out for dinner again tonight."

"I'll come to the hospital now."

"Thought you might. See you in a bit."

Azumi was asleep when I got to the room an hour later, hooked up to so many beeping machines I almost lost count. I tiptoed over to Rico and hugged him. "How is she?"

"New doc said we have to give it time, see what happens with the antibiotics they're pumping into her. She said she's…hopeful."

I took a seat next to him. "Where's Noa?"

"Work. His boss was breathing down his neck, so he had to get some stuff done. He should be here a little later." When his phone rang, he glanced at the screen, his face turning pale.

"Who's that?" I said, craning my neck to see.

"Insurance company."

"No way, again? How many times have they contacted you now?"

"Who knows? Five, six? I told Noa I'll handle it so he can focus on work. Truth is I'm not handling it. They've been pretty vocal about what they're not going to cover, hassling us about the insurance fine print and reimbursements. Noa said to ignore the calls. He thinks he might have a plan."

The little voice in my head whispered things I didn't want to hear about the Jake's Cakes coffee cup in Rico's car and the fact Dad's insurance policies would give them immediate financial relief. I swatted the voice away once again, still asked, "What kind of plan?"

"Not sure. Didn't have time to get into it. I had to call my clients and tell them about project delays. A few weren't impressed. Two said they'd find somebody else because they couldn't wait."

"God, Rico. I wish there was something I could do."

"I know," he said. "Honestly, I'm worried about Noa. He's a wreck, and—"

"I'm fine." Noa stood in the doorway, a tired smile on his face. "How's our baby girl?"

"So far so good," Rico said, getting up to kiss his husband, but when Noa waved at me, I saw the hat clutched in his hand. A dark gray slouchy beanie, like Edith had said. *It doesn't mean anything*, I told myself. Half the Portland population under forty had one.

"New hat?" I said, my voice strained.

Rico looked at me with a quizzical expression and Noa

frowned. "Those are some pretty keen observational skills," he said.

"When did you get it?"

"A few weeks ago. Why?"

"Just wondered."

Noa didn't seem otherwise concerned. Was it because he had nothing to hide and he wasn't the person whom Edith had seen in the hallway, or because he was pretending? I couldn't tell. Didn't know if he had a Nike backpack, either, and why would he leave flowers and chocolates for me anonymously? It didn't make sense.

Nevertheless, unease slithered up my spine. Perhaps I'd been looking at this all wrong. Maybe the beanies meant nothing, and I was dealing with two separate attackers with two different motives. Someone who was targeting the other people on my list, and…Noa, who'd only gone after my father but ended up hurting Sandy instead. I hated myself for thinking my brother-in-law was involved somehow, but now I'd done so, I couldn't stop.

I decided to sit and watch. Rico was right. Noa was stressed, there was an intense restlessness about him as he bounced his feet when he sat, unable to stay still for more than a minute before he rose to pace the room. Hardly surprising for a father whose daughter was sick, and yet…

"You heard Sandy's going to be okay?" I said, watching Noa for a reaction, wondering if he'd flinch or look aghast because he'd caused the wrong person to plummet from the first floor of a building.

"It's great news," Rico said. "We can't believe how lucky he was, can we, Noa?"

"Incredibly lucky," he said. "The guy must have nine lives or a guardian angel. Or both."

Was he really that good an actor? I stayed for another while, observing Noa, but still couldn't tell. I decided I wouldn't spend more time here trying to guess. It was unproductive, Dad was probably out for dinner by now—presumably with Geraldina—which meant it was time for me to pay my old house a visit in stealth mode.

CHAPTER TWENTY-EIGHT

The rain had stopped again, leaving the air cool, the heady smell of damp leaves lingering. With Dad's front door key, which Rico had given me before I'd left the hospital, safely tucked in my pocket, I drove to Riverton. Once certain my father's truck wasn't anywhere to be found, I unlocked the front door and crept inside, looking around as if I were a burglar. Chip padded over, barking and wagging his tail, but before I'd made it to the end of the hallway, my phone beeped with a text message from Dad.

What are you doing in my house?

I froze, took a few steps back as my cell rang.

"Didn't spot the new door cam outside, did you?" Dad said when I answered my phone because I hadn't known what else to do. "I suppose Rico gave you the key." When I didn't answer he continued, "You two were always thick as thieves. What you're looking for isn't there for exactly that reason. Leave the key on the kitchen counter and go out through the garage. Do it now."

"Dad, I want those documents. They're mine. You can't control—"

"I'm not telling you to leave again. If I don't see you driving away within the next thirty seconds, I'm calling the cops. They can arrest you again for all I care."

"You wouldn't."

"Try me."

It took me twenty seconds, and once I'd gone far enough down the road for his security system to not see my truck anymore, I parked on the side, chest heaving. I couldn't believe what my father was doing. The audacity of it all—making my choices for me as if I were still a child. Saying he'd call the police. If I hadn't believed he'd carry out his threat, I'd have driven back to his house, except I couldn't risk it. But damn it, helpful or not I wanted those photos, and I needed to find Shay's information however I could.

I thought back to my conversation with Trish from the adoption agency. Even if I was a world-famous hacker like Kevin Mitnick and capable of infiltrating their systems in my sleep, it wouldn't have been useful. She'd said the documents were in archive boxes. I knew what that meant. Somehow, I had to get inside the adoption agency's offices, preferably more expertly than I'd done at Dad's. I wondered if it might be better to try during the day, but how would I steal anything in a manned building? No, I had to do it under the cover of darkness. And it had to be tonight.

Once I'd located the address for Abbot & Dean on Pearl Street, I drove back to town, dumped the truck on Exchange Street, and doubled back on foot. It was almost eight, the roads relatively quiet. I slowed down as I approached the office building. The main door was made of oak and steel. Big, heavy, but unlocked. I walked into the foyer, which vaguely smelled of sugared almonds, saw a sign saying the adoption agency was on the second floor, and went up the curved, stone stairs.

My recon mission ended abruptly. While the agency had glass double doors, there was no chance of picking the lock, I wouldn't know where to start, but one of those keycard entry systems was mounted on the wall to the left. The only thing standing between me and finding an archive box with my case file in it was an employee's badge. I scoured the floor in case I got lucky, which I didn't. It was only ever that convenient in crime shows where the character had forty minutes to solve a mystery. I headed back to my truck, and when I spotted the Beehive pub a few doors down from the agency, the one Trish had mentioned on the phone, a plan formed as I went inside.

"Hey," I said to the host who was dressed in a black-and-yellow-striped shirt. "Is the team from Abbot and Dean here tonight? I'm new and I think I missed our get-together."

He looked down at his tablet, tapped and swiped the screen. "Standing reservation every Thursday at five thirty for karaoke. Want me to add a seat?"

"No, it's okay. I'm sure Trish will do it." I backed away, pissed I had to wait forty-eight hours before I could take action, but unable to determine a different and immediate way to get into the office.

I decided I'd make good use of my time by tracking down the rest of the people on the list, and hoped the fact I hadn't included Shay's last name would make him difficult, if not impossible, to identify, let alone find.

In the meantime, Adrian Costas and Trina Smith were two individuals I needed to locate and warn they should watch their backs. I headed to my place, ready for more research, and decided to work on my former colleague Trina first.

When I'd come back from university, I'd worked at the

grocery store where I'd had a summer job the previous years. It was only going to be a temporary fix, a place I could earn a bit of money while I decided what to do next now that I'd messed up my education so badly.

Trina was a peer, although she behaved like everyone's supervisor. It didn't bother me at first, not until a month later when there were rumblings of a new store being opened on the other side of town. Rumor had it one of the staff at our location might be chosen to manage it.

That was when the trouble began. One of the more senior employees got fired when he allegedly left a cold room door open, and thousands of dollars' worth of frozen food had to be thrown away. Another colleague resigned because of a story she was mistreating her elderly mother. Nobody knew if it was true, but she was a quiet person who couldn't stand the whispers and stares.

I knew a bully when I saw one, presumed sneaky Trina was behind everything, manipulating people out of the way so she'd be the last one standing for the promotion. That's the kind of person she was, cold and calculating, always out for herself, so I watched her more carefully, but she was smart, not one to make a careless mistake. Not until I caught her trying to stash a half-full bottle of whiskey in my locker.

"What are you doing?" I said.

Trina spun around, her mouth agape. "I know you must be hurting from getting kicked out of university and all," she said, holding up the bottle. "But, I mean, drinking on the job?"

I walked over and grabbed the alcohol right before our boss walked in. In a masterful, Oscar-worthy performance ten times better than what Chelsea could've done, Trina spun a tale. Told the boss I'd been the one trying to get ahead by setting colleagues up, and she'd caught me trying to hide the booze in her belongings.

I protested, lost, and found myself out of a job, the threat of police action hanging over my head. Nothing ever happened—they wouldn't have been able to prove the allegations—but once again it was something I had to explain to Dad, yet another failure on my part. At that point I'd felt pretty sure it was all he expected from me, but the ensuing arguments had raged for weeks.

I had no clue where Trina was now, had never seen her again after I'd walked out of the store. As I sat on the sofa, I searched social media but couldn't find an account with any up-to-date information. The last Facebook post was over eight years ago, and she was nowhere on Twitter and Instagram.

LinkedIn seemed a little more promising. She hadn't included the grocery store in her employment history, but I saw she'd been an assistant at a wholesale company for about a year before she moved to California. Apparently, she was still there, working for a dentist. I looked them up, saw they were open late most evenings, and dialed.

"Trina Smith?" the receptionist said as soon as I explained whom I was looking for. "No chance. Far as I know she's got another few years left."

"What do you mean? Is she sick?"

"In the head. They locked her up. Bank robbery gone wrong a few years back and a guy died. Oh, got a patient coming in. I'll leave you to it. If you search for her name and Mission Viejo, you'll find the details."

Sure enough, Trina, along with three other female accomplices, had tried to rob a bank in the middle of the day. When it ended in a standoff with the police, one of the hostages had been shot and killed. The judge hadn't bought Trina's story of having been forced to participate, called her a charlatan and the mastermind behind the operation. "Clever, almost convincing, and, most of all, extraordinarily unrepentant," he'd said during the sentencing, handing her fifteen years without parole. My former colleague had finally ended up where she deserved.

I had one more person to track down. Someone I'd been putting off because I wasn't sure I could handle it. Adrian Costas, Shay's father. With hesitant fingers, and hoping he'd left the area or was in prison somewhere, too, I opened Facebook, typed his name, and hit Enter.

CHAPTER TWENTY-NINE

When Adrian's profile picture appeared on my screen, my stomach contracted, anger mixed with bile rose to my back teeth, and I forced it down, tried doing the same with the surging memories, but they weren't quite so easy to handle.

While I'd never spoken to Adrian after I'd told him about the baby, I'd still had to endure six months of us being in the same building, which had been torture. Not because I pined for him—I'd developed a hatred for my ex-boyfriend so vast, I thought it might consume me whole—but because I lived under the constant threat he'd share the naked pictures.

For all Adrian's talk about keeping our relationship a secret to preserve its integrity, he and Chelsea had long been a couple officially. The two of them would show up at the cafeteria arm in arm, and sit next to each other, his hand on her upper thigh, Chelsea snuggling into his chest as he whispered in her ear. My loathing for them both burrowed deep, digging into my soul where it took root and spread, hardening my heart, wrapping it in a thick protective layer until it almost became impenetrable, something I'd carried with me ever since.

Now, seeing his Facebook profile made me shudder. I

couldn't help it. It was a visceral reaction my body didn't have control over. I sometimes wondered if Adrian thought about the child he'd helped create, but I bet it wasn't something that crossed his mind, much less anything he dwelled on. The way he'd treated Shay and me made me want to close the app and walk away. He deserved whatever, whoever, came for him. So what if he had an *accident*? Why would or should I care?

I pushed the vengeful thoughts away as I stared at his picture, holding his static gaze. His face was slightly angled to the left, his designer beard and shaggy brown hair perfectly trimmed and styled. He'd placed a hand under his chin, one finger adorned with a thick silver ring mounted with a square onyx stone. The jewelry itched a memory, but I couldn't quite place it, making me think it must've been something he'd already had when we'd briefly been together.

Despite the pose being obvious and staged, he looked approachable and kind, as he had in school, making me wonder if he'd changed his true self, grown into a decent man, or if this, too, was a ruse to disguise the real him I'd known.

When I wanted to dig a little further into his background, tried to see if he was married or had kids, I couldn't get anywhere because he'd locked his privacy settings down tight. Only his friends had access to the details about where he lived and worked, and I sure as hell wasn't about to send him a friend request.

I swapped Facebook for LinkedIn and learned Adrian was an event manager at one of the hotels in town. There was no way I'd go there, not after what happened with Evan at DoNation. I could practically guarantee I wouldn't be able to control my temper when I saw Adrian, meaning Detective Willows or Officer Armstrong would happily slap the cuffs back on me. No, this conversation needed to be held in private, which meant I had to find out where he lived.

Once again, I debated why I should make the effort, the little devil on my shoulder crooning *Adrian had it coming.* What he'd done to me was unforgivable. He'd never apologized. Never been made to suffer a single consequence for any of his actions. If nearly two decades had bestowed him with a certain amount of wisdom or hindsight, he'd not once attempted to contact me, not to express regret, ask for forgiveness, or enquire about the whereabouts or well-being of his child.

He didn't deserve to be warned. For all I cared, whoever was attacking the people on my list, regardless of their reasons, they could have Adrian Costas for breakfast, lunch, and dinner.

Except...it wasn't so simple. If something happened to him that I didn't try to prevent, I'd be responsible, at least indirectly. As much as I despised Adrian Costas, I didn't want his injuries on my conscience, not when it would give me something else to hate myself for. I wasn't warning Adrian for his safety. It was for my own sanity. I logged in to LinkedIn and composed a message.

Adrian,
It's been years but it's important we talk. Can we please meet?
Frankie

I removed the *please*, not wanting to beg or sound desperate, and was about to hit Send, my index finger a fraction away from flinging my words—and potentially evidence—into cyberspace. Because if Adrian got hurt, and the cops found this message, they'd haul me in for questioning.

Leaning back in my seat, trying to slow things down, I wondered if I was missing the point of the attacks completely.

I'd once watched an episode of a crime show where multiple people had been killed, seemingly at random. Turned out only one person had been the real target, all the other victims were pure distraction and misdirection on the perpetrator's part. Could it be I had only one common enemy with whoever was harming the people on my list? Was everything else just noise, a way of sending any potential investigation into a tizzy? It was possible, but it still didn't answer the questions of who the intended victim was, who was hunting everyone, why, or how come it was happening to all the people on my list.

I rubbed my eyes. No matter what was going on, I wouldn't contact Adrian directly and leave an electronic trace of our interaction, not when doing so could lead the cops to asking questions about our past relationship, which I had no intention of answering. My best bet remained finding out where he lived and paying him a visit. But how...?

As I sat there, Adrian's onyx ring and a long-forgotten image of the high school reunion I'd attended five months ago zoomed into my brain, and when they clicked together, I almost laughed out loud.

Chelsea had organized the party, which had been held at a downtown hotel—none other than the one where Adrian worked. And that wasn't all. The place had a fancy rooftop bar where we'd congregated until it had rained, and we'd moved inside. I'd stayed outside a little longer, enjoying the view as well as the peace and quiet, avoiding the chatter amongst old friends that didn't much include me. I hadn't wanted to come in the first place, and swiftly decided I could slip out the rooftop fire exit and down the stairs, escaping without having to fight my way through the crowd.

Mind made up, I headed for the stairwell on the left side, immediately realizing I wasn't alone when I opened the door and heard a set of loud moans. Peering over the banister I saw Chelsea pressed against the railing with a man behind her, their bodies largely concealed by the shadows. This was a *without partners* reunion, meaning the guy screwing Chelsea on the hotel stairs was not her husband, and this I knew for sure because she'd bragged earlier about how he was on a business trip in Zurich, heading for Grindelwald thereafter to purchase a chalet so they could ski in the Swiss Alps over Christmas.

It may have been dark in the hotel stairwell, but there had been enough light to see Chelsea's lover's hand gripping the railing as he thrust into her. A hand I now remembered had a large silver ring, complete with onyx stone. *Adrian.* Her—and my—ex-boyfriend.

Heart thumping, I flicked to Chelsea's Instagram, was amazed at how social media could make finding someone so terrifyingly easy. The latest photo of her had been posted an hour earlier. As she had both hands in plaster, presumably someone else had shared the picture on her behalf. Her long blond hair was in one of those casual-looking updos. Her face looked bruised but clever makeup and a good filter had lessened the mauve and yellowish sheen. The caption read *Going home tomorrow. Can't wait to be back with my darling family.* #warrior #IGotThis #Strongwoman #FamilyLove.

Come morning, Chelsea and I would be having another reunion.

CHAPTER THIRTY

I walked into Chelsea's hospital room before visiting hours began on Wednesday, dodging two nurses on my way. I found her alone, exactly as I'd hoped. Her eyes widened as soon as she saw me, and I think she tried to look surprised but the copious amount of Botox in her forehead must've stopped her.

"Frankie? This is a surprise. You're the last person I expected to—"

"Don't flatter yourself. This isn't a social call. We need to talk about Adrian Costas."

She looked about as taken aback as I thought she would, but quickly recovered. "Adrian? Why would I—"

"Cut the crap. I think it's safe to assume you know where he lives considering you were screwing the guy on the night of the reunion."

"Get out of my room."

"Make me."

She swallowed. "Maybe you've forgotten that I'm *married*. I'd never—"

"Oh, *please*. I saw the pair of you in the hotel stairwell." As I took a few more steps into the room, I tapped my hand.

"Onyx ring. Ten minutes later you judged me for working construction. You're lucky I didn't know what I saw until now or I'd have climbed onto the bar and made an announcement."

"*Nurse!*" Chelsea yelled.

"You sure you want to do that?" I said, and a standoff ensued. We stared at each other, and I imagined Chelsea hoped she could draw on her old ways and intimidate me. No chance. I took another step. "Does hubby know you're banging your school sweetheart? I wonder what he'd say."

Her face turned crimson as a few more beats passed, and finally, she surrendered. "Close the door," she said, waiting until I'd done so before continuing. "Why did you come here? What do you want?"

"I told you, it's about Adrian. I—"

"Oh, no…" She gasped and something in her gaze shifted. "Don't tell me you're jealous."

"*What?* Of course not."

"Yeah, sure. Did you get together before the reunion? Is that why you're here?"

"Eww, *no.*"

"I can't tell if you're lying," she said, eyes frigid. "But if you are, let me spare you some heartache by telling you it won't last. No matter what he says."

I let out a snort. "Doesn't surprise me. He was the same in school."

"Truth," Chelsea whispered, melting a little. "Anyway, tell me what you want so you can leave."

"His home address."

"Why?"

"Unfinished business."

As I waited for her reply, my eyes darted to the table where I noticed a pink book with a picture of a tiny pair of baby feet, the words *Our Little Angel* in silver. I looked around the room, took in the *Get Well Soon* cards interspersed with others I remembered all too well. Muted colors, words such as *My Sincerest Sympathies* written on the front with doves and crosses.

"Chelsea…" I said. "Did you lose…were you…*pregnant*?"

Her steely facade warped and crumbled. Tears pooled in her eyes and when they ran down her cheeks and she was unable to wipe them because of the plaster casts on her arms, I grabbed a handful of tissues from a box and dabbed her cheeks. Once done, I suddenly felt like an intruder, started walking to the door, but Chelsea spoke, her voice a low whisper, rooting me to the floor.

"Six months."

Six months. The reunion had been five months ago. "She was Adrian's?"

A pause. Three blinks. The tiniest of nods. "You can't tell anyone."

"Did he know?"

"He insisted I say she was my husband's."

"Uhm…without sounding crass, how can you be sure she wasn't?"

"Owen was away for ten days, so it's unlikely." She bit her lip, looked down.

I didn't know what to say, taken aback by her display of sincerity and openness, particularly as it was in front of me, ended up offering a hollow sounding "I'm sorry."

Chelsea looked at me. "Why? I was awful to you in school."

I half smiled. "Yeah, and not just in school."

More tears flowed, and I reached to catch them again, wondering who this person in front of me was.

"Trust me, I've had a lot of time to think over the past

few days and I've had more than one epiphany. I know I was a total bitch to you."

"Truth," I whispered, making her smile again.

"School was awful for me."

"For *you*?" I scoffed, my back stiffening once more. "Are you kidding? You ruled the place. You had everyone at your command, even the teachers couldn't see what you were doing. You…you were this evil sorceress who ensnared everyone. God, I hated you."

"I hated myself," she whispered. "I hated everything. The pressure from my parents was crushing. If I got under a ninety-eight percent, I was grounded for days. They expected me to get those kinds of marks and spend upward of twelve hours a week in competitive gymnastics and take dance classes on the weekends."

"But you were on all the teams."

"I had to be. It was all about appearances, making sure they could tell their friends about my wonderful exploits. I was a show horse, trained and groomed to always be better than everybody else." She shrugged. "It taught me to take anybody who was a threat out of the game."

"Hold up. You saw me as a threat?"

"Of course I did, what do you think? You were so smart, and it didn't seem you had to work anywhere near as hard, and you got better grades."

"That's why you tortured me for years?"

"I thought if you were at the bottom, I'd rise to the top." She took a breath. "Man, I can't believe I said all that out loud. I've never told anyone." Letting out a laugh she added, "Must be the morphine. But it feels good."

"The drugs?"

"That, too. But I *am* sorry for what I did."

"Uhm, thank you," I said, meaning it. Never would I have

believed Chelsea Fischer's words could act as a balm for my broken soul. "It's...kind of you."

"God, it's the least I can do. As is saying how sorry I am about what happened to your mom. I know it's way over-due, but I've found out people don't know how to handle another person's grief."

"We're not taught what to do when somebody loses a loved one," I said. "We're worried about saying the wrong thing, so we say nothing, which makes it worse in my opinion."

"So much worse." She blinked hard as her bottom lip started to quiver. "Losing my baby...do you...do you think it's a punishment for how horrible I was...*am*? Is it penance for the way I treat people?"

"I don't think that's how it works. Anyway, wasn't it an accident?"

"They're investigating. We don't know for sure, but I hope it was. Otherwise, it means someone deliberately tried to harm me, and what the hell do I do with that?"

We were silent for a moment, her last words galloping around as another potential angle opened up. "When did you tell Adrian about the baby?"

"About three weeks ago. We'd been meeting at the hotel for a few months before the reunion, to...well, you know. Anyway, I hadn't seen him since the reunion because I'd de-cided I wanted to try to work things out with Owen, but then I found out I was pregnant, and finally decided Adrian should know."

"How did he react?"

"Badly. We met for lunch and when I told him, he was gone before the drinks arrived. Haven't heard a peep from him since, including after the accident. Maybe he doesn't know."

I wouldn't have bet on it. "Can you tell me where he lives?"

"North Deering." She closed her eyes, another set of tears

running down her cheeks as she gave me the street and house number. "If he asks, tell him I never want to see him again."

"Promise." I squeezed her hand. "I'm sorry about everything. Truly. It's not the same but…I know how devastating it is to not have a baby to hold."

"Thank you," Chelsea whispered. "For what it's worth, I never hated you. I admired you, and there's no excuse for what I did. I can't imagine you'd want us to be friends, but I hope one day you'll forgive me."

As I looked at her, a huge boulder shifted inside me, sliding down my back, and crashing to the floor. Maybe her confession had been caused by the drugs. Perhaps her epiphany wouldn't last, and in a few days, weeks, or months she'd be back to her old condescending, cruel ways, leaving a trail of psychological destruction in her wake. But the memories of what she'd done to me in the past were her burden to carry now, no longer mine. They didn't serve me anymore.

I reached for her hand again and gave it a long squeeze. "I think maybe I already have."

CHAPTER THIRTY-ONE

After a quick visit to see Azumi, who still looked so fragile and sick, I left Maine Medical and phoned the hotel where Adrian worked so I could get an idea of his schedule, pretending I was interested in meeting him to discuss a large wedding. When I found out he had the day off, I decided to visit his address in North Deering to see if he was home.

Before I'd left the hospital, Chelsea had told me Adrian was still single, had never married, and consequently I hoped he'd be alone if he was at his house. I wondered what he might be doing on a day off in the middle of the week, if he had any particular hobbies other than screwing married women in hotel stairwells.

The answer appeared evident when I crawled past the bungalow with a sailing boat in the driveway, and an ATV a little farther back, half covered by a military-green tarp. I turned my truck around and parked a few houses down from Adrian's place, while the war between the angel and devil on my shoulders still raged on about the merits of warning him, and if I did, how I'd do so.

When I got out of my truck and looked around, the white net curtains of the house in front of which I'd parked fell back into place. Undeterred, I pressed on and walked to Adrian's. The porch was empty. No shoes or chairs or decorative items, but a few empty beer bottles stacked in the corner. I could see the flicker of a light through the glass on the front door, and I removed my phone from my pocket, clutching it in my hand in case things went bad and I needed to call the cops. As soon as I rang the bell I heard footsteps, making me plant my feet so I didn't run.

And then, there he was.

Adrian stood in front of me in 3D. Real, up close, and personal. Older, but still undeniably handsome, wearing a pair of black jeans and a blue Green Day *American Idiot* T-shirt, the one with the bloodied heart that looked like a grenade.

A frown crossed his face when our eyes met, almost as if he were running through a catalogue of women to decide who I might be, settling on someone unimportant from his past, a vague and distant memory he barely remembered. But then he smiled, ran a hand through his thick hair, charm oozing from every pore. If I hadn't known better, I'd have almost believed he was pleased to see me.

"The shirt suits you," I said, lacing my voice with sarcasm. Honestly, if the guy was going to make it this easy, he only had himself to blame.

Instead of looking insulted, Adrian's grin broadened further, his eyes twinkling with mischief as he slowly looked me over, reminding me of the wolf hoping to devour the three little pigs. "Frankie Morgan." The way he said my name made it sound thick and lush, like luxurious, opulent velvet. He opened the door a little and gestured for me to come inside. "To what do I owe this delightful, way overdue pleasure?"

"I'll stay out here, thanks," I said, his arrogance making my plan of telling him to watch his back crumble before I'd begun. Buoyed by how the conversation with Chelsea had turned out, I decided there were other things to address first. I was never going to come back and see him after this. It was a case of confront him now or never, and I chose now.

"What you did to me was horrendous," I said. "You were an utter bastard."

His gazed hardened in an instant. "What the…? What do you want?"

"An apology to start with."

"For what?"

"I had a child, remember? *Your* child."

"Alleged."

"Oh, the baby was yours."

"Yeah? Well, it can't have been that important to you. You gave it up for adoption."

"*It* has a name, you jackass." I took a step toward the house, my backbone growing some more, turning into titanium. "Shay. You didn't know, did you? And for your information, the terminology is *placing* a child for adoption. Got it?"

He rolled his eyes. "I'll ask again, real slow, so you hear me. What. Do. You. Want?"

"An. Apology."

He laughed. An actual, goddamn put-his-head-back guffaw. The sound swirled around the hallway, making the anger inside me twist and grow, digging sharp roots and anchoring them into my very being. "I see you've been drinking the hashtag me too Kool-Aid. Whatever you think may have happened between us was years ago. Move on, sister."

"I had a kid, Adrian. *Your* kid."

"There's no proof it was mine. And it was almost two decades ago. Get over it already."

"Then apologize to Chelsea." The shock crossing his face, however briefly, made me smirk. "Yeah, I know all about you guys. And the baby. Did you threaten her, too?"

He crossed his arms, a goddamn smug smile dancing across his face again. "You know, I always thought you were a prude until I got my camera." He let out a long wolf whistle making me want to gouge his eyes out with a blunt spoon. "Boy, did you ever want some that night."

"Fuck you."

"Oh, yeah, you wanted that all right. And I'd have given it to you if Mom hadn't arrived. Would've fucked you to kingdom come if you hadn't reverted to being a killjoy. Shame. Still, I had those pictures. Maybe I still do."

"I don't care," I said.

"Oh, Frankie, be careful. I might share—"

"I don't give a damn what you do. Post them wherever you want. I'm not scared of you, Adrian. You don't have any power over me anymore, you hear me? I can't believe I ever thought you did when you're such a pathetic, vindictive piece of shit."

"Watch your mouth."

I stared at him, realizing he was still as mean and pathetic as ever. I meant what I said. I wasn't scared, not of him, not of the photos. The hold he had over me fell away, like shackles clattering to the ground. I put my hands on my hips.

"Why? What are you going to do, Adrian? Try to hurt me like you did Chelsea? Mess with my car?"

His mouth dropped. "The hell are you accusing me of, you crackpot?"

"You heard. But in case your thick brain can't decode my words, I want to know if you tampered with Chelsea's car."

"Fuck off!"

"Were you hoping she'd die because she was carrying a child you didn't want her to have? Did you hear me? Do you understand what I'm saying?"

Adrian walked forward, towering above me, but I refused to move. When he was only a few inches away he growled,

"What went down between me and Chelsea is exactly none of your business, so I suggest you get off my property and never come back." He grabbed my arm, making me yelp as he practically shoved me off the front step.

Before I could stop him, the door slammed, leaving me standing in the cold with my fists clenched, wishing I could pound them into his face instead.

This round was Frankie 0—Adrian 1.

I'd been a complete fool thinking he'd show remorse for, or admit to, what he'd done to me or Chelsea. He hadn't changed one bit, but his extreme defensiveness made me question even more if he'd damaged her vehicle.

Aside from the glimpse of him in the stairwell, I hadn't seen Adrian for almost twenty years. Had no clue what he was capable of, including attempted murder. It had to be a possibility. Maybe I'd speak to Chelsea again, ask if he'd made any threats, veiled or otherwise, if she didn't keep quiet about the fact he was the father of her child.

I headed back to my truck, mind whirring. Voicing my suspicions about him harming Chelsea had been a bad decision. If I was right, he might take it out on her, and if he chose to retaliate, I'd put a woman in danger.

I sat in my truck for a while, watching his house, waiting to see if he left, deciding I'd follow in case he went to the hospital. The desire to warn him had evaporated—he didn't deserve it. Also, I realized as I sat chewing my lip, if he *had* messed with Chelsea's car, and (God forbid) Noa had something to do with Sandy's fall at the building site, perhaps the other incidents weren't related to my forgiveness list. I rubbed my forehead, trying to iron out the permanent confusion parked there.

As I drummed my fingers on the steering wheel, a sharp rap on the driver's window made me jump. I expected to see Adrian's face looming at me despite the fact I'd watched his front door, assumed he must've therefore gone out the back and circled around to frighten me.

It wasn't him, but an older gentleman with leathery skin and a head full of tight white curls, gesturing for me to lower the window. "Good afternoon," he said, the words holding no friendliness behind their strained delivery. "May I help you?"

"No, thank you," I replied with forced geniality. "I'm good."

He stared at me, brown eyes narrowing. "You've been here quite some time."

"Uhm, yes."

"Dear, in case you didn't understand, I'm suggesting you leave."

"Why? I'm not doing anything wrong."

"Maybe." He waggled his phone in the air. "Maybe not. We could ask the police to come by. See what they think."

"Pleasure to meet you," I said, starting the engine and driving off, glancing at him in the rearview mirror until I turned the corner and he disappeared from sight. A hundred yards up I parked the truck again and kept watch on the only exit from Adrian's street. Two hours later, when my bladder threatened to burst and I couldn't rub away the crick in my neck, I admitted defeat and went home.

I spent the rest of the afternoon looking into Adrian Costas. Many, many things about him didn't sit properly. He'd been despicable to me in school, treated Chelsea terribly more recently. What were the chances of him only being an asshole to the two of us? Zero, which meant I had to get out my virtual shovel and dig.

Not long after, the wonders of Google delivered an answer when I found an article. About a year ago, the local news had run a story about a deal falling through between the hotel where Adrian worked and Patrick Davies's Tasty Tomato restaurant chain. I blinked. Adrian had been responsible for the successful completion of the agreement.

Davies had been hurt in a house fire. Chelsea had almost died in a questionable car accident. Both had a relationship gone wrong with Adrian. My heart thumped at the possibility I had been completely mistaken, telling myself again it looked more and more likely Geraldina's fall and Tyler's mugging weren't linked and had nothing to do with my list. Maybe Sandy's accident, too. They might simply be coincidences. Unusual ones, but life could be peculiar sometimes.

My mind shot back to university, more specifically part of a lecture in one of my psychology classes where the teacher had talked about apophenia and confirmation bias.

"It's a psychological phenomenon," she'd said. "People will test a hypothesis under the assumption, often the absolute conviction, it's true. In return, this can lead to overemphasis of any data they have, shoehorning it in to ensure their initial hypothesis is confirmed, and thereby explaining away any and all information to the contrary."

Was that what I'd been doing? Making everything fit together so it worked into my narrative, my paranoia? I'd assumed Evan, from whom I hadn't heard a word, had stolen my notebook, yet it had been at Jake's Cakes. I'd got into a car I'd thought was an Uber and although the company claimed otherwise, it was possible it had been an app or user error, in which case I'd had a heavily discounted ride. But both situations had alarmed me, and with Geraldina's and all the other incidents happening to the people on my list, it was no wonder I saw a pattern that quite possibly—quite probably, I realized—didn't exist.

Maybe Shay wasn't in danger after all, but I couldn't take any chances. I'd thought more about my plan to break into the adoption agency tomorrow evening. Whatever was going on, I still wanted to find my son.

I refocused on the story about Adrian and Patrick, noticed the name of the journalist. Danika Danforth, the woman I'd spoken to on the night of the Davies fire. I called the WPRM line, was told she was out on assignment, covering a legal case in the city, and when I fibbed about having confidential details about a story she was working on, and needed to speak to her urgently in person, they told me where.

The courthouse was a short drive away. Once I'd left my truck in the parking garage and headed down the street, Danika and Eddie were easy to spot among the gaggle of other reporters. Eddie was busy with camera setup, while Danika leaned against the wall about twenty feet from the court's entrance, wearing a yellow ankle-length coat, her dark hair glistening in the sun as she sipped a coffee from Jake's Cakes. Whoever Jake was, he knew how to get around.

"Hi," I said as I walked over to her.

"Hello...oh, I remember you." She squinted at me, snapped her fingers. "Frankie. You were at the fire the other night. The one on Chadwick."

I wasn't sure if I should be flattered or terrified. Probably the latter. "Yeah, uhm, I was hoping we could talk?"

"Okay..." She raised her eyebrows in anticipation as she drew out the word. "But fair warning, if they announce the verdict we're waiting for, you won't see me for dust."

"Got it. I'll be quick. You did a story about a year ago on a deal that fell through with a hotel in the city and the Tasty Tomato chain." Danika did the thing where she didn't speak but continued to look at me, waiting. "I was wondering if you could tell me about it."

"Why the interest?"

"I'm...curious."

"Same line as last time," she said with a laugh. "Honey, I'm a reporter. You'll have to do better than that."

I considered my options, decided they were too limited to throw this one chance away. "Adrian Costas and I go way back," I said. "We were in school together. I'm wondering if…if…"

"Hold that thought." She peered over my shoulder, but thankfully whatever was happening behind me had nothing to do with the case she was waiting on. Still, it reminded me I had no time to lose, and I'd better speed things up.

"I'm wondering if Adrian might have set Davies's house on fire. From what I read online, Davies signed a deal with a different hotel chain or something. I'm not a hundred percent clear on the details, but it looks that way. Adrian wasn't happy."

Danika tilted her head to one side. "What line of work are you in, Frankie?"

"Construction."

"You sure you're not an investigative reporter? Or a cop?"

I let out a snort. "Uh, no."

"Might be something for you to consider."

"I don't think so."

"Why not? You've got some great instincts."

"Then you agree Adrian may have set the fire?"

"No comment. The cause of the fire has yet to be determined."

"Have they checked any door cam footage in the area? He might be on it, or maybe his car?" Danika's expression remained neutral but over her shoulder I saw Eddie taking a step, his mouth opening. She must've noticed because she turned and shooed him away, whispering something too low for me to hear, but she had the same suspicions, I could tell. Did they already have proof Adrian had been in the area that night?

"You say you've known Adrian a long time?" Danika asked.

"Met him when he was in high school. He wasn't nice back then."

"He still isn't," she scoffed.

"No, I agree."

"I can't give you details but what I can say is my interactions with him weren't pleasant when I did the Tomato story. I've put up with a lot during my career, but let's just say I was glad Eddie was around. Costas gave me bad vibes."

"You think he's capable of violence?" I said quietly.

"Isn't everyone given the right circumstances?"

"I guess," I said. "Thanks, you've given me lots to consider."

"You're welcome. Listen, hon, stay away from Costas. He's bad news. But if you can't resist following those instincts and you uncover something, keep me in mind, okay?"

"I will."

"And think about what I said. I might be looking for a research assistant soon. If you give me your résumé, I'll take a look."

I grinned at her, surprised myself by saying, "I'll think about it."

"Please do. Portland's a good training ground for a few years if you want to go to a bigger market after."

"Isn't that what you did? Weren't you in Boston?"

"Almost ten years, but I missed home. I belong here." She dug in her pocket and held out a business card. "If you want to get the skinny on what a career in the media entails, give me a call. We can grab a coffee." She waggled her cup in the air. "This guy makes the best stuff."

"Apparently nobody knows who Jake is. He's a complete mystery."

Danika leaned in. "Ooh, well, you never know. Uncovering his secret identity might be our first story together. What do you say?"

CHAPTER THIRTY-TWO

Going back to Adrian's and confronting him twice on the same day probably wasn't a great idea, but when had I ever heeded my own advice? Trouble was the neighbor who'd chased me off might do so again if I turned up in my truck.

To be a little more covert, I decided I'd wait until I was sure everyone had left Morgan Construction for the day and borrow one of Dad's company vehicles. We had what he called a *run-around car*, which he let employees use whenever they needed. It didn't have any corporate branding, and was a simple, plain, innocent-looking VW Golf with tinted windows. If I brought it back after a few hours, nobody would know.

Before going home, I spent another hour at the hospital with Rico, and Azumi, who was fast asleep the entire duration of my visit.

"Is she going to be okay?" I whispered to Rico.

"We hope so," he said, a tremor in his voice. "God, we really, really hope so."

Noa had gone back to work for an urgent meeting, making part of me relieved because I wouldn't have to look him in the eye while harboring suspicions about him trying to harm Dad. It still felt impossible and ridiculous, unfair, too, and it made guilt crawl beneath my skin.

Thankfully, my brother distracted me a little by telling me they'd found out Tyler had been brought out of his induced coma and was progressing well, but I couldn't bring myself to visit him.

I wanted to check on Chelsea, but she'd already gone home, making Instagram posts of her sitting on her plush teal sofa surrounded by cream cushions. Had Adrian seen these photos? If so, would he pay her a visit? I needed to know if he'd done more than tell her he wanted nothing to do with her or their child, and if he was guilty of arson. Finally, when it was dark, I went to swap vehicles.

Back in North Deering, I parked the Golf on the other side of the street, far enough away from the nosy neighbor's house. A black Acura sat in Adrian's driveway and the lights inside the house were on. He was home, and I still wasn't sure how I'd learn more, but no matter how much I wanted to transform into the Black Widow, the prospect of seeing Adrian again made my insides make a sudden uncomfortable movement I couldn't ignore. There was no choice, and I zipped to the nearest gas station to use the bathroom.

By the time I turned back into Adrian's road, the skies had filled with thick clouds, darkening them still, and the dim streetlamps didn't afford much light. As I parked the car, working up the courage to open the door, I saw someone sneaking down the side of Adrian's house, past the ATV and along the side of the boat. The back of my neck prickled. Was it Adrian? With the lack of light, I couldn't tell for sure, but I assumed so. Why was he sneaking around? Up to no good, that was for sure. He turned and walked down the street with his head bent, and so I followed.

"Hey, Adrian," I shouted when I got a little closer. "Wait up."

One look over his shoulder and he bolted. Despite my better instincts, I gave chase, my feet hammering the asphalt. Man, he was fast, his long strides easily putting distance between us. I tried to catch him, stayed in pursuit when he darted into a backyard. Why was he running if he wasn't guilty of something?

I kept going, arms pumping by my sides, lungs burning from effort, my jacket and boots weighing me down. I slid off my coat, let it drop to the ground as my brain screamed at me to stop, to stand still. Adrian was dangerous and could be waiting around the corner holding a knife or a gun. I might be running into a trap at full speed.

As I came to a halt, I expected Adrian to tackle me, but the only thing I saw was the shape of a man leaping and vaulting over the massive fence at the back. I tried to follow, but on my first attempt I didn't manage to get my fingers over the top. By the time I pulled myself up, my feet scrabbling to gain traction, Adrian Costas had long vanished. I let myself drop to the ground, grateful the house behind me was dark, its owners apparently either not home or unaware of what was going on in their yard, making me even more thankful it didn't belong to the neighbor who'd told me to get lost a few hours earlier.

But what the hell had happened? Why had Adrian scrambled over the fence? Had he snuck out of his house to do more nefarious deeds? A car had been in his driveway, but that didn't mean anything. I hadn't come to his place in my own vehicle. Maybe he had another parked somewhere, ready to use, so he left no trace of whatever he was doing behind.

I had to find out what was going on, and I turned and jogged back to his house, picking up my jacket on the way. If he was running off somewhere, maybe I could get a quick glimpse inside his place if he'd left it unlocked. My mind flicked back to the naked photographs. Was it true he still had them? If he did, and I had a snoop around, perhaps I'd find them. I meant what I said, I didn't care what he did with them anymore. If he shared them, he was the sleazeball, the disgusting pervert, not me, but having them would remove any leverage he thought he had.

When I got to his home, I decided ringing the doorbell was the easiest and safest way to know whether he'd circled back and was already inside. After pushing the button, I took six steps back in case my reappearing for the second time today set him off. I waited a good thirty seconds, and when there was no answer, I rang again. Still nothing.

Glancing around to make sure nobody was on the street watching me, I headed for the back, hoping I wouldn't surprise him in the yard with a shovel or a rake he'd swing at me. But the garden was empty. I turned, saw the back door ajar, and headed over.

Reaching out with one hand, I pushed the door open, my gaze falling to the tiled floor, my fingers instinctively covering my mouth as I tried hard to stop myself from crying out.

A body. Arms splayed to the sides. Someone dressed in jeans, sneakers, and a Green Day T-shirt. The clothes Adrian had worn earlier. Vomit rose into my mouth as I looked at him. He was on his back, toes pointing at the ceiling. His face, or what remained of it, had been reduced to a mass of flesh and bone. The picture of the heart on his shirt was now drenched with real blood, an ever-expanding pool seeping into the fabric.

Adrian was dead. No way could anyone survive having half their face removed, but it took eons for my brain to send any other thoughts or commands to the rest of me. Finally, I stumbled, almost landed on my butt as I tried to put more distance between me and Adrian's corpse, a journey of a few steps that seemed to take years.

I forced myself out of the yard, willed my legs to move

and take me to the front of the house where I pulled out my phone, hardly able to speak as I dialed.

"911. What's your emergency?"

"I need help," I said. "Please come quickly. I—I think someone's been murdered."

CHAPTER THIRTY-THREE

Hours later, it was as if I'd been put through a high-speed washing machine cycle, all my senses messed up beyond reason. Officer Armstrong had descended upon me first, swiftly joined by Detective Willows, both of them demanding to know what I'd been doing in Adrian's neighborhood.

Although I no longer believed it, I offered my theory of Adrian tampering with Chelsea's car, squirming in my seat as I shared the fact he'd fathered the child she'd lost in the accident. I knew they'd follow up with her, and I was betraying her confidence. Although I asked them to be discreet with the information because her husband didn't know about him not being the baby's dad, I still detested myself. Except, there hadn't been much choice. I couldn't tell them about Adrian being Shay's father because it provided motive for me to hurt him. I hoped to God as they searched his place for clues of who had killed him, Adrian had either long destroyed the naked pictures of me, or they wouldn't recognize my face as they'd been taken almost twenty years ago on a shitty cell phone. It was a gamble I was willing to take.

And so, I'd stuck to my story of only knowing him casually at school and seeing him and Chelsea together at the re-union. She might tell them I'd asked for his address because I had *unfinished business* with him, and I explained my initial trip to Adrian's place had been to question the link between him and the Davies fire because it could cost Morgan Construction a project, something I suggested they explore although I didn't think it was necessarily true anymore either.

"He was really defensive when I mentioned my suspicions about him messing with Chelsea's car," I said. "I was watching his house because I felt guilty I may have set him off and he'd try to hurt her again."

"You should've come to us immediately," Willows said.

"Maybe," I said. "But you didn't seem like my biggest fan in front of the judge."

Forensic experts examined my hands and took my clothes, presumably to search for blood and other evidence. I didn't think they'd find any, other than on the soles of my shoes as I'd taken a step into the hallway. With the state of Adrian's face, surely they already knew if I'd beaten him to death I'd have been covered in blood. I also wouldn't have picked up the phone to dial 911, or chased the perpetrator into a neighbor's yard, something I presumed they'd find sufficient proof of to confirm my story.

From what I understood about crimes and criminals, Adrian's murderer had been more than angry. The extent and violence of his injuries meant the assailant had been downright furious. I knew someone with anger issues. Someone who'd had access to my list. A person I'd continually added to and discounted from my suspects. Evan Randell. I pressed my hands over my eyes, trying to fit everything together, but nothing would stick.

More time ticked by as the clock slowly passed midnight,

another hour or more during which Armstrong and Willows came and went, asked me a round of questions before, or so I presumed, leaving me to stew, hoping I'd unravel, and they'd trip me up when I changed my story. They'd have a long wait, and as I sat in the tiny, bland room, I knew I could've asked for George, my lawyer, but no way did I want them thinking I had something to hide.

I almost decided otherwise and confessed when they came into the room around 1:30 a.m. and Armstrong set an iPad in front of me. "You know Tyler Vance?" she said.

"Yes, from high school, and he's my niece's surgeon."

"And how do you feel about that?" Willows said.

"What do you mean?"

"Are you happy he's your niece's doctor?" Armstrong said.

"Yes, of course. Apparently, he's one of the best in his field."

Willows leaned in, tapped the screen, and I watched as a truck identical to mine drove down a street, footage presumably captured via a door cam, my profile clear enough despite it being dark. The date stamp was from a week ago. "Care to tell us what you were doing near Mr. Vance's place this early in the morning?"

I shrugged. "Couldn't sleep, I went for a drive."

"Which happened to take you past Tyler Vance's place?" Armstrong said.

"Tyler who was attacked in his home, like Adrian Costas," Willows added. "Quite the coincidence."

"Not really," I said. "I told you, I knew Tyler from high school. He was a pompous ass then and I was curious about where he lived, you know? Wanted to see if he was still all flash and no substance."

"Sounds like you were envious of him," Willows said. "Of his lifestyle. His success."

"No." I shook my head. "And I'm devastated Tyler got hurt. My niece needs her doctor, and from what I gather he's the best. He's been really kind to my family this past week." I sat back and crossed my fingers, hoping Armstrong didn't remember my being at the scene of Patrick Davies's fire. Visiting three different crime scenes would've been one too many to explain.

As they asked for more details, I remained cooperative, answered their repetitive questions, all while trying to quash the anxiety building inside. Somebody had brutally killed Adrian. But who? It might've been Chelsea's husband, Owen, if she'd told him about her affair. If nobody else on my forgiveness list had been hurt, I'd have bought it, but I didn't think it was him. Whoever had done this was the same person who'd gone after Tyler, my father, Patrick Davies, Chelsea, and Geraldina. Unless Noa had tried to harm Dad, but that connection was only based on a slouchy beanie and a hopefully incorrect hunch.

Like I'd believed all along, these attacks had to be linked, and the only finger I saw was pointing back in Evan's direction. He'd had access to my notebook. Known about the sunflowers. Probably followed me to the hospital, which meant he could've been driving behind me when I'd visited Adrian earlier today, following me to get to the rest of the people on my forgiveness list. Or he'd put a tracker on my car, and I'd missed it. I wasn't exactly tech savvy. But *why* would he do all this? And what would happen when he'd found everyone? My name held the prime spot on the list. Did that mean he'd come for me last?

Evan had to derive pleasure from messing with people he met in anger management. Maybe it really would all end in him bribing me, threatening to show my list, of which I bet he'd taken a photo, to the cops. The guy was sick. He'd escalated things further, going from mugging Tyler to beating Adrian to death. Had killing him been his intention? Was he really a murderer? I couldn't get my brain to reconcile the person I'd met in anger management with a killer, but there was no other answer. My breath hitched as I thought about the fact there were now five people left on my list who hadn't been attacked in some way, including Shay and me, and I needed to find my son before Evan did. And before he ultimately came for me.

Finally, Willows appeared, opening the door wide. "You can go, Frankie."

I jumped up. "I'm not a suspect?"

"Should you be?"

"*No,*" I said quickly. "I told you the truth. I didn't hurt Adrian."

She gave me a curt nod. "We'll be in touch."

"What about my car? I need to take it back to my dad's company."

"Not possible. As part of an ongoing investigation, it needs to be processed. We're keeping it for a while."

"How am I supposed to get home?"

She shrugged and walked off. "Thanks for your help," I called after her, deciding to take a cab.

Twenty minutes later I pushed open the main door to my apartment building. As I walked past the mailboxes, I saw something orange through the open grid at the bottom of mine. "Not another gift," I whispered as I fished out my keys and stuck them in the lock, relieved when I saw an envelope with my name written in Dad's neat penmanship. I unfolded the sheet of paper inside.

Dear Frankie,

I was wrong to deny you these—they're yours, not mine. I hope they help you find the peace you're looking for. Please think about

what I said about not searching for your lad until you've sorted

out whatever's going on. I truly believe it's not fair to him or you.

Love,

Dad x

Once I got to my apartment, I checked every room to ensure I was alone, locked the front door, and shoved a chair underneath the handle. Settling at the kitchen table, I pulled out the contents of the envelope. A one-page family profile on which details were sparse. One drawing and four photographs. Judging by the dates on the back they'd been taken around a year apart.

In the first, Shay was tiny, only a few weeks old, and dressed in a onesie with fluffy lambs, his eyes wide. The second picture showed him sitting in a high chair with a red rattle in hand, face beaming. Age two he was on a swing, his tooth-filled face squealing in obvious delight.

The last photo had been taken on his third birthday. He sat in front of a huge cake decorated with candles and Reese's Pieces, and pointed at the picture on his shirt, Count von Count, one of the Sesame Street characters. There was a drawing in the envelope, too, the one that had made me break down and sob. A smiling sun, toothy flower, and the words *I LOVE YOU* written below.

I ran my fingers over Shay's little face, traced the outline of his cheeks. I wanted more. Couldn't believe this was it, this was everything I had. What had I done? How could I have accepted to not receive any other photos of my son after his third birthday because it was too hard? I'd had no idea. *This* was so, so much harder. And I fully deserved the number one spot I'd assigned myself on my damn list.

* * *

By late Thursday afternoon, I'd lied to my father about the whereabouts of his run-around car because I couldn't face telling him yet about the murder, partially because I was shaken and terrified, but also because I realized I didn't care Adrian was dead, which said an awful lot about me I wanted to ignore.

I'd taken a cab to collect my truck, and was back on Pearl Street, ready to put my adoption agency information extraction plan into action. Once I'd walked past the building housing the offices of Abbot & Dean, I'd headed into the stairwell, checking for cameras, but found none. Satisfied, I set up camp at a table by the window of a burger joint across the street where I drank a sugar-laden soda I didn't need as I watched the building's front door. The agency's *About Us* page of their website indicated they had a staff of nine and I scanned every person who came and went, trying to identify as best I could if they were an employee.

At around five twenty I saw two of the men I recognized as Abbot & Dean members exit the building and enter the Beehive. A few more minutes passed, and another stream of people came out, a few of them heading for the pub. I waited another quarter hour until the last office light on the second floor went out and Trish, the woman I'd spoken to on the phone and whose picture was also on the web, stepped outside. With the office now empty, this was my chance.

I grabbed my stuff and followed them all to the Beehive. Trish's group was at one of the tables in the far corner, eight of them sitting in a cluster. I took a seat on the opposite side, near the entrance to the bathroom. When the server came, I ordered a diet ginger ale, and asked for the menu. Not that I had any intention of having food, but it gave me something to do and hopefully made me appear less conspicuous.

Half an hour later, after Trish had finished a spectacular rendition of "Valerie," one of the women from her table headed to the bathroom. I followed, hoping she'd leave the bag clutched under her arm near the sink. Wishful thinking, because when I entered the tiny bathroom, it wasn't there. She'd obviously been sensible and taken it into the stall with her. I stood in front of the single sink and washed my hands, taking my time until she came out of the stall and set her bag on the top of the trash can where it balanced precariously.

My heart thumped so loud as I dried my hands, she had to have heard it. No clue if this was going to work, but short of pinning her down and frisking her, this was my one shot at trying to find a way into the office undetected. As I went to grab some paper towels to dry my hands, I moved out of her way, deliberately making her bag fall in the process.

"Oh my goodness," I said, kneeling quickly to scoop up and sift through the contents. Bingo. A red lanyard sticking out from a side pocket led to a badge with her beaming face. I grabbed and quickly slid it into my jacket pocket. "Yikes, how embarrassing," I said with a sheepish smile as I stood.

"No harm done," the woman said, taking the bag from me and zipping it up without looking inside. "Happens to all of us."

Hands shaking, I returned to my table, left ten bucks for my drink, and headed to Abbot & Dean. The street was still busy, but nobody paid any attention as I pulled open the heavy front door before moving to the staircase. Peering upward, I couldn't see any sign of movement, and there was no noise either. The air smelled of lemons, as if someone had recently cleaned the area, and I hoped whoever had done so was now gone for the evening. I took the two flights of stairs and found myself in front of the adoption agency's main door.

This was my last chance to back out of doing something illegal, but the urge to find Shay and protect him from harm wouldn't let me. I waved the badge over the black box mounted on the wall. The lock clicked. The door opened. I was in.

I had no idea if or where they might have installed cameras, or if anyone was watching, so I flipped up my hood and put on a pair of mittens I'd stuffed into my pockets, moving around the office. When I'd spoken with Trish on the phone, she'd said the old files were in archive boxes, but I had no clue where they might be.

I snuck past reception and peered into the darkness, trying to get a sense of the layout. From what I could see, the office was one large area, with a short corridor at the far end, which had two doors leading off to the left, and one to the right. The walls were decorated with calming watercolor paintings of landscapes, and they'd hung a few photographs of families, presumably those they'd helped.

I wondered if I should boot a computer and see what I could find in case Trish was mistaken and the files were digitized, knew it was likely pointless. They'd have security settings and passwords for which I couldn't venture a guess. No, I needed to find those old paper files. They had to be somewhere. I headed for the corridor, had taken three steps when the main lights came on. Heart thumping, I fell to my knees and scurried under a desk as a male voice rang out.

"Stop."

Shit. In no time I'd end up in Armstrong and Willows' clutches and there was no way Judge Orr would let me go with a warning. I was about to crawl out, contemplated holding up my hands and moving to the door in the hopes I could somehow make a run for it. Before I moved, the man continued talking, his voice full of frustration.

"No, stop. *Stop.* Not fair. I'm not home late *every* day. You're exaggerating."

He was on the phone, not speaking to me, which meant he hadn't seen me. I curled into a ball, quietly pressed myself against the back of the desk, praying this workstation wasn't his.

"I didn't mean to forget," he said, and I watched his shiny brown brogues approach, getting way too close. My eyes widened as he bent at the knees, his hand reaching for the small filing cabinet attached to the desk under which I'd hidden. I closed my eyes. Heard a drawer slide open.

"Yes, yes. I have it." Pause. "Uh-huh. The silver one with the soccer charm, gift wrapped, exactly as per your instructions. I told you I didn't forget." Another pause, a big huff. "No, I won't go back for more karaoke. I'll be home in thirty. Bye."

He mumbled something about missing his chance to sing "Karma Chameleon," and finally his footsteps retreated to the entrance. At last, the office was plunged into darkness, but I didn't dare move for an excruciating eternity until I was certain he wouldn't return.

My legs and feet cracked when I stood and made a run for the corridor so I could begin my search for the archives. One small cafeteria and a conference room later, I found a storage area. I used the flashlight on my phone, saw shelves filled with office supplies and almost backed out of the room again until I spotted the stack of archive boxes at the far end, tucked away beneath the photocopy paper and a tower of plastic-wrapped multicolored sticky notes.

I closed the door, took off my jacket, rolled it up and laid it down to stop the light from shining underneath, and flicked the switch. This part wasn't something I could easily do in the dark and the quicker I got out of here, the better.

I searched through the boxes, heart sinking when I noticed they weren't organized by year. Instead, folders had been thrown in with no apparent logic or reason. There were twelve boxes in all, and so I settled on the floor, working my way from the one farthest to my right, pulling out folder after folder and flipping through them as fast as I could, searching for my name or any specifics indicating the papers were about Shay.

It took twenty long minutes to find my file, and my intention had been to read through the details, take a few pictures, and put it back, but once I had it in front of me, I couldn't. I removed my jacket from the floor and folded it over my arm, hiding the adoption folder underneath before opening the storage room door quietly and tiptoeing down the corridor, half expecting someone to shout or side tackle me as I made my escape.

The weather had flipped again in the time I'd been inside. Drizzle fell from the skies and the wind whistled through the trees. Pearl Street was almost deserted and when I got back to the comforting warmth of the Beehive, the pub was heaving.

The woman from the adoption agency whose badge I'd borrowed stood on stage singing "I Will Survive." I lowered my head and went to the bathroom where the stall was unoccupied. I yanked the badge from my pocket, wiped it on my jeans, set it on the floor, and used my toe to slide it against the back wall. For good measure I grabbed a handful of paper towels, bunched them up and chucked them back there, too, covering the badge as much as possible.

Hopefully someone would find it and hand it in, and Trish's colleague would think it had fallen from her bag when I'd knocked it over. Like she said, no harm done. Pausing for a second, I still couldn't believe I'd pulled it off. Tucked away on the inside of my jacket were the details I needed to find Shay.

This was Frankie 1—Abbot & Dean 0.

CHAPTER THIRTY-FOUR

My knuckles turned white from clenching the steering wheel as I drove home, and when I got back to my apartment, which seemed to take forever because I kept looking over my shoulder to make sure I wasn't being followed, I slid off my jacket and let it fall to the floor. Heart thumping against my rib cage, I sat at the kitchen table, not daring to touch the folder, the seemingly innocuous bundle of papers that would, at last, give me insight into what had become of my son.

All this time I'd wondered who'd adopted him. Where they lived, what they did, if they were good people. In my daydreams he was happy, healthy, accomplished, and lived close enough for me to visit on a regular basis. In my worst nightmares his adoptive parents were awful, despicable human beings who'd mistreated Shay or put him back into the care system. I'd read similar stories, and knew if that had happened, I'd never find him. Maybe it was for the best because at least it meant he was safe.

I wondered if I should talk myself out of opening the folder because the contents and where they might lead terrified me, but when I'd run out of excuses not to look, I turned the page. And suddenly, there they were, the answers to the questions that had near consumed me.

According to the new birth certificate, Shay's name was now Jeremy. His parents, whom my father and I had only known as S. and L., were Sherry and Lawrence Norton. The report on their suitability as adoptive parents was extraordinary, and reading through it, there was no wonder my father had chosen them. Sherry taught computer engineering at the University of Southern Maine in Gorham whereas Lawrence worked in environmental science. They'd been married ten years at the time, had tried to get pregnant for eight, and had what doctors called *unexplained infertility*. After three rounds of IVF, they'd turned to adoption.

My life has become so much more since I met my husband, Sherry wrote in one of her letters. *He is without a doubt the most gentle, caring, and loving person you could ever meet. He wouldn't just give you the shirt off his back, he would make shirts and give them to everyone in need. I can't imagine him not being able to share those qualities with a child and I want to see him become a father more than anything. Picturing him with a baby in his arms fills me with such immense joy, its power could run our entire town forever.*

I touched the page, studied the swirls of Sherry's writing, an invisible boulder of crushing weight sliding off my back. Judging by the accompanying character reference letters, it sounded as if Shay—*Jeremy*—had a good home, a great one.

I kept reading, discovering at the time of the adoption, the Nortons had lived in Westbrook, a mere six miles away. Were they still there? Would they be easy to find? I grabbed my phone and opened the browser, fully expecting a research-filled night, but with the wonder of modern technology, finding my son's parents took all of thirty seconds. They no longer lived quite so close, but they weren't far either—the address

I found for them was in Gorham. According to the university's website, Sherry still worked in the same department.

After waiting all these years, now suddenly things were moving almost too fast. It wasn't enough time for me to fully comprehend how easy it would be to meet Shay. *Jeremy*, I corrected myself again. I had to remember his name was *Jeremy*. I searched social media for his profile, hoping to find a picture and finally see what he looked like all grown up, but found none. Was that out of the ordinary? Or had I somehow passed my aversion to a large digital presence down to him? The thought made me smile, although it disappeared when I couldn't find his parents anywhere online either.

Fidgeting, I pushed my chair back so hard it tipped over. I jumped up and paced the room, trying to work out how best to approach this. Call the Nortons' home number? No, not the best solution. If Jeremy answered, I'd be incapable of getting out a single word. Perhaps I could drive there, wait awhile, and discreetly survey the house, more inconspicuously than I had Adrian's. Thinking about him made me shudder. When I did finally meet Jeremy, how could I possibly tell him that not only his life might be in danger, but his biological father, who wasn't named on the birth certificate, was dead? Should I tell him? It would be so much to take in, so much for me to unload *onto* him—if he had any desire to meet let alone speak with me. But I had to try. I couldn't run the risk of him being attacked.

It was almost seven twenty now, and I had to go. Minutes later I was in my truck driving into more rain, running through every scenario as to what I'd say, and how. The trip to Gorham took under half an hour, not nearly enough time to calm my spinning mind.

At first glance, it seemed the Norton family lived comfortably. Even in the dark, and despite the weather, I could tell the single-story house was large. It had an attached three-car garage and the yard had to be more than sixty feet deep. The wraparound porch, which had a ramp for easy access on one end, could've comfortably held a dozen people without it being a squeeze.

I parked and sat in the truck staring at the Nortons' home, wondering if Jeremy's childhood had been a happy one. The area certainly seemed to offer plenty of possibilities for riding bikes and playing street hockey, wooded areas close by for games of hide-and-go-seek and places to build tree forts, all of which would've been far better than my trying to raise him. I wondered if Jeremy had followed in his parents' footsteps and gone into the field of STEM, or if he'd explored a different avenue closer to the interests I'd had at his age.

I let out a groan when I realized the possibility of Jeremy being away at college somewhere. As inconvenient as it might be for me now, I hoped if it was the case, he'd gone someplace on the other side of the country—maybe overseas—and was thereby out of harm's reach.

As I weighed my options, headlights appeared on the road behind me, and I ducked down when a dark Subaru Forester pulled into the Nortons' driveway. I watched as a woman got out—Sherry, I presumed—and headed to the trunk from where she retrieved a wheelchair, making me gasp.

Had Jeremy been hurt? Had the stalker who was working their way through my forgiveness list already got to him? I wanted to clamber out and run over, but instead I pushed my butt firmly into my seat and continued observing as Sherry assisted her passenger into the wheelchair. It was dark, and while I couldn't clearly make out a face or age, from the glimpse I managed to get as they went up the ramp and into the house, it wasn't a young man.

I needed to speak to them, and if Jeremy wasn't home, perhaps I could convince Sherry her son was in danger. Surely, he'd listen to her more than me. There was a risk she'd demand we go to the police, in fact it was almost a certainty, but in that case so be it. Now I'd found him they could investigate me all they wanted as long as they kept him safe.

I waited another while, on a whim reached underneath the front seat for a dusty beige baseball hat with the word *Maine* embroidered on the front, slapped it on my head, and tucked my hair underneath. After running across the street and to the front door, I pressed my finger against the buzzer without hesitation, knowing if I thought about it too much, I might still change my mind.

When Sherry answered the door, I took in her huge blue eyes, the smattering of freckles across her cheeks and her tentative smile, something to be expected considering a complete stranger stood on her doorstep.

"Can I help you?" she said.

While I opened and closed my mouth a few times I took a step back to convey I wasn't any kind of threat. All my words, everything I'd imagined saying now seemed to have fallen out of my head. I pressed a fist over my mouth as I tried to buy myself time to regroup.

"I, uh, I'm here about Jeremy," I said, my voice so quiet I wasn't sure she heard me.

She put a hand to her neck, eyes widening in fear. "Did you find my boy?"

"Uhm, no—"

"Oh, thank God." She exhaled, her hand moving down to her stomach. "Gosh, I know that must've sounded strange. What I meant is I thought you were going to tell me you'd found his body. Only, it's what happens on TV, isn't it? An officer always comes to the house when it's bad news."

I tried to process what she was saying. My son was missing. Since when? And she thought I was the police? She expected me to say something, and I plumped for, "No, it's nothing like that."

"And you haven't found him?" she asked, and as I tried to summon the courage to explain why I was there, she exhaled slowly. "To be honest, I wasn't sure you'd ever follow up. Your colleague didn't give us the impression he was taking Jeremy's disappearance seriously."

I wanted to ask so many questions, but a male voice rang out behind her. "Is everything okay, darling?"

As Sherry opened the door, I saw the man in the wheelchair rolling up to us. She turned to me. "This is my husband, Lawrence, and this is... I didn't catch your name, officer."

"Uhm...Miscione," I said. "Pleased to meet you both."

"There's no news," Sherry said to Lawrence quickly. "They haven't found him."

"I, uh, wanted to check on a few details," I said, trying to anticipate what she might do, and when Sherry offered for me to come inside, I couldn't resist, found myself following them to the kitchen, a bright, airy space with slate gray cabinets, a huge white granite island, and the counter and stovetop mounted lower than usual, indicating whatever had happened to Lawrence wasn't recent.

While he retrieved glasses and a pitcher of water, Sherry gestured for me to take a seat at the heavy rectangular stonetop table. Nerves clawed at my stomach, and I couldn't wait any longer to ask, "When did Jeremy go missing?"

"Seven months ago," Lawrence said. "Two days after his eighteenth birthday."

I nodded, tried not to let my shoulders drop with relief. My forgiveness list hadn't existed seven months ago. Did that mean he was okay? "Where did you see him last?"

"Here, at the house," Sherry said. "I told your colleague

this already. When we got home from work, Jeremy was gone, as was his car."

"What kind of car?"

"A blue 2013 Hyundai Genesis Coupe," Lawrence said, a hint of irritation creeping into his voice. "Apparently, he sold it for cash a day or so after he left. I'm pretty sure your colleague made a note."

"Yes, yes, of course," I said quickly, realizing I hadn't spoken for a little too long because I'd been trying to picture what his old car looked like, and Sherry was giving me an expectant gaze. I couldn't blow this opportunity to get a whole lot of answers, including why he'd run away. Were they responsible? Had they done something? They seemed so unassuming, so nice. I put my crime reader game face on, thought about what the heroine in one of my books would do.

"And, uh, you had the impression my colleague wasn't taking your report seriously?"

Lawrence and Sherry exchanged glances. "When we told him Jeremy had taken clothes and a few other things from his room the day he left, but not his cell phone, he lost interest. He said our son's an adult, and when we mentioned Jeremy had run away before he really didn't seem to care."

"He'd run away recently?" I asked.

"No," Sherry said. "A few years ago, when he was fourteen." She swiped the backs of her hands over her eyes. "When he overheard us talking one night, and he found out he was adopted. Didn't your colleague tell you any of this?"

I tried to remain calm as a throng of questions shouted for attention. "To be honest, his notes weren't great. It's why I'm following up."

Lawrence reached for Sherry's hand and gave it a tender squeeze. "Jeremy was angry with us."

"Oh?"

"Not about being adopted," he continued. "Actually, he said he'd always suspected it because he looks nothing like either of us, but he was livid we'd lied to him. Said we'd manipulated him since the day he was born."

"He wanted to know who his parents were," Sherry said.

"What did you tell him?"

"The truth," she said. "We don't know who his biological father is, and only had his birth mother's initials. She had him very young and couldn't take care of him. Her own mom had recently died, you see, so the poor thing was obviously in a difficult situation."

"Obviously." I shifted in my seat, trying to keep my expression neutral as I hoped they wouldn't see the guilt spread over my face in a three-inch-deep layer. "That must've been a lot for Jeremy to take in."

"It was," Lawrence said. "He knew it was a semi-open adoption, and at age eighteen he'd have access to her information. If she ever wants anything to do with him. When he was three, the agency told us she no longer wanted the annual updates we'd agreed on."

"It broke our hearts when he overheard us. We wanted to tell him properly," Sherry said as Lawrence rubbed her shoulder. "And then he ran away. He was only gone for about three days, but we were so worried. Things got worse, especially after Lawrence was injured a few months later. He refused to spend much time with us after that."

"May I ask what happened?" I said.

"Car accident. One of those things, you know. Rear wheel came off."

"The wheel came off your car?" I said slowly. "How?"

"Not sure," he said. "All I remember is—" he smacked his palms together, making me jump "—bam. Off the road

I went. I got lucky. Could've been a whole lot worse if the damage had been higher up on my spine. Or I could've died."

My brain was screaming at me now. The rear wheel of Chelsea's car had come off, too. A coincidence as well? Lawrence's accident had been about four years ago. There couldn't be a correlation…could there? "Do you have any idea where he might be?" I said, mouth dry.

"We asked everyone we could think of," Lawrence said. "To be honest, we were certain once he ran out of money he'd come home, but so far we haven't heard anything."

"What about friends?" I said, saw them exchange another glance.

"He wasn't really close with anyone," Sherry said. "Nothing wrong with that. Kids can be so mean, especially teenagers. I was always happy with my own company at that age."

"Same," Lawrence said. "Jeremy spent hours reading in his room. It's his favorite thing in the world, especially crime fiction. He's passionate about it."

"I showed your colleague a photo of him," Sherry said as she stood up, my heart bursting from the fact my son loved books of the same genre apparently as much as I did. "Maybe you can take a picture of it again in case he…mislaid it."

She only left the room for a matter of seconds, but by the time she returned, a pool of cold sweat had collected under my arms. This was one of the moments I'd dreamed of, seeing my son's face. I was sure they'd be able to hear whatever tune my heart was playing as it thumped against my rib cage, and when she passed me the silver double frame, there was no way they didn't spot the tremble in my fingers.

"This is him when he was seven," she said. "The one on the left is the most recent. We took it on his birthday, before… before he left."

My eyes prickled as I stared at the boy I'd known as Shay.

Not only because of the intensity of his gaze, the shade and shape of his eyes so similar to mine—but because I *knew* him. Or at least I'd seen him, multiple times. He'd been the new employee my father had fired when he'd bumped into the ladder and sent a colleague flying. He was the young man wearing the plum jacket, whom I'd walked into as I'd come out of the Thai take-out place, the guy who a couple of days later had bolted to the kitchen in the back. And I'd have bet money he'd been lurking in Lonny's deli, dressed in a mulberry hoodie.

That wasn't all. I'd been in Jeremy's new car, the mysterious Uber. I was convinced of this because the smiling, green-eyed seven-year-old boy wore a Barney the Dinosaur T-shirt, reminiscent of the figurine dangling from the rearview mirror. Purple, or so it seemed, was Jeremy's favorite color. Without me noticing, my son had orbited my life for months.

And I knew exactly where to find him.

CHAPTER THIRTY-FIVE

I'm not sure how I made it back to Portland in one piece, or without being stopped by the cops for speeding, but somehow, I arrived at the Thai restaurant without incident. I tried to stay calm as I burst through the doors but judging by the glances the customers and hostess threw my way, I didn't do a good job.

"Excuse me," I said, giving up and rushing over to her. "Is Jeremy working tonight?"

"I'm new," she said, shaking her head. "I don't know who—"

"He works in the kitchen." I grabbed my phone showing the photo I'd taken of Sherry and Lawrence's picture frame. "Tall, dark hair, and really green eyes."

"Oh, yeah. He left about a minute ago. Said it was an emergency. You might catch him if he's still out back."

I barreled out the way I'd come and headed for the rear of the building in time to see a car driving out of the entrance. I waved my hands and yelled, but the driver didn't slow down. My gut instincts roared at me to follow. Running faster, I darted to my truck and gunned the engine, hoping Jeremy, if it was him, hadn't got too far ahead.

Sure enough, I saw his taillights about fifty yards out, and I pressed the gas pedal before falling back, deciding to remain at a distance. If I could see where he was going, I could maybe take a breather and decide if I should confront him immediately or wait until I'd calmed down. The last thing I wanted was to freak him out, accuse him of following me when I was mistaken. He'd left home and was probably trying to make ends meet, working multiple jobs in the city, taking whatever opportunities he could. I shook my head. *No*, enough of insisting everything was coincidence and random. There was more to this situation, I could feel it, and I had to find out what it was.

He drove up Congress Street and when he headed out of town toward Westbrook Street, I thought he'd turn in the direction of Gorham, and had decided to go home to his parents, but he went straight. Congress turned into County. We passed the Husson campus, after which the road narrowed to single lanes either side. I fell back a little more as there were hardly any other vehicles around, which meant fewer opportunities for me to lose him. I presumed he'd turn soon. Maybe he'd found an apartment somewhere out of town as it was cheaper, but it seemed Jeremy had other ideas.

We kept going, past North Scarborough until he took a right onto Long Plains Road, driving farther still. He finally slowed down and turned left through a set of open gates. I went past in case he'd noticed someone was following him, but still had more than enough time to read the big signs. The top one made from carved wood read *Connie's Campground*. The one below, *Thanks for a great season! See you next year!* The place seemed deserted. What was Jeremy doing here?

Sixty yards down the road and I doubled back, coming to a crawl as I turned into the campground. I couldn't see much past the welcome booth, had no clue why Jeremy had come here. Was he meeting people? For all I knew this was where teenagers hung out and drank, busting into a closed campground fewer than thirty minutes away from Portland where the cops potentially wouldn't come looking. Or it was something nefarious, and my thoughts leaped ahead, wondering if Jeremy was involved in drugs.

Maybe Sherry and Lawrence hadn't been completely truthful. Perhaps he was an addict and they'd kicked him out but didn't want to say so because they felt it would make them look bad. If it was true, if Jeremy had an issue with drugs, I vowed I'd help him. Do whatever I could to get him into rehab so he could recover. It was the least I could do.

When I was sure my Ford wasn't visible from the main road anymore, I killed the lights and pulled over to the side, deciding I'd continue on foot. It would be much quieter, and I figured finding one or a few cars on the campsite couldn't be hard. I'd approach Jeremy gently, quietly, and if it wasn't an option I'd regroup and wait until there was a more opportune time, especially now I knew one of the places he worked.

I wasn't wearing my jacket and didn't bother going back for it as I set off down the road, using the flashlight on my phone to guide me. The rain had finally stopped, the sky now clear enough to let the moon break through on occasion, casting eerie shadows, turning trees and shrubs into something more ominous-looking. An owl hooted in the distance, reminding me Jeremy and I weren't the only ones out here, there were animals, too. Preferably small ones considering I didn't have anything to defend myself with.

A hundred yards later it became apparent I'd underestimated the task ahead when I reached a crossroads. I had three options; keep going straight, turn left or right. I held my flashlight to the signpost. The arrow to the left pointed to a picnic area, splash pad, and playground. The one to the right had an icon with a tent. If Jeremy was staying here longer term, I didn't believe he'd be roughing it, not when there were other options, as indicated by the last sign, showing, amongst other things, that there were cabins straight ahead.

I kept going, past a boarded-up restaurant, a beach volleyball court, and concrete all-weather Ping-Pong tables. When I rounded the corner, I spotted a few cabins in the distance, and a crack of light shone through the curtains of one of them. This had to be it. I crept forward, taking my time, and when I saw a dark Mazda CX-3 parked out front with a Barney the Dinosaur figurine dangling from the mirror, I knew I'd found him.

As I reached out to knock on the cabin door, rabid butterflies flapped their wings in my stomach. This wasn't how I'd imagined the reunion with my son, but this wasn't a Lifetime movie, and I knew I might not get the happy ending I'd dreamed of. I rapped my knuckles three times and took a step back as I heard footsteps. When the door opened, I exhaled, letting my arms drop by my sides, watched as Jeremy peered behind me. I put my hands up.

"I'm not the cops or anything," I said. "I don't mean you any harm."

Pathetic, considering he towered over me. He had to be at least six feet and so slight I wondered when he'd had his last meal. With the light behind him, his face was shadowed, and I couldn't make out many of his features, or his expression.

"I need to talk to you," I said. "I...I'm..." I swallowed, took another deep breath, but before I could finish my sentence, Jeremy spoke.

"Frankie," he said, his voice soft, friendly. "You're my birth mom."

CHAPTER THIRTY-SIX

He held the door open and stepped aside, and as he turned, a smile spread across his face, unabashed delight and excitement brimming from every pore. He wore a pair of jeans and a magenta shirt, more confirmation of his favorite color. His dark hair had a shaggy, floppy look, almost touching his shoulders, a little longer than in the picture I'd seen of him at Sherry and Lawrence's home. But his eyes…it was as if I were staring into mine. I didn't move but continued gazing at him as he spoke again.

"Come in, come in," he said. "You must be freezing."

I hesitated for a second before doing as he asked, still utterly bewildered by what was going on. He *did* know me. I *had* seen him before, and not only when I'd climbed into his car last week when he'd driven me back to my apartment. But if he'd known who I was, why hadn't he said anything?

Unable to utter a word, I looked around. The cabin was small, maybe three hundred square feet at most, with a compact kitchen and living room combo that included a sofa, a dining table for four at a push, and a wood-burning fireplace, sitting empty. Two pine doors led off to the left, presumably to a bathroom and bedroom.

"It's not much," Jeremy said, grimacing when he caught my gaze. "Anyway, how did you find me?"

"I, uh, saw a picture of you," I said, skimming over the details for now. "And I remembered you from the Thai place. When I got there, they told me you'd just left, and I…I followed you." I waited a few beats for his reaction, expected him to freak out, but when he didn't, I babbled on. "I know that must sound really strange, and this isn't the way I wanted us to meet, but—"

"It's okay, it's okay." He smiled again. "I've been following you, too."

All the air seemed to leave my lungs. My mouth opened and closed a couple of times before I managed to say, "I thought so…but why? You knew I wanted to meet you. You had my details."

"I—I was scared." He shrugged, looking embarrassed. "I wanted to be sure. You wrote the agreement over eighteen years ago and I thought you might have changed your mind."

"No," I whispered, wanting to put my arms around him but too afraid of him pushing me away. "Never."

"I've been working up the courage to speak to you again," he said. "Properly, I mean. Other than when I walked into you at the restaurant and when I drove you home."

"It really *was* you. Are you actually an Uber driver?"

"No, I improvised," he said quickly. "You were waiting in the rain, staring at your phone. You looked so angry, and I took a chance you'd called a rideshare. It was a gamble. Probably not the smartest. I hope it didn't freak you out."

"How did you recognize me? I mean, sure, you had my name, but how did you know what I look like?"

"Easy," he beamed, pointing at the laptop on the table. "Social media. And I'm pretty good with computers and stuff."

"And did you work on one of Morgan Construction's sites?"

"Yeah…"

A blush crept over his cheeks, and I gave him a moment to handle his embarrassment by looking around again, taking in the eggplant-colored slouchy beanie hung next to a jacket on the wall, and the black Puma backpack on the floor. Not Nike, *Puma*, but Edith could have easily mistaken the logo of a lunging feline for the classic swoosh when she'd peered through a peephole into a darkened hallway.

"Did *you* leave flowers and chocolates for me?" I said, and Jeremy nodded. "But why didn't you include a note or a card? I thought I had a stalker or something."

He hung his head. "I wanted to do something nice for you."

"It *was* nice," I said, daring to take a step. "So, you got my details on your birthday?"

"Oh, no, it was before then," he said, his face lighting up again.

"It was?"

"Yeah. About a month before when I finally managed to hack into Vital Records. I'd been trying for ages and then I got in and found my original birth certificate." He puffed out his chest when he caught the confused expression on my face. "Told you I was good with computers."

"But…"

"I wanted to find you earlier, but my *parents* wouldn't help." His face turned dark again, brow furrowing. "They said I had to wait until I was eighteen, it was the rule. I begged them to let me find you as soon as I knew for sure I was adopted, but they wouldn't. They *refused*. Can you believe it?"

"Those were the terms we'd agreed on when I placed you

for adoption," I said gently. "They couldn't have shared my details even if they'd wanted to. They didn't have them."

"I bet they could've found a way. Though they're not resourceful. They wouldn't give me the name of the adoption agency either."

"Maybe they were afraid they'd lose you."

"Well, they did," he said, eyes flashing with a burst of fury. "As soon as I left home, I sold my car so they couldn't track me down, and I only use burner phones now."

I let that sit for a second, wondered what had really happened at the Nortons' home, if I should mention I'd spoken to them, and they were worried about him, but decided against it in case he ordered me to leave. We'd have plenty of time to unravel what had gone on and where we'd go from here. I waited another moment for his anger, which was so akin to mine, to disperse a little, and changed direction. "Why are you living all the way out here?"

"It's where I had a summer job during the holidays. The owners are in Florida until spring. They go for almost six months every year."

"Hold on. You can't possibly stay the winter. Is there even electricity?"

"I borrowed a small generator," he said quietly, looking at his sneakers.

"You didn't happen to *borrow* it from one of our sites, did you?"

"Might've," he said with a small grin. "I didn't want to light a fire in here in case someone saw, and I shower at the YMCA every day. I know the janitor, he's fine with it."

The decision was easy. He was my son, I had to help him. "You can stay with me until we decide on a better plan," I said. "I can't let you live here. You'll freeze by Christmas."

"With you? Really?"

"Yes. There's so much I have to tell you." I swallowed hard. "I'll explain everything when we get back to my place. You know where I live but come in my truck, okay? I'll drive and we can talk. Get to know one another. We'll pick your car up later."

"Sure," he said, excitement filling his voice. "I'll grab my things."

He headed into what I presumed was the bedroom while I hung back. This kid, *my* kid, had been following me around, desperate to talk to me but too shy to approach. It was sweet, adorable really, him leaving me chocolates and flowers and...

How had he known I loved sunflowers? Was it something we had in common, a lucky guess, or...*wait*. Had he stolen my notebook? Had I dropped it in his car after all? He'd have easily been able to take it back to Jake's Cakes and pretend he'd found it there because he'd seen me come out of the coffee shop before picking me up. I decided to ask him outright, walked to the bedroom, pushed open the door, and froze.

Sheets of paper were stuck to the walls, filled with photos, names, and scribbles in black marker. Bang in the center was a picture of me, one I'd never seen before, but I could immediately tell where it had been taken. The church hall where I'd attended anger management sessions, and this photo was of me at the back of the room by the coffee supplies table, where I'd first spoken to Evan.

I remembered the tall, thin participant who'd worn an eggplant hoodie and had sat folded into themselves, head bent, not saying a word. *Jeremy.* He'd been there, too, pointing a camera at me, taking my photo. But how had he got into the session? It wasn't a walk-in group. You had to sign up.

I didn't have time to answer the question because surrounding the picture of my face were many others, and I recognized each one. Patrick Davies, Adrian Costas, Chelsea Fischer, Tyler Vance, Geraldina Hoyos, Edith Bryant, Trina Smith, my father, each one linked to me with arrows and more scrawls, and one blank spot filled with the words *The bastard who killed my grandmother* in angry black pen.

My stomach tied itself into knots as I stepped farther into the room while my brain shrieked at me to turn and run. I couldn't, it was as if an invisible string was reeling me in, pulling me closer and closer to the deranged map of people pinned to Jeremy's wall.

"Wh-what's all this?" I whispered.

Jeremy whirled around, his eyes widening. "You're not supposed to be in here."

"Why do you have all this stuff? Jeremy...what did you do?"

"Don't be afraid," he said. "I'd never hurt you. You're my real mom."

"But...these are all the people on a list I made," I said, pieces falling together for certain. "And you came to the anger management session, didn't you? *You* stole my notebook?"

"I was going to talk to you that night, but you bailed, so I did as well."

"You followed me and Evan?"

He shrugged. "I was curious about the list you'd made. I wanted to take a photo and put it back, but I wasn't quick enough when Evan got your coffees, and you were in the bathroom." He scowled as he raised his chin. "I don't like him. I hope you don't either."

I couldn't speak. Fingers trembling as I put them over my mouth, my knees almost gave way and I pressed a hand against a chest of drawers to stop my body from sinking to the floor, shrinking back when Jeremy came toward me.

"Please don't be afraid," he said again. "You don't need to be scared. I did all this for you, Mom." His eyes went wide as he beamed at me, face full of hope as if he were expecting my approval. "I got your list and found everyone on it. It wasn't hard, not with social media, yearbooks, and your LinkedIn profile. I love research. I'm good at that, too, and—"

"My dad's name was on that list. Your *grandfather*."

"He deserved to be punished!" Jeremy shouted, and when he saw me flinch, he lowered his voice. "And I didn't mean for the boards to break completely, I just wanted to scare him. But I heard the way he spoke to you. I don't think he believed what you said about Davies touching you. *I* do. Davies is a pig."

"How could you possibly know about that? And who told you I'd signed up for anger management sessions? I never put any of it on social."

He pointed to my pocket. "I, uh, put some stuff on your phone and in your apartment a few months ago."

"Wh-what did you say? You mean spyware? And you've been listening to my conversations? Watching me at *home*?"

"I didn't put the cameras anywhere bad," he said quickly, waving his hands around. "Only in the living room and kitchen."

"*What?* When? When did you do this?"

"Remember when I knocked the guy off the ladder at work? I needed a diversion so I could install a hidden program on your phone and grab your house key to make an impression."

"I...I can't believe... How did you even know my password?"

"It's my birthday." He looked at me and *smiled*. Unable to speak, I let out a noise somewhere between a gasp and a cry.

Jeremy took a step in my direction, his placating voice almost reassuring. "I wasn't doing anything wrong."

"You broke into my apartment!"

"I just wanted to *see*. And we're so much alike, Mom. We read the same books and everything. Lisa Unger's one of my favorite authors. I read all her novels last year and you have the entire collection, even the ones she wrote as Lisa Miscione. Isn't it amazing?"

"I can't cope—"

"But I wish I hadn't sent you the wrong bouquets. I thought you liked sunflowers, but you kept throwing them away." He smacked the side of his head with his hand. "It was careless of me. I'll do better for your birthday. I promise."

I almost sank to the floor again as my brain tried to register what I was hearing. Jeremy, my own son, had stolen my key, broken into my apartment, and installed cameras. He'd listened to my phone conversations. Signed up for the same anger management sessions where he'd got his hands on my notebook. He'd tracked down the people on my forgiveness list, he'd…

"You loosened the wheel on Chelsea's car," I gasped, barely daring to voice the suspicions I'd carried with me since leaving Sherry and Lawrence's house. "Did…did you do that to your dad's?"

There was no shame or remorse on his face. He was happy. Worse still, he looked proud. "When my parents told me your mom was killed when you were fourteen, I thought if they died, I'd get to live with you. But only my dad was in the car."

"He was paralyzed," I said. "How could—"

"I wanted to be with *you*," he said, his voice going up. "But then I found out I wouldn't have been able to anyway. I still had to wait until I was eighteen."

I could barely speak. How could I have got everything so completely wrong? Evan hadn't done anything, hadn't harmed anyone. He was innocent, and so was Noa, but my son… "You set fire to Patrick Davies's house."

"I didn't think he was home."

"You *killed* Adrian."

"I heard what that man said. He threatened you."

"Jeremy, he was your biological father."

"Who cares?" Jeremy shouted, his temper flaring. "He didn't! He deserved to die after what he did to us. Why don't you understand? Don't you see, Mom? You don't have to forgive *anyone*. It's a revenge list instead. It's so much *better*."

"Jeremy," I whispered. "No, it isn't. We have to go to the police."

"Why would you say that? Those people hurt you."

"You don't know what half of them did!"

"I don't care. I did it for you. I did everything for *you*."

I could hear the anger in his words, see it spiraling out of control, ripping him apart. Holding up my hands and forcing my own fury back down, I very, *very* gently said, "I know you understand hurting those people, their families, was wrong. It doesn't matter what anyone on the list did. It was between me and them."

"But I—"

"Listen to me, Jeremy. We'll explain everything to the police, and I'll help you. I have a lawyer who—"

"*No*. No way. I'm not done."

Fear trickled down my back in an icy wave. "What do you mean?"

He pointed at the blank spot on the wall. "The person who killed your mother, my grandmother. Don't you want them found? Bring them to justice like they do in the stories we love so much?"

"Of course I—"

"Let me help you. We'll work together, get into the police system somehow, I'll find a way. We'll review the case notes, see what we can find. There's new tech all the time and we'll go interview people. Somebody, somewhere, must remember *something*."

"Jeremy—"

"Tell me you don't want to find them," he whispered. "Tell me you don't want to inflict the same amount of pain as they have on you. They killed my grandmother. Ran her over in the street and left her to *die*. We have to give them what they deserve."

Twisted, malicious desire snaked its way into my core, tempting me to go on this wild vigilante quest with Jeremy. Throw myself into searching for the person who'd mowed Mom down one summer evening and hadn't bothered to stop. That wouldn't happen if I delivered my son to the cops, he'd be charged with murder and multiple counts of attempted murder. I'd barely found him and now I was supposed to put him behind bars? Yes, what he'd done was terrible, but wasn't the world better off without Adrian Costas in it? How many times had I silently wished him away? Geraldina only had a broken nose. Chelsea, Patrick Davies, and Tyler Vance would all survive their physical injuries.

The spiteful, callous part of me expanded, whispering perhaps the three of them would become humbler as a result of what my son had done. He'd taught them a lesson. Wasn't that a good thing? Wasn't that what people deserved? And nobody else on my list except for my mother's killer, if we found them, would get hurt. I hadn't taken care of Jeremy for over eighteen years. Wasn't it my duty to do so, and to protect him now?

As I wrestled with malice, Jeremy must've taken my prolonged silence as tacit agreement because he grabbed my hands. "I never got to meet my grandmother because of the person who murdered her," he said. "Let's find them. Punish them properly. *Together.*"

"No," I whispered, still trying to convince myself more than him. "No, we can't."

"We *can*. We're almost there. Nobody suspects anything. All the incidents so far are different—the cops can do their profiling and victimology assessments all they want. Only the two of us know what's on your list."

Logic and reasoning set in. Adrian had been murdered. Chelsea lost her baby. When I yanked my hands away, Jeremy looked as if I'd punched him full force. "Revenge isn't the answer, not this way. We need to go to the cops."

"You're going to tell on me? But I'm your son. They'll lock me up. I'll never see you again."

"You will. I'll help you. Please, please let me help you. I'll figure it out. *We'll* figure it out."

Jeremy stared at me, his eyes filling with fear as he backed away, sank onto the bed, and pulled his knees to his chest, looking small and terrified. "I can't. I'm scared."

"Don't be." I knelt beside him. "Everything's going to be all right. I promise."

"I wanted to make you happy," he said, tears rolling down his cheeks now, his green eyes pleading with me. "That's all. Please don't hate me. I can't live with myself if you hate me."

"I don't and I'm not going anywhere. I'm going to help you."

For the next twenty minutes I cajoled and reassured Jeremy, convincing him to do the right thing, and finally, we were outside. We'd left everything in the cabin's bedroom as it was, and I presumed once I alerted Willows and Armstrong, they'd want to see all the evidence for themselves. "I left my truck at the entrance," I said. "We can walk—"

"I'll drive my car there," Jeremy said, his voice tiny and frightened. "I can hide it behind the reception building where nobody will see."

I wasn't about to risk him taking off, and it was only a few hundred yards. "Fine," I said, opening the door and getting into the passenger seat.

"I really didn't mean to hurt you," Jeremy said as he started the engine.

"We're going to work through this," I said. "Together."

"You don't mean that," he whispered as we drove away, the car lurching as he pushed down on the accelerator, hard. "You're going to abandon me."

"No, I'm not. I promise."

"I don't believe you. You spoke with my parents today."

"How…?" The tracker on my phone, that's how he knew. He must've been following my movements since he'd installed it. He may not have heard our conversation because my phone had been tucked into my bag, but he'd seen me coming to the restaurant, that's why he'd bolted, trying to get away. Or had he lured me here? "Yes, I did, but—"

"Are you colluding with them? Trying to get me home? Now you'll tell them I caused my father's car accident. You're all turning on me."

"We're not, I promise, I—"

"Liar!" he shouted, speeding up some more. "You put my name on your list. You *hate* me. You've always hated me. I didn't want to believe it, but I bet you wish I'd never been born."

"God, no, no, that's not true. I hoped you'd contact me as soon as you turned eighteen." I looked down. "I was angry when you didn't. It was selfish of me to include you. I have nothing to forgive you for, it's the other way around. Can you please slow down?"

"You think I'm a bad person."

"No—"

"Don't lie." Jeremy pressed his foot on the accelerator again as we sped past the shuttered restaurant, and kept going, flying through the crossroads.

"I'm not lying. Stop the car, my truck's up ahead. I'll drive us."

"No." The word bounced around our heads as he went faster, zooming past my vehicle and heading for the exit. I thought he'd flip the car, but he managed to turn left, driving in the opposite direction of Portland and farther into the countryside.

"After everything I did for you," he said, teeth clenched. "I searched for those people on your list. Got revenge for *you* and you want me arrested?" He pressed his foot down. Sixty miles per hour. Seventy.

"What are you doing?" I yelled. "Stop. I said slow down."

Jeremy refused, his jaw set, knuckles white. "You don't want me in your life. Nobody does."

"That's not true, I promise!"

"I told you to stop *lying!*"

"I'm *not.* Jeremy, please."

I wanted to grab the wheel, but if we went off the road we'd be in big trouble, and if I threw myself out of the car, there was no chance I'd survive the impact at this speed. But if I could somehow get through to him, perhaps make him slow down enough for either option to become viable... "Please calm down," I whispered. "We'll talk—"

"Don't tell me what to do," he yelled. "You're not my mom. You didn't want me, remember? I *hate* you."

"It wasn't like that. Jeremy, pull over before we get hurt."

Instead of doing as I asked, he accelerated again, the speed-ometer getting close to eighty. "Nobody will want me after what I've done," he said. "Nobody."

I knew there were large animals out in these woods. If we hit a deer or a moose, we might not come out the other end alive. A signpost flashed past us. Too fast for me to read, but shortly afterward Jeremy hit the brakes full on, tires squeal-ing as he turned left, cutting across the road. This time I saw the sign ahead of us. Chudley's. I remembered the name. A disused quarry, a victim of the last recession, putting dozens of people out of work. A place abandoned ever since.

What was Jeremy doing? Why were we heading there? I didn't have to wait long before the answer came. My son stared at me for three seconds before he hit the gas again, buildings and piles of rocks whizzing by until I saw a large red-and-white wooden sign indicating what appeared not only to be the end of the road, but the edge of a cliff. I screamed, scrambled to loosen my seatbelt which looped around my arm and shoulder as I fumbled for the door.

Jeremy hit the central lock button. "You put both our names on your list," he shouted. "You want to forgive your-self for what? Abandoning me? You don't have that right and I don't forgive you. You're going to die. We both are. That's what we deserve."

I yelled again when I understood he had no intention of slowing down. With a sickening crunch the car burst through the crumbling wooden barricade. The gravel disappeared and there was nothing underneath us but air. I cried out as the nose of the car tipped down, sending us plunging into the darkness below.

CHAPTER THIRTY-SEVEN

Fear gripped me by the neck as I fell forward, barely restrained by the loosened seatbelt, arms and legs flailing as I scrambled to push my legs into the floor, my palms pressing against the ceiling for stability. I don't know how many seconds passed. One? Two? Thirty? Time had taken on an elastic quality, stretching, distorting, making it impossible to think properly or cling to any kind of comprehension.

I didn't see the ground below us, and braced myself for impact, imagined the front of the car smashing into concrete, crumpling into an accordion, crushing my knees, my hips, my back. But we didn't hit the ground, instead it was water, the car falling backward, making me smack my skull first on the window, and then on the headrest. The force brought bright white stars for a few seconds, enough time to hear the car was already filling with liquid, pouring in through gaps, cracks, and crevices.

We bobbed a little, the hood slowly tipping, making my feet scramble again. It was so dark I could barely see my hands, but I could hear water, smell it, too—damp, musky, cold. I looked over at Jeremy. His head was slumped and when I reached to shake his shoulder, he let out a soft moan.

There was no time to think about the fact he'd tried to kill us both. Not long and we'd be submerged.

I fumbled around for the door handle with one hand, reached for Jeremy's shoulder with the other, shook him as hard as I could. "Hey," I yelled. "Come on, we have to get out."

He didn't answer and I wondered if he'd lost consciousness again. I tried to open the door, forced my entire body weight against it, but it wouldn't budge. We were sinking too fast. I tried again, and again, but it was too late.

This was it. This was how everything would end for me. In a watery grave at the bottom of the lake of Chudley's quarry. I'd never see Rico, Noa, Azumi, or my father again. Never have the chance to tell them I loved them. I'd been so fixated on and angry with my past, I hadn't paid attention to or tried to repair my present. Would they find us? Would they know what happened to me? Might they ever understand why?

As I was about to give up and accept it was all over, anger grew in my stomach, grabbing hold of me. No, this wasn't anger. This was total raging, white-hot fury. Something, if used properly, I could tame and direct to get me out of here. Because this was *not* how I would die. I would not give up. I would not put my family through losing someone again.

With a guttural scream I crawled into the back seat of the tipping car, lay across the seat on my back, lifted my legs, and pounded my boots against the side window. Over and over. Harder and harder, crying out again and again with every beat, rage filling my legs and heels. At last, the glass splintered and gave way. Freezing water gushed into the car so fast, it felt like a thousand pins were being driven under my skin. As the water kept coming, I scrambled, had almost made it out of the window when Jeremy grabbed my leg.

He yanked me back, pulling me down. "No," he screamed. "You're not leaving me again. *You're not leaving me.*"

I kicked, shouted, wrestled, and heaved my body toward the broken window, my last chance at freedom. At life. When he tried pulling me back, his hands on both my legs now, I managed to free one foot and kicked as hard as I could. My boot connected with something solid. It made a cracking sound and Jeremy cried out as his grip finally loosened. I didn't waste time by turning around to see what was happening but thrust my legs again and gave myself one last heave out the window. A yell rang out, echoing off the quarry walls, and I flinched until I realized the voice belonged to me.

No clue how big the lake was or which direction the shore was in, but I swam, frantically pushing my arms and legs, tears streaming down my face and mixing with the frigid water. It was so cold, my fingers were already going numb, but I couldn't stop. As I moved, I tried to listen for Jeremy, imagined his hands reaching upward for my feet, my legs, ready to pull me into the final resting place he'd chosen for us.

He'd attempted to kill me. My own son had fully intended on ensuring both of us died here tonight. Survival instincts hit me full on as I made myself continue, not knowing if I was swimming into the middle of the lake or closer to the edge. Another ten kicks, and another, before my hand hit a rock wall in front of me, grazing my knuckles and making me yelp. I tried to touch the bottom with my feet, but it was out of reach.

My phone had survived the impact in the sense it was still in my pocket, but when I fished it out as I treaded water, I knew it was dead before I looked at the lifeless screen. I felt around the rock face, trying to grab hold of something to pull myself up with, but even if I had, there would be no chance of scaling a cliff in the dark. It was suicide.

I changed my plan, edged my way along, hoping at some point I'd find an exit before I froze to death. My teeth chattered, and I could barely wiggle my toes, but I kept going, counting the strokes in my head—one, two, three, four—over and over, lips moving silently. Five sets of four, and three more, before my feet hit solid ground. I clambered onto a path as the clouds parted, affording enough moonlight to see. As soon as I was out of the water I stopped and turned, eyes darting across the shimmering surface. There was no movement, no indication I'd almost drowned, and Jeremy had...

Oh my God, I'd left my son to die.

I opened my mouth to shout his name, thought about running up the hill as fast as I could to get help, but the fear of what he might do stopped me. I let myself sink to the ground and fall to my knees as reality hit. What would the police say if I walked into the station and told them Jeremy was dead and I hadn't helped him escape? What would they do if I told them he was responsible for hurting all the people on my list? There was proof in the campsite cabin that my son had planned something, but now he was gone. Would they say I was his accomplice, we'd worked on this *revenge* project together, I'd coerced him, especially as we were mother and son? How would they react when I told them Adrian Costas was his father?

Would they believe me if I said I'd only found Jeremy's cabin this evening? With my prior arrest, the warning, the footage of my driving past Tyler's house, and the fact every single person who'd got hurt could be tied back to me, would I be charged anyway? Wrongly convicted? I couldn't put Rico and my father—or myself—through more than I already had.

I looked around. Nobody on the road had seen us drive in. The quarry was abandoned, the water deep. Somewhere nobody would come looking. Jeremy had chosen this, all of it, but while his choices weren't any of my doing, I was responsible, too, and we'd be bound by this deadly secret together. Forever.

I turned and ran.

CHAPTER THIRTY-EIGHT

I've no idea how long it took to reach the campsite, but when I saw my truck, I almost cried. The keys were still safely tucked away in my pocket, but as I climbed inside and reached for my jacket, grateful to get out of the cold for a few seconds, I knew I couldn't leave this place yet. I had work to do. I inched the truck forward and drove to Jeremy's cabin.

Although the place was shrouded in darkness, I crept up the porch before quietly opening the door. I quickly searched the rooms, making sure they were all empty before locking the front door and heading back to the bedroom.

I ripped down all of Jeremy's papers, made sure none of them fell to the floor, and stuffed them in a garbage bag I found under the sink. Next, I swept the entire cabin. By the looks of things, Jeremy hadn't left any of his belongings behind, including his phone and laptop, which were in his bag at the bottom of the quarry lake, but I still checked everywhere three times to make sure.

There was a bottle of bleach under the sink, along with a roll of kitchen paper, and I set to work, wiping down everything and anything we may have touched. As I cleaned, I searched for the shreds of my forgiveness list in case Jeremy really had lifted them from my garbage during one of his *visits* but couldn't find them anywhere. It didn't matter. The lake water would've already destroyed the ink.

When I was done and surveyed the rooms, nothing looked out of place, in fact, it didn't appear as if anyone had been in the cabin at all. I opened the front door, half expecting Jeremy to jump out and attack me. I threw the garbage bag into my truck, went around the back to grab the generator he'd stolen, and headed out, setting the heater at full blast as I tried to warm up.

A few miles later a cop car appeared behind me, making my hands quiver. The cruiser followed me for the next five miles before turning in the other direction at a crossroads, and I let my shoulders drop as the enormity of what had happened hit full on. The tears didn't come until I saw the Portland lights glowing on the horizon, but I made myself take the I-95 to the building site where Jeremy had stolen the generator, and let myself in. On my way out, I swiped a pair of coveralls and changed in the car under the cover of darkness, thankful I could finally get out of my sopping clothes. I started the engine of my truck again, and this time, I pointed it in the direction of home.

When I parked and headed to my apartment, I couldn't imagine collapsing in bed and falling asleep no matter how exhausted I was. My brain was going a thousand miles a minute, and I didn't think it would ever slow down, not with what I'd done. My encounter with Jeremy played on a loop, and part of me wanted to go to the police and tell them everything, but I still couldn't bring myself to. I needed to calm down, put more distance between me and the events so I could decide what to do, and when. I thought about Sherry and Lawrence, the fact our son would never return, and as

I stripped off and let myself sink to the floor in the shower, I cried until no more tears came.

I spent the next two days in a state of disbelief, at times unsure if what had happened with Jeremy had actually taken place, still wavering about whether I should go to the cops and confess or return to the quarry to search for my son's body, self-preservation and fear kicking in, telling me I had to keep quiet. My brain shut the rest of me down, and while I didn't think I'd ever sleep again, somehow it was all I seemed capable of doing, allowing me to escape reality and my anger, if only for a while.

On Sunday morning I was woken by the doorbell shortly before seven thirty. I jumped up, expected the police on my doorstep, ready to haul me away. Part of me was glad, relieved to tell the truth, hoped they'd believe I was innocent, except for my leaving Jeremy at the bottom of the lake. I clasped the door handle and opened it, letting out a small gasp when I saw Evan.

"Frankie," he said. "I hoped you'd be here."

"Why?" My voice shot up. "What do you want?"

"To talk to you. Before I lose my nerve."

I noticed his expression, the way he pushed his hair from his face, moving from one foot to the other. Why was he here? Did he know about Jeremy? Had they been in on this together, working their way through my list for some incomprehensible reason? It didn't make sense. Jeremy said he didn't like Evan, then again, at this point I couldn't trust anyone.

"I don't want to speak to you," I said. "I need to be alone."

As I started to close the door, Evan put his palm against it and blurted out the words I'd been desperate to hear for almost twenty years. "I know who killed your mom."

I stood there, fingers still wrapped around the handle, entirely immobile. I didn't tremble. Didn't flinch. I couldn't move. Couldn't breathe. Didn't want to in case I broke the spell he'd cast. Evan knew who killed my mother. He *knew*?

His expression wasn't one I'd ever seen on anyone before. Sheer terror mixed with absolute desperation. The way he was still shifting from one foot to the other made me think he was about to cut and run. I needed to say something, *anything*, and fast, before it was too late.

"Wh-what do you mean?" I whispered. "How could you possibly know?"

"Let me come in," he said. "Please, Frankie. Let me tell you."

I acquiesced. The need to have whatever knowledge he possessed was so strong, so urgent it eclipsed all other emotion, and any fears or doubts about letting him inside my apartment faded away. He walked past me, taking a seat at the kitchen table, gestured for me to do the same but I refused, standing by the front door, which I left open a crack, just in case.

"Got any alcohol?" Evan said, with a pitiful laugh.

"You said you never drink."

"I don't, but I might have to make an exception for this."

"Tell me what you know. Or what you think you know."

Evan was silent for a long moment, and when he began to speak, his voice was barely a whisper. "I'd been at a friend's all day. We'd spent the afternoon playing together in Riverton, and I was there…when your mom…when she got hit."

"You saw who ran into her? Were you in the street? At your friend's house?"

"No." He wrung his hands before continuing. "She said she'd stopped. She'd promised. Swore on my life."

"Who? Swore she'd stopped what?"

"My mom. She'd said she'd stopped drinking. But it was a lie. It was always a lie."

I finally understood what he'd come to tell me. "Your mom was driving…"

"Yes." The word came out strangled followed by a huge sob. "I…I was in the front passenger seat. Mom didn't care where I sat when she'd been drinking. Front, back, seatbelt or not. She didn't care. She didn't care about anything." He began to cry harder, tears streaming down his cheeks as I stood in silence, trying to grasp what he'd shared. "I'm so sorry, Frankie," he said as I put my back to the door, my weight pushing it closed. "I'm so, so sorry."

"You were in the car?"

"I tried to grab the wheel," he said, blinking away more tears. "As soon as I saw someone in the street, I shouted at Mom to watch out, but she was too slow because of the booze, and she batted my hands away. When I looked up again, your mom was ahead of us, and then she was gone, lying behind us in a heap on the ground."

"She was in a crosswalk. There was a stop sign."

"I know, I *know.* It was an accident."

"Why didn't your mother come forward? Why didn't you?"

"Mom had DUIs. She said she'd go to prison if we told, and I'd be taken away. My dad had left, there was no one to look after me. She begged me to keep her secret and I have, but it's been eating me alive."

I stared at him, wanted to open my mouth and shout at him, rant and rave he should feel guilty. He was responsible, at least partially, for the hell my family had gone through, but as I looked at him, saw the remorse, humiliation, and pleading in his eyes, my anger—or what was left of it since I'd used it all up escaping from Jeremy—melted away.

"It was almost twenty years ago," I whispered. "You were a kid."

"I was ten," he said. "Not that small, and I've never forgotten."

"But you *were* a child, and you've been dealing with it all this time? Alone?"

"It doesn't matter how old I was. I knew what we did was wrong. She made me swear—"

"Your mother was protecting you."

"She was protecting *herself*. Covering her own ass. It's all she ever did."

"Didn't you say your mother raised you on her own?"

"Yes."

"And no family close by?" When he shook his head, I continued. "She was right about what would've happened to you. You'd have ended up in the system."

He gave a so-what shrug. "Probably. Or maybe with my aunt in California, although she and Mom hadn't spoken in years. Why aren't you angry? You should be furious."

"I'm done being mad," I said, for the first time in my life actually meaning the words. "I'm exhausted. I can't keep being angry about everything. It's been eating me alive, too." I paused, looked at him. "Where's your mom now?"

"She died five years ago. Cirrhosis."

"Oh my gosh, Evan."

He waved a hand, not dismissively, but as if he didn't believe he deserved any of my sympathy. "The messed-up part is I didn't know she was sick."

"She didn't tell you?"

"Nope." A shake of the head. "Not me, not anybody. We hadn't been in touch for over a year, but it was her fiftieth, so I went to see her." He clenched his jaw, looked down for a few beats before wiping under his eyes with his fingers while I waited for him to continue. "Her car was at home, but when she didn't answer the door, I let myself in. I found her on the living room floor."

"Was she…?"

"Dead? No. Covered in vomit and unresponsive so I called the ambulance. They took her to hospital, but she never woke up again. She passed two days later. God, I should've done more, been there for her, you know?"

"Sometimes it's not that simple. Relationships are…difficult," I said.

"No kidding. I mean, what kind of a mother doesn't tell her own son she's dying but leaves a hefty life insurance as a reward for him keeping his mouth shut? Who *does* that?"

"Perhaps she didn't want to burden you more. It wasn't your fault she drank herself to—"

"Wasn't it? I moved out as soon as I could. Avoided seeing her for years at a time. I knew she still had a problem, and do you know what I did? Nothing. I walked away."

"She was sick. It's an illness."

"I know, but generally when people are sick, you help, you don't turn your back on them, which is exactly what I did. I was so ashamed, Frankie. I read about the accident in the papers, saw your mom's obituary, and as I got older, I'd look for your profiles online to see how you were doing, you know?"

"That's…kind of sweet."

"No, it's pathetic. I should've told. Instead, I used a third of the money to buy my apartment and donated the rest to AA and MADD, but I was still so angry, so…*furious*. It's why I eventually signed up for the sessions with Geraldina, and when I walked in and thought I recognized you, I had to be sure."

"That's why you wanted to see my driver's license at the coffee shop?"

"Yeah. And when you came to my apartment and Do-Nation, I was freaking out, thinking you'd somehow figured out what had happened the day of your mom's accident. I'd imagined telling you for years, but when I had the opportunity, I couldn't do it, I still wasn't…ready." He put his hands up in surrender. "I know how pathetic and selfish that sounds."

"Why are you telling me now?" I asked as gently as possible.

He looked away at first, then forced his gaze to meet mine. "It was something Geraldina said at the last session. She was talking about closure, and I realized it was my responsibility to help you with yours, even if it meant I couldn't protect Mom or myself anymore."

I hesitated for a moment before reaching forward and touching his arm. "Thank you."

He exhaled a long, nervous breath. "I should've told you when you came to my apartment. Or when you showed up at the office."

"I'm not surprised you didn't, considering how angry I was. My turn to apologize."

"No, it's fine. But what did you mean when you said something about people getting hurt? What was that about?"

I waved a hand, hoped he couldn't see how badly it trembled. "A misunderstanding."

It seemed enough for him. When he spoke again, it was as if he thought his words might not come out if he didn't make them do so quickly, blurting, "I want to tell the cops everything about the accident. About what happened."

"But—"

"No, I want to. I *need* to. Unless you don't think it'll help your family? I mean, Mom's gone and will never be prosecuted."

I gave him a small smile. "I think it's very compassionate of you. And I'm sure my dad and brother will be grateful. We can tell them together if it'll make it easier."

"You'd do that for me?"

"Of course," I said, shoving the guilt of Jeremy's death deep down, deciding in a few months, once I was certain enough all my DNA had disappeared from his car, I'd make an anonymous phone call and report a vehicle in Chudley's quarry.

I'd never tell the rest of the story to anyone. I knew what I was doing, understood Jeremy's parents would forever wonder how he'd ended up there. Unlike Evan, I'd never be able to provide them with full closure. But wasn't it better than knowing he was a murderer? That was something I'd have to be prepared to carry for them in exchange for keeping my own secrets.

CHAPTER THIRTY-NINE

Four months later

Sometimes I can't believe how much has changed, or how far my family has come after being on the brink of destruction last year. It's Sunday, and Dad has invited all of us for one of his legendary meals for my thirty-fourth birthday, a celebratory dinner that includes a brand-new dessert he's mastered and won't divulge yet. I glance around the table, the dining room bursting with people. Not long ago, Rico told me I should let people into my head, and my heart. I didn't think doing so would change everything.

There's Tyler, helping Azumi with the peas on her plate and it makes my heart sing to see how kind and caring he is to her. He's fully recovered from his attack now, and although he's frustrated the police have no suspects, he's delighted how well my niece is doing and says there won't be any long-lasting consequences from Azumi's infection. We all cried when he told us.

Tyler and I had a long-overdue conversation during which he apologized for what happened at Northwestern, and I listened without interrupting, without being rude. He said he had no excuse for his actions, he'd been selfish and wrong, an arrogant spoiled brat who'd finally been humbled by the kids he'd treated. He offered to pay for whatever education I wanted to pursue. When I refused his generous suggestion, he set up a foundation for sick children. Azumi is the first recipient, meaning Rico and Noa no longer have to worry about money.

I was wrong about so many things. Noa had been trying to sell his share of the start-up to raise funds for the medical bills, and I felt so guilty for suspecting him. Tyler, once a brash show-off in high school and college, had long become a gentle man, telling me how much he regretted how he'd behaved in the past.

Even Edith and I have had the occasional conversation in the hallway, and we go to our local bookstore together about once a month. Penelope still hisses whenever she sees me, but I guess I'll have to live with that. I've discovered people can and do change, including me, and I've eaten about as much humble pie as my father's fine cooking, happy to swallow every bite.

A shiny solitaire sits on Geraldina's finger, catching the warm, late February sun streaming through the windows. Dad proposed to her on Christmas day, and when he asked Rico and me what we thought of the idea a few weeks before, I hugged him so hard he wondered if I was congratulating or trying to strangle him.

They're adorable together, and Geraldina has helped me so much with my anger, enabling me to understand it's a normal, healthy emotion, and useful depending on how I handle it. When she told me that, images of me in Jeremy's car, pounding the glass with my feet, flashed through my mind, and I pushed them back down. What happened still haunts me. It's my deepest, darkest secret. I've forgiven myself for many things. Deserting him in the lake isn't one of them.

The guilt lives with me, a constant reminder of what I did, and something I'll never allow myself to forget. It's not only my not going for help, it's also the fact his personality—and with it the propensity toward anger—came from me. Yes, Adrian was a terrible person, but that only made up fifty percent of Jeremy's DNA. The rest was mine, meaning I may have passed on more than a few physical features to my child. Finding out I'd placed him for adoption may have catapulted him over the edge, but I'll never know either way for sure, and I'll never be able to discuss it with anyone. It's something I'm going to have to learn to live with for the rest of my life without letting it destroy me.

"She's not listening," I hear Evan say as he waves his hands at me from across the table. "Hey, Frankie, you with us?" He's become another regular at our Sunday dinners. I wasn't sure how Dad and my brother would react when we sat with Evan to share the story about him being in the car that hit my mom. Rico gaped and went silent, gripping Noa's arm so tight I thought both of them might need surgery. After running a hand over his face, the first thing my father said to Evan was, "I can't imagine how horrific this has been for you."

We're all healing together now, and Dad's and my relationship has made progress. Two weeks ago, I finally asked if he'd ever forgive me for Mom's death. He stared at me for a long time before asking if I blamed myself because of something he'd said or done. Turns out I really was projecting my guilt onto everyone. He'd never blamed me, not for a second, but I'd pulled away and he felt like a failure for being unable to reach me, both of us closed off in our individual cocoons instead of folding ourselves into the same protective bubble. Giving and accepting forgiveness has been hard, and our relationship may always be somewhat fractured, but we're committed to working on it.

As for Evan and me, we have a growing connection other than the one linking us because of our mothers. It's developing slowly, a touch of a hand here, a look there, and I've no clue where it'll lead. I'm hesitant because while he knows I had a son, I didn't share what happened with Jeremy last year. Although I care for Evan, very much, I don't know if I can start a relationship knowing I can never tell him the truth, but whomever I choose to be with, it'll be the same. For once I'm taking it slow, thinking things through, much to Rico's astonished amusement. He thinks I should get Evan into bed already.

My brother pokes me in the ribs, bringing me back to the conversation around the table. "Evan said you're excited about starting your new job," he says, and I smile.

"A thousand percent."

"Traitor," Dad laughs, and I know he doesn't mean it because his eyes are filled with something I haven't seen him have for me in a long time. Pride. "I can picture it now, you on my TV screen, holding a microphone and saying—" he lowers his voice, putting on an announcer-type cadence "—this is Frankie Morgan, reporting live for WPRM."

"I'm going to be Danika's research assistant," I say, waving a hand. "Not a reporter."

"All in good time," Geraldina says. "We think you'll be fantastic."

In the end, making the career move was an easy decision. After another long conversation with my father, we decided he wouldn't sell Morgan Construction, but it was high time I pursued something I was truly passionate about. Danika was delighted to give me the skinny on what working as her assistant would entail when I called. We arranged to meet for coffee at Jake's Cakes, which has quickly become my favorite spot—their coffee really is glorious—and she offered me a role she agreed to hold for a few months until I was ready.

I promised Dad I'd stay with him until he brought in a new business partner and got them up to speed, and since a woman named Sally Wozniak joined, things have exploded. Turned out we didn't need Patrick Davies's business after all. Good job considering he was arrested almost as soon as he was discharged from the hospital after the fire, and charged with sexual harassment and assault.

Dad's apology for questioning what I'd said about Davies was profuse, Danika's in-depth report on him cutting as she divulged a series of allegations ranging from groping to rape. The trial begins in a few months. Davies's wife is taking over the Tasty Tomato chain and she's already contacted Morgan Construction about revamping all their locations.

Helping Dad's company through the transition wasn't the only reason I delayed going to WPRM. Danika might be reporting on another story today, and the anticipation is the reason I've pushed Dad's food around my plate, feeding scraps to Chip under the table, trying to not seem distracted.

We've had an abnormally warm winter so far, with a huge thaw this last week that opened a window of opportunity. Two days ago, I made an anonymous phone call to the police, told them about a car in the lake at Chudley's quarry. They located it quickly but so far, Jeremy's body hasn't been found and they're sending in divers today.

I'm hoping by the time Danika has finished her story of the tragic accident in which a young man drowned, and I start working with her Monday after next, there'll be little chance of her sending me to talk with Sherry and Lawrence. I don't know if they'd remember me as the fake police officer who arrived on their doorstep one rainy October night, and it isn't a chance I want to take. But I want them to find their son.

Adrian's murder and Patrick Davies's house fire are as yet unsolved, and I hope it stays that way because I'd like to shield Sherry and Lawrence Norton from the pain of knowing what Jeremy did. I don't want them blaming themselves like I do.

When Dad asks if I can help him with dessert in the kitchen, I get up, follow him out of the room. Instead of presenting me with another of his succulent creations, he hands me a printed sheet of paper.

"What's this?" I ask.

"Information about Maine's Adoption Reunion Registry Program," he says. "You may already have heard of it, but in case you haven't… It's another way for you to find Shay, something a little more proactive than waiting for him to make contact."

Tears fill my eyes, which Dad mistakes for gratitude, although I *am* grateful for this because it means the chasm between us is closing. He pulls me in for a hug. Since I've managed to mostly get control of my anger and we can talk without my exploding, he hugs me often. Turns out not everything was down to him to fix. Admitting when I'm wrong has been oddly satisfying.

"I hope you find him," he says. "And when you do, he'll be part of the family, if he wants to be. I'm so sorry for what you went through. God, when I think back how young you were…"

"It's all right."

"No, the way I treated you, the whole situation…it *wasn't* right. I should've listened more. I didn't know what to do.

Without your mom, I was lost. Sweetheart, I was scared. Can you forgive me?"

"There's nothing to forgive," I say, more ancient, suffocating weight sliding from my back although it's swiftly replaced by something else. More guilt. Because Dad will never meet his grandson, and I can't tell him why.

"We can do something for Shay's birthday next month if you like," Dad says gently. "Whatever's best for you. It's what we should've done all along."

I wipe away my tears, knowing I'll refuse the offer and light another candle for my deceased son instead, crying for what could've been, and hoping he has found peace. "Thank you," I say, putting the envelope in my back pocket.

Dad fishes an elaborate cake with choux pastry buns and spun sugar from the fridge. As his back's turned, I can't help looking at my phone, scanning the WPRM website, hoping for a headline screaming BODY FOUND IN CHUDLEY'S QUARRY LAKE but there's nothing.

The doorbell rings, and I shove my phone away while Dad busies himself with whipping cream. "Would you mind getting that?" he says. "I hope it's Amazon with my new door cam. Can you believe the old one broke already? What a waste of money."

"They might give you a refund," I say, walking to the front door with Chip on my heels as happiness fills my heart when I think about all the people I have in my life and now call family. I haven't been able to forgive myself, but like Geraldina said all along, setting down my animosity toward others like a set of oversized baggage has allowed me to let go of some of the past and focus on my present, and future. I understand how precious life is, and if I'd known how much better this feels than holding on to so much hatred, I'd have done it years ago. If I had, nobody would've got hurt, and I'll have to live with that, too.

My jovial expression changes as I look down, the smile sliding off my face, fear prickling my skin. There's a bouquet on the doorstep. A bunch of sunflowers. I see an envelope with my name on it, and it makes a crinkling noise when I snatch it and break the seal.

Time slows down. My hands tremble as I retrieve the single piece of paper and unfold it. It's a list. *My* list. The one I wrote in the first anger management session, tore up, and threw away. Someone has stuck the pieces together with transparent tape, but their contents are clear and perfectly legible. FRANKIE MORGAN has been circled three times with thick, dark red pen that almost looks like blood. The words *GOOD LUCK!!!* scribbled in handwriting I instantly recognize.

The world spins, and as protective instincts and terror take hold, my legs buckle. The anger I've worked so hard to tame these past few months saves me. It rushes back, filling my body, supporting me, strengthening me, and I greet it like a dear old friend. I know what to do with my rage now and I'm going to need it, because Jeremy—my son—who tried to kill us both and whom I left to die, didn't drown. He's alive. He's coming for me. It's Frankie 1—Jeremy 1.

And when we meet again, I plan to win.

★ ★ ★ ★ ★

ACKNOWLEDGMENTS

Writing the acknowledgments is such a thrill. Not only does it mean I've finished another book, but I also get to thank the most incredible individuals to whom my boundless gratitude extends.

Dear reader—whether you picked up this novel in a professional or recreational capacity, thank you for choosing *The Revenge List* and taking this journey with Frankie and me. I hope you enjoyed the ride and are keen for more of whatever my imagination cooks up next. Thank you for sticking with me!

To Carolyn Forde, my stellar agent who's so smart and talented—thank you for guiding me through the world of publishing with such a steady hand.

To Emily Ohanjanians, my lovely former editor, and Dina Davis, my lovely new editor, who picked up the project partway through—thank you for your guidance, insights, and support. Your abilities to bring out the best in my work are extraordinary, and it's truly a privilege to work with you.

To the wonderful Harlequin, HarperCollins, HTP, and MIRA teams, including Cory Beatty, Peter Borcsok, Nicole Brebner, Audrey Bresar, Eden Church, Heather Connor,

Lia Ferrone, Emer Flounders, Heather Foy, Olivia Gissing, Miranda Indrigo, Sophie James, Amy Jones, Sean Kapitain, Meena Kirupakaran, Ana Luxton, Ashley MacDonald, Leo MacDonald, Lauren Morocco, Lindsey Reeder, Justine Sha, Alice Tibbetts, Evan Yeong, and colleagues: a standing ovation to you all!

To HarperAudio, BeeAudio, and Lauren Ezzo—thank you for bringing my stories to life and for taking such great care of my characters. To Brad and Britney at AudioShelf—love you two. Brad—thank you so much for your thoughtful input. Please keep writing.

Another massive thank-you to fellow crime author and retired Detective Sergeant Bruce Robert Coffin, and Forensic Detective Ed Adach, who assisted with all things police and court related. I adore our yearly "how would you (insert crime)" chats and your ideas are phenomenal. Any inaccuracies are of my own doing.

Often you send out a call for help via email or social media and meet the most extraordinary people. In this case, huge shout-outs to Dr. Ali Kopelman in Maine and Ha Nguyen from OMC Oakville, who gave up their time to share their medical advice and expertise. More thank-yous to Heather Stultz for the adoption insights, Janine P. Salevsky for the hospital billing help, and Kristin from Vital Records in Maine for the adoption registry details. May every author encounter such limitless generosity. Again, any errors are entirely my fault.

Big, big hugs to my wonderful friend and First Chapter Fun partner in fictional crime, Hank Phillippi Ryan, for input on an early version. More big, big hugs to P.J. Vernon—you're the absolute best for bouncing the initial idea for this novel around with me. I owe you one (or ten!). Mwahs and thank-yous to Cool A.F. Brady for pointing out some plot holes where I'd obviously lost it. You can go NY on my manuscripts any-time, darling!

To Jennifer Hillier, who inspired me long before we met in person, and to Sonica Soares, whose enthusiasm for books and life is infectious; you truly are my BFFs! Brunch soon, please.

To all of my author friends in the GTA and beyond, I'm so grateful for you. We may kill people on the page, but you're truly the kindest, most hilarious, and wonderful individu-als. Thank you for continually supporting and inspiring me. I hope to see you soon. Waving at Lisa Unger, who's such a powerhouse author and incredibly generous to boot—thank you for all your help.

To Dad, Joely, Simon, Michael, and Oli; my in-laws Gil-bert and Jeanette; and my extended family everywhere—your support means the world and I'm so grateful for everything you do as you tirelessly champion my work.

And finally: to Rob, Leo, Matt, and Lex, who are the best husband and sons I could ever have wished or hoped for—thank you for listening to my wacky plot ideas and for not judging my search history too much (it *is* research, I promise!). My writing career wouldn't have happened without you, and I love you more than anything in the world. Even books and chocolate (gasp)! You'll always be my everything.

1. What did you make of Frankie's anger issues and the way she dealt with them? Were they justified? What might you have done in the various situations Frankie found herself in?

2. How did you feel about Frankie's guilt surrounding her mother's death? Can you imagine blaming yourself in that situation? What could or should Finn have done to help her through it?

3. How do you think Frankie may have grown up to be as an adult if her mother hadn't died? Was that the life-defining event for her from which everything in her life spiraled or was it something else?

4. What do you make of Frankie's statement "Truth is, we all carry some degree of anger inside, every single one of us"?

5. What do you make of Frankie's belief there's a double standard when it comes to how anger is perceived in men and women? Have you encountered the same disparity? How do you think anger should be managed?

6. Did your allegiances shift at any point during the story? Toward whom, why, and when?

7. What scene was the most pivotal in the story for you? How would the novel have changed if it had been different, or hadn't taken place? What did you expect to happen?

8. What surprised or shocked you the most? What didn't you see coming? What was obvious?

9. How did you feel about Frankie wanting to shield Sherry and Lawrence from what their son did? Would you have told them the truth if you'd been Frankie, never mind the consequences?

10. How do you feel about the ending? What do you think might happen if or when Frankie and Jeremy meet again?

THE
REVENGE
LIST

HANNAH MARY McKINNON

Reader's Guide

mira

only because it's interesting to learn new things, but mainly because I get to speak with such brilliant and knowledgeable people.

How has your writing process changed since your first book was published in 2016?

I've become a lot more streamlined because of deadlines. I've figured out what works for me (plotting and structure) and what doesn't (winging it), all of which goes a long way. Having written seven published and two yet to be published novels means I have a good few years of experience in the industry, and I've learned to trust my instincts and process more and more. When I find myself thinking, "Gah! This is terrible!" I remind myself I said that about the previous book. Actually, that's a lie. It's my husband who reminds me of it every single time and he's always right.

Your books are filled with many plot twists and turns. How much of the stories do you map out in advance?

I love twists and turns, and the more books I write, the more I plot them, but it's impossible for me to foresee everything in advance. While detailed outlines make me more productive and efficient because I know where I'm headed, it doesn't necessarily mean I'll end up at the destination I mapped out. Things change as I write. I plot, but I'm flexible and still need my manuscript to surprise me as it evolves.

You often set your novels in Maine. Can you tell us why?

I prefer writing about places I've been as there's only so much you can do online to visualize a town (which is why I make them up in certain novels, too). We have family in New Brunswick, and when we visit, we often drive from Toronto via the United States, which takes us through Maine. It's a beautiful state and

I loved Portland in particular, which is why I've set a couple of my books there now. I hope to return in the near future.

What can you tell us about your next novel?

My upcoming novel is a bit of a departure for me, as I've penned a holiday romantic comedy called The Christmas Wager. This rivals-to-lovers story set in the snowy town of Maple Falls in the Colorado mountains releases early fall 2023. It's written under the pseudonym Holly Cassidy, and I had such a fabulous time exploring the romantic, lighter side of life—and Christmas, of course. I hope you'll enjoy it, too.

If romantic comedies aren't your speed, fear not, because another thriller will follow in 2024. We don't have a title yet, but I can say it's about the rise and demise of an all-female pop rock group, and the lengths some of the members go to hold on to their fame. After all, aren't rock bands potentially worth more dead than alive? I can't wait to introduce you to my brand-new protagonist, drummer Vienna.

This is your seventh novel. What was your inspiration for The Revenge List?

I can usually pinpoint exactly where the inspiration for my novels came from. Typically, it's a news article (You Will Remember Me and Her Secret Son) or a radio segment (Sister Dear), maybe some daydreaming (The Neighbors) or a specific character (Never Coming Home).

With The Revenge List, *it was after batting various plot ideas around with my agent Carolyn and former editor Emily that a random idea popped into my head: "What if an anger management exercise went terribly wrong?" That was it—we all needed to know what might happen next.*

Do you come up with the plot or the characters first, and how do you develop them?

It depends on the book. With The Revenge List, *I knew from the outset my lead character would be female and it was incredibly interesting to write from the perspective of a so-called angry woman. There's still such a double standard when* it comes to society's perception of how men and women are supposed to handle emotions, anger in particular.

Frankie became very dear to me as her story developed. She was incredibly damaged and had been through so much, it was no wonder she had anger issues yet there was still a vulnerability and softness to her that was wonderful to explore. Most of the time I just wanted to give her a hug.

Do you have a favorite chapter or scene?

Gosh, there are quite a few. I adored writing the scenes with Frankie and Rico because I loved the brother/sister relationship and dynamics. I don't have a brother, but if I did, I hope it would be someone like Rico as he was such a wonderful, caring man who clearly adored his sibling but wouldn't put up with her nonsense either.

Another scene I thoroughly enjoyed writing was when Frankie sees Dr. Ali about her pregnancy. It made me quite teary, which doesn't happen often. Oh, and the one where the car goes off the cliff gave me the shivers!

How do you research your novels?

I don't do a lot of research before I start writing but tend to put placeholders for areas that need fleshing out and go back to them after I've finished my first draft. That way I'm not spending hours on facts that don't make the cut, or getting sidetracked by stuff that's interesting, but potentially irrelevant to the story.

Regarding The Revenge List, our eldest son had appendicitis when he was ten, so I drew on that experience, which thankfully was far easier than little Azumi's. I called in the experts for more in-depth advice on medical, police, and court procedures, and how adoption in Maine works, which was all fascinating. Research is one of my favorite parts of writing a book—not